ISLA GORDON

The Wedding Pact

sphere

SPHERE

First published in Great Britain in 2021 by Sphere

1 3 5 7 9 10 8 6 4 2

A CIP catalogue record for this book
is available from the British Library.

ISBN 978-0-7515-7450-0

Typeset in Caslon by M Rules
Printed and bound in Great Britain by
Clays Ltd, Elcograf S.p.A.

Papers used by Sphere are from well-managed forests
and other responsible sources.

Sphere
An imprint of
Little, Brown Book Group
Carmelite House
50 Victoria Embankment
London EC4Y 0DZ

An Hachette UK Company
www.hachette.co.uk

www.littlebrown.co.uk

Dedicated to Mum and Dad
♥

Chapter 1.

August

There is a starting point for all our dreams, and a tipping point where we, and sometimes fate, decide if it's time to follow them, or walk a different road. For August Anderson, the starting point had happened many years ago, nearly twenty-five in fact, but the tipping point had only just arrived.

When it finally came, August hadn't expected it to be marred with tears and disappointment, and she resented James for that.

Her dream had begun in the same spot she now sat, outside a four-storey Georgian townhouse on the crest of a hill at the edge of the city of Bath. The ribbon of properties that ran all the way up one side of the hill and down the other formed Elizabeth Street, and at the very centre was Number Eighteen.

Across the road from Number Eighteen was a spacious

opening between the houses, allowing for a courtyard with a low wall to showcase the views that swept down across the city of Bath and the green fields beyond. At golden hour, the setting sun would pick up the honey tones in the Bath stone architecture, casting a warm glow over every building and every steeple, while liquid gold would drift by in the distant river.

Taller and grander than the neighbouring homes, Number Eighteen sparkled from within thanks to glittering chandeliers framed by long, rectangular windows. It sat proudly behind a wide pavement, with a wrought iron railing painted a rich black, and a matching archway, in front of the fanlight-topped door, from which a gas lamp hung.

If you pictured a character from a Jane Austen novel colliding into her roguish lover while out for a stroll, Elizabeth Street is a safe guess for what you might be picturing. Number Eighteen, in particular, had a Regency air, which hung around it like an invisible mist, and it was somewhere very special for August. A thousand memories bound her to this house, and this dream.

Over the years, August had climbed to the top of this hill and sat in this very spot many times. The house on Elizabeth Street had become a sort of Pole Star for her, a place to come to escape into her imagination, to dream about her future, to wallow in heartbreak, or to celebrate her achievements. One day she'd hoped to finally live here, and it had briefly felt as if that day might be just a whisper away.

Until James had kicked the idea to the immaculate curb with his stupid, too-clean trainers.

It was Friday evening, the summer sun having lowered so far beyond the skyline that the only light now visible came from streetlamps and from behind windows, and August was sitting on the wall in front of the house on Elizabeth Street, feeling very alone. Tears had dragged mascara down her face, her lipstick, once a quirky, neon pink, was now subdued, partially wiped off by her sleeve.

'Arsehole,' she muttered into the night, mainly directed at the long-gone James, but also a little bit to herself.

She'd waited *so long* for a chance to move into the house she now sat in front of. As a little girl she'd dreamed of the day she would somehow be wealthy enough to own it, and as she grew up – and her expectations lowered – she watched as it was converted into flats, which then became rentals, and still she waited. Though August had left the Bath area for a while, first for university and then to London to dip her toes into the world of professional acting, she had now returned. And she knew that with a little motivation she could transition from dipped toes to diving right in.

Last week, August spotted an advert in the paper, and it had felt as if fate had sensed she was back in town. The next day it was there again, and then again the day after, begging her to take notice. The first-floor apartment of Number Eighteen was vacant, and a tenant was required as soon as possible. Two bedrooms, one bathroom, only a smidge unaffordable as long as she had a flatmate to share it with. It was *vacant*.

She'd felt it: her dream could come true. This could be the start of the life she longed for.

Earlier that evening, she'd met up with her boyfriend James for a pre-dinner drink at a coffee shop at the bottom of this particular hill.

'This is such a random place; do they even serve alcohol?' James had said when they'd sat down, cleaning a speck of dirt from his shoe, before she'd launched into her proposal.

August had delayed until her date with James this evening to share the news with him. Sure, they'd only been seeing each other for four months, but they were serious enough, and it made sense to her: if she was going to move into a new flat and needed someone to share the rent with anyway, why not move in together?

'Why don't I want to move in with you?' he'd asked, letting a laugh escape like he wasn't even sure if she meant it. 'August, we've only been seeing each other for, what, three months?'

'Four months,' she corrected him. 'I know it's soon, but we spend lots of nights over at each other's homes anyway, and believe me, this house is amazing. Let me take you over there.'

James shook his head. 'I can't move in with you,' he said.

'Come on,' she said, trying to twist his arm. He usually liked this impulsive, spontaneous side of her, though lately he'd seemed a bit off. Maybe he just needed to know that as playful as she was, she could be serious when it came to the two of them. 'If you don't move in with me I'll need to find a flatmate, and who knows how long that will take. I can't afford this place on my own, even for just a matter of weeks.

And really, how long would it be before we wanted to live together anyway? I think we should just go for it!'

'I know that's what *you* think we should do, but I *don't* think we should. And it's not all about you.'

She did understand his hesitation, of course she did. It was sudden, and he hadn't had any warning she was thinking of asking him to move in with her. Hey, August hadn't had any warning herself, but the flat was available *now*. Not in six months' time, not next year, but now. But while August had leaned in with every inch of her heart, James had leant so far away that he fell right out of her life.

And it felt like her dream had fallen right out of reach along with him.

Chapter 2

Flynn

That night, a hundred miles east of where August stood watching the lights make a bokeh effect over Bath through her tears, an aeroplane touched down at London Heathrow. Flynn Miyoshi sat in his seat until directed to unclip his belt, his belongings – headphones, a water bottle, his phone, glasses and a well-read book – piled upon his lap. He watched England pirouetting outside the window, showing him her runway, her terminal and her skies, as much as was possible at this dark, late hour and thanks only to strings of bright, uniform lights.

He was home. Though it felt like nothing of the sort.

Flynn, born Fujio Flynn Miyoshi but who went most commonly by his middle name, was born and raised in the UK by his British mum and Japanese dad. But for the past four years, he had lived in Japan, following his parents when they'd moved back to Tokyo after spending the best part of their married life in England.

Now, after three delays, one change, one emergency stop and zero sleep for almost thirty-three hours, Flynn had British soil under his feet once again.

As he waited to exit the plane he checked his phone. He checked it again before he entered the immigration hall and again at baggage claim. Aside from two missed calls from the owner of the house he was to be lodging in from tonight onwards – no doubt checking on his journey and letting him know where they'd left the keys – there was nothing. Flynn decided he would return the owner's calls once he was settled on the coach.

He yawned. It would be a long journey from Heathrow to Bath, nearly two hours according to his itinerary, maybe longer now due to the knock-on effects of all the delays he'd faced.

It was the height of summer, but this particular night time was cool, and Flynn felt a chill creep under his stained sweatshirt as he stepped out of the arrivals hall and took his first breath of fresh air. He couldn't wait to get to his new home and shower, change into PJs and have a good sleep. He felt as if he'd been in the same clothes for a week, his skin was dry, and someone's baby had thrown up on him on the flight during some turbulence.

Eventually his coach arrived, packed with tired holiday-makers either arriving home or just arriving, piling themselves on in a herd of elbows and overhead bags, neck pillows and separated children.

Flynn found a seat near the back, his eyes drooping before the coach had even pulled away from the airport.

He didn't wake again until he was forty-five minutes outside Bath.

With a stiff neck and a parched mouth, he reached for his phone to see if she'd messaged him. Not with a declaration of love or a plea to return to Japan, he didn't expect that, not really. But maybe a small question, a 'How was your flight'; something that might have made him feel like he hadn't just been erased.

But still nothing, at least from her. He had a text and a voicemail now from his new landlord, the text containing an address he didn't recognise. He'd forgotten to call back and it was now approaching one in the morning. Grabbing a pen and the back of a magazine from his bag, ready to note down any instructions in the message, he pressed play, the volume low so not to disturb the nearby sleeping passengers.

'Hello, this is a message for Flynn Miyoshi,' the voice said on the end of the line. 'Flynn, this is Chris, of Chris and Donna. I'm very sorry to tell you this in a message, mate, and I hope you pick it up before you hit Bath.'

Oh no, what more could go wrong on this journey? Flynn was beginning to wish he'd never left Japan.

'Donna and I have just made the decision, the very difficult decision, to separate. It's not good, mate, it's not good, and we just can't play host to someone else in the house at the moment, as much as we were looking forward to the extra money.'

Flynn's mouth fell open. Did he hear that right?

'Anyway, we need the spare room now and I don't know what's going to happen, but ... Listen, we'll ... ' There was a pause on the line, then a sigh. 'We'll pay for you to stay in a hotel until you find something, all right? It's our fault for messing you around. We've booked you into a place near the bus station for your first night; I'll text you the address now, and the directions. It's not a great hotel but we can move you tomorrow if you want. I'll swing by and sort the bill in the morning. Text me or something just to let me know you got the message, yeah?'

The line went dead but Flynn had to listen to it again to make sure he had heard right. That poor couple. They'd seemed so lovely on email, after he'd responded to their advert on the rental website looking for a lodger. They'd seemed happy when he FaceTimed with them a few weeks ago. They'd talked about how it would be nice having him in the house and how he was really helping them out because they could do with some extra cash. Donna especially had looked so lovingly at Chris as she talked about how maybe they could finally take a holiday together again, as they hadn't had one since their honeymoon. He remembered that because it had made him wonder at the time if Yui ever still looked at him in that way. What had happened to rock Donna and Chris's world so completely? It seemed likely he'd never know.

The coach quietly sliced its way through the night, following the ribbon of the M4 before it would turn off towards Bath, and Flynn sat back in his seat.

Although he was surrounded by fellow passengers gently sleeping or lit by the glow of their phones, he'd never felt more exhausted, unanchored and very, very alone.

Chapter 3

August

August woke early on Saturday morning after a light and troubled sleep. She rolled over and pushed aside the half-drunk bottle of San Miguel on her bedside table to reach for her phone.

'Good morning, sunshine!' a chirpy voice said on the end of the line.

'I broke up with James.' August declared, her voice raspy.

Bel paused and then said, 'I'm on my way.'

'No, don't, thank you, though. I'm a festering stink bomb at the moment and my flat is a tip. I just want to lie face down in my beer-soaked duvet cover. In other words, I'm not quite ready for company.'

'What happened?' asked Bel. Thank god for Bel, August's favourite person and best friend.

August rested the phone on her cheek so she could flop her heavy arms back down beside her. 'The most amazing flat came up for rent, so I suggested we move in together and he suggested I take a hike.'

'I didn't know you were flat-hunting?'

'I'm not, but this wasn't just any apartment, it was in the house on Elizabeth Street.'

'Ohhh,' replied Bel, having heard August make passing comments and declarations of love about that house for years. 'So he freaked out because you suggested living together?'

'I am unlovable.'

'You are *dramatic*. And very lovable.'

'But the thing is, couldn't he have just said no? That he wasn't ready to live together? We didn't have to split up over it.'

'What exactly did he say?' Bel probed.

'I told him that the perfect flat had become available, and that I really wanted to live there, with him, and that it would be a perfect next step in our relationship. Although, maybe instead of "our relationship" I might have said "our blossoming love", but I was clearly only joking.'

' ... And what did he say?'

August sniffed. 'Well, he said no, that he wasn't ready to live together. Then we got into a huge argument and I think ... that's when I started acting like a toddler being told I couldn't have what I wanted.'

August could practically hear Bel rolling her eyes at her over the phone.

She continued. 'I said something about how, if he didn't want to live with me I'd find someone else who would, and move in without him. And he said, "Okay, sounds great," and then somehow things escalated, and the last thing I remember screaming at him was how *clearly* he had a problem with the way I buttered my toast in the morning, and if he couldn't get past that he could just fuck off for ever.'

Bel sighed on the end of the phone. 'Wow. How did your weird toast buttering come into it?'

'I do not have weird toast buttering!'

'Who else in the world slices lumps of butter and presses it between two slices of blackened bread?'

'Whatever,' grumped August. 'I just felt like he was always judging me for it.'

'Are you sure you've split up completely? This isn't just a fight?'

August knew. She was glossing over the details to her best friend, but they'd said some mean things to each other. The flat had just been the catalyst, a reason for James to put the brakes on like he'd been intending to before things went any further. They'd been on different pages and that was painfully clear now. Yes, four months was early to ask to move in with someone, but August had felt ready. Or, at least, she was willing to be ready if it meant having someone to help split the cost of living in the flat on Elizabeth Street with.

August picked the phone off her cheek and pulled herself into a sitting position. 'Yes, we're done. But it's fine. What are you doing today?'

'Steve and I had been planning to pop out to Marshfield to visit his mum, but I can come over to yours if you like? We could go to the spa? Or the Pump Room for an afternoon tea, because we haven't played at being tourists for months?'

'No, that's fine, let's do that soon, when I'm feeling a bit stronger, but for now, you and Steve go ahead to Marshfield.'

Bel paused. 'Would you like to come to visit Steve's mum?'

'No really, I'm fine. I just needed a little vent. Thanks, though.'

'Okay, sugarplum. Well, take care today and call me if you need another vent,' said Bel.

'Will do,' answered August, and she bid Bel goodbye.

August sat on her bed staring into space, feeling like she wouldn't look out of place as a background player in a sad music video right now.

Something was bothering her, and it wasn't just the break-up.

Her eyes scanned her bedroom, resting briefly on the shadows James had left behind on his last visit: a note-pad with a message scrawled in his handwriting, a pair of his headphones, a book of hers which he'd taken off the shelf and not put back (stupid prick). Try as she might, she couldn't convince herself that James, or rather his departure, was what was needling her. It was the loss of an opportunity; the feeling that her long-held dream, which she'd always believed would be a catalyst to her other dreams coming true, was slipping away from her grasp, after being so close.

August's grandmother's voice entered her head, as clear as it was before she'd passed away. *'One day you'll grow up to be successful enough to live in that house,'* she'd told her, pointing at Number Eighteen, Elizabeth Street while August's six-year-old self looked ahead in awe.

August stood up. She didn't need James, not at all. Why the hell should she tangle her dreams up with him? Sure, it would have been easy to rent with him, and logical, she thought, but she could probably, somehow, string together enough rent to keep her going until she did manage to find a flatmate. Perhaps her temp job in the press office of a historical holidays company, which wasn't actually so temp, if she were honest, would fancy giving her a raise? Or maybe she could try and get some more acting work ...

Either way, all she'd need was a little creativity and a stroke of luck that somebody would materialise who would be ready, and willing, to move in with her at the drop of a hat. It would be fine. Where there's a will there's a way, and all that.

This had been August's dream home since she was six years old, and now, aged thirty-one, she had a chance to make that dream real. She wouldn't let it drift by; she would grab it and force it to become her real life. 'Come back!' she said out loud.

Chapter 4

Flynn

Elsewhere in Bath, Flynn woke up, if that's what you call it when a zombie takes its first parched gasp as it comes back from the dead. That's how Flynn felt when he came to, following a night – more like half a night – on the lumpiest of all the hotel beds in the world. The hotel wasn't as close to the bus station as he'd imagined, so he'd ended up wheeling his large case up and down several streets for a good fifteen minutes in the middle of the night, passing a number of more appealing accommodations, before he found it.

His room was hot, but with the window open it was noisy. Inside it was no better, with the people next door shouting at the TV until at least four in the morning. Then, when he finally sank down onto his pillow, he'd not been able to switch his brain off.

His original plan had been to arrive in Bath early evening yesterday, try to stay awake at least a couple of hours before turning in for the night safe in the comfort he was home, even if it was a brand-new home. The jet lag would be beaten almost immediately, and he'd wake bright and fresh on Saturday morning ready to spend the weekend getting to know his new city, picking up some extra homely goods, some additional clothes, stretching his legs. All ready for an early start at his new role at a law firm on Monday, and ready for what he already knew would be two full-on weeks at work, including an all-weekend conference starting on the Friday.

Like many plans that are made, that one had whooshed its way out of the window in record speed, doing a runner at the first sign of delays on the plane. And now he was not bright, he was not jet lag-free, and he was distinctly homeless.

As he made himself a cup of tea in the hotel room, in a tiny white china mug with a crack in it, using warm, long-life milk, he scrolled through a property rental website on his phone.

Studio in city centre, available in two months' time.

One-bed basement flat, available in December.

Fourth floor apartment in the next town over, over-budget and would cost him a fortune travelling into work every day.

He bookmarked the handful of places available immediately, and once he'd forced down the watery tea, he started making phone calls, setting up viewings throughout the day with all the enthusiasm his zombie brain would allow him.

Flynn showered under a cold drizzle of water and made his way to reception, ready to get out of here and get some decent coffee before his first flat viewing. The receptionist eyeballed him as he got closer.

'Hello,' he said, while she ran her eyes up and down him. 'I'm in room twenty-eight, but I wondered if I could move rooms. My neighbours are a bit loud and there seems to be something wrong with the water temperature.'

She regarded him for a second or two, sizing him up, and eventually she answered with a, 'No more rooms, sorry, we're booked out.'

'You are?' he couldn't contain the incredulity from his voice.

'It's the summer holidays now, Saturday night, town centre,' she stated by way of an explanation.

'Oh. I don't seem to have any hot water – could someone come in and fix that at least?'

'No,' she offered, and added with a shrug, 'Sorry.' After the two of them stared at each other for a moment she followed it up with, 'When the hotel's full the hot water just runs out. Maybe get up earlier tomorrow?' Flynn was about to protest when she leaned in closer and lowered her voice. 'Or I could come up to your room and make you *appreciate* that cold shower, if you know what I mean—'

'*Lorna*!' yelled a voice from behind a Staff Only door.

Lorna, the receptionist, stepped back and sighed, shaking her head.

As Flynn was weighing up whether he had time to pack up his things and find a new hotel – one with some availability and thicker than two-millimetre walls – the receptionist plonked a paper bag on the counter.

'What's this?'

'Breakfast,' she replied, and turned back to her computer.

Flynn took the bag and opened it up to find a bruised apple and a box of apple juice. His stomach growled at him fiercely, and he left in search of a good bacon sandwich.

He looked back at his hotel and thought for a moment that even Yui, who was always trying to encourage him to be more adventurous, would agree this place was crossing a line. Nevertheless, finding a home had to take priority over finding a new hotel in the city.

A decent coffee and a decadent amount of bacon later, Flynn felt revived enough to head to his first appointment. Just about.

Flynn looked at the list of property appointments he'd made on his phone this morning with despair. He'd just seen his seventh flat of the day, and it was almost like Bath didn't want him to find somewhere to live. He didn't mean to be a Goldilocks about the situation, and actually he hadn't told any of the agents a flat-out no, just in case, but if he had to pick between the damp basement studio under the pub, with the hole in the ceiling, or the creepy room inside the terraced house where all the shelves and cupboards were filled with dusty lifeless dolls (that the landlord would like to not be moved, thank you), it would be a tough call.

Bath seemed beautiful – at least what little he had seen of it while he was rushing between appointments. He had no doubt there were many wonderful places he could call home . . . if he had the luxury of time. And if he'd picked a better time to move over – rather than after the start of the British summer holidays – then maybe he could have got a short-term Airbnb to keep him going, but even those were in short supply unless he considered moving as far as Bristol. It might well come to that.

The business hours of today were drawing to a close. He had one more place to see, which, like the others, sounded maybe promising. But also like the others, it turned out to be a non-starter.

'Hello, mate,' the agent greeted him as he got to the top of the hill, the other side of the town from his last viewing.

'Hi,' Flynn panted in response.

'You're here to view number four Elizabeth Street? I'm afraid that one got let this morning.'

'This morning?' Flynn's mouth hung open. 'But I only made the appointment this morning.'

'I know,' the agent replied. 'But it got snapped up, it's a popular road, this one. You sounded keen though so I wanted to show you another place we have that's not even made it online yet, just in case. It's a short walk away from here. It's more than your budget, if I'm honest, but it's not available until October, so maybe you could look into your finances and see if that would be doable by then.' The agent started to walk away, expecting Flynn to follow him.

'So it's over budget and not available for three months?' he clarified.

'Erm . . . yep.'

If he could have given up, got back on a plane, and pretended that this whole 'adventure' had never happened, in that moment he would have. 'I think I'll leave it,' he told the agent. 'I need something now.'

The agent nodded. 'Slim pickings for something immediately, I'm afraid. Come back to us on Monday? You never know.'

Monday he would be at work, all day, but he nodded nonetheless, tiredness pulling him to sit on a low wall at the top of the hill.

The agent went to leave before turning to Flynn and shielding his eyes from the dipping sun. 'I shouldn't say this because it's not one of ours, but I saw in the paper this morning that there's another flat on this street having an open house tomorrow, looking for tenants ASAP. I didn't pay attention to which place it was, or if it was in your budget, but you won't find a lot else to go and look at tomorrow so it might be worth a try?'

'In today's paper?' Flynn asked.

'Yeah, the local one. You'll find it in all the newsagents.'

He sat on the wall for a little longer, taking in the view before he lost it to the shadows. Then he straightened out the cracks and crumples from his back, and allowed one last trickle of hope back in at finding a place to call home.

Chapter 5

August

On Sunday morning, August arrived on Elizabeth Street early for the open house. Not a little early, but three hours early. It was 7 a.m.

August lifted her face to the sunshine, which beamed strong over Bath, a warm pool of summer light even at this time. She sat on the wall at the top of the hill in front of the house and pictured herself coming out through the front door of a morning, coffee in hand, slippers on feet, and breathing in the city. Before her, Bath, yellowed by the dawn, stretched and yawned. The cream stone of the buildings wove like threads beside wide, nearly empty streets and green flashes of parkland. And where the city blended into countryside, the green became denser and took the eye on a journey to the horizon.

This view had always soothed her, in the way that a feeling of home often does. August glanced back at the house behind, and hoped she would, indeed, be able to finally call this home. Just as her grandma had predicted.

Three hours to go.

Hmm. Maybe this was a little *too* keen. After a while, she needed something to distract her from the anxious merry-go-round of thoughts that whirled through her mind: *What if I don't get the house? What if a bidding war breaks out between prospective tenants and they eat me and my meagre salary alive? What if I do get the house and then can't find a flatmate and have to go into debt trying to pay for a swanky two-bed flat by myself? What if I do get the house, do get a flatmate, but then don't have the talent or ability to make any of my other dreams happen after all?*

Standing, with one last look at the house, she dragged herself away and made her way back down to the bottom of the hill, for now.

August pushed open the door to the coffee shop with a tinkle, taking a huge inhale of the warm, sweet pastries piled in powdery mountains on the counter. Even her showdown here with James on Friday night couldn't taint her love for this place, somewhere she considered her 'local' coffee shop even though she, at the moment, lived a good thirty minutes' walk away. Not for much longer, though!

'Good morning,' she sang to the barista, whose sleepy face visibly woke up at such a sunny greeting.

'Morning; what can I get for you?'

'Please could I have ... ' August looked up at the menu as is compulsory even though she knew exactly what she wanted. 'A double shot, whole milk latte with whipped cream and hazelnut syrup. No! Vanilla syrup. No! Hazelnut syrup. Extra large. And an almond croissant. Please. Thank you.'

'Will you be having those in or to take away?'

August checked her watch. 'In, please.'

'Coming right up.'

She was the only one in the cafe at this time on a Sunday, though it would certainly be filling up soon, so she took her coffee and croissant to sit at the bench in front of the window and let it frame her beloved Bath for her.

The sun was dazzling in, hitting the pane of glass and glinting throughout the coffee shop, kissing the dangling copper lights, and stroking the hot-chocolate-coloured walls. For a moment she closed her eyes and imagined herself coming here every morning. The door tinkled with another customer coming in, and with her eyes still closed, she smiled. As predicted, the place was already coming alive.

At the sound of a man's voice chatting to the barista and asking what she'd recommend, August brought herself back to the present, lifting her cup up to her face and taking a big sniff of the delicious cinnamon powder sprinkled atop the whipped cream.

Slightly *too* big a sniff.

Without a second's notice, the cinnamon shot up her nose, and expulsed itself back out again as a sudden sneeze that sent the whipped cream topping flying splat onto the window.

'Bless you,' said a man's voice from the counter.

'Thank you,' August called without turning around, too

busy using her single napkin and her sleeve to try and clean the window, and wipe away her embarrassment.

August left her chair and stepped to the side of the counter to search for some more napkins, peeping in a mirror on the wall en route to mop the whipped cream from her nose. In doing so, she caught a glimpse of the man whizzing back to the counter having wiped the mess clean for her.

'Oh! Thank you,' she turned, and the man, tall and slim, wearing a suit and with his back to her, half turned his head as he paid for his order, and she saw a flash of a smile.

'You're welcome,' he replied.

August dragged her eyes from him, from his black hair, and the way he ran his fingers through it, tousling it ever so slightly, while he awaited his own Sunday morning pick-me-up. Instead, she looked at her whipped-cream-less coffee, which looked a bit sad and naked now. Bugger it, this was a big day for her and she needed that whipped cream (though perhaps not up her nostrils this time). Picking up her cup she swung around to head back to the counter.

Her cup was still very much full of coffee. An extra large serving of coffee, in fact. So of course she was staring hard at it, to make sure it didn't spill.

Staring so hard at the coffee that she didn't look ahead.

In fact, she was still staring at the coffee, her eyes widening, as it tidal-waved out of her cup, into the air, and straight towards the man she'd just collided with.

Chapter 6

Flynn

The irony.

Flynn watched with wry fascination as the coffee lunged for his only clean clothing. The suit he planned to wear for his first day at work tomorrow. The suit and shirt he'd worn today because being overdressed to flat-hunt seemed a better plan than showing up in stained and smelly sweatshirts.

He watched as it splashed a milky brown wave across his front, the heat prickling his skin beneath, the scent of hazelnut catching in his nose.

He watched the woman's face, the one who'd just sneezed her whipped cream all over the window and seemed determined to redecorate this entire coffee shop, as she gasped in surprise.

The last dregs of coffee splashed onto the floor and everyone was silent for a moment, until the barista let out a small sigh.

'I am *so sorry*,' the woman said to him, reaching forward her arm and pressing her sleeve into his chest before backing away.

'No, I'm sorry,' said Flynn, because even though he'd been out of Britain for four years, the impulse to apologise for everything hadn't gone out of him. 'I turned too fast and didn't look where I was going.'

'I wasn't looking, I was too busy, well, trying *not* to spill my coffee.'

Flynn raised his eyebrows and she shrugged.

'I should have seen you,' she continued. 'You're very tall.'

Not tall enough, Flynn regarded, looking down at the front of his shirt, once pale blue, now marbled brown. He hadn't worn a tie this morning, leaving his collar unbuttoned, as he'd seen no need to go overboard. Now he wondered if a tie would have taken the brunt of the liquid, leaving him with his final clean shirt intact.

'I'll pay for your dry cleaning,' the woman continued, thrusting paper napkins into him, while the barista brought a mop out from behind the counter. 'And for your coffee. Do you happen to have another, erm, outfit with you?'

'No,' Flynn answered. No, he didn't.

'Right . . . ' She looked around, even eyeballing the barista's own shirt for a moment. 'Well, the shops will be closed for a few more hours so I can't offer to take you shopping.'

Flynn held his hands up, trying to keep the grump from his voice. This wasn't a big deal. It was only spilt milk-plus-some-other-ingredients. *It's the awful sleeps making you like this, not her*, he told himself. 'I wouldn't take you up on it even if we could. Really, it's fine.'

'It's not fine,' she argued. 'I just ruined your look. Now you have to wear coffee stains to ... church? Oh God, you aren't off to a funeral are you? Did I just make your day even worse?'

'No, no funeral, I'm just ...' Flynn didn't think it was quite worth getting into the whole sorry tale of how packing light had been a great idea until his few changes of clothing had one by one been ruined from a series of unfortunate events, and his plan to go clothes shopping had been over-taken by the need to find a home. Instead he said, 'I'm new in town, and I need to go shopping later today anyway.'

'You're new in town? From where?'

'From Japan.'

'Whoa.'

'Yep.' Flynn paused for a moment, unsure what to say, and the woman took her purse from her pocket.

'Welcome to Bath!' she smiled, shrugging, and he found himself smiling along with her.

'Thank you. It's quite an introductory service you have going on there.'

'Listen, first things first, I'm going to buy us both another coffee, because you lost half of yours during the collision too.'

'You don't have to do that.'

'I want to. I have enough on my plate today without the crushing anxiety of having cocked up your day too. Let me make it up to you, starting with coffee. And then we'll figure out what to do next.'

She turned to the barista and ordered two more coffees, 'To go, please. Is that okay?' she asked him.

'Where are we going?'

'I don't know, but I've overstayed my welcome here for one day, and I think I need a cup with a lid.'

There was a pause in conversation while they waited for the new coffees to be made, and Flynn noticed the woman side-eyeing the damage to his shirt. He looked down at the large brown stain and tried not to sigh.

'So where were you off to at this time of day in your Sunday best? Work?' she asked him.

'No, I start a new job tomorrow, actually.'

'Is that why you moved here? For the job?'

'Yep,' he answered.

'. . . Were you planning to wear that tomorrow?'

He couldn't help but smile at the way she contorted her face in anticipation of his answer. 'Yep. I didn't bring a lot of clothes with me and this is far from the first food and drink-related soaking I've taken since leaving Japan. I was kind of out of options this morning.'

'More so now,' she commented, and paid for the coffees.

The two of them stepped outside the coffee shop and back into the morning sunshine, the air fresh in a way that felt reviving to him. 'Thank you,' he said.

'You're welcome. I'm August, by the way, and I'm not always a walking disaster.'

'August. Like the month.' He felt like an idiot for saying that.

'Just like the month,' she smiled with the kindness of someone who has heard that comment a thousand times.

'I'm Flynn.'

'Hi, Flynn.' He observed her for a second, holding his coffee close to him in case of any more sudden movements. She had caramel hair in loose curls to her chin, a rainbow of clothing, bright pink lips and green eyes that looked like they were studying him, or plotting something.

'Is this your first time living in Bath? Did you visit much ... from Japan?' August asked.

'This is my first time in Bath, full stop. I arrived on Friday night, or yesterday morning, strictly speaking, and don't really know anything, or anywhere, or anyone.'

'You moved here without ever having been here? That's adventurous.'

Flynn raised his eyebrows. He'd never been called adventurous before. In fact, it became something of a needle between him and Yui. He could hear her voice now, her sigh, after she'd suggest something for them to do and he'd brush it off with a 'maybe one day'. *'You're so unadventurous,'* she'd tell him, and walk away. It stung to remember those missed opportunities. It stung to think that's how she thought of him.

'Well, guess what?' August asked, pulling him from his memories.

'What?'

'You now know somebody in Bath.'

Flynn smiled at that. 'That's true. I feel like a local already.'

'So what do you think so far? Of Bath I mean. Of here.'

'Oh. It seems nice. I've not had a chance to explore yet. I got a bit caught up with ... things ... yesterday.' No need to tell this stranger about his house-hunting debacle, or his godawful hotel, which by the way, offered just as little cosy comfort last night as it had the night before. He might have dozed off for an hour or so in between the corridor parties happening outside his door, the pub life outside his window, the stifling night-sweats, the drip-drip-drip of the tap in his bathroom and the anxious worry of never getting out of this place.

'I could be your tour guide!' August stated all of a sudden, slapping him on the arm and causing him to hold his coffee far away from him just in case.

'What do you mean?' he asked.

'Now, I could show you around. I know Bath like the back of my hand, and if I can't go and buy you another shirt at this time of day then let me give you a whistle-stop tour.'

'You don't have to do that.'

'I want to, please, it's the least I can do. Come on, it'll be fun. Bath is lovely and quiet at this time on a Sunday morning, and the sun is shining, and no offence but at the moment you look so fed up you might just jump back on the next flight to Japan, so let me show you that Bath isn't made up of people throwing coffee at each other.'

He hesitated. It did sound appealing, actually getting to see some of the city, and he didn't really have much else going on for a while.

'Come on,' August cajoled. 'I'm an actress, you know, so I can make all the stories really interesting.'

'Don't you have anything better to do with your day?' he asked her.

'Yes,' August nodded, and looked at her watch. 'But I have about two hours free. Do you?'

He was this close to saying, *Maybe another day*, when he thought of Yui again. Shaking her head at his lack of adventure. So instead he nodded at August. 'That would be great. Where first?'

Chapter 7

August

This was great. August loved being a tour guide; it allowed her to boast about the city she adored and test out her amateur dramatics on unsuspecting visitors. And besides, by the sound of it, this guy needed a break. She didn't know why he'd not brought shitloads of stuff with him from Japan (maybe he'd fled! Maybe he was a fugitive!) and she didn't know why he looked like he hadn't slept for twelve weeks. But she owed him some good karma, and this was the least she could do.

August was wondering where to take him first when he asked her, 'Do you live in Bath?'

'I do, I moved from London about six months ago,' she replied. 'But I have – had – family here so I grew up coming to the city a lot. What made you decide to move from Japan to Bath?'

'Work. I work in international law, and the firm I was

with in Tokyo has an office here. I saw an opening and went for it.'

'You'll like Bath,' August nodded. 'It's a cool city. Just pick your team out of the Romans and Jane Austen and you'll find lots of interesting things to do.'

As they walked, August noticed he was about a head taller than her, that his suit was well-fitting and he had a nice after-shave fragrance emitting from him. He was maybe a couple of years older than her if she had to guess.

'So where first, Tour Guide August?' Flynn asked. 'If you're sure you don't mind?'

'I don't mind at all, in fact, it will help time go quicker, and stop me stressing about something I'm doing later.' He looked at her inquisitively but she waved her hand to show she didn't want to talk about it, instead changing the subject. 'First things first, let's take you to the most photographed hotspot in Bath. Be prepared to wish you were rich.'

August took Flynn on a highlights walking tour of Bath, showing him where the Royal Crescent and the Roman Baths were, pointing out the architecture of the abbey, and Pulteney Bridge, which had old Florence and Venice vibes with its lines of shops. She directed him to the main stores and the best spots for alfresco picnics, runs, or river walks. She gave him tips on pubs and cafes, threw in some history and lots of Jane Austen trivia which she bet he loved.

They grabbed Danish pastries from a bakery, whose doors had so recently cracked open that the smell of sweet dough wafted out into the street. With their treats, August and Flynn began a slow walk back towards the coffee shop where they met.

'You know a lot about Jane Austen,' Flynn commented. 'Which came first, the love of Bath or the love of her?'

'Bath, for sure. My grandma lived here and she got me to see all the beauty of the city. She would tell me all about the Regency period and I just became obsessed. From there I learned about this awesome author who wrote funny, complex women set in this time period I loved, and now, my biggest goal in life is to be a theatre actress starring in an Austen play.' *Maybe my second biggest goal*, she thought.

'You said you were an actress?' Flynn said.

August took a beat before answering, trying to form the right words. 'Yes, I'm a voice artist, mainly, but I don't do as much of that as I did back in London, to be honest.' She drifted off for a moment, a guilt settling onto her. She sometimes felt like an imposter when she referred to herself as an actress, now that she'd let that side of her life all but dry up. But it's okay, living in her dream home was about to change all of that.

'All right, we're changing the subject now,' said August, coming to a stop in front of a small cottage that sat at the foot of the hill, one street away from where Elizabeth Street began its ascent. The home was shaded on all sides by thick, emerald-hued trees and tall bushes. It was painted a pale yellow and had round windows and a thatched roof. The low oak tree in the front garden was still there, after all these years, though the old tyre swing had been replaced with a smart, rattan swing chair, which swayed in the slight morning breeze.

'Whose house are we looking at?' Flynn asked.

'This was my grandmother's house, when she was alive,' she replied. A lump formed in her throat, which was silly really because she'd visited this place many times since her grandmother passed last year, in fact she walked past it every time she came up to the top of the hill to sit on the wall, and she said a silent hello to it whenever she did. Living close to this memory was something she wanted so badly.

Flynn stayed silent, giving her a moment.

'We were pretty close,' she explained after a while, and then forced a big smile back onto her face. 'I used to come and stay with her a lot. It's only a bungalow, really, though she'd turned the attic into a sort-of secret den that you could get to by a ladder, and I always wanted to sleep in there.'

'Did she let you?'

'Yeah, but we had to tell my mum I'd slept in the spare room because she would have freaked out about me falling down the ladder if I got up to pee in the middle of the night,' August laughed at the memory of her funny, conspiratorial grandma.

'And did you ever fall down the ladder in the night?'

'Meh, once or twice.' She turned to him. 'Are your grandparents still around?'

'Just the one grandmother. My mum's mother lived in England and she died around five years ago. It was one of the reasons Mum felt it was a good time to move over to Japan. My dad's mother lives over there too, and she's very much still alive, living on one of the islands in the south. I'm not as close to her as I should be though.'

August gave him a sympathetic smile, and then turned back to the house, bidding a silent farewell to her grandma, for now. 'I'm running out of time,' she said. 'Want to walk with me up to what I consider is the best viewpoint in Bath?'

They made their way slowly up the hill of Elizabeth Street, side by side, sunlight dancing on them.

'I was here yesterday,' Flynn remarked, but before she could question him, he harked back to her earlier comment and asked, 'So I guess all this means you're Team Austen rather than Team Romans?'

'Oh yes, Austen all the way,' said August, pleased that he remembered. 'I remember the first time I ever walked up this hill. I was six years old, and I was staying with my grandma for the whole summer after my parents split up. On the first morning when I woke up I was confused and sad and missing my parents, and she took my hand, and took me right up to the very top of Elizabeth Street, and we ate Bath buns for breakfast on the wall I'm about to show you.'

'Did you feel better after that?' Flynn asked, probably wondering what a Bath bun was.

'So much better. And every single morning for the rest of the summer we did the same thing. And every single morning my grandma would tell me these stories about women in big skirts and men in top hats who used to live here in Bath and have these great romances with one another. There were always a million sisters and everyone fancied the wrong person and there was a lot of sitting and sewing and waiting for invitations to great balls that would then happen down in the Assembly Rooms in the town.'

'She sounds like a good storyteller,' remarked Flynn.

'She was, and she always did different voices for all the characters, and added details to make it really real.' August smiled at the memory. That was one of her favourite things about voice acting – creating characters and voices and playing around, like her grandma used to do. 'For example, in every story she always had somebody living in the house at the top of this hill, you'll see it in a minute. So I would sit on the wall and instead of looking out at the view I'd look at the windows of the house, at the chandeliers I could see twinkling inside, at the steps up the front door, and the whole thing was like a tableau coming to life before me. Am I being really boring?'

'Not at all, are you kidding? You've just entertained me for about two hours straight on a private walking tour. You aren't boring at all.'

'Well, thank you,' August replied, and they carried on their trek upwards. 'Of course, years later I found out that all the stories she was making up were actually stolen from the one and only Jane Austen. I was reading *Sense and Sensibility* one day for school and was like: *This is really familiar!* It turns out my grandma used to take the gist of the storylines, and the characters, transport them all to Bath, even those that weren't set here, and pass them off as her own stories to me. I lapped them up like she was a genius.' August laughed at the recollection. 'Sometimes I credit her with my acting gene, or at least my acting bug.'

They reached the top of the hill and looked out across the city as it woke up only to remember it was Sunday and it could have a wonderful lie-in.

Her grandmother *had* inspired her into acting, actually. Not that she had been an actress herself, but something about the way she shone at storytelling, and the way she carried herself like a movie star from Hollywood's golden age, all pearls and rubies and a streak of wickedness. Her grandmother's penchant for taking risks and living wildly and to the fullest had rubbed off on August from a young age.

Now, when August looked back, she could see her gran's effect on so much of who she'd shaped herself to be.

Her gran's influence had been there in every money-making scheme she'd had as a child, from selling flowers that she'd pilfered from over her neighbour's fence (her parents had quickly put a stop to that) to carol singing in July (she'd even been offered money to *stop* singing at some houses).

Her gran's influence had been there every time she took a backpack and a Bel and went zipping around the world, finding detours and drama aplenty. She smiled, remembering the time she and Bel had jetted to the south of France on a whim to attend the Cannes Film Festival. They had blagged their way into a party on a superyacht by pretending to be London socialites from a reality TV show that they made up. August had felt out of place for about two minutes, until she realised they weren't the only fakers there. She could still remember Bel's faux-Chelsea accent slipping more after each sip of Prosecco.

Her gran's influence had been there every time she'd embellished her CV with skills and credentials and then allowed a fake confidence to push her to finish the job she'd been hired for. '*Sure, I can do the splits!*' she'd told her first on-screen job, a commercial for yogurt, before having to spend two weeks wrestling her hips into ungodly positions so that when it was time to film she was able to hold the pose and a faux-smile just long enough for the three-second panning-shot to whizz past her.

'*Don't wait around for someone else to make your dreams happen, girly,*' her grandmother had told August once. '*Everybody has dreams, not just you, so they're rightly all too busy fannying about with their own to take on yours too.*'

She taught her to take risks and throw caution to the wind and just see what happens. But lately, since her grandmother had passed, really, if she had to pinpoint a time, August had grown more reserved. Not in personality, but in actions. She'd become more afraid of failing. More fearful of what would happen if things *didn't* work out. Moving to Bath had been her step to countering this, to taking a plunge and continuing with her plans even without much of a plan, but what then ... ?

So no, she wasn't successful enough to be able to afford the whole house on Elizabeth Street yet, like her gran had predicted. But this felt like a sign, a kick up the backside sent by her grandma. *Live here and remember who you are, who you dream of being.*

August turned to Flynn. 'Well, that's the end of the tour. What did you think?'

But instead of taking in the vista, he was looking at her soon-to-be house, and then down at something on his phone.

'Hmm?' he looked up. 'Oh, thank you so much, I really appreciate it. You've helped me feel like the weekend wasn't a total washout. I can now go to work tomorrow knowing what city I live in.'

'Good,' replied August. 'That's enough of a rave review of my services for me. What are you looking at?' she asked.

'Is that house number eighteen?'

'It certainly is. And this is where I need to leave you,' she said, beaming.

'Do you live here?' he asked, turning to her in surprise.

She hesitated. 'I will be living here.'

Flynn's lips curved into a smile. 'You're here for the open house too?'

But August did not smile. Instead, shocked, she pointed between Flynn and her dream home. '*You're* here for the open house?'

Chapter 8

Flynn

'You're here to view this same flat?' August asked. She was pointing at him, and at the house that was his last hope of lining up somewhere to live before starting work the next day.

'Yes,' Flynn replied. 'Don't you already have somewhere to live here in Bath?' He wasn't sure why she was so taken aback, but he had a strong gut feeling he was more deserving of this house.

'B-but ... I have to live there ...' she stammered in response. 'Why were you creeping around here so early if you were coming for the open house?'

'Thanks to jet lag I was awake and thought I'd come up and check it out, make sure it wasn't going to be a waste of time like all the places I trudged around yesterday. Why were you here, "creeping around" so early?'

'Because I'm going to get that house.'

He laughed. 'I see, so you were staking claim like

someone who turns up hours before a concert begins, to make sure they're in the front row.'

'Something like that,' she said, nodding. 'Only you have to share the front row with other people. This place is mine, and you – you distracted me.'

'I did not distract you. How was I supposed to know you were house-hunting?'

'Well, I am, and I've got to live in that house, man.'

Flynn put his hands on his hips. 'So have I. I have nowhere else to go. This is my last shot.'

'What are you talking about? There are a million places to live in Bath.'

'Yes, there are,' he agreed. 'But very few of those are available to move into soon. And those that are, that I can afford, well, I'd frankly rather stay in my hotel.'

'Great!' August cried. 'Then you should do that – wait for something you really like to come up.' She paused and then pointed her finger at his outfit like he'd duped her. 'Is *that* why you're wearing a suit? So that you make the best first impression at the open house? Damn, that was a good idea,' she muttered.

'No, it's like I told you, I'm just out of clean sweatshirts, now even more so,' he looked down at the dried coffee stain. 'I packed light coming from Japan. A baby threw up on me on the flight, I then threw tea on my only other jumper yesterday, and I've not had a spare minute to hit a launderette because I've been viewing flats since I arrived.'

'Well, it sounds like you have choices. I think you should pick one of them.'

He shook his head. 'Believe me, they were not good choices.'

She threw her hands up in the air and huffed, which made him smile. 'Why didn't you get a flat sorted before you arrived?' She demanded. 'You didn't think to line something up before packing up your life and flying around the world?' She gasped and lowered her voice. 'Are you on the run?'

'No, I'm not on the run,' Her life must be a lot more dramatic than his to even ask that. 'Actually, I did have something lined up, a room in a house, but it fell through last minute. How come you're looking to move already, if you've only been here six months? Is there a problem with your flat?'

'No, it's fine. It's great, in fact, you should move in there,' August teased.

'Then why? At least tell me *why* you're getting all huffy with me and trying to convince me not to go in there.'

August paused for a minute, as if finding her words. 'There's just something about this house. I've always wanted to live there. As in, not just in the six months I've been back in Bath, but like, always, at least for maybe twenty-five years. But although it's divided into four, maybe five flats, it's really rare for one to become available. Really rare.'

'I see. Have you ever been inside?'

'Just once, only into the entrance hall, when I was little, and my grandmother told me that one day if I worked hard and followed my dreams I could live here, ' August replied.

Flynn assumed she was going to elaborate, but instead, after a moment, she said, 'You know, this is a really rough neighbourhood.'

43

'Is that so?'

She nodded. 'Crime, debauchery, noisy neighbours.'

'That's bad news.'

'Yep.' August sighed. 'You'd be much better off getting a flat down there somewhere, near the park perhaps,' she pointed down the hill towards Royal Victoria Park.

'You're so helpful,' Flynn smirked. 'But you know what, if it's that bad, maybe you should just stay living in the flat you already live in.'

'No, no, I'll take one for the team, I'll move in here, and you can take my old flat.'

'That doesn't seem very efficient.'

'Why does life need to be efficient?' August shrugged. 'Anyway, back to your question. You asked me why this house was so important to me. It's because this house is *why* I moved back to Bath, in a way. No matter what big thing has happened in my life, from exam results, to break ups, and other life decisions, I've come back to Bath, stood at the top of the hill right here in front of this house, and let the magic of the city lights guide me.'

Flynn raised his eyebrows. 'That's not really a reason. You're very welcome to come and hang out on this wall after I move in.'

'No,' August cried. 'I have to live in there. It's hard to explain but I've been waiting so long, like my life has been on hold, to live here. And now I have the chance, and I know that when I live here I can move on and be successful and make my grandmother proud.'

Flynn sighed. 'I feel like you're just saying this so I back off.'

'I'm actually not,' August laughed. 'It's true. I even had my first kiss in front of this house.'

'Really?'

'Yes.'

'It must have been a good kiss to want to live in front of the memory of it?' he asked.

'Yuck, no, it was horrible – wait, was your first kiss good? Did you have a movie-version of a first kiss?'

'My first kiss was okay; the back of my hand is pretty sexy. But if yours was such a bad memory, why would you want to live somewhere you'd have to stare at that spot every day?'

'I said it was a bad *kiss*, not a bad memory,' August said, wagging a finger at Flynn. 'You're not getting me to back down that easily. This is my greatest aspiration; you could live in a million other houses.'

'I need somewhere to live now – this is my last hope.'

'You're in a hotel.'

'But I can't stay there for ever, and I'm out of time to house-hunt.'

'There's always time. We all have the same number of hours in the day as Beyoncé,' August reasoned. 'Anyway, I can't stay where I am because there are too many memories wrapped up there with my ex-boyfriend.' The twitching at the corners of her mouth gave away that this wasn't neces-sarily the entire truth.

'That's a shame,' Flynn concurred. 'But I went to the doctor who told me my jet lag may never pass if I'm kept awake by the stress of not having a home to call my own.'

'That's not a thing,' August cried. 'You'll be over your

jet lag in like, three days. I however, may never get over my ex-boyfriend. Not unless I can move out of there and into here.'

Flynn shook his head. 'My hotel room has a ghost. A poltergeist actually. It keeps throwing things at me at night – little bottles of shampoo, the TV remote. I need to get out of there before it does me any serious damage.'

'Well, luckily you work in law, maybe you could sue your ghost. I, on the other hand, have chronic bed-bugs and the only way to get rid of them once and for all is to move out, otherwise they might eat me to death.' She shrugged at the unavoidable nature of these surely made-up bed-bugs.

'That's a big shame for you, but if you have bed-bugs you could bring them onto Elizabeth Street and then be exiled. I think you should stay away. However, I'm not so lucky. I'm pretty sure my hotel is a front for a criminal underworld.'

'Oh, really, what a shame.'

Flynn nodded. 'And they're trying to recruit me because of, you know, my sharp suits, and whatever.'

'It's nice to have extra income . . . '

'I just don't look good in trilbies.'

She laughed. 'Is that what you think criminals wear?'

'I'm pretty sure I've seen pictures of James Cagney in one.'

'What a modern reference. But look,' August sighed. 'A criminal underworld is one thing, but I need to move out of my current flat because it doubles as a porn studio. It's very hard to keep the place clean, Flynn.'

His face went mock-serious. 'Maybe I *should* move in . . . '
August gave his arm a slap and he laughed, and they stood

in silence for a few moments before he added. 'It would be some really nasty porn with all those bed-bugs.'

August checked her watch as another person went into the building. 'It's started, and I keep seeing people go in. Look, I'm not trying to tell you what to do, but I have a history with this place, and like I told you, it was my grandmother's dying wish that I lived here. Not you, *me*.'

'It sounded more like a pep talk for you, than a dying wish for her. And didn't she say that to you when you were a child?'

'Yes, but, we're all dying Flynn, all the time, so even back then it still technically counts as a dying wish.'

'As sobering a message as that is, I can't give up *my new home* on a technicality, sorry.' Flynn started to make his way towards the door, while August scurried beside him.

'I'm glad I spilt coffee on you now,' she hissed.

At the bottom step they looked at each for one moment longer, August with her chin tilted in subtle defiance, Flynn with a glint in his eye.

'I guess this is it,' Flynn said. 'Time to find out which one of us is going to be moving in.'

'Time for you to go on back to that hotel and keep looking, because I am witty and charming and having that house.'

'Is that so?'

'That is so.'

'I can be pretty charming myself, you know,' he said.

But August appeared ready for battle; like she'd been ready for this since she was six years old. 'Let the games begin.'

Chapter 9

August

They stood at the door of the house together. August had had it all planned out, from the smile she was going to dazzle the owner with, to a perfect handful of compliments to scatter between the front door and the door of the flat. No matter what the inside was like, and no matter who was showing them around, they were a perfectly curated collection of not-too-needy, gracious accolades.

This was it. The door that was going to open up all her dreams. The life she'd imagined for herself, the person she wanted to be, who she'd always thought she *would* be, the goals and visions that had been reignited inside her were one door away.

August stepped up and rang the bell. *Hello, future.*

She leaned forward slightly; mouth already open to impart her wonderful opener. The door swung open and she hesitated for a millisecond at the sight of an attractive man in his late thirties, all tensed jawline and brooding eyes, a light tan to his skin that gave a hint that there was more to him than the businessman façade that the world was seeing in this moment. That hesitation proved fatal, as Flynn swept in and bellowed, 'Hello! I'm Flynn, I'm ready to move in and let you get back to your Sunday,' diverting the man's attention upwards.

She was going to kill Flynn. And then move into her new flat.

August wracked her brains for something to say, because her sparkling opener, which wasn't far off what Flynn had exclaimed, now seemed like it would fall flat. She tried to pull inspiration from the improv classes she'd taken when she'd first moved to London, but the best she could come up with was declaring 'August!' rather loudly, followed by, 'That's me. I'm August.'

The man just nodded, seeming distracted and flustered, and said, 'Jolly good, nice to meet you. I'm Abe. I'm not the landlord though, that's my mum, Mrs Haverley, so you might as well save your gushing for her.'

Yeah, Flynn, save your gushing, August thought, raising her eyebrows in smugness at Flynn as they followed Abe in through the door.

It was just as August had remembered it, that time she'd come over here as a child. The staircase with the sweeping bannister, and how the sun streamed against it causing those pillars of light to dance their way up the wall. The chandelier glittered overhead, as ornate yet understated as it ever was. August gazed up into it, remembering how her younger self had felt as if it was an ice castle she could climb up and get lost in.

Halfway up the stairs the doorbell rang again, echoey and mellow from inside the walls of the house. Abe sighed and turned around. 'The apartment that's available is just at the top of this staircase, on the first floor. You can't miss it.' Abe disappeared down the staircase, muttering away to himself, and August and Flynn approached the door of the flat.

Of *my* flat, August thought.

A woman of about August's age, early thirties, stomped out from within the apartment, pushing past them on the landing. 'Waste of time,' she was mumbling, clearly irritated. She stopped short after she passed the two of them, looked right at them in a way that August couldn't tell if she was being scrutinised, or if the woman was lost in thought about what to say, and then she stated, 'But I'm sure *you two* would be just right for this place.' The woman flounced off down the stairs, her red hair flying behind her.

August was lost for words for a moment – something that very rarely happened.

'What was that about?' Flynn asked no one in particular.

'What did she mean by "you two"?'

They shrugged at each other. Whatever, there were more important things at play.

The door was partially open, and when Flynn pushed it, they were greeted with a sight August hadn't fully antici-pated. August and Flynn weren't just competing against each other for this place, oh no, the flat was teeming with potential residents. Way more than August had expected there would be. The crowd shuffled through the living room, pottered in and out of the bedrooms, opened the kitchen cupboards, gazed out the windows, touched the lampshades, caressed the sofa cushions, leant against doorframes and sniffed at the potpourri like it was a tray of freshly baked cookies. They did all the things August wanted to do.

'That must be the landlady,' Flynn said, tilting his head towards the one woman in the room who didn't seem to be in raptures about her surroundings. Instead, she stared out of the window glumly.

August was going to approach her, but saw her sigh as a man in his fifties loomed, talking at her before he'd even come to a stop, waving his arms and saying loudly how he'd 'love to discuss numbers'.

Instead she turned to Flynn. 'Well, I'm going to start looking around, so I guess this is ... goodbye?'

'I guess so.'

'You sure you don't want to just give up and go home now?'

'I can't, remember ... I have no home.' He replied, but with a smile.

Dammit. 'You'll find one,' she sang and turned away.

'Thanks for keeping me company this morning,' Flynn added to her as they began to go their separate ways.

'You too,' she smiled, and felt a pang of sadness at the broken connection. But she pushed it aside. He was her competition. So she added loudly, 'Excuse me sir, you seem to have a large stain on your shirt,' before throwing him a wicked grin and scuttling into the nearest room.

Inside, August took a deep breath, remembering where

she was. She was inside her dream home. It was just as lovely as she had hoped. The living room, the main hub when you walked in the front door, was large and bright thanks to the long Georgian windows with the view that flowed down the hill. The ceilings were high. Two bedrooms, beside each other, led off from the living room, though one was used as a snug in the current set-up, with a sofa bed billowing with cushions beside a bookshelf, and French doors acting as windows that led to a small balcony overlooking a private park behind the house. The other bedroom was larger, definitely the master, and it had the same lookout as the living room, which would be quite the thing to wake up to every day.

August couldn't decide which of the two rooms she'd actually rather sleep in when she moved in.

Oh, she could see it now, sort of, if she blocked out all of the other people milling around.

Would August be heartbroken if she didn't get the flat? Probably. And she knew it was her own fault for getting so caught up in the fantasy as soon as she heard about one of the apartments becoming available. She'd poured way too much hope into something that now seemed far more out of her control than she imagined. Sure, she could try and dazzle the landlady. She could even offer to pay over the monthly rental asking price. Well, she couldn't really afford that at all, but she would find a way, temp more hours, sell online acting workshops on the side. She could even ask a higher price from whoever she sublet the spare room to, perhaps, if she added some extras on the side, such as housekeeping being included. They could even have the master bedroom.

Her thoughts were running away with her and she knew she needed to centre herself and come up with ideas to stand out from the crowd before it was too late, so she moved back towards the front door of the flat, imagining herself walking in again for the first time, and all the excitement and motivation she'd felt.

Standing in front of the partially open door and trying to block out the noise, as if she were about to enter from stage left to a crowd of adoring fans, August heard hushed voices outside. She moved over a little in case the door was about to swing open into her back, and in doing so glimpsed the landlady, huddled on the landing with her son, Abe, the grumpy greeter.

August tried not to listen. She really did. But in the same way as trying not to think about laughing can cause you to laugh, her attempt at not listening meant her ears became hyper-sensitive.

Could she have moved away? Yes. Should she have moved away? Of course. Did she move away? *As if.* You see, she'd just overheard something that rooted her to the spot.

'So what *would* make you happy, Mum? What kind of person *would* you be willing to have live here?' Abe asked, exasperation apparent even in his low voice.

'I just want a nice, dependable couple. Married. And young.' Her voice was stubborn and firm. August raised her eyebrows.

'You can't be that specific, Mum, that's not how it works. Please tell me you haven't been turning people away for that reason again.'

'It's my house, I should be allowed to decide who lives here. I want someone who will be around for a long time, I don't want ancient people who'll be carted off to the funeral parlour in six months. I don't want flighty singletons coming and going at all hours, moving in and out, bringing home their sexual conquests.'

Wow. The landlady was a tough cookie. August stayed silent, though her heart was sinking like an anchor in the ocean.

Mrs Haverley continued. 'I don't want somebody constantly ringing on my doorbell asking me to fix this, and fix that. A nice couple will be able to maintain the place by themselves.'

'You don't know that,' Abe replied.

'Well, it's a good bet,' snapped Mrs Haverley. 'And that's what I want. Married. Solid. Dependable. I'm too old to have to deal with anything else.'

But August knew she *would* be in it for the long haul. She *wouldn't* be moving in and out. She *could* handle maintenance on her own (or at least she'd rope in Bel and give it a good go). She'd be Mrs Haverley's ideal tenant, if only she could see past her lack of a husband, or wife. It was just so outdated, and so unfair.

August heard Abe sigh, in a way that indicated this was a bigger conversation he'd had with his mother many times. He then said, 'Well, there must be twenty or so people in there, and quite a few are couples. I showed a couple up here only about ten minutes ago, have you spoken to them? Short girl and dark-haired chap?'

Now hang on, thought August. Were she and Flynn the short girl and the dark-haired chap? Her eyes darted to other couples moseying around and they certainly seemed to fit that description the most closely.

Mrs Haverley sighed one of her resentful sighs again, and said, 'No, and I suppose I'd better go back inside, otherwise this blasted morning will never end.'

August tiptoed away from the door quickly. An idea was forming in her mind, a spark that hadn't quite had time to burst into flames, but was thinking about it, reaching out ready to ignite. But she needed to find Flynn.

Spotting him by the window in the master bedroom, she started towards him and then paused. 'Oh, crap,' she whispered, realising she had some backtracking to do. No, she couldn't do this. She couldn't ask *him* to do this. Could she ... ?

But if she didn't ... it would be game over.

Chapter 10

Flynn

Flynn walked away from August, shaking his head. Luckily, he didn't think the landlady had heard August basically shout to the entire room that he was a mess – which had been *her fault* – but even so, he felt self-conscious. He really needed to make a good impression and stand out in front of all these people . . . and not because he looked like he had a problem getting a cup of coffee safely to his lips.

He'd enjoyed chatting with August this morning – in fact it had been quite the tonic he needed after the past forty-eight hours – but it was definitely time to cut ties. He hadn't missed the faraway look in her eyes when she spoke about the house, the history, what it meant to her this morning. She wanted to build on those memories, she wanted to be happy, and although part of him wanted that for her, she had a home already. He didn't. He could step back now, but for what? A stranger?

In normal circumstances he would be that person. He

would take himself out of the running. Acts of kindness keep the world turning, right? He just didn't have the luxury to do that this time. The cold hard truth was that if he didn't find a place to live today – and being a Sunday he wasn't going to have a lot of luck using an estate agent today – then who knows when he would next fit in a house-hunt.

Though, looking at all these people, the whole thing might be a moot point anyway.

And then suddenly, there she was again.

'I need to speak to you,' August hissed, leaning into Flynn and putting her hand on his upper arm.

'Oh no you don't,' he took a step back. 'For all I know you have another coffee stashed, ready to lob on my crotch and tell everyone I wet myself.'

'Nothing like that,' she smiled sweetly and shuffled closer again. He eyed her with suspicion. What was with the fluttery eyelashes?

'What are you doing?' he asked.

'Nothing,' August replied, taking her hand in his.

What on earth was happening now? 'Are you trying to flirt with me to get me to back off the flat? It's not going to work. Have you seen this place?'

'Yes, it's beautiful, come with me and I'll show you it from a different angle.' August gripped his hand even firmer, and he saw her teeth grit through her smile.

Flynn shook his head and tried to pull his hand away. 'August, I'm sorry, I know you want the flat, but I really need a fair shot at it too—'

'Please, give me just one minute. Please.'

The way she looked at him, a sincerity in her eyes, is what made him follow her. If she hadn't dropped the bravado, and the gentle rivalry, for a second, he might not have relented, and all that happened after would have been nothing more than a what if.

So he followed August as she led him briskly back through to the balcony off the snug. She stepped out into the sunshine, pulling him after her, and closed the metal-rimmed glass doors behind them.

Outside the light flooded the balcony, the only shade coming from a few swaying branches of the large oak tree opposite. Here at the back of the house, they were looking down on a private, compact green park which Flynn guessed was for use by the residents. How he'd love to sit out there with a beer on a hot summer's evening after his first week at his new job . . .

August leaned over the balcony, looking above and below as if checking for other sunshine-dwellers or open windows, but finding everything closed.

'Are you . . . planning to push me off the balcony?' he asked her.

She turned to Flynn and spoke in hushed tones. 'What if I told you there was a way we could seriously increase our odds at renting this flat?'

'We?'

'Yes. We. We both want to live here, and you'd be looking for a flatmate anyway, right?'

'And so would you.'

'And so would I,' she agreed. 'I think we should move in together.'

'August, this feels like a trap. What are you talking about?' Flynn didn't mean to sound annoyed; it was just the tiredness catching up with him, but he really needed to get back in there and get to work with whatever he needed to do to secure this as his new flat.

But to his surprise, August shook her head. 'This isn't a trap. I'm serious. I can't get it on my own. I need to move in with you.'

'Why?' Flynn asked. 'For all you know I could be a serial killer.'

'Are you?'

'No. But I'm sure Ted Bundy would have said the same thing if you'd asked him. In fact, I think he did. I could be a stranger who followed you into that coffee shop and mirrored everything you told me you were doing today.'

She paused. 'Why are you trying to convince me you're a murderer?'

'Probably because I'm too polite to imply *you* might be one.'

'I'm not, I swear.' At that moment, she seemed to spot something out of the corner of her eye, somebody coming into the room behind the glass doors.

August laced her hand into Flynn's again, swivelling him to face the small park, and rested a head against his upper arm. Flynn mused that to anybody looking at them from within the snug, they must be the picture-perfect image of a happy couple.

On the balcony, Flynn side-eyed this suddenly, strangely, tactile creature. 'What are you doing?'

'I will explain everything, just kiss my hair.'

'*What*?' he started to pull away and August smiled up at him, adoringly.

'I'm really sorry about the shirt thing and all the stuff I said, but just act with me,' she said through her gritted teeth. 'Please. Trust me.'

Flynn sighed. 'Um ... ' He leaned over and rested his cheek for a moment on her head in a way that he hoped was affectionate-looking. He did *not* kiss her hair like she asked, because even that was one step too far into what-the-hell-was-going-on-here-ville for his liking. Nevertheless, he still felt her hair, soft against his face, the scent of banana and coconut drifting into his thoughts. Their hands entwined. 'So what the hell is going on?'

'This place is perfect, right?' she said, her voice softening.

'It is really nice – the best place I've seen so far this weekend.'

'And we both want to live here. Me because it's been a lifelong dream, you because your life has just turned upside down and you need somewhere to call home as soon as possible. Am I still right?'

'You are ... '

'We can't afford to live here long term on our own, we'd have to get a flatmate.'

Flynn nodded. That certainly seemed likely. 'So you think we should live, and apply, together?'

'It makes perfect sense to me. I mean, you have no other friends in Bath.'

'Ouch.'

August chuckled. 'You know what I mean. You, and

60

probably I, would end up advertising and then sharing with a stranger anyway. So . . . '

'Better the devil you've known for five seconds . . . '

' . . . than one you've known for zero!'

Flynn glanced down at their hands, still clasped together. 'But what's with the amateur dramatics?'

Chapter 11

August

August glanced back behind her. A minute ago, from the corner of her eye, August had spotted the landlady and her son wander into the snug and look towards the balcony doors. Now, the landlady was still there, talking to her son and looking irritated at what he was saying, but watching August and Flynn with interest.

Was this idea too out there, even for August? She could almost sense her grandmother chuckle at that. In parallel, she could almost sense her mother pursing her lips in disapproval.

No, it was fine, it was *essential*. This was nothing more than an acting role.

Time to delve even further into character. August dropped Flynn's hand and wrapped both arms around his waist, smiling up at him with as much fake love as she could muster. 'I know this is really weird,' August pleaded through her smile, keeping her voice low. 'And I am so sorry for manhandling you, but I know how we can have a good shot at landing this apartment. And believe me, if you don't follow my lead, we *will not* be living here.'

Flynn studied her face for a moment, as if guarded. Perhaps he had a girlfriend and felt uncomfortable. But before she could question him, he seemed to shake away whatever thoughts were mulling, and turned to her, wrapping his arms around her too, their bodies close together, and their faces looking directly into each other. 'Go on,' he coaxed.

August lost her words for a second, distracted by the intimacy. She cleared her throat. 'I overheard something, from the landlady. She was talking to her son and she really only wants to rent to one type of person, or people: a couple. A married couple.'

'I'm not sure that's legal,' Flynn replied, a small laugh escaping.

'Well, it probably isn't, and I think her son's been trying to tell her that, but the fact is that's what she wants, she's already been turning people away, and us arguing with her might make a point but it won't get us in the door.'

'Why does she want a married couple?'

'Something about stability and not wanting fickle singletons coming and going and moving in and out.'

'I'm beginning to see where this is going,' Flynn said, noticing the landlady in the snug for the first time, and how August was still nestled in his arms.

'We'd just need to pretend we're married for the *tiniest* amount of time.'

'Whooooa,' Flynn laughed and on seeing that the landlady and her son had left the snug, he dropped his arms and took a step away from August. 'Pretend we're married? I thought you were going to say pretend to be a couple.'

'It's the same thing!' August cried.

'It's not the same thing at all. If we tell her we're a couple we can then tell her we've split up the next time we see her. If we tell her we're married that's a whole different . . . everything.'

'It's just semantics,' August said, waving his concern away. And even if it wasn't that easy, she'd find a way to make it work. It would be *fine*. 'Have you seen how much interest there is in this place? There are other couples in there *right now* trying to prove they'd make the best tenants. We need to fit the bill, exactly.'

'But . . . married?'

'Yes. Married. It has to be, because she's not going to want just a couple who might split up and move out. She wants people who are dependable, solid, that's what she said.'

'But what if we aren't in it for the long haul? What if I don't like my job and decide to move out in six months? What if you decide to move on?'

'I *am* in it for the long haul,' August said, certainty in her voice and in her heart. 'I will not move out; I won't let her down. And if you need to move on that's fine, we can handle it, and I'll have proved myself as a great tenant by then.' She didn't want to plead with him, but every part of her was in fact silently begging him, this virtual stranger, to help her.

Her grandmother's hand. The feel of it inside her own

flashed into her mind at that point, out of nowhere. Being a school child, climbing this hill with the woman who had meant more to her than anyone in the world, who had looked after her, homed her in the holidays, especially after her parents' messy divorce and subsequent leaving of her dad, told her stories and explained how to grow up. And the memory of that warm hand, skin soft from years of thick cream applied daily but wrinkled like the soft folds of worn leather, now tingled against her palms. August turned her face away from Flynn for a moment and looked out across the gardens.

'What are you thinking?' he asked her.

'Nothing,' August answered. It wasn't fair to lay what she was really remembering on him. Eventually she said, 'Just that I'd be willing to give you the bigger room ... So what do you think?'

Chapter 12

Flynn

What did he think? He thought the whole idea was utter madness. He thought he was wasting time even being out here with her at this moment. He thought he had it all figured out before he'd even left Japan, and that everything was going to be easy.

Who even was this girl, and why would he get himself involved in this? Flynn stifled a yawn as he processed his feelings, the exhaustion of moving hemispheres, battling jet lag, flat-hunting, feeling anxious about starting a new job in the morning, all weighing down on him. It would be nice to just have a home sorted. Even if he had to stick it out in the hotel for another couple of weeks, knowing he wouldn't need to try to book flat viewings into his evenings was pretty tempting.

But this wasn't him; he wasn't one to take chances and get mixed up in hairbrained schemes.

'Come on,' August cajoled at that exact moment. 'I know you have an adventurous streak, you just moved here from *Japan*, for crying out loud.'

A memory of Yui hit him like a sucker punch, again, the image of her face before him, her eyes disappointed, her lips exhaling a sigh. *I was never adventurous enough for you*, Flynn thought.

Perhaps . . . perhaps he should take more chances. Perhaps he should throw caution to the wind from time to time. What would he tell Yui if they spoke, if he didn't? *'Oh, I had the opportunity to have a great home but I didn't want to take a chance on it not working out.'*

Flynn didn't know if pretending to be a couple would even work. He wasn't about to lie in any documentation, but then equally the landlady shouldn't be discriminating against non-marrieds, so the whole thing was just an ethical mess. But, was there really any harm in trying? August was right, they would be good tenants. They seemed to get along, for the most part, and they both really wanted to live here. He *needed* to live *somewhere*.

Flynn took a deep breath, and, with Yui's face in his mind, asked, 'The bigger room would be mine?'

She snapped her head back around to look at him, her eyes wide. 'Yes, yes, it could be all yours.'

'All right, then.'

'All right? All right you'll do this?'

'Yes, let's give it a shot.'

August threw her arms around his neck and hugged him so hard the heels of her feet lifted off the ground. With her lips beside his ear and his arms around her back she asked, 'Are you sure? Are you really sure?'

'Yes. I'm not making any promises though, we don't know if she'll even like us. And if it involves anything illegal with the paperwork I'm out.'

'Of course, of course,' she agreed, that would indeed be stepping too far. 'Thank you, Flynn, you don't know what this means to me.'

Actually, he thought he did.

To anybody watching August and Flynn embracing on the balcony, framed by tall French doors, they would have seen a couple of people who, right now, looked very much in love.

Chapter 13

Flynn

Stepping back inside, Flynn and August walked hand in hand through the apartment, making their way towards Mrs Haverley, who was just finishing talking with another couple before they walked away looking pleased with themselves.

Mrs Haverley however turned and muttered, 'Bloody hippies.'

Flynn glanced toward the couple, who were smiling, arm in arm and taking one last look before exiting the property. Apart from her nose stud, and the shell necklace he was wearing, they didn't look very hippy-like to him.

'Mrs Haverley?' August spoke first, dropping Flynn's hand to reach out and shake the landlady's. August's voice had dropped a touch, like when somebody has a posh 'phone voice', only this silky, confident tone was like the room had been silenced and a pleasant audiobook had been started.

'Hello,' Mrs Haverley said with suspicion, looking between them.

'Mrs Haverley, thank you for giving up your morning to allow us – to allow us *all* – to have a look around your beautiful home. It must be a great pain to have all these people traipsing through, and on your Sunday, no less.'

Mrs Haverley tilted her head. 'Well, it is a little, yes,' she said. 'But no matter, it has to be done.'

Flynn was impressed. August seemed to know exactly what to say. He wondered if she'd taken improv classes in her past, or whether she just had a natural ability for reading people and reacting to them.

August continued, reaching a hand to Flynn's arm, sliding it down in an oh-so-familiar way. Comfortable and close without being too intimate or showy. 'May I introduce myself and my husband, Flynn. My name's August.'

'Hello,' Mrs Haverley said again, with a respectful nod.

'I'll cut to the chase, if I may, because I'm sure you've had quite enough waffle from people extolling the virtues of this place: the views, and the space, and the ceiling height,' August hesitated. This was a tightrope she was walking on. Perhaps Mrs Haverley *did* want to hear those things, after all, who doesn't like flattery? But if Flynn had to guess, which August also appeared to be doing, he'd place his bets on the landlady being a factual, rather than emotional, person.

A small smile played on Mrs Haverley's lips, and Flynn noticed August let out a tiny exhale of relief. 'My husband and I would like to move in, as soon as possible. We are dependable, we are extremely self-sufficient and we would be fantastic tenants for you.'

'Is that so?' Mrs Haverley asked.

Flynn felt he better jump in quick before she labelled him a doormat or some such thing. 'That's right, Mrs Haverley. We would be honoured to start our married life in this very apartment.'

'And what do you both do?' Mrs Haverley asked.

Relieved she hadn't pressed on the marriage issue, Flynn said. 'I work in law. International law.'

To which August added, 'He works for one of the top law firms in Bath. I am employed within Bath tourism and also do theatrical work.'

'Theatrical work?' Mrs Haverley asked.

Flynn stiffened and he felt August tense against his arm. Was that the right or wrong thing to say? Was August about to be labelled a hippy?

But Mrs Haverley smiled again, one of her small, tight smiles. 'I do enjoy the theatre.'

'Oh, I'm so glad,' August said. 'Did you catch *The Mousetrap* when it came to the Theatre Royal last autumn?'

'I didn't – were you in it?' Mrs Haverley's interest had clearly been piqued.

August laughed, pleasantly, bashfully, and said, 'Sadly not.'

'I don't actually get to the theatre that often,' Mrs Haverley added. 'Not as often as I'd like.'

'Well, perhaps we'll have to change that.'

Flynn watched as August went from another-prospective-tenant to Mrs Haverley's companion in a matter of breaths.

Is this how she'd talked him around too? It was quite something to watch. But it didn't seem fake. It didn't seem as though she was acting. This appeared to be August's genuinely warm personality, embellished and adapted to suit the current company. That's not a bad way to get by in life, Flynn thought.

Mrs Haverley looked from August to Flynn and back again for a moment, seeming to think things through, and then said. 'You say you could move in right away?'

'As soon as you would like,' answered Flynn.

'Would two weeks be suitable? There's a little maintenance to be done, unfortunately.'

'Two weeks would be perfect,' August nodded. 'Wouldn't it, darling? Just enough time to get our other affairs in order.'

'And you're certain this is the apartment for you?' Mrs Haverley confirmed. 'Not looking to buy a semi-detached out in the countryside?' She asked this with a curl of her lip, as if she couldn't imagine anything worse than suburban life.

'Oh no,' August answered. 'We're far too committed to living here in the city, and on this street in particular. My grandmother lived not too far away, so I know the roads around here well. I'm actually rather fond of this house.'

'Do you sometimes sit on the wall out there, eating ice cream?' Mrs Haverley asked, all of a sudden.

Flynn saw August stumble for words for a millisecond, and was about to jump in when she regained her composure. 'Um, well, yes, actually. Often in my lunch breaks I walk up here. I mean I don't always have ice cream for lunch, but you know, once in a while, or once a week, doesn't do much harm ...'

Mrs Haverley just nodded. 'I'd like to speak to my son now, if you'll excuse me. Perhaps you could stay around for a while longer, or leave your telephone number somewhere I might find it. What were your names again?'

'Flynn and August,' Flynn said, feeling August's hand lace with his and squeeze tightly.

'Flynn and August. Unusual names.' Mrs Haverley nodded to herself. 'Memorable though, and not as unusual as some names people are giving their children now.' And with that, she'd walked away.

'Do you think we're getting the apartment?' August asked in a whisper, her voice shaking a little, her hand sweating against Flynn's.

'It sounds like we might be,' he replied. 'What do you reckon our chances are with the son?'

August pondered. 'Not bad. He seems like a bit of a grouch, but also like he just wants his mum to get on and pick someone to live here. That might work in our favour if she's been hard to please up until now.'

'You might be right.'

They waited for a bit, looking out the window, both trying not to let their hopes get too high. He could sense, though, that August's hopes were practically clawing their way through the roof, and up into the atmosphere, until she asked, 'Is this idea a bit bonkers?'

'Yep,' answered Flynn.

'Are you annoyed at me?' she asked, quite serious.

'Not at all. You didn't force me.'

'I forced you a *little* bit.'

'It takes more than a pretty face and some skilled persuasion to force me to do anything.'

August shrugged. 'Well, that's all it takes for me, so luckily *we* won't have a problem,' she joked.

Abe walked into the living room, clapped his hands together and the gathering stopped whatever corner of wallpaper they were admiring to face him.

'Thank you for coming, everybody,' he said, with all the sincerity of a tanked lobster inside the entranceway of a restaurant. 'I have an announcement to make.'

Chapter 14

August

'Mrs Haverley has now settled upon tenants, pending paperwork,' Abe said to the room. 'If any of you would still, truly, be interested should this arrangement fall through, please take an application form on your way out and return it promptly so we may keep it on file.'

August and Flynn held their breath, and their hands, not that they strictly needed to still be holding hands at this point, but it felt like moral support.

And then it happened. Abe's gaze swept the room and landed on their faces. He walked over, all immaculate and handsome and formal, and asked, 'Remind me. You are ... ?'

'Flynn Miyoshi, and this is August ... my wife.'

'August Anderson. I kept my name.' She held her hand out to shake, but instead Abe placed an application form into it.

'Abe Haverley. You two are the "winners", as it were; my mother has deemed you suitable to rent this apartment from her.'

'That's very kind,' August squeaked, really trying to keep her cool.

'Fantastic news,' Flynn said a little too loud, causing a few sneers from the other hopefuls, now exiting the flat.

'Yes,' said Abe. 'Would you mind completing this application form so we can make it official? I'll also need to see some documentation to prove your right to rent in the UK, that could be a passport—'

Before he'd even finished his sentence, both Flynn and August had whipped their passports out of their pockets.

'Right, thank you.' He took the passports and used an app on his phone to take a digital scan of both passports. Afterwards, he pulled two contracts out of his briefcase and handed them over, along with their returned passports. 'Here's the contract. If you could have a read through and sign them – you can either both sign one or sign one each, it doesn't really matter. Could you return both the contracts and application form within an hour or two, please, as I need to head back to London late this afternoon.'

'Of course,' said August, taking the items from his hands. 'Are you just here for the weekend?'

Abe smiled for what seemed the first time. 'Just this weekend, and the last, and the one before that. But I think we're finally there.'

'Well, we'll go and get a coffee nearby right now, go over these, and then drop them back over.'

'Thank you,' Abe said, back to formalities. 'I'll then have my mother look through everything and counter-sign before I leave, and I'll make copies of the contracts and get them in the post to you, first class.'

Better use my address on the application form, August thought.

With Abe leading the way, August and Flynn left the apartment that would soon be theirs, and as the three of them descended the staircase August ran her hand on the bannister, saying a silent hello and asking it, *remember me?*

At the bottom of the stairs, as he opened the door, Abe said, 'Just to be clear, Mrs Haverley, my mother, will be your landlady. This house belongs to her. She is who you go to for any questions before and after you move in. However,' he lowered his voice a little. 'Here is my card, please store my number. She won't like to think you're coming to me behind her back, but if you need to, this is how you reach me.' He paused, fiddling with the card before handing it over, a small wash of sadness seeming to drift past his eyes. 'She's ... well ... we're all getting older I suppose. I really don't mind, please do let me know if you need anything.'

With that, Abe seemed to pull himself together, right as August was about to reach her hand out to touch his, probably very expensive, suit arm. 'Right, so you'll be dropping the contracts back around in an hour or so?'

'We will,' answered Flynn. 'Thank you,' he said.

'Yes, thank you,' August said, genuinely.

'And thank you,' said Abe. 'I'm glad my mother has found some very nice new people to share her home. People that she's actually happy with.'

He closed the door with a nod, and August watched his face disappear from view, hoping that she really would live up to expectations.

August waited. She waited until the two of them were out of the house and curling their way down Elizabeth Street's hill before she let herself breathe and happy tears spilled over. She dropped Flynn's hand and covered her mouth.

She looked up at him with soggy eyelashes and a pink face, unable to speak any words.

August was going to live there. Finally. Finally, her dreams were coming true. 'I can't believe this is happening,' she managed to choke out.

'It's happening,' he laughed. 'And there's nothing on this application form about marriage, or proving we are married.' He was flicking through the document on the street. 'We need to give a deposit, which will be put into a tenancy deposit protection scheme, but if you want you can transfer me some money and I'll do that. Or the other way around. And we need to give an address for at least one of us, so we'd better put yours if that's okay?'

'Yes, that's okay. Flynn?'

He looked up. 'Yep?'

'We're going to live together!'

And luckily, instead of this realisation dawning on him and him running for the hills, he just let a huge grin cross his face. 'I don't know anybody else in Bath I'd rather live with.'

August was happy. 'Come on, let's go and get that

paperwork out the way, and then tonight I'm taking you out for dinner. Pizza?'

'You don't have to do that,' he said.

'Oh, do you have big plans with room service in front of terrestrial TV?'

'Good point, pizza would be great.'

She nodded, satisfied. 'Back to the coffee shop at the bottom of the hill? I hope you liked it, because it's soon going to be our local.'

Chapter 15

August

August floated about the rest of the day, making imaginary plans about how she'd spend her days on Elizabeth Street, drafting an email notice to her landlord about leaving her current flat, lapsing into long daydreams where she remembered visiting the house with her grandma.

This really felt like the start of something. A new beginning. The first, and longest, dream coming true and paving the way for her other goals to follow suit. She knew she'd returned to Bath at the right time, and that the temporary flat she was in now, and the temporary James whose heart hadn't aligned with hers, were just fillers, warm-ups for the bigger acts of her life.

When the time came to head out for dinner, August was still on cloud nine.

She walked down the narrow street towards the pizza restaurant, and paused on the corner, seeing Flynn already inside, seated by the window. He'd changed out of his suit jacket and into a blue sweatshirt, and seemed to keep pushing the sleeves up, then pulling them down, then pushing them up again. His dark hair flopped on his forehead as he looked down, and his strong, open face was framed by the window pane. He was quite a pretty picture really, August observed.

Her circumstances were very different from his, but there was something soothing about the knowledge things were slotting into place. He was a nice guy. *I'm glad I met you today*, she told him, silently.

She opened the door of the restaurant with a tinkle, and Flynn looked up, beaming when he saw her. She was the only person he knew in the city, and although he'd only met her this morning, to her it seemed that he relaxed with happy familiarity that fizzed through seeing her again.

He grinned as she came towards him, and she kept her smile as bright as the colours of her outfit, which bounced against the cool, dark tones of the pizzeria, and seemed to contrast against the cool, dark tones of him.

'Hello, again,' she said.

'Hello, again to you,' he replied, and stood up.

There was a moment when they weren't sure how to greet each other. They'd gone from strangers to sharing a home together in less than a day. A wave? A handshake? A hug? A kiss on the cheek? All of the above?

They wavered, both let out a nervous laugh, and made the joint decision at the last minute to go in for a hands-on-arms, quick-peck-on-the-cheek hello. For a tiny fraction of a second when the skin of their cheeks touched, a breath of August's perfume and Flynn's aftershave fused together in the air between them.

Chapter 16

Flynn

Sitting in the window of the pizzeria, Flynn couldn't quite believe how much his fortunes had changed in twenty-four hours. This time last night he was eating instant noodles courtesy of his hotel kettle, nursing his blistered feet and desperately re-scouring the property websites for anything he'd missed. He'd widened his searches to nearby villages, upped his budget as much as he could possibly stretch it, and then spilled tea on what had been (until now) his last remaining sweatshirt.

And now, he had a home. Even with a two-week delay before moving in, at least he had it sorted. It was strange and satisfying and sad all at once because he wouldn't be living with Yui this time, but he would be *living* again, rather than in this strange twilight zone of jet lag and hotel room.

August, this woman who had gone from stranger, to

potential flatmate, to fake wife, and was now maybe a new friend, asked him, 'What did you do with the rest of your day?'

'I bought some shirts and a clean jumper to wear,' Flynn said, gesturing to himself. 'The last thing I needed was to drip melted cheese over my suit before my first day tomorrow.'

'It looks nice,' August commented, taking a seat and signalling to the waitress for a beer also. 'I mean, it's a nice jumper.'

'Thanks. It's a little too warm if I push the sleeves down though, and a little too cold if I push them up.'

'Poor Goldilocks.'

'I know, right? My life is so complicated.' They smiled at each other, and there was a brief pause in the conversation. When August's beer arrived, along with some smoked almonds to nibble on, they both made a comment about how the food 'hit the spot', and then fell quiet again after placing their pizza orders.

Flynn leaned forward and said in a low voice, 'We haven't run out of things to talk about already, have we?'

At that, August laughed, a big, head-thrown-back laugh. 'Why are we being so weird?' she said.

'My mind has gone blank! I could tell you about my new jumper again?'

'Oh my God, that was so fascinating, could you go over the parts about the temperature of your forearms one more time?' They paused again, sipping their beers, and August said, 'I don't think we've run out of things to talk about, I think I just don't know where to begin.'

'I think you're right. I keep nearly saying things and then thinking, did I already cover that this morning?'

'We talked for a long time this morning. But . . . don't take this the wrong way . . . ' August hesitated. 'I don't remember a lot of what you said.'

It was Flynn's turn to laugh hard. 'I thought it was just me! I can barely remember a thing from our conversations!'

'I know I had fun talking to you, and I found you interesting, but most of the time I was just thinking about the open house.'

'I'm really a good listener most of the time, I promise, I just need a good night's sleep.'

'Do you think you'll get that tonight?' August asked.

'Almost certainly not, but I hope so. Just knowing I have a place lined up again now makes me feel a lot calmer. I can put up with another couple of weeks of the hotel now there's an end in sight, and I don't have to try and squeeze in house-hunting after hours.'

They ordered another round of beers, and both relaxed into their surroundings. August looked at Flynn. 'Let's slow things down and start again from the beginning. If we go over old ground, so be it. Tell me again what happened to the house you were supposed to move into when you flew in from Japan – you said something about the owners splitting up?'

'Yes, exactly that. Quite sad really. It happened while I was on the flight over, but I didn't check my voicemail until I was already on the coach heading towards Bath, and they broke the news that they couldn't take in a lodger anymore, and would I mind finding somewhere else at this time. They offered to pay for a hotel for me until I found a new home, but I didn't want to do that to them. Divorce can be expensive enough, and I was supposed to be helping them out, money-wise, not costing them more.'

'So, if you'd found out as soon as you got off the plane, would you have gone straight back to Japan?'

'No,' Flynn said, and for a moment he drifted to somewhere else, to the other side of the world, before he returned to the present. 'No, but I might have just stayed at an airport hotel in London for the night instead.'

'Do you miss Japan?' August asked, catching Flynn's faraway look.

'I mean, I've only been back in England for forty-eight hours,' he replied.

'That doesn't answer my question.'

'It's a hard question to answer at the moment.'

'Fair enough. Did you miss England when you were out there?'

'Yes,' he considered this while he sipped on his beer. 'I missed it, but not because I felt like I was missing out. I loved living in Japan, but loving Japan didn't stop me from loving the UK too, and the same is true vice versa.'

The pizzas arrived, Flynn's a classic pepperoni, laden with mini bell peppers, a scattering of basil leaves and reams of stringy mozzarella. August had a Hawaiian, with fresh, grilled pineapple chunks scattered over big pieces of thick-cut bacon.

'I get what you're saying, that you like both countries and

missing one doesn't detract from valuing the other. But what caused you to swap Japan for England again?'

'I guess it was time for a change,' he said, eventually, and then looked her in the eye. 'I can always go back, I guess.'

'Of course,' nodded August. 'Just not for a while, okay?'

Flynn picked up another slice. 'You moved here from London, right? Did you say last year?'

'Six months ago,' she confirmed.

'What made you decide to make the move?'

August looked out of the window at Bath. 'I just wanted to come home.'

'This is where you grew up?'

'Not really, but not far. It was more my grandma's home, and my best friend Bel's, but I only grew up maybe an hour or so away. For me it wasn't that I wanted to come *back* home, but that this is the place I wanted to *call* home. Bath, for as long as I can remember, felt like it would be my home one day. I just knew it.'

'What is it about Bath? You mentioned that you came back all the time for big life events. It can't just be the house – *your new flat* – on Elizabeth Street?'

'The whole place is perfect to me,' replied August. 'The architecture, the history, the way the past – both real, and fictional, thank you Jane Austen – feels like it's soaked into the pavements of this city. It's just inspiring, and feeling inspired makes me feel excited. And happy.' She shrugged. 'I wanted to be happy.'

'That was a good answer, did you rehearse that?' Flynn teased.

'A little. You'd be amazed the number of people who seem surprised that I'd give up living in London to move to Bath.'

'Really? How come?'

'Because I'm an actress and I left a city with probably two hundred theatres to come to one with maybe a handful. But something you should know about me, Flynn, is that I like a challenge.'

'I can tell,' he laughed. 'Remind me what kind of acting you do?'

'Mainly voice work, which is just the most fun. I love it.'

'It sounds really fun, and you have a nice voice.' He cringed because that felt like an odd way to compliment someone, but she just smiled at him and continued.

'I do a lot of audiobooks and educational material. "A lot" might be an overstatement though. And it's been a while, to be honest, though I'm planning to change that. I also voiced a squirrel in a videogame once.'

'That's very cool!'

'It was pretty awesome,' August agreed with a sparkle of pride.

From there, and over the remaining slices of their respective pizzas, the conversation between Flynn and August flowed easily again, as easy as it had that morning. He told her about his life in England before he had returned to Japan with his parents, then about his job, and his anxieties about his starting work the next day.

Flynn had already been fully versed that morning about August's long history with their new house, but chatting to her now over beers he understood what her grandmother meant to her, and began to see glimpses, like sunlight reflecting off glass, of who she wanted to become.

When they were both full, August yawned and said, 'Do you mind if we call it a night? I'm worn out from all the talking we've done today. And that's coming from a voice actress.'

'Ha, not at all, that's fine,' Flynn said, yawning also. They stood up, leaving money for the bill. 'Shall I walk you back home?'

August waved him away. 'No, that's fine, it's not like we're on a date. Go and get some sleep. And good luck tomorrow.'

As they exited the pizzeria, Flynn asked, 'Should we get rings? Prop ones, I mean?'

August thought it about it for a moment and then chuckled. 'No, I don't think we should. You know we'd forget to put them on, or worse, we'd forget to take them off and then be unlucky in love for a year and be wondering why nobody was hitting on us.'

'Good call. If the landlady comments about the lack of rings we can just say they're being cleaned.'

Outside, the air had grown cool, the streets close to empty, it being a Sunday night. A breeze ruffled the leaves of a nearby tree, and August and Flynn's goodbye suddenly felt as awkward as their hello had.

'I'm really glad I met you today,' Flynn settled on. 'You saved my bacon.'

'Right back atcha,' August said. And with that, they turned to go their separate ways, before she called after him, 'Flynn?'

'Yep?'

'I'm sure you're going to be kept super-busy with your new job and all your new workmates, but if you need someone to hang out with over the next couple of weeks, just drop me a message.'

Sadly, he feared he wouldn't have much time for hanging out at all, but it was something he didn't want to dismiss out of hand. So he simply smiled, nodded, and said, 'I'd like that.'

Chapter 17

August

There was a breakfast spot in Bath that August could always count on to make great coffee, and even better pancakes. On Monday morning she'd hauled herself out of bed super-early in order to meet Bel before her friend had to get to the practice where she worked as a dentist. For two self-proclaimed morning people, both had arrived late, dashing in the door and making snap-decision orders at the counter.

'I'm *starving*,' declared Bel, sitting down at the table by the window, the dawn light just beginning to paint the pane of glass a soft peach.

'Same,' August answered. 'I had a piece of toast to keep me going before I left home, but now I'm famished again.'

'I just had, like, a tiny bowl of cereal. Just in case food took a while.'

'That's good thinking. I mean you've probably got a busy day at work and breakfast is important. I had peanut butter on one of my bits of toast and cherry curd on the other. Oh, I guess I had two bits.'

'Cherry curd sounds nice. I had an apple too, just for some vitamins. Oh and a Pop Tart but that's just like having a biscuit with a cuppa.'

'Exactly,' nodded August. 'Let's hope our food arrives soon.'

Bel removed her jumper as the waiter set down two big white mugs full of creamy coffee. 'It's hot out today. So what did you want to chat about? How are you doing?'

'I am *good*.'

'You are?' Bel looked puzzled. 'Did you and James get back together over the weekend?'

August sipped her coffee and shrugged her shoulders. 'James who?'

'*Yas*, James who!' Bel laughed. 'But seriously, when we spoke on the phone on Saturday you were pretty cut up about him dumping you—'

August cleared her throat pointedly.

'Sorry, about *you* dumping *him*. Now you're all bright-eyed and bushy-tailed. Are you drunk already?'

'No, it's like seven-thirty in the morning! I wait until at least nine.'

'Then what is it? What changed?'

Their pancakes arrived, two steaming stacks on wide white plates. 'I had some time to think,' August explained. 'James was but a blip and not worth wasting any more energy on.' Even though the words were coming from her mouth, August wasn't entirely convinced by them. She and James

92

had been growing closer over the four months since their first date, and it still stung her heart, and her pride, that he'd broken the news that he was done with getting to know her. So yes, in theory, she was grateful not to be wasting energy on someone who wasn't genuinely interested in a future with her, but her soul still needed a little feeding before it caught up. With that in mind, she became impatient for the bottle of syrup Bel was hogging. 'You know, for a dentist you eat more sugar than anyone I know.'

'I know, right?' She continued to pour on the syrup for what felt like an age, before relinquishing it to August. 'But don't shame me, and don't tell my patients.'

'Oh, I'm not shaming you,' August said, starting her own waterfall of syrup upon her pancakes. 'And I am one of your patients.'

'Don't tell the ones that pay.'

'Deal. So, I have news . . . ' August declared, diving into her stack, finally. 'I'm moving.'

'No! Not back to London? You only returned to Bath six months ago!'

'Nope, not back to London, I'm staying here, I just got a new flat.'

'But not with James?' Bel clarified.

'No, not with James.'

Bel hesitated, realising why her friend had that familiar, excitable bounce about her. She'd done something a little crazy. 'Wait, is this to do with the house on Elizabeth Street?'

'Yes!'

'Are you renting that apartment you told me about? The one you couldn't afford to rent alone?'

'Yes!' August was grinning.

'But you can't afford to rent it alone . . . Did you come into some money? Are you planning to squat? Aug, I've told you that's not the way—'

'Relax, I'm not squatting, I'm renting, all above board and legitimately, pretty much.'

'Oh God. What does that mean?'

'Can you believe I'm finally going to live in that house?' August said by way of reply.

'I mean, it's about time,' Bel agreed. 'Most people's dream home is some mansion in Beverly Hills, but you've been banging on about that place since school.'

'I'm obsessed with it, and I have no problem admitting it. And now I can live there!'

'How come though? Like I've been saying . . . Isn't it too expensive? Did you find someone to rent with?'

'Exactly. I'm going to give notice on my place today and I should be able to start moving in within a couple of weeks.' August took a big, satisfied gobble of her pancakes.

'Who are you moving in with?'

'How are your pancakes?'

'Incredible, but who are you moving in with?' Bel pressed.

'Just this guy.'

Bel put down her knife and fork and sat back in her chair.

'"Just this guy?" "Just this guy", she says. Which guy?'

'A guy called Flynn.'

'Flynn?'

'Yes, Flynn. It's a cute name, huh? Don't you want any more of those?' August reached across the table but Bel slapped her away.

'People called Flynn aren't just "some guy". Flynns are bad boys. Flynns wear leather jackets, and will ask to put their hands up your blouse at the drive-in. Flynns are Casanovas.'

'Okay,' August scoffed. 'I'll be on guard at the next drive-in I go to. You don't even know any Flynns.'

'I know hundreds of Flynns.'

Now August put down her utensils and folded her arms, sitting back in amusement. 'Name one Flynn who fits this Casanova theory of yours. In fact, name just one Flynn you know.'

'Flynn Rider.'

'The guy from *Tangled*?'

'He was a wanted criminal.'

'He was the hero! I mean along with her.' August added, 'Plus he was a cartoon, so I'm discounting him. Who else have you got?'

'Jerome Flynn.'

'That's a surname, and he's a national treasure.'

Bel thought for a moment. 'Well, his character in *Game of Thrones* was quite the ladies' man.'

August rolled her eyes. 'Next.'

'Oh, I know,' Bel leant forward, clicking her fingers. 'That guy I went on a couple of dates with before I met Steve. The one who tried to take me on a ski holiday for the second date.'

'Wasn't he called Jordan?'

'Yeah, but he was *such* a Flynn.'

Laughter popped out of August. 'You have nothing, your evidence isn't even circumstantial. This case is dismissed and you have to go to prison for filing a false claim.'

'All right, all right, so who is this "Flynn" and how come you're moving in with him?'

August resumed her pancake eating. 'He's really nice, and I met him just before the open house yesterday morning—'

'You *just* met him?'

'Yes, I just met him, but that doesn't automatically mean I'll let him feel me up at a drive-in movie.'

'I need more coffee,' Bel signalled for the waiter. 'May we get two more coffees, please, and can you double-shot the hazelnut syrup in them? Thanks.' She turned back to August. 'How do you know he won't do that, or worse, if you've only just met him?'

'Because I asked him if he was a murderer, and he said no.'

'Oh well, that's fine, then.'

'And I told him I wasn't one either. Seriously though, he seems like a really nice man, and I would have had to advertise for a flatmate anyway. They would have probably been a stranger.'

'Not ... necessarily.' Bel said.

August looked at her. 'Well, were you about to leave your fiancé to live on his own so you could shack up with me?'

'No ... But I could have put some feelers out. We could still find you someone who's maybe a friend of a friend.'

'No, it has to be Flynn.'

Bel raised an eyebrow. 'Why? Why does it have to be him?'

'I *want* it to be Flynn. We talked for hours yesterday, before the open house even started, and then we went out for pizza in the evening to get to know each other more.' She still felt as though she was only scratching the surface of why he'd left the Land of the Rising Sun for the Land of the Infrequent Sun, maybe over time she'd get there.

'You went on a date with him?'

'*No*, it absolutely wasn't a date.' The last thing she needed was to mess this all up by trying to date the man who'd agreed to move in with her.

Bel got out her phone.

'What are you doing?' August asked.

'I'm texting Kenny to tell him I'll be in late today because my friend is having a nervous breakdown.'

August batted the phone out of her hand, stopping Bel from contacting Kenny, her dental nurse and friend. 'I am not having a nervous breakdown; I am actually very happy with the decisions I've made.'

'Back it up then, and tell me what's going on.'

August took a breath and explained how both she and Flynn had arrived on Elizabeth Street early, how he'd just flown in from Japan and was desperate to just get some accommodation sorted before starting his new, really busy job, and about how the place was perfect for both of them, so it made sense to just rent it together.

'There's something you're not telling me,' declared Bel when August had finished.

'Nope, that's everything.'

'No . . . ' Bel leaned forward and studied her friend's face. 'No, you're leaving something out, I can tell by your twitchy eyebrows.'

'I do not have twitchy eyebrows, I am an actress and I have full control over my face, thank you very much.'

'Tell that to your eyebrows. What's going on?'

August hesitated. 'Well, there is one thing . . . ' Bel waited, without saying a word. 'It's only a small thing, but there is a reason it has to be him that I move in with.'

'I knew it. I knew that nothing is ever just easy breezy with you. What's the reason?'

'We just have to, very occasionally, just for show, no big deal, pretend to be . . . um . . . *married*.'

Bel sighed. 'You and Casanova have to pretend to be *married*?'

'Yes, but only to the landlady.'

'Oh, good, I thought it would be to someone integral to the contract, like the postman!'

'All right, Sarcastic Sue.'

'What do you mean you have to pretend to the landlady that you're married? Why do you need to do that?'

'Because I heard her telling her son she only wanted to rent to a married couple therefore this was our only way in. It was this or both of us be homeless.' August shrugged.

'Homeless? You haven't even handed in the notice to your current flat yet.'

'But Elizabeth Street is my real home, I can feel it.' August spent the next couple of minutes explaining to Bel and her rolling eyeballs all of the arguments she'd put forward to Flynn only the day beforehand out on the balcony, of why it wasn't worth fighting the landlady, and how the arrangement was advantageous to both of them. By the end, Bel was shaking her head, but smiling.

'This scheme is so typically August,' she said. 'And so is stubbornness, so I know I'm not going to change your mind.'

'You're not,' August said, firmly.

'And I won't try, you're obviously happy.'

'I am.'

'You're finally going to live in your dream home.'

'I am,' August replied, sighing softly, relaxing her shoulders. 'This feels like the start of something for me.'

Bel reached across and squeezed a sticky hand over August's. 'And Flynn really is a nice guy? You aren't just letting the dream home cloud your judgement?'

'He really is nice. He seems kind, and funny, and clever. I think you'll like him.'

'Okay, then, I'm happy for you.' Bel smiled and checked her watch before pulling out some cash. 'Listen, I'd better get going for work, but let's catch up again soon. And I want to meet this husband of yours.'

August gave her friend a thumbs up, and then lingered in the cafe a while longer after she'd gone. She wasn't letting the house cloud her judgement; she was sure of it. Flynn really did seem like he'd make a great flatmate. Though if she was honest with herself, really honest, she probably would have shacked up with Charles Manson if he was residing in the house on Elizabeth Street.

Chapter 18

Flynn

Flynn had a recurring tension headache that pulsed at his temples every time he gave himself thirty seconds to stop for a breather on his first day. He felt like a rookie, a fresh graduate, rather than someone with close to eight years working in law. The still-present jet lag, worsened by the still-present lack of sleep in his hot hotel room, the mountain of corporate policies and jargon for his new firm to learn, the volume of new names to remember and the knowledge he wasn't going to be getting a day off for nearly two weeks thanks to the conference at the weekend all culminated in this little gift to himself: the headache.

'It's a lot to take in,' said Shelly, his new manager, presenting him with a coffee he hadn't asked for but accepted gratefully. 'Is everything at your desk working okay?'

'Yes, seems great,' Flynn replied, clearing his throat,

pasting on a smile, and pushing acknowledgement of the pain quite literally to the back of his head.

'Bath must seem pretty different to life in Tokyo,' she smiled.

'It's definitely a culture shock,' Flynn laughed. But possibly not for the reason Shelly was thinking. Sure, Tokyo was a million times faster paced than this cathedral city in England, but right now he felt a lot more frazzled than he ever did in Japan. It would be different when he was settled, in his own place, caught up on sleep. He thought back to his apartment that he'd shared with Yui, with its calming décor, clean lines and tranquil lighting. Oh to be back there, napping on the window seat under a soft, cloudy sky, listening to the gentle rain on the glass.

He wondered if Yui was there now, on the window seat, dressed in her light grey dressing gown that she always wore. She said she might keep living there even when he was gone, but part of him wondered if she was just saying that to spite him.

Shelly walked away, leaving him to continue navigating his way through the company intranet. And it was at that moment his phone flashed up with a text.

A smile spread across Flynn's face. He hadn't noticed that she'd done this when he'd given August his phone at the end of dinner yesterday, to put her number into his contacts. She'd named herself 'The Wife'.

'Still want to live with me? In other words, do you have enough jet lag brain to make you still want to do this?'

He replied with, *'Yes, to both. And you?'*

August replied with four house emojis, four wedding ring emojis, and a gif of Chandler from *Friends* doing a happy dance. He took that as a yes.

In truth, he was a little apprehensive about moving in with a stranger, especially one he had to act like he was married to should the landlady ever come around. But this person had a way of bringing smiles to his face and bubbles of laughter from out of him, which felt like an energiser in this upheaval of a time.

Now he just had to get through the next two weeks in that hot hotel room and he would be in his very own home.

The days were busy, full of learning on the job, conference preparation and coffee-fuelled mornings, and, thankfully, those two weeks rushed by like a fast-moving river after a heavy rainfall.

Chapter 19

August

August spent the fortnight packing up her flat, removing traces of James, and having a clear-out. Come the weekend before the big move on Monday, her abode was wonderfully organised chaos. On one side of the living room (if you could even call it a room, it was sort of a snug with a kitchenette at one end) were bags of clothes, books and objects that hadn't 'sparked enough joy' during her Marie Kondo-style clear out. She was proud of those bags.

On the other side of the living room were all the boxes of clothes, books and objects, that, apparently, *did* spark joy. And so she'd kept them. Though looking at the shell lamp teetering perilously out of the top of one of them, she wasn't sure she'd been entirely ruthless enough. And then on the floor, like a scene from the latter half of *Home Alone*, were little mounds of 'stuff'. Stuff that didn't fit into a neat category and so didn't belong to a box. Stuff that was an odd shape. Stuff August couldn't decide if she loved or actually hated. Stuff that was tiny and looking to be swept up together with other tiny things in a pretty pouch of some kind to be forever left in the back of a drawer because who knows what to do with tiny things like that.

Her doorbell buzzed and August sighed, picking up the smallest box from the pile and tiptoeing over her things.

She opened the door to James. Seeing him again was ... well, what was it exactly? She had expected in this moment to feel a rush of sadness, or embarrassment, or something akin to the feelings she once held for him. But although it was strange not to reach for him or kiss him, she was missing a longing to do so.

'All right?' he asked, looking like he wanted to be done with this as fast as possible.

Relax, she wanted to say to him. *This isn't some ruse to try and get you back together with me.* 'Hi, James, thanks for stopping by, here are your things.'

He peered past her into her flat. 'Are you moving?'

'Yep.'

'To that house at the top of the hill?'

August laughed a little. 'On Elizabeth Street, yes.'

'Without me?'

She looked around. 'Well, I don't think I'm moving there *with* you. I'm pretty sure that's why we broke up.'

James nodded, lingering on her doorstep.

'Are you okay?' August asked.

'Yep,' he said, taking the box. 'Thanks for this. See you

104

later.' With that, he left, and August found herself wondering if Flynn was that weird.

Then she asked herself, *Why are you comparing Flynn to James?*

Chapter 20

August

It was move-in Monday and August was on Elizabeth Street before the sun had even had time to reach the top of the sky. Having enlisted the help of Steve and Bel to help her shift her boxes of stuff over before they started work, including the beautiful, and ginormous, jade velvet armchair she'd inherited from her grandma, she was now seated upon her throne on the opposite pavement, in front of the wall, gazing lovingly towards her new home.

A curtain twitched inside the building, and was then flung open. A blonde woman visibly jumped from behind the glass on seeing a stranger in an armchair staring up at her apartment.

August shuffled to try and make herself appear less creepy, and looked instead down the street, searching for signs of Flynn. When she glanced back towards the window, the curtains were firmly closed again.

There were four storeys to the townhouse: a top floor, with windows that angled themselves towards the sky and had a sort of stone balcony running across in front of them, then three levels of big, rectangular windows. Below that were the whispers of a basement level, peeping out from behind the eyelashes of the wrought iron railing. August didn't know if that was a whole separate flat, or part of the ground floor dwellings. The flat she and Flynn were moving into was one floor up, nestled in the middle. It currently had sunshine beaming against the panes of glass.

The front door of the house opened a crack, and the blonde woman poked her head out. 'Hello?' she called towards August, sitting with her belongings.

August scrambled from the armchair and waved. 'Hello! Sorry, I'm not a weirdo, I'm just moving in today.'

'Are you August?'

'I am!' She waved again, for good measure. 'I'm just waiting for my – my – my – Flynn, he's bringing the rest of, um, our things.'

'Great,' said blondie-head, and her head disappeared back in the door, only to reappear – along with the rest of her – a moment later, carrying two mugs, a bag of caster sugar dangling from her mouth. She set the mugs down on top of one of August's boxes and said, 'Sugar?'

'Oh, um, no, thank you. Thank you so much!'

'No problem,' said the woman, who August could now see was probably in her forties, athletic looking with a tan, dressed in floppy yoga pants and a Detroit Red Wings T-shirt. 'I'm Callie, your neighbour. I live up there with my mum.'

'Your mum isn't Mrs Haverley, is she?' August joked, checking that not everybody she ran into at Number Eighteen, Elizabeth Street was one of Mrs Haverley's offspring.

'No, no, though they get on like a house on fire, those two.'

August couldn't imagine the grumpy Mrs Haverley having a roaring time with anyone, but okay.

Callie continued. 'Mrs H's great, she let me move into Mum's spare room about a year ago after my marriage broke down. Mum needs a little extra help anyway, though she'd be pissed off if she heard me admitting that to you, so it's our little secret. Mrs H lives on the top floor.'

August looked up, surprised, shielding her eyes from the sunlight and looking at the top level of the house, with its skyward-windows. 'Oh. I didn't realise she actually lived in the building.' Oh no. This could make things a lot more awkward than she'd promised Flynn.

'Oh yeah, she loves this place. We all want her to move down to the ground floor though and swap with the couple that live there. They're more than happy to switch, at least they say they are, and Mrs H could do with less bloody steps to climb every day, but she's stubborn as anything. Don't tell *her* I told you *that*.'

'Okay,' laughed August.

At that moment, Flynn appeared, walking up the hill towards them. He rolled a large suitcase behind him and wore a bulging rucksack on his back. Compared to August's great pile of clobber he looked like he was just going on a weekend away.

August put down her mug and reached for Flynn, pulling him straight into a hug and whispering in his ear, 'Go with it.'

'Hi, darling!' she then said out loud.

Flynn looked from August to Callie and replied, 'Hello . . . sweetheart.'

'Callie, this is Flynn, Flynn, this is one of our neighbours, Callie.' She squeezed Flynn's hand. 'Callie lives in the flat above ours, and Mrs Haverley lives on the top floor. In there. In our building.'

Flynn followed her gaze up to the top floor and then blinked at Callie before pulling himself together and sticking out his hand. 'Hello, I'm Flynn.'

'Great to meet you,' Callie replied. 'Would you like a cuppa? Or a hand bringing in your things?'

'I'm fine, I just filled up on coffee,' Flynn replied, with an easy smile. August watched him, happy to see his face again, glad it was still as friendly as she remembered and it hadn't just been a trick of the light across his jet-lagged five o'clock shadow.

'And we can manage bringing these things in,' August added. 'I guess we didn't have a lot of stuff between us, once it's all in boxes.'

'Did Mrs H let the flat to you furnished?'

'Partially furnished,' August answered.

Callie nodded. 'Makes sense. The older couple that lived here before made a move to a retirement village near their kids, which probably would have had some furniture in already. They still went off with a whole removal van though.'

'I'm looking forward to seeing what's been left,' August said, excited to get inside and start flinging her colourful wares about the place.

'Before we do,' said Flynn, putting an arm around his 'wife'. 'Let's just take a moment to take it all in.'

Callie picked up her tea and the sugar bag and said, 'That's my cue to head back inside, I was just about to force my mum to take a yoga sesh with me so I'll catch up with you love birds later. August, just pop the mug outside my door when you're done.' She waved at them and disappeared back into the house, and Flynn and August turned, arm in arm, to look out across the view.

'So our landlady lives here in the building?' Flynn asked quietly, glancing towards August with an amused smile.

'Apparently so,' she agreed. 'I'm sorry, I didn't realise. It'll be okay though, right? How often do people run into their neighbours anyway?'

'Well, we just ran into one and we haven't even moved in yet. So what are we doing, pretending to everyone that we're married, or asking everyone else to pretend to Mrs Haverley?'

'I don't think we should ask anyone else to lie,' August replied, chewing on her lip. 'Let's just not make a big deal of it to anyone else. If we just act like close friends who are a bit touchy-feely, will they really know any different? I mean, my friend Bel and her fiancé have been together for years and it's not like I'm always catching them snogging, and they don't talk dirty to each other when I'm there.'

'Friends who are touchy-feely?' he clarified, and laughed.

'In front of other people,' August stated, firmly.

They made their way in through the door and up the stairs to the flat, murmuring quietly about the small fly in the ointment, and August was about to open their new door when a man stepped out wearing a baseball cap and a hoodie, looking down at his phone. August shrieked, causing him to drop his phone. He looked up, startled, and she realised it was Abe.

'Oh my God, I'm so sorry!' she said. He looked so different from the stuffy, suited Abe they'd met two weeks ago. This was off-duty Abe, she guessed.

'Hello,' he said, a little bewildered. He cleared his throat, bringing himself back to the 'Business Abe'. 'Just doing a final check that the lights were all working, before I catch a train back to London. Again. I wasn't expecting you here so early.'

'Oh, no problem, sorry about that,' August said, and reached behind her to hold Flynn's hand, hoping Abe hadn't heard anything they'd been saying.

'That's okay, I'll leave you to it.' He nodded a smile to both of them and high-tailed upstairs.

When he'd gone they stepped into the apartment, both being hit by the wonderful light streaming in through the windows again.

'Is this okay?' August asked Flynn. 'All this, I mean? I'm sorry it's more complicated than we – I – thought it would be.'

She watched as Flynn breathed in and savoured the moment. She imagined he was probably just glad to have a day off work, and to be finally out of the hotel. 'This is more than okay,' he confirmed. 'I just can't wait to have a bed of my own tonight.'

'Uh-oh.' Turning, August and Flynn noticed the problem at the exact same time.

Chapter 21

August

From the living room August and Flynn had a perfect view into the two bedrooms. One of them had a large, solid oak, king-sized bed that appeared to be brand new. The other: as bare as a naked lady. No bed, no furniture, nothing. One bed. Two people.

'Crap,' said August. 'I thought both beds were included.'

'Me too,' replied Flynn, and noticed a handwritten note atop the one bed. 'Look at this.'

They both leaned over the letter, written in the beautiful penmanship of someone who hadn't spent their lives predominantly typing to the point that five minutes with a biro caused hand-cramp. August read it aloud.

Dear Flynn and August,

Welcome to your new home, and welcome to Elizabeth Street. I hope you make many happy memories here, as I have.

I hope you can forgive the bed situation. When my previous residents moved out, my son and I took a look at the beds and decided they were too scruffy and dated. We have therefore replaced the master bed with a brand new one. Because of this, will you mind awfully purchasing a second bed for the spare room by yourselves? I wasn't sure what size bed you would like for the second room, or frankly whether you wanted it to be a full bedroom at all, or had other plans for it. The previous tenants simply had a sofa bed in the second room, which worked quite well for their set-up.

Should you need anything, you can find me at the top of the staircase in apartment 4. Though if the thing you need involves heavy lifting or a sharper mind, you may have better luck calling upon some of your other neighbours.

Warm wishes,

Mrs W. Haverley

'She's so nice,' August said, on finishing the letter. A pin-prick of guilt at misleading the woman stabbed at her. But they hadn't done anything very wrong, she was sure they would be ideal tenants, and she had no plans to move out, frankly, ever, which had been Mrs H's only concern about singletons.

'She is,' Flynn agreed, and their eyes met.

'Are we both thinking the same thing?' asked August. 'That we should just get married for real so this isn't awkward?'

'That wasn't quite where I was, but we're in the same area,' he said. She'd been joking, of course, but she felt him watching her as worry etched its way across her features, and he added, 'It's fine though, it's good that she's nice, and she seems to genuinely be happy we live here. We're still us, in holy matrimony or not.'

'You're right,' August shook herself out of it, determined to let moving-in day remain magical. Because she was here! In her dream home! With no bed . . .

'Right, then,' she said. 'I'll see if Bel could drive me over to Ikea or something after she's done at work so we can pick me up a flatpack bed and a mattress. In the meantime, could you give me a hand bringing my boxes up and into my room? Some of the stuff is living room/kitchen but I just shoved a lot of it in together so it'll be easier for both of us if I can just empty it out onto the floor of my room and ignore it for a few days.'

The two of them carted all the boxes and suitcases into the flat, and Ross-Geller-Pivoted the armchair up the narrow staircase without, mercifully, scuffing the wall.

'No,' said Flynn, stopping her before she could take a box marked 'bras', that he'd lifted previously and found to be surprisingly heavy, into the second bedroom. 'You take this bed.'

His chivalry, though appreciated, was betrayed somewhat by his own eyes, which gazed at that big, comfortable bed with the longing of someone about to eat their last slice of pizza before going on a month-long cabbage diet.

'No way,' she said, walking into the master bedroom with

Flynn following her. 'Your room, your bed. And no offence to those bags under your eyes, but you look like you need a good night's sleep. Jeeeesus.' She sat on the edge of the bed and immediately flopped backwards. 'And you are going to get a hell of a good night's sleep on this baby.'

Flynn sat down beside her. 'Why don't you just take this one? Wow, this is ...' He too lay back on the bed, so they were side-by-side, staring at the high ceiling above them. He cleared his throat. 'This is horrible,' he said, clearly lying. 'I hate this bed.'

'You do not hate this bed,' August said, turning her head to face him.

'How do you know? How do you know my back isn't seizing up as we speak?'

'It's obvious you love this bed; you're practically snogging it.'

Flynn laughed. 'I am not.' He faced her. 'But seriously, you take it. And the room.'

'Nope. This is your room; this was part of the deal. I wouldn't feel right going back on my word. And I don't need some white knight to give me his coat – or room – thank you very much.' She said it with a smile though.

'August,' Flynn said, and sat up, so she did the same.

'Flynn.'

'You don't need to keep acting like you pushed me into this, or apologising for unexpected turns of events. I'm very much a grown up, and we're in this together now.'

'But it was my idea,' she pressed.

'And I went along with it, very willingly. It was a good

idea. An idea that *I* would never have thought of, but that's just because I don't have your imagination. But we're here, the flat is great, I've finally got a place to call my own and you're finally getting to live in your dream home. So let's enjoy it.'

'Let's enjoy it,' she said, nodding. 'Shall I open a bottle of wine?'

'I mean, it's ten in the morning, but if that's what you're into.'

'Oh. Maybe tonight, then.'

'You know what else we should do tonight?' Flynn asked. His eyes flicked towards the bed, and then he slapped his forehead, as if he immediately regretted what he'd said. 'Not that! Oh God, I'm not a sex pest, I promise!'

Sleeping with her flatmate would be a b-a-d idea: August did not want him to run a mile, which was her current MO when it came to mixing housing and boyfriends. But right now if he suggested she *literally* slept next to him in this heavenly cloud of a bed, August would seriously consider it. 'What?' she asked.

'Have a strategy meeting.'

'Oh,' she crinkled her nose. 'That sounds dull. Can't we just agree you'll always do the bins if I always clean the toilet?'

'Not that kind of strategy, I think we need to figure out us, in relation to them,' he pointed above and below, indicating that he meant their neighbours.

August nodded. 'I see. We need to bump uglies to decide what we tell people in the building about us being married.'

Flynn looked very surprised. 'We need to do *what* now?'

'Bump uglies.'

'Um ...'

'You know, Flynn, bump uglies,' she tapped the side of her temple. 'Like, put our heads together.'

He started to chuckle. 'I don't think you know what bumping uglies means.'

'Okay, don't give me your mansplaining bull—'

'This is not mansplaining, this is just ... friend-splaining. Bumping uglies means ...' he paused, a dryness seeming to take over his mouth. Flynn was clearly feeling awkward, and in the end mimed it with his fingers like a school boy and mouthed '*Sex*.'

'No.' August said firmly, shaking her head. 'No it doesn't.' She stood up and walked to the door, then turned back to look at him. 'No it doesn't.' Grabbing the box of 'bras' (dandruff shampoos) from the floor she walked them into her room, pausing briefly to say again, 'No it doesn't.'

August reappeared at Flynn's bedroom door. 'Does it?'

'It does,' he nodded.

'Well, that explains why I didn't get called for a second interview for an office job a while ago.' She shuddered, remembering telling the interviewer that she and he ought to 'bump uglies' as soon as she joined the company in order to explore the full potential of his ... upward trend. Oh God.

'Anyway,' August pressed on, never one to be deterred by past mistakes for long. 'Yes, let's have a strategy meeting over some wine tonight. No, let's not bump uglies, no need to complicate things. Yes, you're taking the bed,

118

and the bedroom, because I've already been plotting how to decorate my space anyway. And do you want anything from Ikea?'

'I don't know,' he stood up, letting any embarrassment slide away. 'Shall we unpack and see where we are?'

'Good idea. And Flynn?' August picked up another box, and Flynn leaned against his doorframe to listen to her. She took in his form for a moment, assessing his kind face, his tall physique, his dark hair and his at-home posture. 'Thank you for moving in with me. I think we're going to get along just fine.'

He appeared to take her in for a moment too, so she flashed him a sunny smile which he returned. 'Thank you for convincing me. I think we'll have a lot of fun.'

Chapter 22

Flynn

Three hours later, August walked through the door of the apartment and lobbed a tube of tin foil at Flynn. He caught it reflexively with one hand, and then realised it was a tightly wrapped baguette sandwich.

He looked from her to her closed bedroom door. 'What's this? I thought you were in your room!'

'This is lunch, because I know all the best places to eat around here and you know nothing.'

'Thank you, I think.'

August pulled two cans of Fanta from her handbag and cracked them open, sitting down at the round table in the centre of the living room and beckoning Flynn to join her. 'I didn't know what you like, apart from pizza, so I asked for yours to be cheese, pepperoni and peppers. Is that okay?'

'It sounds delicious.'

'I would have asked you first but you seemed deeply

invested in organising your shirts by colour, so I thought I'd better leave you to it.'

Flynn took a seat and a long, grateful gulp of Fanta. 'How else would I organise my shirts?'

August mulled on this for a minute. 'I don't know. I guess I never organise mine, so I don't know all the wonderful ways it could be done.'

'How's your unpacking going?' he asked.

'Well, firstly, thank you for the chest of drawers that we took out of your room. I now have some of my clothes and all my underwear put away. I also nicked a side-table that was under the window in here for my bedside table, so now my book and two used tea mugs have somewhere to live. And then I wanted to make sure our Wi-Fi was all up and running, so I watched two episodes of *Brooklyn Nine-Nine*.'

'Good progress,' Flynn nodded, and reached for his phone to open the notes app. 'All right, let's make a shopping list. What do we already have?'

August looked at the living room. 'We have a sofa, my armchair, a TV and this table with four chairs. We did have a small table by the window, but that's now in my room. And it's very small. More a stool.'

'We don't need loads of tables in the living room. Might we want a coffee table though?'

August pondered this. 'Not with any great rush. A coffee table's always the kind of thing you can just find, anyway.'

'It is?'

'It is if you're happy with an old pallet with a blanket draped over it,' she said with a shrug.

Flynn smiled. That sounded good to him. 'So nothing else for in here for now?'

'Pictures would be nice,' August replied. 'Although the view is pretty picturesque in itself.'

'What would you like pictures of?'

She thought about this and then joked, 'Of our honeymoon?'

'And where do you think we would have gone on our honeymoon?'

'Let's not get ahead of ourselves, the strategy meeting is tonight. But maybe New York?'

'How about Japan? I have a lot of photos of that?'

'But none of them have me in.'

'If the criterion is that you – and I – are both in them we'll have to have honeymooned in Bath,' Flynn pointed out.

August looked to be thinking through the logistics of photoshopping herself into his travel pictures, before saying, 'This isn't important right now. If we come across a great picture, we can always claim we bought it on our honeymoon, even if it doesn't show a destination. What does your bedroom need?'

Craning his head back to look through his door, Flynn said, 'Not much. The wardrobe is built-in, there are curtains, the bed, a bedside table ... I feel terrible, you know,' he turned back to her with a bashful smile.

'Don't,' she said, firmly. 'I'm fine with it, it was always the deal. All right, my room. So I have a built-in wardrobe in there too, plus curtains. I think storage is basically fine – you might not believe this, but I did actually have a clear-out

122

before I moved in. So I need bed, mattress ... I brought a lamp with me but ... do you need a lamp?'

'I could take a lamp,' Flynn agreed, noting it in his phone. 'Hey, do you want us to get some bolts for our doors?'

August paused. 'I'm not sure we'd be allowed to add such things, to be honest. But thanks for the suggestion, it's noted that you're a gentleman.' She stood and performed an elaborate curtsy.

'All right, well, if you change your mind that's totally fine, I can fit them. I want you to, you know, know you're safe.' He felt himself blushing, but she just smiled, and moved on past him.

Poking her head through the door, she called, 'Bathroom seems fine, nothing we need there.'

'Wait, I could do with a couple of towels.'

'Let's also get a couple of bath mats.'

'How about we also get one of those "his and hers" tooth-brush stands?'

August raised her eyebrows at Flynn. 'Okay.'

'Okay.'

She moved onto the kitchen. 'I brought a big load of pots and pans and utensils and I'm happy for us to both use them if you like, at least until we figure out what we're short of?'

'Are you sure you don't mind?' asked Flynn.

'Of course, though ... ' August paused. 'You know what I always imagined about living here?'

'Having the place to yourself?' Flynn joked.

'Well, yes. But drinking coffee while I looked out across my kingdom of Bath! Do you drink coffee?'

He nodded. 'Probably too much.'

'Would you like to split the cost of one those coffee machines, not a pricey one, just one that makes filtered coffee in a jug and you can pour it pretending you work in an American diner?'

'Yes, I'd love one of those,' enthused Flynn, adding it to his list.

They took a few moments to check there was nothing they were missing, and added hangers, a clothes horse, some coasters.

'What do you want to do about grocery shopping?' Flynn asked. It had been a really long time since he'd had a flat-mate; he'd forgotten how much there was to think about.

August thought for a moment and said, 'Maybe we buy our own things but have a kitty for essentials like milk, dishwasher tablets, etc.?'

'That sounds fair. But let's trial it for a bit and adjust it if need be. I have a feeling I eat a lot more than you, and I'll be swindling you on the essentials.'

'We'll see about that. We could also add into the essentials a few things like pasta, and then sometimes cook meals together?' August looked at Flynn with hope.

He was happy with this. He didn't want to overstep the mark with his flatmate, but one of the things he missed about living with Yui was both of them coming home after a day at the office and being able to let their thoughts pour out over a tasty meal, so that by the time they were done their minds were free from thinking about work. Since living in the hotel, he'd felt as though he couldn't ever turn his brain off.

'All right, let me just text my friend Bel,' August said. 'And we'll see about a man with a van to take us to Ikea. Or at least a woman and her VW Polo.'

August's friends Steve and Bel were both pretty adamant a flat pack bed would never fit in the back of their car, and neither of them was free to help that day anyway. So instead Flynn found a van hire company where you could book two-hour slots, and they did a mad dash from Bath to Bristol Ikea. They zoomed around the store like they were on *The Crystal Maze*, before arriving back at the house and unloading, both of them sweating by then.

By the time they'd put the bed together, the sun was dipping, and August and Flynn were ready for something to eat again.

They called for takeout pizza, and Flynn popped out to a nearby store to pick up a couple of drinks, and when the food arrived, the two of them collapsed on the sofa and the armchair, their feet propped on leftover boxes and empty packaging.

'I can't believe we have to work tomorrow,' August commented. 'We should have done this on a Friday so we had the weekend to recover.'

Flynn groaned. 'You're so right.'

'Do you think you'll be extra busy tomorrow because you took today off?'

'Yeah, I think so. It seems really full-on there. I'm not sure if it's because they downscaled so I'm actually doing the job of more than one person, or I'm just slow because I'm new, but yeah, it seems very busy. Today has actually been a tonic, just doing something different! What's your work like?' he asked, realising he knew about her voice acting, but not a lot about her day-to-day job.

August sighed into her wine. 'It's fine. No, it's good, they're really good to me there. I'm temping, but I've been with the same company since moving to Bath, it's the press office of a historical holidays company. The work is interesting – because I've been there a while they give me proper, in-depth tasks so I'm not photocopying all day or anything, and they're really flexible regarding time off if I need to go off and record or go for an audition or anything.'

'Auditions?' Flynn asked with interest.

'Any kind of freelance acting work,' she waved it away and didn't elaborate on that further, so Flynn let it pass for now. 'So the people are lovely, the work is good, I just ... when I came to Bath I thought I would just temp for a month or two while I found my feet, and I feel like I've become complacent. Or scared? One of the two.'

'What did you hope would happen after a month or two?'

'Well, I thought I might become the most celebrated actress in the land and win both a Tony and an Oscar,' August joked. 'Anyway, we're here now and I think *this* is the new baseline point to start my Tony and Oscar campaigning. But not tonight, because we have other strategies to discuss.'

They both sat up straighter, refilling their wines, and leaned in.

Flynn started things off. 'So, the big question. Are we just going to pretend we're married when we're with Mrs H, or with everyone in the building?'

'I think everyone in the building. I don't think we should drag everyone else into a secret.'

'Agreed.'

'But I think with everyone else, and Mrs H, really, we don't need to be super-explicit about it.'

'Explicit?' Flynn raised his eyebrows. He hadn't planned to be. Was she imagining they'd be making out on the steps into the building?

'As in, I don't think we need to start marching the corridors referring to each other loudly as "DARLING HUSBAND" and "MY EXTRAORDINARILY BEAUTIFUL WIFE" or anything.'

Flynn smiled. 'Gotcha.'

'I really think we can get away with being pretty normal around people, nobody will be expecting us to start snogging in front of them.'

His eyes flittered to her lips, just for a millisecond.

August nodded, and seemed satisfied with that agreement. 'The next step is that we need a backstory.'

'Like, how we met, when we married, etc.?'

'Exactly.' She paused. 'So how did we meet? When did we get married?'

'How about we met at uni?' Flynn suggested.

'Which uni did you go to?'

'Edinburgh, you?'

'Ahh, I love Edinburgh. But I went to Exeter.' August paused. 'I don't think we should say uni, it could open up

127

a whole new can of worms. We could say we had a holiday romance somewhere?'

'Sounds fun. We should pick somewhere we've both travelled to though, the devil is in the details and all that. Where have you been?'

August thought for a moment. 'Where would be a romantic place to have met someone . . . I'm thinking ours should be a tale of "love at first sight, I knew right away he'd be my husband", so maybe not a crowded bar in Mykonos. Ooh, how about a vineyard tour under the Tuscan sun? Have you been to Italy?'

Flynn shook his head. 'I'm afraid not.'

'What? You've never been to Italy? But it's gorgeous!'

'How about we go there for our anniversary,' he teased. 'Have you been to Portugal?' He was picturing a pretty cove and August paddling in the water in the distance, probably wearing some billowing, rainbow-coloured kaftan.

But she shook her head. 'Canada? Snowy mountains, meeting over a hot chocolate by the fireplace?'

''Fraid not. I've been to the US . . . '

'Me too!' said August. 'Where did you go?'

'New York – you?'

'Dammit. West Coast only.'

'I've always wanted to travel around California, driving up that coastal road,' Flynn mused.

'It's amazing. I'll take you there for our second anniversary.' August smiled at Flynn.

'Did you say you've never been to Japan?' he asked after a while, but she hadn't.

'Morocco? Hungary? Cuba?' August suggested, and Flynn shook his head for each one.

'Mexico? Switzerland? Spain?' he proposed, and suddenly August sat up.

'Spain, I've been to Spain, and I travelled all over. It was the summer right after I finished uni and I was out there for three months.'

Flynn sat up straighter too. 'I was there over the summer too, after I'd finally become fully qualified in law.'

August did some quick maths. She knew Flynn was a couple of years older than her, and that law degrees, along with the placements, can take – was it six years? 'I left uni in 2012.'

'That's the year I went! I just did the south coast and the Sierra Nevada National Park.'

'So we actually *could* have had a holiday romance,' August laughed, and then brought her wine up to her lips to hide her blush.

Flynn pushed past it. 'Shall we settle on the national park then? Maybe we met on a camping trip?'

'Where we slept under the stars? Yes! We could have been cold and besotted and ended up sharing a sleeping bag.'

'Ha ha, okay,' he agreed.

'I would have even put out on the first date, that sounds so frickin' romantic,' added August. She picked up a notepad. 'I'm just going to make a note of this so we can look back on it, like revision notes.'

'All right,' Flynn said, shaking himself out of that image when she put the notepad down. 'So we met in the Spanish hills in the summer of 2012, where we had a holiday romance. Then we stayed in touch and got together back in the UK?'

'Yep. You lived in London for a while, before Japan, didn't you?'

'On the outskirts.'

'That'll do. Nobody's going to ask us about those details, I'm sure. People only care about the fun stuff, things like how we met, the proposal, the wedding, the honeymoon. How many babies we're going to have and when, and if I'm not drinking because I'm pregnant.' She took a drink of wine.

'People wouldn't ask about babies, would they? That's so private.'

'That's *all* people ask women my age about. And yes, it's private, but apparently my fanny and its goings on are fair game if the b-word is involved.'

Flynn cleared his throat. 'Okay, well, shall we do the proposal next?'

'I have an idea for this one,' August sparkled. 'Can I take the proposal story?'

'Okay, shall I take the wedding?' He held his hand out for a piece of paper from her notepad, which she tore off for him.

August paused when handing it over. 'I think we should both plan the wedding. Do you want to take the honeymoon?'

'Sure,' he shrugged, and the two of them sat in silence for a while, thinking, making some notes, pausing to sip on their wine, their eyes meeting briefly.

Flynn watched her write, her head bent over the page, her

130

legs crossed, swamped by that big, ugly, jade armchair. He enjoyed her gung-ho attitude and her colourful outfit topped with a messy bun. And he tried very hard not to think about the image of them sharing a sleeping bag under the stars.

Chapter 23

August

It felt so strange for August to be sitting here making up romantic stories about this man she'd just moved in with. Strange, but – now this might be the wine beginning to spread its fingers into her system – also a little thrilling. She was going to have to watch herself around this one. *You do have a habit of flirting with the dark, handsome strangers after a little liquid stimulation, Missy.*

But of course, as was always the way for August, she didn't pay a lot of attention to her conscience, and sat forwards to pour them some more wine.

'Finished?' Flynn asked, putting his own pen down.

'Yep.'

'You go first.'

August cleared her throat. 'This is my idea for the proposal. We're in London, taking our final walk beside the Thames on a quiet, Sunday morning. You've been transferred to an office in Japan, and you're leaving today. We're promising each other that it isn't the end, and I'm crying and you're holding me, and we know you're going to come back lots to visit because your company has a private jet.'

'Nice,' Flynn nodded.

'I know, right? And I thought this way it ties in with you going to Japan for a while, in case that ever comes up.'

'Good thinking.'

'So, it's a sunny morning, I have tears in my eyes, you tell me how pretty I am and how you'll remember my face every time you see a sunrise, it's all very Vera Lynn. And *then*,' August stopped, chuffed with this next part. 'I surprise the hell out of you by getting down on one knee, and asking you to marry me.'

'You propose to me?' Flynn asked, surprised.

'Yep. On one knee and everything. And I tell you I've never known a more handsome and kind man, and that I don't want to lose you, and *then* ... '

'There's more?'

'There's more! And then you say that I would never lose you because I am your everything, and the only way you can travel across the world is so that you can come back home and be my husband. And then *you* get down on one knee and pull out a ring, and propose to me!'

'So we propose to each other?' Flynn seemed impressed.

'We were just always so in sync that we both knew it was the exact right time on that morning.'

'But I still went to Japan? Weren't you mad?'

'No, not at all, because absence made our hearts grow

fonder, and I used that time away from you to pour my everything into training with the Royal Academy of Dramatic Art.'

'You went to RADA?'

'I did in *this* version of my life.'

'Very cool,' Flynn nodded.

The truth was, August would have loved to have gone to RADA. Ever since she was young, she'd been keen on acting, though fear had held her back from a lot of opportunities. She'd been so excited when she started landing regular voice work in London, but a gnawing insecurity told her she wasn't skilled enough, didn't have enough in her repertoire, that it was too hard. She was so fearless in so much of her life that she worried, *if I'm scared of* this, *maybe it's not right for me*? And so, acting was her passion, but she kept it part-time.

'So how does all of that sound to you?' August asked, hopeful, shaking herself from her thoughts.

'It sounds perfect.'

'You don't mind that I proposed to you first?'

'Of course not,' he said. 'I'm flattered.'

August beamed. 'Okay, what did we do for our honeymoon?'

Flynn took a moment, looking at his notes.

'Come on, spill,' August coaxed, softly. She wondered why he was hesitating.

'All right,' Flynn started. 'I know it's not the most far-flung place and you probably want a honeymoon that takes you all over the globe ... '

August smiled at that, not that Flynn saw as he was staring at his paper. She didn't necessarily need those things . . .

He continued. 'But I thought our honeymoon could be in Edinburgh. You said you'd been to Edinburgh, right?'

'I have, I loved it,' she answered, surprised by his choice. She thought for sure he was going to suggest some little bolthole in the Japanese countryside.

'So. We had our wedding, whatever that looked like, and then we took the train up to Scotland. Just you and me, and a couple of small bags each. We'd sleep on the train. I guess it could even be a sleeper train, depending on how far we were coming from. Either way, we'd probably be tired from the big day, and dozy, and so we'd travel and eat and watch the world go by for a while.'

August could just picture it. She sat back in her armchair and closed her eyes, listening to Flynn talk.

'Once we made it to Edinburgh, we'd stay a couple of nights in one of the castle hotels, somewhere with a spa and a good restaurant. We'd explore the city, enjoy the history and the skyline, and then we'd travel further north and stay in a cabin by a loch, somewhere in the Outer Hebrides.' He paused, and then said, 'August? Did you fall asleep?'

Her eyes fluttered open and her smile widened. 'Not at all, I was enjoying the imagery.'

'I thought maybe you'd found the whole idea extremely dull-sounding.'

'No way, I think it sounds perfect.'

'You do?' Flynn smiled.

'*I do*,' she proclaimed with a chuckle.

Flynn stood up and stretched. The evening was rolling into night and August could see he was beginning to tire, but he seemed to be enjoying himself. 'I'm going to have myself a comfort break, grab another bottle, and then shall we figure out the wedding plans?'

'Do you think we can plan a whole wedding in just one evening?' August joked, standing up also and stretching her legs by pacing the room.

'We became a married couple over the course of a couple of hours, I think we can do anything.'

Chapter 24

Flynn

'August?' Flynn called a few minutes later, returning to the living room with a fresh bottle of wine.

'In here,' she called from somewhere.

He looked around the room. He then glanced into his own bedroom and hers. 'Where?'

'In here . . . '

'In the bathroom?' Surely she didn't want him to come in there with the wine?

All of a sudden, a section of the wall swung open, wallpaper, mouldings and all, and inside stood August, illuminated by an orangey lightbulb hanging from the ceiling. She was looking around her in awe. 'It's perfect.'

Flynn stuck his head into what appeared to be a storage cupboard, not much bigger than the inside of a wardrobe, hidden in the living room wall. 'It is?'

'*So* perfect. Flynn, could I have this? We don't have anything else we need to store, do we?'

'I don't think we do, but what do you need it for?'

'I could record books in here. Remember I told you that before I came to Bath I was a voice actress and I used to do loads of audiobooks? Well, I don't put myself forward for as much work as I did now that I'm further away from London and Oxford, where most of the audiobook action is. But if I could have my own in-house studio I can offer myself out as truly freelance.'

Flynn put his head further in, nutting a spider's web on the way. 'You can make a studio out of this?'

'Easily. I mean it won't really be a studio, more of a booth, but if I soundproof it and get a decent microphone, I know I could make it work.'

Her face was lit up, even in the dim of the closet, with an excitement he hoped to find also with his new job. She continued. 'And best of all, I'll once again be able to get my voice nice and trained up and I could add the next string to the bow of my grand masterplan.'

'What is the grand masterplan?'

'Let's have more to drink before I tell you that. But can I have this? Do you mind?'

Flynn pretended to consider it for a minute, looking up and down and side to side inside the closet. 'It is beautiful, I'm not sure I'm ready to let it go.'

'Oh, shut up,' August thwacked him.

'The musty old secret cupboard is all yours,' he relented.

They stepped back out into the living room, and August

closed the door with a respectful gentleness. And just like that, it was one wall again.

'Why do you think it's hidden, designed to look like there isn't a door there?' Flynn questioned.

'Well, you know how things were in the Regency period,' answered August, heading back to her seat and dimming the lamp on her way past.

'Not really . . .'

'You don't know what they used to do? To the maids who worked in the houses?'

'. . . No . . .'

'When the women began to know their minds too much and started to speak out about the poor living wage and unfair conditions, the master of the house would shut them in the cupboard in the wall, for hours, as punishment. He would make them stand in there when they had guests, and they were not to make a *sound*.' August dropped her voice down low, causing Flynn to lean forward. 'Only, sometimes, the residents of the house would forget they'd shut one of the maids in there, and they'd go out for the day, and the maids, fearing making a noise, never protested. And then, you can probably guess what happened to them.'

Flynn blinked. 'That's awful.'

'You just have to watch out, if you're ever here alone and hear a tap-tap-tap that for a second you could mistake as a bird on the window ledge. But listen closely and you might just be hearing the ghosts of the women in the walls.'

'That is not true, you shut up,' Flynn cried, and he saw August's eyes crinkle in the corner. 'It's not true at all, is it?' She laughed. 'You *are* a good actress! Did you make all that up?'

'Every word of it. I have no idea why this cupboard is all wallpapered over, but I expect it's because someone, at some point in history, whacked a bloody great MDF door in and it looked unsightly.'

'I don't know if I want to plan a wedding with you now,' he said, to August's amusement.

'Yes, you do, come on. First of all, where do we get married. Would you like us to say we got married in Japan?' she suggested.

But Flynn answered quickly with a definitive 'No'. He'd thought a lot about having a wedding in Japan, for a long time, but he didn't want to revisit that again in his mind for a moment, and it felt wrong bringing August out there – even as make believe. It felt like a betrayal to Yui, somehow.

'All right . . .' she moved on. 'Shall we stick to the UK?'

'Yes, but nowhere local to here because you know somebody else in the building will have got married there and we'll find ourselves down an even deeper ditch.'

'Good thinking,' August agreed. 'Let's not go with Edinburgh because I like your travelling-by-train-to-our-honeymoon idea. Have you been to Cornwall?'

'I have, actually, just once when I was little.'

'How about we say it was at a beach in Cornwall. There's a nice beach at Watergate Bay with some good places to get a drink nearby. Fancy a beach wedding?'

'Sounds great,' he agreed. 'Does it matter that I don't know the area?'

'No, I don't think so, we can bump out the details with the wedding itself. So, beach wedding, summer?'

'How about September? Less busy, still good weather?'

'Or October? Still sunny but a nice chill in the air?' suggested August, to which Flynn nodded. 'Did we allow kids?'

Flynn shrugged. 'Sure. Did we have regular cake or one of those cheese tower cakes?'

'Both. Was it religious?' They looked at each other, religion not having come up before. 'Are you religious?'

'To be honest, not really,' he admitted.

'Me neither,' she said.

'And we said no prop rings?' Flynn asked.

'No rings. I can always claim I lost mine,' replied August. 'It won't take the neighbours long to realise I'm a loser. Ha!'

Flynn made a note on the pad that August was a loser. 'Shall we just say the reception was on the beach too?'

'In a marquee?'

'Yeah.'

'Okay. How many people did we have? A hundred?'

'If we did, then ninety-five of them would be your guests,' said Flynn. They settled on keeping it smaller, around fifty people.

'That's probably enough, don't you think?' August said, stifling a giant yawn.

'I think we have everything covered, at least for now.' It was late. Flynn put down the pad of paper, so ready to call it a night. 'Quick test; where did we honeymoon?'

With droopy eyelids, August smiled. 'Edinburgh, and

then the Outer Hebrides, and we got there by sleeper train from Cornwall. Did we have kids at our wedding?'

'We did. Who proposed?'

'I did. Actually, we both did. What was the name of the beach we got married on?'

That stumped him. ' . . . Waterloo Beach?'

'Watergate Bay,' she corrected.

He had one last question. 'And what's the grand masterplan?'

August stood up, did a cat-like stretch, and started off towards her room. 'It's waaaay too late to get into all the intricacies of that. But in a nutshell, I wasn't entirely joking about the Tony thing. I'm going to be on the stage one day.'

And then she saw something that made her stop in her tracks, and Flynn in his.

Chapter 25

Flynn

'Oh my God,' August and Flynn said in unison.

August looked at her bed, all completed, all ready to be slept on except for one thing.

Flynn looked at his own bed, all comfortable and inviting and tempting him to call it a night and climb in, except for one thing.

The two of them turned at the doorways of their bedrooms and faced each other, wine-stained mouths agape.

'I didn't buy the mattress,' August declared, crestfallen. She must have just completely forgotten to pick it up from the Ikea warehouse section. It was those bloody tealights that had distracted them.

Flynn was equally dumbstruck. 'I don't have any bedding.' How could he forget bedding? It was literally Bed 101. It just hadn't occurred to him in the slightest when they'd been making the shopping list.

One bed with a mattress, but no pillows, duvet, blankets. One bed with pillows and a duvet, but no mattress to put them on.

Suddenly they were both talking at once.

'I'll go back to the hotel,' said Flynn.

'No, no, I'll go and stay the night at Bel's,' answered August, seemingly happy to give him her bedding for the night.

'It's getting really late, please. You stay here. You take the bed and all the toppings. I'll kip on the sofa, or maybe the floor, it's fine. I can use a sofa cushion for a pillow and . . . it's not cold so I don't really need a blanket.'

'That sounds awful, and you wouldn't even fit lying down on this sofa,' August said, shaking her head. '*You* take all the bed and bedding and all that jazz, and I'll sleep on the armchair under my dressing gown.'

It had been such a long day, and their bloodshot eyes betrayed how tired they both were, overwhelmed by the enormity of moving into a new home, and both a little woozy from the wine and excitement comedown. They breathed for a moment, silently, staring into each other's eyes from across the living room, wondering if they should do what they both wanted to do.

It was August who took the plunge, raising her shoulders in defeat, and said in barely more than a whisper, 'Shall we just both sleep in the bed?'

Flynn struggled with what to do. A big part of him wanted to just give her the bed and find somewhere else. It was the only right thing to do if he wanted her to feel completely at ease with him.

'Stop battling with yourself, I know you aren't taking advantage,' August yawned and stepped into her room, coming out a moment later clasping her huge, warm-looking duvet in her arms. 'It's just one night, we'll both stay fully pyjama-d, and no spooning.' She stopped en route to his room. 'Are you okay with this? Not just because of this chivalrous, Mr Darcy thing you're doing, but for you? Am I making you uncomfortable?'

Flynn softened. Maybe it was only a big deal if he made it one. He knew he wasn't going to do anything untoward to her, and she seemed confident he wouldn't either. He was also certain she wasn't about to try it on with him. 'I think I'll be far more comfortable with you than either of us will be sleeping on that armchair,' he admitted.

'Great,' she dumped the bedding on his bed and went back to her room. 'I'm going to put on my most nun-ly PJs now, and I think you should do the same. Then I'm going to wash this makeup off my face, so get mentally prepared for that. Then I'll see you in bed. Darling.' August walked off towards her bedroom, leaving Flynn to stand for a moment, wondering if he even had any PJs.

Remembering a long pair of joggers he owned, he pulled them on quickly, adding a clean T-shirt to cover his chest, and then made the bed. By the time August returned, he was already in, snuggled down in a state of bliss, his reading glasses on and a copy of an old Stephen King novel on his lap. He looked up as August entered, not taken aback at all by her makeup-free face. Not even a little bit.

She regarded him. 'Hmm.'

'What?'

'I like your glasses.'

'Thank you,' Flynn felt himself blush, just a little.

'Also, we appear to sleep on the same side.'

'Oh I'm sorry,' he said, gathering up his things. 'I'll move over.'

'Stay where you are,' she waved him back down and walked around the end of the bed before sliding under the covers. 'I really don't care where I sleep. Whoooooa, this bed is so comfortable.'

'I like your jim-jams.'

'Thank you,' August replied, looking down towards her long white PJs, adorned with a hundred hot pink flamingos. 'You can borrow them any time you like.'

August and Flynn bid each other goodnight, sleep rolling in towards them both as soon as the light was off.

'By the way,' August said. 'I twitch just before I go to sleep. Don't be alarmed.'

Flynn smiled into the darkness. 'Okay, I won't be.'

A few minutes later, August spoke again, her voice drowsy and light. 'Flynn?'

'Mmm-hmm?' he replied.

'Do you have a girlfriend, somewhere?'

Flynn's eyes fluttered back open and he turned his head to face the window. Before he could answer she spoke again, saying, 'I'm not hitting on you, I just want to know if I'm sharing a bed with another girl's man, and I want her to know I'm sorry.'

'No,' he murmured after a moment, after Yui's face had

started to fade away from his mind again. 'There's no girlfriend.'

August didn't reply, but before he could ask her about her situation in return she spasmed a huge twitch, snorted, rasped the words, 'By the way, I also snore,' and had rolled over into a deep slumber.

And with that, Flynn turned on his side, his back to August, and did the same.

Chapter 26

August

The following evening, Bel popped over for a post-work cuppa, to check out August's new place, and new flatmate. Two cups, and half a packet of custard creams later, and Bel was just finishing off the latest gossip about her dental nurse, Kenny.

'... And so now, Kenny's decided he is completely in love with the new receptionist, Mark, and is showering my patients with free toothpaste samples just so he has an excuse to keep going over and getting more.'

With that, the door opened: Flynn was home.

'Is this him?' Bel said, her eyes sparkling, and the two of them stood up and took a step towards the door.

In walked Flynn, dashing in his suit, his shirt untucked and his collar loose, his dark hair swept casually to the side.

'Welcome home, hubby, I'd like you to meet someone,' August chuckled.

Flynn scanned the two of them for a microsecond,

appeared to assess the situation, and stepped forward with a big smile, sticking out one hand to shake Bel's and throwing his other arm around August. 'Hello, I'm Flynn, August's husband.' And to August he said warmly, 'Hello, sweetheart.'

'Oh—' August started, realising Flynn mistook Bel for a neighbour. She turned to face him, to explain, just as he turned to plant a kiss on the side of her head.

The result: Flynn kissed August. On the mouth. They both pulled their heads back instantly, surprised and unsure where to go from there, until August untangled herself, a blush on her face, and said, 'Flynn, this is actually my friend Bel.'

'Your friend?'

'Not a neighbour. Bel. I told you about her. She knows we aren't married.'

Flynn composed himself. 'Yes, yes of course, I've heard lots about you, Bel, it's nice to meet you … I'm sorry.' He turned back to August, flustered. 'I didn't mean to just lunge at you. I was going for your head.'

'That's okay,' said August.

'He was going for your head, Aug,' teased Bel, and August laughed it off but she could still feel the imprint of Flynn's lips on hers. He'd felt soft, with a tiny whisper of end-of-day stubble and faded aftershave.

'Right,' Flynn said. 'Well, I'm going to go and change out of this stuffy suit and hide my shame in the shower for a few minutes. Bel, will you stay for dinner so you can see I'm a perfectly normal guy and not someone who's coercing your best friend into ill-timed kisses?'

'I believe you,' Bel said. 'She speaks very highly of you.

149

But maybe next time, because I need to get going. Nice to meet you, Flynn.'

'And you, Bel,' he waved a goodbye and went towards the bathroom, turning to mouth *'I'm so sorry'* to August on the way past.

Once he'd closed the door, Bel gathered up her things, plus one custard cream for the road, and walked with August to the door.

'You two are kissing already?' Bel hissed.

'Just that one time, and it was an accident,' August proclaimed.

'He's gorgeous.'

'He's very *nice.*'

Bel nudged her towards the bathroom. 'I think you should go and join him for that shower.'

August thwacked her friend and pushed her towards the door. 'Would you shut up and leave? I'll call you tomorrow.'

After she'd left, August leaned her back against the door and breathed out. She listened to the sound of the shower running inside the bathroom.

Stop it, she scolded herself. *Stop trying to picture what's behind that door.*

Chapter 27

Flynn

Behind the door, Flynn was mortified. He'd kissed her. And he truly hadn't meant to, but what if she thought he had? Why had he even done that anyway? Even if she was his real wife, there's no law to say you have to plant one on her when you walk in the door from work, it wasn't the fifties. He'd just had a spring in his step about coming home to his new house, that was all.

The last person he'd kissed had been Yui, when they were saying goodbye. His last kiss with Yui hadn't felt right, it hadn't felt like their other kisses over the years. He'd been expecting it to feel like their worlds were crashing together one final time, like all the sadness and longing and farewells were being shown to each other through that kiss, but it had felt cold. Like she'd already shut the door, and that this kiss was just a formality. Like returning a key.

It was one of the saddest memories he'd taken with him.

Now he couldn't quite recall the feel of Yui's lips. Only August's.

Chapter 28

August

It was the kind of late-summer early morning that you see at the start of a movie. A montage of joggers and cyclists passing by, the first leaves tinged with red on the trees, the sun casting a warm pool of lemon light below.

August made her way down Elizabeth Street and curved through a few nearby lanes holding her brand new, lime green yoga mat.

Inspired by her neighbour Callie, who she'd met on move-in day, August had decided yoga would be a great addition to The New Her. The new House-on-Elizabeth-Street Her. Also, practising yoga would be a way to focus and get her creative juices flowing, just like all the real actresses did.

Because for the first time in a while, she didn't feel like an imposter, but she felt like a real actress today; she'd had a call she'd been waiting for.

A couple of months ago she'd auditioned for a role at the

Roman Baths, playing a Roman woman in full costume, staying in character and chatting to visitors. And she'd finally had news to say she'd been accepted. It was only a couple of times a month, but it felt amazing to be a part of something like this.

It was the house, she could *feel it*. It was already bringing her good luck and fortune and the promise of academy awards.

Yes, yoga was very fitting to her new lifestyle. And there was a studio no more than a five-minute walk away that she was trying out for the first time today.

The studio was situated within a small spa, and August was ushered through by the whispering receptionist to a room with amber-coloured wooden walls, candlelight and a water feature trickling in the corner, complementing the music that hummed softly.

'Find a space anywhere, lie down and *relax*,' the receptionist purred, barely audible. 'Your teacher will be in shortly.'

August lay her mat down next to a woman who was flat on her back, under a blanket and an eye mask, snoring softly. Unsure quite what to do with herself, August tried lying down and closing her eyes, but kept peeping to check she wasn't the only one who hadn't shape-shifted into warrior pose.

This was *lovely*, she thought, settling in. What a find. August could see herself coming here every other morning to start the day, before heading to auditions and eventually a recurring role in a revered play. The reviews would say how the leading lady displayed such poise and clear skin and she would say in interviews that she owed it all to yoga.

There was a snort beside her, followed by a cry of, 'Oh, hello!'

August turned her head to the side, where the woman beside her had lifted her eye mask and propped herself up on her elbow. Her heart sank. 'Callie. Hi.'

'I didn't know you were a yogi too!' Callie said, her voice seeming very loud against the serene quiet.

'I'm not really,' August confessed. 'This is my first time; I'm just testing it out.'

'You're going to bloody love it,' continued Callie, nudging the person on the other side of her until she too opened her eyes and looked up. 'Pam, this is my new neighbour August, the one I told you about with the delicious husband.'

Pam waved and closed her eyes again, thankfully. August really didn't want to bring her 'husband' into this place.

Was she going to have to find a new yoga studio now? she wondered. It wasn't that she had anything against Callie, not at all, but this had felt like part of her new beginning, a sanctuary where she could be herself and centre herself, not a place outside her home to have to keep performing.

At that moment the teacher walked in, who said in the most soothing of voices, like cream blended with honey, 'Good morning, friends. Time to let everything go and allow yourself to truly be you.'

August let herself do exactly that, and for the next hour, through slow stretches and mindful challenges, she found herself sinking into a feeling of contentment. It was the same feeling she had that first night in her new home. *Hello, me*, she said to herself.

As the hour drew to a close, the yoga teacher told them to pull their blankets over themselves for fifteen minutes of quiet rest. August allowed her mind to drift, her thoughts exploring the steps she could take and the doors she could open next. Perhaps it was time to find a local amateur dramatics group again. Perhaps it was time to put herself out there again for voice work and turn those ideas of converting the living room closet into a mini sound studio into reality. Perhaps it was time to—

Beside her she heard, so faintly, the sound of a wobbly intake of breath. August opened her eyes and turned her head towards Callie, whose eyelids were firmly closed, though a single tear was escaping down the side of her face towards her ear.

What should she do? Ignore her? Say something? Instead August reached her fingertips out and lay a hand over Callie's, who jumped a little at the human contact before turning her palm upwards and squeezing August's.

'Sorry about the sniffles,' Callie whispered to August as they rolled up their mats a few minutes later. 'I'm getting better but there's something about that time at the end when we're all quiet, and all my thoughts and feelings come barging in.'

'Don't apologise,' August replied. 'I'm all for a dramatic scene. Are you okay?'

'Yes, yes, I'm fine,' Callie waved her away. 'It's a release in a way, and I'm glad to do it here rather than at home in front of Mum. I guess I'm just not quite over my divorce yet. But I'll get there.' She smiled, and they left the studio together.

August squinted at the bright light and observed Callie

for a moment while she got herself tangled up in the straps of her yoga mat bag. It didn't take a genius to see that Callie was lonely.

'What did you think?' Callie sorted herself, her voice hopeful.

'Really lovely,' August answered, truthfully, and the two women started to walk back up the hill. It would be a shame to find somewhere new ...

Callie exhaled, sounding genuinely relieved. 'I'm so chuffed you liked it. I don't mean to sound all needy-new-friend, especially after you already had to deal with my waterworks today, but it's really nice to have somebody to talk to besides Mum around, you know? Nothing against Mum, she's great, but you and I, well, I don't know, I'm just glad you moved in, that's all.' Callie blushed, and then laughed. 'Sorry, you must think I'm intensely pathetic!'

'Of course I don't!' August cried. Actually, it was rather nice to hear about people who had good relationships with their mums – she and her own mother always seemed wary of each other, always at arm's length. 'I'm glad we've moved in too. And the yoga was lovely, I'll definitely go again.'

True to her word ... at least, some of her words, August became a regular at the yoga studio near her new home, lying beside Callie and having pleasant chats to and from practice. August had to get a little creative whenever the conversation steered to her and Flynn's relationship, which it often did, but at least during yoga she could switch off from any distractions and allow her mind to run free.

*

Over the weeks, which rolled into a month, Flynn and August lived side by side, getting to know each other when they crossed paths at the start and end of their workdays and at weekends.

While Flynn worked late into some evenings, August came home from her day job and began to turn the little closet into a recording booth, tinkering nightly with some of her old, and some new, equipment until she thought the sound was just right, her voice crystal clear, the background noise non-existent, and calming. She'd hung spare blankets as soundproofing, and spent as much money as she could afford on a decent microphone and a popshield, plus an interface to connect the mic to her laptop. After much deliberation, she'd signed up to an annual subscription of the audio editing software Adobe Audition, but in monthly instalments, as it was a little more cost effective.

She put out small feelers to previous voice acting companies she'd worked with, and to authors she'd got to know, and added herself to freelance lists. It was exciting, and nerve-wracking, but moving into Elizabeth Street had started the ball rolling, and she was moving towards her dreams. It was like one win gave her the nudge to try and achieve the next one. And taking charge of her voice acting career again fuelled her motivation.

August reached out to her mum, inviting her to come over for a cup of tea at Elizabeth Street 'sometime', despite her mum always having something to complain about when it came to August's life or her decisions. But as expected, the visit hadn't materialised. Mrs Anderson had never visited

August in her previous flat either, and certainly wasn't the type to pop by unexpected, so August was just fine to keep to their usual arrangement whereby she visited her mum's home, an hour's drive away, once a month instead. Mrs Anderson had, however, 'met' Flynn. It had happened during an impromptu FaceTime call that August had arranged when she was feeling uncharacteristically sentimental towards her mum (Callie's influence, no doubt). He'd walked past the screen without a shirt on, not realising she was on a call, until August's mum shrieked out, '*Who is that man?*'

'That's Flynn, Mum, my flatmate.'

'Why's he naked?'

'Hello, Mrs Anderson,' Flynn waved, covering himself up. 'Sorry, I was just coming back from the bathroom.'

'August,' her mum leant closer to the screen. 'Is something going on between the two of you? That's a very bad idea, you know.'

'No, he's my flatmate, we literally met a few weeks ago.' August angled the laptop away from Flynn, who caught her eye as he went into his bedroom, and grinned. Her mum knew nothing of their 'arrangement', and August would keep it that way, thanks very much. Her mum just wouldn't understand.

Over time, Flynn and August met their neighbours properly – Callie, of course, and her mum in the flat above, Maud and Allen, who lived in the flat below. And the basement flat seemed to be some kind of holiday let but mainly for the use of Mrs Haverley's family, or if anybody else in the building had family to stay and needed some extra space.

Talking of Mrs Haverley's family, August had noticed that Abe Haverley seemed to be visiting his mum often. Sometimes he'd appear and disappear like he'd just travelled over from London for the day, sometimes she'd see him heading into the building late on a Friday evening, and run into him in the hallways over the course of the whole weekend, as he brought up shopping, or helped his mother down the stairs. He was increasingly polite, like a layer of his initial gruffness peeled away with every meeting. It had come to the point that August felt a smile washing over her when he was near, and she had begun to hope they might become friends.

August and Flynn held hands when walking in and out of the building, and made a small show of standing with an arm around each other or glancing at one another with affection when they spoke to neighbours. The few times they'd been asked about their history or their wedding they smoothed over it with some loose details; white lies that drifted away on the breeze.

They were good flatmates to each other. A good team. Everything had worked out perfectly; everything about living together was easy. It was all fairly uncomplicated.

At least it was at first ...

Chapter 29

August

'Callie,' August cried, answering the door. 'What a nice surprise.'

'Hi, love, just wanted to pop down and give you a tub of these brownies my mum's been making upstairs. I always meant to give you a welcome-to-the-building pressie, so here it is.'

'A welcome pressie? You didn't need to do that!' They'd lived there a month already, but those brownies looked damned good, so August accepted the box. 'Thank you so much. These look like they'd go well with tea!'

'They sure would!' Callie replied.

Keeping her eyes on the brownies, and Callie, August gestured to Flynn to run and close the bedroom doors.

'Would you like to come in?' August asked, loud enough for Flynn to hear. 'I'm sure you could manage one too?'

Flynn had leapt up from his seat on the sofa where

he'd been doing a little evening work wearing his new PJ trousers and his work shirt. In his glasses and with a pen jammed behind his ear, he hot-footed from August's room, to his, and into the kitchen like a parkour expert. When Callie entered the flat, she wasn't faced with very obvious his and hers separate bedrooms, but instead with a serene scene of wedded bliss, topped off with Flynn, in the kitchen, holding the kettle, looking every bit the perfect husband.

'Hi, Callie,' he said smoothly. 'I hear you brought some treats over; thank you. Can I make you a tea? Coffee?'

'I'd love a tea. *Love* one.' She went to the sofa and pushed his paperwork to the side. 'I like your glasses, Flynn, they suit you.'

'Thanks. I like your . . . scrunchie.'

August gave him a look that said, *nice try, Casanova* and joined him in the kitchen to get some plates. 'I like your scrunchie,' she whispered to him.

'What?' he whispered back, trying not to laugh. 'I was just trying to be nice.'

'You *are* nice, you don't need to try so hard.'

'Right,' said Callie when they joined her in the living room. 'These are just normal brownies, I'm afraid, not funny ones with cannabis in. Sorry about that.'

'Normal brownies are actually my favourite kind,' answered August, helping herself to a big one.

'I wasn't implying anything, just letting you know. It would be fun if they were though, wouldn't it?'

They all tucked in to the delicious, and thankfully quite

normal, brownies, when Callie suddenly looked around and said, 'Where are all your pictures?'

August froze mid-bite. 'What do you mean?'

'You don't have any holiday snaps in frames, or any wedding photos up. Didn't you have a lovely beach wedding?'

August and Flynn locked eyes, excuses twirling in their heads and trying to form into sentences, when Callie continued, 'I suppose we just keep it all on our phones these days, don't we – I must have been living with Mum for too long.'

'Yes, that's it,' August said, relaxing, while Flynn stuffed a brownie in his mouth.

'Let's see them, then,' Callie said.

'Let's see what?'

'Let me see your wedding photos, I want to see your dress.'

August felt sick, the brownie having turned dry in her mouth. She looked at Flynn who said, 'I don't think we have the wedding photos on our phones.'

Callie turned from one to the other. 'You must have something, everyone has something. I even have my wedding photos still and I had a better time at my divorce party than my wedding day!'

'Water damage!' August cried, her improv training kicking in. 'We had water damage in our last place and the box with all our printed wedding photos got ruined.'

'Oh no,' said Callie. 'Thank God everybody uses digital now so you must have backup.'

'Yep,' August shook her head. 'Yep, we have them on … CD. We just need to get them reprinted.'

'That'll be nice,' Callie nodded. 'This place will feel

really lovely and romantic once you've got a bit more of yourselves here in your space.'

With that, she finished her brownie and her cuppa and pattered back off up to her own apartment.

August felt bad lying to Callie, especially over the subject of weddings and marriage, something Callie was so open with her about. Should she just come clean? Maybe sooner would be better than later. Yes. She'd have a good think about that … maybe she'd do it tomorrow … or the next day. Anyway, she'd do it soon.

Flynn, meanwhile, pushed his glasses up onto his head and rubbed his eyes. 'So where's the nearest beach?'

The beach, however, would have to wait, as would the whole should-I-confess-to-Callie thing, because during ten days of every September, Bath transformed into a Regency paradise with the Jane Austen Festival. Dance workshops, readings, balls, bonnet-making classes, street performances, it was, quite frankly, how August imagined heaven might be, as long as she could bring a few mod cons along with her. And some Pop Tarts. Oh, and her phone.

Bel cursed, shoving her parasol under August's arm and retying the ribbon that looped her body underneath her bust, converting her maxi dress to a high-waisted Regency-style frock. 'This damned thing keeps falling down. How did I think making my own dress was a good idea?'

'The same way you do every year, my darling,' August replied with a smile, fluttering at her face with her paper fan.

'Next year, please remind me to take you up on your offer

164

of helping me. I don't know why I think I can do it myself every time.'

The two of them were strolling slowly through the centre of Bath, dressed to the nines, as part of the festival's Regency Costumed Promenade, along with about five hundred other people, all bedecked in Austen-like finery. August had, as usual, needed no cajoling to get Bel to take part, her friend being just as into all the pomp and circumstance as she was. Now here they were, in long dresses with temporarily stitched-on puffball cap sleeves, hair curled and piled on their heads, and an air of two sisters on the lookout for mischief.

'Guess what?' Bel said. 'My practice is finally getting the big renovation we've been waiting for.'

'That's amazing!' August said, knowing how long her friend had wanted, and campaigned, for this. 'When?'

'Next summer.'

'*Next* summer? A whole year away!'

'But,' Bel added, a smile on her face. 'Next summer it'll be closed for a whole month while the renovations happen, so Steve and I have decided ...'

August gasped, stopping in her stride and causing a small pile-up behind her. 'Is this it?'

Bel dragged her forward. 'This is it. Next summer, after all these years of being engaged, we've decided to get married. And take a nice long honeymoon.'

'Bel, that's brilliant news!' said August, so happy for her friend. 'And I'm not just saying that because I'm an expert at weddings and marriages now. I am genuinely over the moon for you both.'

The promenade led them down Great Pulteney Street, August's favourite road in Bath (aside from her own) due to the charming horse-and-carriage look it had about it. After that, they'd stroll across the bridge, through a small portion of the town, skirt around the abbey and end in the Parade Gardens beside the river. It was a nice walk on any day, but dressed up like a couple of Austeneers it was all the more special.

Around them, gentlemen tipped their hats, ladies linked arms, the odd dancer twirled past and the town crier bellowed to keep everyone in order. Spectators gathered, including some of Bath's new fresh-faced university freshers watching in mild bewilderment. When they reached the gardens, August and Bel lay in happy contemplation upon the grass, letting the warm autumn air sink over them, and chatting about potential wedding ideas. The Jane Austen festival would have made August happy enough, but an excuse to spend some time with her favourite Bel-lisima too made the day perfection.

However, after passing time for a long while, Bel sat up. 'Right,' she said, getting off the grass, wiping herself down, and untying the ribbon from her underboob. 'I'm going to love you and leave you, Aug, because this September sun is begging for me to lie in the garden in my knickknacks with a good book.'

'Sounds like a good plan,' August replied, and hauled herself up. Her own dress wasn't so easily converted, so she'd have to totter all the way back up the hill under a sweat-inducing swathe of taffeta.

August took her time crossing the Parade Gardens, staying under the shade of the trees and smiling to other festival-goers like she thought she was Lizzie Bennet herself. She stopped in front of a wooden noticeboard, where flyers for festival happenings and other 'of interest' advertisements were displayed.

Something caught her eye. The word Audition.

Her eyes flew over the poster, a simple informational sheet printed on white paper, detailing auditions being held the following month. An in-house production of *Northanger Abbey* at the Old Theatre Royal. Full wage, two-month run, starting next spring.

August blinked at the words in front of her. This was it: this could be her big break. An Austen play, a proper production, in her town? This was her next goal, her grand masterplan! She longed to move forward from her fears and become a full-time actress, working both in studios and on the stage, and here was the perfect opportunity to go after her dream of bringing down the house. Surely her previous amateur dramatics work, and her voice acting, would put her in a good position?

Wouldn't it? No, maybe it wouldn't. She couldn't go for this; it was too big a step up. No, of course she couldn't.

But she overcame the obstacles to getting her dream home. Maybe it was time to move forward with her dream career.

Chapter 30

August

August ran all the way home. Not literally. She actually shuffled at a fast pace, as fast as her heavy, noisy skirt would allow her, the parasol she'd lent Bel banging against her legs all the way. Even though the whole end section was uphill, she never slowed.

She sped up the Elizabeth Street hill feeling like Rocky. She was pumped, full of adrenaline, and by the time she crashed through the door of her flat, pink and sweating, August, in her mind, had already landed the role, been spotted by a casting director, given the leading part in a BBC Austen adaptation, made her London stage debut and won that Tony award.

Flynn looked up from where he was chucking what seemed to be a whole bunch of bananas into a blender. He took in her panting, her face the colour of a strawberry, the way she gripped the stitch in her side and asked, 'Did you run instead of walk the promenade?'

She gave him a thumbs up and scrabbled for her phone.

'Banana smoothie?' he asked.

August double-thumbs-ed-up him this time, and he poured in a load of milk and half a tub of yogurt, and started whirring the blender just as August rasped, 'Audition!'

Flynn turned the blender off again. 'What?'

She waved him away for a moment, still trying to catch her breath, and then said 'There's an audition,' just as he turned the blender on again.

He switched it off. 'Pardon?'

'You go,' she panted.

'No, you go,' Flynn said.

'I'll just show you. Carry on.'

And so Flynn powered up the blender again, and by the time the contents were a pale yellow, frothy liquid, August had her phone thrust in his face. 'Look, an audition, for a Jane Austen play down at the theatre.'

He squinted at the phone, trying to read the print on the poster she'd taken a photo of. 'The Old Theatre Royal.'

'Right.'

'Is that different from the Theatre Royal?'

'Yes, it's the old one, but they still have performances there sometimes, including this one. They're putting on *Northanger Abbey*, which was actually set there, or at least some of it was, next May. And they're holding auditions.'

Flynn poured the smoothies into two tall glasses and handed one to August, who gulped it down in one and tried to disguise a burp. 'You're going to go for this, right?'

'I don't know,' August replied, surprising herself with the

answer as much as Flynn. Isn't this why she'd run all the way home? Now she struggled to put it into words. 'I don't think I'm good enough for this.' Flynn opened his mouth to protest but August held her hand up. 'Don't worry, I'm not fishing for compliments, I'm just … no … I can't audition for this. But maybe I could see if I could volunteer with the production or something.'

'Volunteer with the production?' Flynn said. 'That's some rubbish-old-flat-August talking there, not Elizabeth-Street-August. I thought you went after your dreams these days, instead of being content with being a wall shadow.'

'A wallflower.'

'Huh?'

'The expression is wallflower.'

'Well, you wouldn't be a very good one of those anyway because you can't keep flowers alive.'

August laughed and grabbed a towel to mop her face. 'But this is a big deal, and I haven't done much acting work in months.'

'You literally have built a studio inside the wall and have been getting all amped up to start taking on more voice work.'

'But theatre acting uses all sorts of skills, which I haven't flexed for a long time.'

'What about your new role at the Roman Baths?'

'I've not done much flexing there yet either.'

'Then let's flex them.'

'What do you mean?' she asked.

'Come on, you're warmed up from your run, you've just

had a big, protein-filled smoothie, let's run some lines.' He picked up a copy of *Gone Girl* from the bookshelf and tossed it to her. 'You be the man; I'll be the woman.'

'Why would you be the woman? Why can't I be the woman?'

'Because you already are a woman and you need to flex those acting muscles.'

August flipped through the pages of the book. 'I have all of Jane's books in my room, you know, we could read one of them.'

Flynn shook his head. 'We'll do that tomorrow. For now, we're starting with this.'

'Aren't you in the middle of something … else?' she asked, really not sure she wanted to do this.

'Hey,' Flynn said, coming over to her and slinging an arm over her shoulder. 'You've shown me some of your audiobook voices before. Why are you shying away from this?'

'I'm not. I'm just … ' An audition like this is what she'd been waiting for. In fact, part of the deal she made herself when she left London was to try and expand her career to include the theatre, specifically in period acting. But shouldn't she start smaller? Join a local amateur dramatics group first or something, like she'd been thinking about? The only in-person acting of any kind she'd done since moving here was her recent first day at the Baths as a costumed character. 'I can't go for this audition, Flynn, what if I don't get it? What does that say about me?' *What does that say about my dreams*?

'What if you never try? You'd feel like a right … ' he searched for a word and landed on, ' … bell-end.'

'I would not feel like a bell-end,' August insisted, but she laughed. 'What a thing to say. But I want to pick something I'm a bit more familiar with.'

Flynn succumbed. 'All right, you choose the text, whatever you want, but you can't play you, or someone like you. Even if that's the role you're going for. We'll get to that but I really think this will take you out of your head for a minute.'

August disappeared into her room for a moment and brought back out with her a tatty old paperback of *Romeo and Juliet* that she'd had since school. She loved this play so much. She also loved Leo DiCaprio playing Romeo in the movie so much. 'How about this?'

'I guess this could work,' Flynn answered. '*But*, I'll be Juliet and you have to be Romeo. Shall we do the fish tank scene?'

'From the movie? But there wasn't any talking in that bit, plus we don't have a fish tank.'

'Oh. Can I take a look?' He reached his hand out and she handed him her book.

'Shall I change first?' She pulled her damp dress away from her skin.

Without looking up Flynn said, 'No, don't shower, it'll make the scene more intense if you're a bit disgusting.'

'Ha, thanks.'

'Got it,' he said. 'Let's do the big fight scene between Tybalt and Mercutio.'

'Juliet's not even in that scene – even Romeo is barely in that scene.'

'Doesn't matter. You're playing Tybalt.'

'I am?'

Flynn handed the book back to her, open on Act Three, Scene One. 'Here, you take this, I'll find the script on my phone.'

'That's okay, I don't need it. I know this play like the back of my hand.'

'Whatever you say. You're Tybalt, I'm Mercutio. And just so you know, I'm picturing the movie version. We'll start from where Benvolio says *By my head, here come the Capulets* and then I say,' Flynn cleared his throat and stood proud. '*By my heel, I care not!*'

August laughed, involuntarily. It wasn't that he'd done anything wrong, it was just funny to her, and endearing really, that he was willing to stop what he was doing on a Saturday to help her with some acting. And he seemed very into it.

She then realised she didn't know the next line. 'I need the book, sorry, I guess I'm a little rusty.'

They read the lines together, August reserved to begin with, doing no more than read what was on the page aloud, until Flynn said. 'You're supposed to be mad. Tybalt is mad here with Romeo and his cronies. Be mad with me.'

'I can't be mad with you.'

'Of course you can, you're an actress. If you can be married to me you can be mad at me.'

'What do you know about this stuff?'

Flynn's eyes narrowed and he folded his arms, a smirk appearing on his face. 'I do know a little, you know. Just because you're too afraid to go on an audition, even though that's what you say you want more than anything to do, don't take it out on me.'

August was shocked. 'I'm sorry, I just—'

'Don't be sorry, just read the damned lines or let's stop wasting time.'

The pink that had been fading in her face flared up again and August fumed, 'Wasting *time*? This was your idea, not mine, I didn't even know if I wanted to do this stupid audition, and I really don't think I need your help with it.'

'Prove to me you aren't a coward,' he provoked, that smirk staying put though she wanted to wipe it clean off his face.

'I don't have to prove anything to you!'

Flynn shook his head and put down his phone. He turned and muttered, 'Coward.'

August Anderson was *not* a coward. Her eyes flickered to the book, but she was remembering now, she was remembering the words she'd learned and practised over and over again in her youth. '*Romeo, the love I bear thee can afford no better term than this – thou art a villain.*'

Flynn switched roles and read Romeo's line, glaring at her every time he looked up. '... *Villain am I none. Therefore, farewell. I see thou know'st me not.*'

August was inside Tybalt now, full of rage, bitterness, she felt the character, she empathised. '*Boy,*' she snarled, stepping close to Flynn, right up to his face. '*This shall not excuse the injuries that thou hast done me. Therefore turn and draw.*'

She was close to Flynn's lips now and something unexpected happened.

August wanted to kiss him.

That was most certainly not part of the script, but the instinct was so overwhelming that she nearly toppled, sensing he wanted it too.

The adrenaline pumped through her, keeping her on a knife edge, until before her eyes Flynn's face changed, and he stepped back, saying, 'There she is! Brava, brava, and the Oscar goes to Ms August Anderson for playing Tybalt with such ferocity I was afraid for my own testicles for a moment there.' Seeing August's confused face as she came down from the sugar-high that was being fully in character, he stepped forward and gave her sweaty frame a hug.

'That was an act?' she said into his chest.

'Are you angry?' Flynn asked. 'I didn't mean any of it, I just wanted you to forget your insecurities and go for it. I just said things that might make you a little pissed.'

'It worked,' she said, nodding. 'You're a good actor.'

'Hardly, but thanks.'

August was still a little dazed, but that was okay, because it actually felt good to have her insecurities contested, to feel accountable for making her dreams happen. 'I think I'll do the audition, you know,' she stepped back from Flynn but kept a hand on his arm. 'I'm still a little surprised you knew which buttons to press to kick me into gear, but I appreciate it.'

'You know I didn't mean any of it, right? In actual fact, you're the least cowardly person I know. And I know you can handle this audition.'

She spent a long time in the shower thinking about what

just happened. And she just kept coming back around to two things: one, it felt good to surround yourself with people who challenged your own self-doubts. And two, a question more than a thing, really. Where did that near-kiss come from?

Chapter 31

Flynn

'Does this feel a little over the top to you?' Flynn called.

'Whatever do you mean?' August shouted back, trying to be heard over the howling wind, and the flapping of the hem of her dress.

Flynn rubbed the sand, that was swirling in mini tornados around them, out of his eye. They were stood on Weston-super-Mare beach at dawn, on a day which was both sunny and enjoying forty-mile-an-hour winds. Because this morning, pre-work, August and Flynn were getting married.

'So what kind of photos do you want?' Bel hollered to the happy couple, as she'd been roped in as the photographer.

'Let's just get a couple of us looking, um, coupley, here in front of the waves. Try not to get the pier or anything in the background. This has to look like it could be any beach in the UK.' As August said this, another great gust caused her to nearly flash the lot of them.

She was wearing the only white dress she owned, a cotton sundress which didn't quite fit any more so wasn't done up all the way at the back. Flynn was in his work suit, and August had fashioned him a faux-pocket square out of a pair of her satin undies, which she'd made him promise he wouldn't look at. They'd plucked a couple of flowers on the way down to the beach which were to go in his lapel but all the petals had blown off before they'd even made it onto the sand.

Bel got snapping, with Flynn and August grinning into the camera the best they could with the wind whipping at their cheeks, their arms around each other.

'Do you want a kissing one?' Bel called, in her most innocent, 'whatever the client wants' voice.

August gave her a look and shouted back, 'No, that's okay. Let's just get one more with us looking lovingly at each other.' She faced Flynn and added, 'You need to look lovingly at me now.'

If Flynn stepped back for a minute and removed himself from this situation, if he let himself really think about what was going on, he'd notice how crazy this whole thing was. He was a grown up, why was he out here on a beach at the crack of dawn, taking make-believe wedding photos to fool their strict landlady, if she ever were to ask to see them?

August placed her arms around his neck and gazed up at him, *lovingly*, and that was why.

Bel took a couple of snaps and was just yelling 'That's a wrap!' when a whoosh of mint fabric swooped past Flynn and August's faces.

'My knickers!' August cried. Flynn's makeshift pocket

square had broken free and was dancing in the breeze above them. He reached a hand up but just missed, and they flew off into the waves.

August ran in after them, screaming at Flynn, 'Get them! Catch them! No, don't touch them! I've nearly . . . '

Eventually she caught them on the crest of a wave, but by this point she was soaked, and in no state to be in any more wedding photos. Flynn, whose suit trousers were also soaked, wrapped his jacket around August.

And just for a moment, it was as if he was watching himself on an old home movie, a memory playing out before him as though it wasn't happening in real time but was being treasured and tucked away and kept for ever. Splashed with salty water, wind whipping at their faces, August wrapped and laughing inside his jacket, he found himself imagining what it would be like if he really was marrying this girl today. In that moment, with tendrils of her hair catching the sun, his feet in the ocean, he couldn't imagine being happier.

'Do you think we got good pictures?' Flynn asked, when they were all safely back in the car and could stop shouting.

Bel nodded, and handed her phone back to August while she started the car to drive them back into Bath. 'Take a look.'

August leant forward, showing Flynn, who was in the passenger seat, the photos Bel had taken.

They were good – nice even! 'We look very cute together,' August joked to him, and Flynn couldn't find a way to reply, the moment from the beach still on his mind, like a dream he was trying to cling to that was fading. And then she got to the final few pictures, where Bel had kept snapping, capturing the knickers in the air, August jumping through the waves, and Flynn walking a laughing August back up the beach, his jacket and his arms around her.

August peered at their faces in the photo. 'I tell you what, it took every ounce of acting skill in me to play the adoring newlywed in all that wind and freezing seas. But you really got it there,' she said, showing him. 'This one is really good actually, you nailed the "looking lovingly" brief.'

Flynn laughed, agreed, and let the dream-like moment go without saying another word.

At the end of that week, a week in which Flynn had worked from dawn until dusk with the exception of one morning when he'd had a quick wedding on the beach (and had needed to work even later to get through his mass of paperwork), two of his co-workers invited him to The Bath Brew House – a smart pub in the centre of town with a rustic vibe and a lively Friday evening drinks crowd.

He was tired, and as much as he liked the company of these guys, he wanted to at least try and put anything work related behind him for the weekend.

Flynn went up to the bar – it was his turn to buy a round, and then he'd probably call it a night – and found himself wondering what August was doing this evening. Maybe when he headed back to the flat, if she was there, he could see if she fancied going through some her lines for the audition next month. Or even just watch a movie and switch off altogether.

He sighed. He had to shake off these thoughts of August that kept floating through his mind since their 'wedding shoot'. She'd made it clear she was just acting, and yes, he'd had a moment of feeling like there was something more between them, but it was nothing but his imagination. Perhaps he was just lonely. Perhaps he was beginning to feel ready to move on from Yui, and he was just projecting it onto August because she was right there.

'Has she stood you up?' a voice said beside him, and he looked over to see a pretty redhead smiling at him.

'I'm sorry?' he replied. He knew a pick-up line when he heard one, but he was never very prepared with a slick answer.

'Your wife, has she stood you up?'

She looked vaguely familiar but he couldn't place her. She definitely didn't live in any of the flats in his house. Maybe she worked on a different floor of his office or something. 'I'm not . . . no, I'm not waiting for anyone, just getting some drinks for some friends.'

'My mistake,' the redhead shrugged. 'You just looked like you were waiting for someone.'

'Oh,' he nodded, and went back to trying to catch the barman's eye, which was difficult in this crowd.

'So you aren't married?' she persisted, and then leant in closer and said, 'Indulge me, will you? I'm with that hen party over there and they're doing dares, and my dare was to come and chat you up. Very high school, I know. And so even though this doesn't have to go anywhere, I still don't want to be batting my eyelashes at somebody's husband.'

'Ah, I see,' Flynn relaxed and gave her his full attention for the first time. 'Well, no, not married.' *Unless you count a fake wedding on Weston-super-Mare beach a few days ago.*

'Girlfriend?'

'No.' It still stung him though to be reminded that he was no longer part of a couple. August never pressed him on it, so Yui was beginning to cross his mind less often. When she did though ... Maybe he wasn't as over her as he thought.

'Great,' the redhead propped herself against the bar, creating a place for herself amidst all the business. 'I'm Poppy.'

'Poppy,' he repeated. 'Named after the hair or is the hair to match the name?' *Smooth, Flynn, could you sound any more like a sweaty-palmed retired businessman?*

But she just laughed and said, 'Don't tell anyone, but the hair is dyed, so it came afterwards. What's your name?'

'Flynn.'

'Good to meet you, Flynn.' She studied him for a moment while he racked his brains for something to say. He felt so unpractised at flirting with a stranger.

'What's the end goal here? Of the dare, I mean; what are they expecting from you?' he asked.

'Honestly?' Poppy gave him a direct look, her eyebrows raised. 'I don't think they'd be satisfied unless you threw me on this bar and made out with me.'

'What can I get you, mate?' the bartender interrupted them at that moment and Flynn had to splutter out a response.

'Erm, three pints of London Pride, please, and ...' he

looked at Poppy. He hadn't intended to buy her a drink too, but he could hardly not after that line.

'I'll have a Merlot, thanks,' she said over her shoulder, her eyes on Flynn, a teasing smile on her lips. 'Don't worry though,' she said to Flynn as the bartender went to fix their drinks. 'I'm not about to accost you. Maybe you could just take my number instead?'

'Okay,' Flynn replied, and opened up a new contact on his phone, handing it to her to input her number.

'Until next time, Flynn,' Poppy said, taking her wine and heading back to the table with a wink.

Flynn paid for the drinks and paused for a moment, feeling like a whirlwind had just hit him.

Back at the table, he tried to focus on the conversation, but, like it or not, his eyes kept flitting towards Poppy, the redhead in the corner, surrounded by friends. And she seemed susceptible to glancing his way too. Flynn didn't even mean to, it's not like he was looking to meet someone, but it was one of those situations where you want to keep your eyes fixed forward but accidentally keep being drawn towards the flame.

He drank his pint swiftly, tiredness and confusion taking over, and made his exit.

At home, August was sprawled on the sofa wearing a sheet face mask – which made him jump out of his skin – and re-reading *Persuasion*. As he stood there, looking at her, all thoughts of Poppy drifted away like petals on the wind.

Chapter 32

August

I would like to perform an inspection on your apartment in 24 hours' time.

Oh, crap.

It was Saturday morning, and with August's big audition next month still at the forefront of her mind, she'd been planning to spend the entire two days in character. Wasn't Hilary Swank a method actress? And she had an Oscar. Really, it was the least August could do.

'Flynn?' August called out, the letter that had been slipped under their door in her hand. 'Flynn?' She knocked on his door – was he even home?

She heard a big, manly yawn, followed by a sleepy, 'Come in, August.'

August cracked open the door, her eyes scrunched closed.

'Are you sure? Are you alone?' She wasn't sure why she'd asked that.

'Yes, of course I'm alone,' he laughed, his voice husky, like he'd just woken up. Which he had. 'What time is it?'

'Ten. Did you have a late night?'

'Yes, but only catching up on work,' he yawned, gesturing to his work laptop, which lay closed on the other side of the bed. He was all messy hair, among the crumpled bedsheets. The room was dark and cool, though morning sun filtered through the closed curtains so it wasn't pitch black. 'Come and get into bed with me so I don't feel like a lazy sod.' Flynn rolled onto his front and closed his eyes again, the duvet down to his waist, and he patted the gap on the mattress beside him.

'I'm not getting into bed with you,' August said, taking a step forward.

'Come on, baby, climb on in,' he slurred, but one of his eyes opened and he peeped at her, and she could see he was playing.

Instead, August *sat* on the bed with him, propping the spare pillow up behind her back, and thwacked his back with the letter. 'You're such a tease.'

'You're a tease,' he shot back, and slung an arm over her outstretched legs. Flynn's skin was warm and his arm heavy, and she liked this familiarity between them. It felt light, like it always had with him from the start, and sometimes she felt it transfigured with the complications of . . . life . . . and their situation. But sometimes, on lazy mornings or long evenings, she liked to just forget everything else and just be like this. Enjoying each other.

'We've had a letter,' August stated.

Flynn yawned. 'Post is nice.'

'It's from Mrs Haverley.'

He lifted his head to look at August. 'Everything okay?'

'Yes. At least, hopefully. She wants to do an inspection tomorrow morning.'

Flynn looked over his shoulder at his room, which was a bit of a state with piles of clothes, bigger piles of paperwork, coffee mugs scattered on surfaces. He really needed to cut back on his hours.

'It's part of the contract, just a standard thing during the first couple of months,' August continued, skimming through the letter. 'Tomorrow morning at 10 a.m. She likes to do things on Sunday mornings, doesn't she?'

'Mmm,' Flynn agreed, closing his eyes again.

August sighed and shuffled down in the bed, so she was lying next to him after all, moving his arm to rest across her stomach instead of her legs. She pulled the duvet over her, succeeding in not glancing down for a peek as she moved it, and tried to formulate a plan. She loved living here so much, so this needed to go well.

'Hi, there,' Flynn said, his face close to hers.

'Hello.' She gulped.

'Nice of you to join me.'

She knew he was joking around, but ... they were sure finding themselves in a lot of situations where they were 'joking around' since moving in together. August focussed on the present. 'Don't try anything. We need to have a house meeting is all, and you're too lazy to get up for it so I guess we're doing it in here.'

'Don't *you* try anything,' stretched Flynn. 'I'm the one not wearing any clothes.'

'You're naked?' August screamed.

'Ah relax, I'm not naked, I have boxers on.' He rolled onto his side to face her properly. 'All right, so the landlady is coming on down tomorrow morning.'

'At 10 a.m. You'll be up, right?'

'I sure will.'

'Our biggest problem is that we're going to need this pigsty to look like we share it. And my room to look like the spare.'

Flynn scanned his room again. 'Luckily, this is all just surface mess because I've not had a minute to breathe this week. It's actually pretty clean and tidy underneath.'

'But even cleaned, it still doesn't look like the room of a married couple.'

'How should a married couple's room look?'

She thought about it. 'It's fine that all my clothes are next door, if she comments on it we just say we each had too much stuff to fit the built-in wardrobes, so rather than split it we use the spare room – i.e. my real room – as my walk-in closet, as it were. But . . . '

'But?'

'I don't know exactly what it needs, I just know that right now this room feels one hundred per cent "Flynn" and zero per cent "August"'.

'You could just move in here with me permanently, and then it would always feel like you,' Flynn joked, and immediately looked as if he regretted it, like he'd given away his subconscious.

'Flynn! What are you suggesting?'

'Nothing, I'm just messing with you.' He sat up and she followed suit, pulling the duvet higher to cover them both.

August didn't quite know what to make of all this. He seemed extra flirty today. But was it teasing, was it his tired, sleep-deprived mind trying to make jokes she wasn't quite getting? Either way, it was having an effect on her, and now she couldn't shake the thought of sharing a bed with him every night, what that would potentially lead to, and—

Stop it, August.

'Right,' said Flynn, getting a hold of himself, and running a hand through his hair. 'So, let's put your dressing gown on the back of the door along with mine, and bring in your bedside table. Then we should also put a little pile of your scripts or books on the windowsill. That looks like you've been in here practising, which you wouldn't do if it weren't your room . . . would you?'

'Of course not! If I was rehearsing for something and you were out, and I had this whole beautiful apartment to myself, I'd hardly come and stand in here and clog my nostrils up with your aftershave.'

'Hey, you don't like my aftershave?'

'Well, actually I do, I was just including it for dramatic emphasis.' She mused for a moment. 'I think I'll get a bunch of flowers and a vase, to go on your windowsill.'

'Uh-oh,' Flynn said. 'Watch out, flowers.'

'All right, all right, we both know I have the least green fingers in the world but I'm sure I can keep them alive for one day.' It seemed like overkill, and slightly clichéd, to try and make the room look 'girly' by putting flowers in there, but August figured that Mrs Haverley and her old-fashioned ways might consider it proper to have fresh flowers around, so August was willing to play the part.

'Come on, then, get up,' she instructed, climbing out of the bed. 'I'll go out and get everything we need for some great bacon sandwiches, and you make a start in here. Ugh, I sound so bossy.'

But Flynn just laughed lightly and sat down, the duvet dropping back down to his waist again. 'No you don't, you're just the boss. I'm on it, in just five more minutes,' he yawned, and after she left his room he snuggled back down under the duvet with a smile on his face.

Chapter 33

Flynn

By early afternoon, the apartment had transformed from a flatshare into a marital home. August had cleared the decks in her room, throwing everything into her drawers and wardrobe, and put some spare towels and a box of tissues neatly on the side, so it looked like they were ready for weekend guests at the drop of a hat. The living room was much as it always was, but with their new 'wedding' photos prominently printed and framed, and a card on display that August had picked up that morning that said 'Husband, just to say I love you'. Flynn had laughed at that.

Flynn's room was looking, well, quite inviting actually. It was neat and tidy, like he usually was, to be fair, but now it had accents of August dotted about. Some of her books on his shelf. Her *Northanger Abbey* script plus a few older ones and the flowers on the windowsill. A few select pieces of makeup and toiletries on her bedside table that they'd moved in. She'd swapped his big, framed, signed *Star Wars* poster for a print that usually hung in her room, a photo of the crest of a wave taken from the side, the sunshine streaming through. It actually went well in his room, coordinating with the Japanese artwork he had up of *The Great Wave*.

They stood at his doorway now, surveying their work.

'I think we did well,' said Flynn. 'Although I might wake up tomorrow morning and forget whose room I'm in for a moment. Let's not drink tonight.'

'Good plan,' August agreed. 'I'll change my bed covers in the morning, so my bed doesn't look slept in.'

'So are we done?' Flynn asked.

'We should clean, I guess,' August answered, and then went and made them both a cup of tea.

'I can do that – you wanted to rehearse this weekend,' countered Flynn.

'You know what though? It's actually been nice taking my mind off it a little. I know that scene like the back of my hand. I know Catherine Morland like the back of my hand. Maybe having a day off is what I need.'

He looked at her. 'Okay, but if you want to run lines while we're cleaning just say the word.'

'You know me so well,' she laughed. 'Are you still all right with this whole arrangement?' August enquired, handing Flynn's mug to him a few minutes later, and they took a walk out of the building to sit on the wall and relax.

'Living with you?'

'That, but also this whole . . .' August checked behind her

to make sure they were alone and then lowered her voice. 'This whole "fake marriage" thing?'

Flynn nodded and sipped his tea. 'Sure. It seems to be working pretty well so far. Are you?'

'Yes. I'm so ...' She inhaled the fresh, Bath air. '... happy ... living here. And you're a great flatmate. But there have been a few occasions where we've had to cover our tracks, or things have got more complicated than I imagined they would.'

'I see what you mean. But I think we've handled it all well so far, don't you?'

'I do, so far.' She crinkled her nose at him. 'Sorry for any tricky bits though. I'm sure spending your Saturday prepping your home to make it look like you're married to your flatmate wasn't how you expected your life to be when you were thinking about moving from Japan. Hopefully tomorrow will go smoothly.'

'It'll go fine,' Flynn replied.

'Did you live with somebody in Japan?' she asked him outright, for the first time. 'Did you live with your ex-girlfriend? Tell me to mind my own beeswax if you want.'

Flynn had been expecting this question at some point. Well, not necessarily that exact question, but he'd never really discussed Yui, or the exact details of his life in Japan, with August. Even when she'd told him about James, he'd still not opened up much. It had felt too fresh, too personal, to start sharing. But maybe now was a good time.

He took a long gulp of his tea. 'Yep, I lived with Yui, for about a year.'

'Oh,' August replied, her eyebrows raising involuntarily. 'I hadn't realised. So it was pretty serious.'

'It was. We'd been together for a couple of years before I moved.'

'Did you ... ' she trailed off.

'Did we ... do it?' Flynn teased.

'No,' August laughed. 'Did you move to England because you broke up?'

'That's a difficult question.' Flynn had never tried too hard to see through the frosted glass window to the end of his relationship with Yui. Sometimes he felt like it ended because he chose to go to England, and that's certainly the narrative she'd chosen. But other times it felt like he'd chosen to move back because he knew things were over between them, like he didn't feel wanted anymore, and that's why he'd started to think about starting afresh.

August let silence fall over them while he thought. She moved her arm like she wanted to put it around him but thought twice. Instead she waited.

'If I really think about it, the break-up started when Yui and I moved in together,' Flynn started, his gaze never leaving the vista ahead of them. 'We had a great first year together, obviously, that's why we took the next step. We found a nice apartment, equidistant from both our work-places, cosy, lots of natural light. It had this big window seat we could both lie out on – you would have liked it.' Why did he say that? He hadn't meant to insert her into the tableau.

'It sounds lovely,' said August.

'But I think Yui ... no, both of us ... assumed moving

193

in together would mean being able to spend more time together. In reality it only highlighted how many hours we both put into our jobs and how neither of us wanted to argue about it when we finally came home.'

'And that went on for a year?'

'Not continually, it's more that the cracks started to form, and niggles became pain points, which became arguments. But we didn't really want to break up, we just didn't know the solution. At least that's how I felt. Then I found this job transfer and I thought maybe if we both moved over here for a while it would be a change of scene, a change of pace, a new adventure. But Yui saw it as a break-up.'

'Did she want you to stay?' asked August, treading carefully.

He looked down then, swirling the remainder of his tea in his mug, and sighed with defeat. 'Not really. I think, for her, it was a light at the end of the tunnel. An escape route. From me.'

'I'm sure she didn't see it like that,' August commented, kindly.

'It's not like we ever got really mad at each other, it was never horrible between us, I just began to feel like she wasn't looking at me the same anymore, like I'd disappointed her and she was done. If I hadn't found this job, I expect we would have split up anyway.'

He went to take another sip of tea but his mug was empty. August took it from his hands and replaced it with her own, a mug which was still half full.

'Do you miss her?' August asked.

'I miss the her from before we moved in together. I can look back on that and smile now. But the Yui from the past year still makes me sad. No, the situation makes me sad, it's really not her fault. It does make me worried about moving in with a girlfriend again though.' He sighed. That was the truth of it really, the reason he would never jump into living with a girlfriend again, and the reason he knew he had to keep his thoughts about August to himself if he didn't want to risk their friendship.

'Why's that?'

'Because what if I ruin it again? What if living with me is a relationship destroyer?'

August thought about this. 'I like living with you.' He smiled into his mug of tea, and she continued. 'I know I'm not a girlfriend, but for what it's worth, I do. And every situation is different. Your next girlfriend won't be exactly like Yui, so why would your relationship?'

Flynn nodded, glancing over at August, at the sun catching her hair, at the way she held her hands around his empty mug, cradling it like she could still feel the warmth. He wasn't sure what to say. Because what he was thinking was about how it would feel if August *were* his girlfriend.

So August spoke again. 'That said, I'm not as wise as I sound, because I have never lived with a boyfriend. My last boyfriend broke up with me at the mere *thought* of living with me, so maybe we're both complete nightmares, destined to just live together for eternity like a couple of misfits.'

Flynn laughed at that; his melancholy moment broken. 'That doesn't sound too bad.'

'No?'

'Nope. James's loss was my gain, quite frankly. Where does he live now?'

August shrugged. 'Same place as he used to, I'm guessing, in a house share across the city.'

Flynn slung an arm around August's shoulders, the weight of it heavy but comforting. They both admired the big, open panorama in front of them, and he said, 'Well, we live here.'

'We live here,' August smiled.

Chapter 34

August

August watched Mrs Haverley's profile as she ever so slowly scrutinised the apartment. She'd been there fifteen minutes and hadn't left the living room yet, barely saying a word. Her eyes were moving along the lengths of the wall, perhaps looking for scuff marks, or signs that August and Flynn were living there under false pretences and needed immediate evicting.

Flynn asked again, 'Mrs Haverley, are you sure I can't make you a tea or anything?'

Mrs Haverley dragged her eyes from the curtains to Flynn's face, regarded him for a moment, and then said, 'I'm fine, thanks.'

She moved towards August's bedroom and stopped, her gaze caught by one of their faux wedding photos, sitting in a silver frame and propped up on a shelf. 'You had a beach wedding,' she stated, with no indication this was a question, nor whether she considered it a good or bad thing.

'We did,' August replied in her brightest voice. 'In Cornwall. It was a magical day.'

'Yes,' Mrs Haverley replied. 'Weddings are quite lovely.' With that, she moved into August's room, and behind her August and Flynn glanced at each other.

August held her breath.

'I see you purchased another bed.'

'We did,' August confirmed, aware she was becoming repetitive. 'We use this as our spare room.'

'Do you have many overnight guests?' Mrs Haverley asked sharply.

'No,' Flynn and August said in unison, and Flynn added, 'August has family not too far away so we like to be prepared in case they want to come into Bath.'

That'll be the day, August thought, but Mrs Haverley nodded. 'Fine. How do you find the bed in the master?'

'Wonderful,' exclaimed Flynn.

'Very soft,' chimed in August.

'Thank you,' they added together.

'I don't like a soft bed myself, too much bounce,' Mrs Haverley said, inspecting the doorframe. She looked directly at August then. 'But I am old and have a bad back, of course, and you are young. I expect young people don't mind a bit of bounce.'

Mrs Haverley stalked past them out towards Flynn's room and August was dumbstruck for a moment. Had that been a twinkle in Mrs Haverley's eye? Had she just made a bit of a naughty joke? No . . .

In Flynn's room it was back to business, and Mrs Haverley

ran her finger over the window pane like Mary Poppins checking for dust, and there was a quiet tap on the door.

August excused herself for just a moment to see who it was, and as she walked away she heard Mrs Haverley spot the scripts on the windowsill and ask, 'What are these?'

'Those are August's – she's an actress and they're scripts, one is for an audition she has coming up,' Flynn replied.

'What has she been in?' she heard her reply from the other room.

Poor guy, she'd be back to rescue Flynn in just a moment. Opening the door, expecting to find her most regular visitor, Callie, to be standing there with her yoga mat or some more baked goods, she was surprised to see a smiling, and slightly dishevelled, Abe Haverley.

'Hello,' August said, taking in his stubbled jaw and just-got-out-of-bed hair. He wore a sweatshirt with the sleeves drooping down over his fingers, jeans, and trainers with the laces tucked in instead of done up.

'Morning,' he said, his expression sheepish. 'Is she here? I completely overslept.'

'She's here,' laughed August. 'I didn't know you were coming along too, we've started "the tour" without you.'

'Mum asked me to come down to Bath at the last minute yesterday – she needed a hand with some things – so I'm a bit all over the place.'

'I have a pot of coffee on if you'd like one?'

'That would be amazing.'

Abe followed her into the kitchen and she watched him as he took a gulp of the strong, black coffee she poured him

199

from the percolator. How was this the same stuffy grump of a man they'd met on their first day? He cleared his throat and stood tall, and for a second she saw a flash of Serious Abe again, until he said, 'Now, if Mum asks, I'm late down because I was on the phone with the internet company, all right?' She nodded, and he grinned, placing a hand on her shoulder for a millisecond. She liked that they had a little secret, a little moment.

Returning to Flynn's bedroom with Abe in tow, she heard that the conversation hadn't progressed too far.

'You're not sure?' Mrs Haverley was asking with incredulity. 'You're not sure if your wife has been on the silver screen?'

Flynn must be wracking his brain in there, August thought as she hurried back in, he must be worried about saying 'no' if she had and he'd forgotten.

'He just means he's not sure of the title,' August said smoothly, entering the room. 'I had a small part in an Italian film, years ago, the title is quite complicated but roughly translates as "Fun adventures on a Tuscan vineyard".'

'Do you speak Italian?' Mrs Haverley asked.

'No, thankfully I just played a tourist on a wine tour, so my couple of lines were in English. Look, Abe's here!'

Mrs Haverley simply nodded at that, and at her son, and opened the window, sticking her head out to wipe her finger along the glass on the outside. Abe walked across the room to join her.

'Is that true?' Flynn whispered to August. 'You were in an Italian movie?'

'Mmm-hmm,' nodded August, and then added, 'Well, actually, no. But I did audition for it. I just didn't get the role.'

Mrs Haverley brought her head back in, sighed, and lingered in the room for a moment longer. Without a word about the state of the window, she nodded and exited, as swiftly as she'd entered. She and Abe moved through the bathroom and kitchen with a similar tight-lipped rigidity, and with every passing minute August and Flynn could feel beads of sweat forming at the back of their necks.

Back in the living room Mrs Haverley faced them, her mouth pinched, and regarded the two of them for a moment.

August reached for Flynn's hand to add an extra layer of happy-couple-dom, at which Mrs Haverley gave a curt nod and turned towards the door. 'Everything seems in order,' she said, her long fingers clasped over the doorknob. Looking over her shoulder back at them she asked, 'Nothing is broken or causing bother, I trust?'

'Nothing,' August and Flynn confirmed in unison, standing before her, hand in hand, like the creepy twins from *The Shining*.

Mrs Haverley's eyes swept the room one more time as she cracked open the door, a draught of September air from the landing wafting in. And then she stopped, her head tilted to the side, and her eyes narrowed.

'You got married in Cornwall?' she asked.

August gulped. 'Yes.'

'On a beach?'

'That's right,' said Flynn, keeping his voice light and chirpy.

Mrs Haverley pointed a finger towards the photo she'd commented on earlier. 'Steep Holm.'

'Pardon?' said Flynn. He could feel August's palm beginning to sweat against his.

'That's Steep Holm in the background of your wedding picture, the island off Weston-super-Mare.'

August turned her head in slow motion to look at the photograph.

Mrs Haverley, her voice low, asked, 'Why is it there if you married on a beach in Cornwall?'

Flynn and August looked at the photo, and the very small blob on the horizon behind Flynn's shoulder. A thousand thoughts raced through August's mind like a lie-based *Wheel of Fortune* machine. It tried to locate, as quickly as possible, the most feasible excuse.

Ratatatatatatat – The wedding pictures had been ruined so they tried to recreate them nearby? A bit far-fetched.

Ratatatatatat – This was actually the engagement shoot? Believable, but would they then need to go and take another set of wedding pictures? She didn't have another white dress.

Ratatata-ta-ta—ta—ta— gaslight a poor lady in her late seventies into thinking she can't believe her own eyesight? She'd run out of thinking time so that had to be the winner.

'It does look like Steep Holm, doesn't it?' August laughed. 'It's actually a cargo ship sailing past in the distance. We asked the photographer to photoshop them all out, but she must have missed this one and we never noticed.'

Flynn laughed with hearty gusto. 'That photographer, we'll have to ask her to redo that one, won't we love?'

'We sure will, honey,' August chortled, angling the two of them between Mrs Haverley and the photo, so that their bodies were blocking it. 'Thanks for pointing that out, Mrs Haverley. And thanks for coming over.'

'Yes, thanks,' added Flynn.

'Lovely to see you,' said August, holding the door open.

Mrs Haverley gave one of her no-nonsense nods once again, and seeming satisfied, left their flat. Abe went out along with her, meeting August's eye for a second as she was closing the door.

As the door shut, August let out a sigh. 'Hubby, fetch me my laptop,' she said to Flynn. 'I appear to have some photo-shopping to take care of.'

As he dutifully went off to get her computer for her, she let her breathing return to normal. But what was normal? Because this didn't feel much like a normal way to live, more like a web they were getting tangled further and further into.

Chapter 35

August

'Happy Anniversary!' cried Callie and her mum, standing on the landing and holding a huge cake covered in mint icing.

August blinked. 'Thank you?'

'I couldn't remember the exact date you got hitched last year, but you said early October, which is now, so I figured you love birds would be celebrating for days.' Callie pushed past August and plonked the cake down in her kitchen, slicing four great slabs and throwing open cupboards until she found plates.

Flynn appeared. 'What's the cake for? Yum!'

'Our anniversary,' August explained. 'Our wedding anniversary.'

'Yep,' said Flynn. 'Yep, it's our anniversary, good memory, Callie. Nothing gets past you.'

'Maud and Allen send their best wishes as well,' said Callie's mum.

'Oh yes, and I know Mrs H probably does but I haven't seen her yet this week.' Callie dug a camera out of her pocket. 'I'll be popping in tomorrow though, so I'll tell her all about it.'

The cake was moist and light, a chocolate centre to the mint icing, making the whole thing taste like a reverse After Eight. Callie's mum had outdone herself with the baking this time, it even beat the brownies from a few weeks ago.

While they ate, Callie nattered away about her new quest for a boyfriend, inspired, she said, by the two of them and their lovely relationship. A twist formed in August's stomach at that, at the thought she was misleading Callie who was so sweet. She really needed to put some thought into whether or not to confess. But, it was a good thing that Callie was moving on from her divorce, whether it was thanks to them or not, wasn't it?

'Must dash, yoga-with-Mum time, come up if you want, Aug,' Callie said, standing up as soon as she was done with her slice. 'First, let's have a photo of the two of you with the rest of your cake so I can show Mrs H tomorrow.'

August and Flynn dutifully stood side by side, holding the plate with the cake in front of them.

'It's not a bloody church coffee morning,' Callie's mum admonished. 'It's your wedding anniversary. Give us a smooch.'

August tilted her cheek towards Flynn and he gave it a chaste peck, to which Callie groaned.

'I don't think Mrs Haverley wants to see us full-on snogging, Callie,' said August, imagining the look of horror on her landlady's face at being forced to look at such a photo.

'You don't know her like I do,' laughed Callie, holding up the camera again. 'And I bet she bloomin' does. Come on, give her something to bother putting her glasses on for.'

August and Flynn looked at each other over the cake, their eyes flittering briefly to each other's lips. It was clear they were both trying to work out the best thing to do in this situation.

August was pretty sure Flynn's look said, *Come on, let's just kiss*, but she couldn't be sure.

She tried to convey to him that she was thinking, *It's okay, let's do this*, but she couldn't tell if he'd read her right.

Callie lowered her camera. 'What's wrong with you two? Did we interrupt you in the middle of an argument or something? Oh bloody hell, Mum, we need to leave them to it.'

'No, you didn't,' said August, seeing the embarrassment on their faces.

'It's me,' chimed in Flynn, a brainwave hitting him. 'I have a cold sore coming, I can feel it.'

'Oh,' Callie stepped away, looking a bit uncomfortable.

'Yep, it's tingling away. I don't want August to catch it.'

'Quite. Listen, keep hold of the cake plate for as long you need, okay?'

'Will do,' Flynn smiled, and August showed them out, though they didn't need much help fleeing.

August leant against the door after they'd left, her heart beating fast. It really caught up with her sometimes, these lies, the spontaneity they required. And that was a close one. Too close.

'Flynn,' August blurted out.

'Hi,' he replied, noting the wringing of her hands, her nervous pacing. 'What's up?'

'That – that is what's up,' she motioned to the door. 'That was a little too close for comfort.'

Flynn laughed. 'Nah, we got away with that pretty well, I'd say.'

'I think we've got to try it, man,' August said, looking directly at Flynn. 'I think we have to try kissing.'

She marched towards the cupboard where they kept alcohol and pulled out a bottle of Malibu, swigging it straight from the bottle, holding eye contact with him, a thousand thoughts darting through her mind. 'What do you think? Are you up for it?'

He watched her, amused. '*Try* kissing? You've kissed people before, right?'

'Millions! Well, not millions, but yes, I have done a lot of kissing. And now I think you and I should.' She waved the Malibu bottle at him. 'If we just get this out of the way and have a kiss then if we're ever put in the position again where we need to kiss each other or whatever in front of other people we won't be awkward and stand-offish, and give the game away. We'll just be like, *Oh yeah sure, I'll kiss my husband, no big deal, we do this all the time.*' She took another swig. 'It'll just be a thing we do, like the hand holding. Just acting. Rather than it being a THING.'

'What's with the Malibu?'

'Liquid courage.'

'You need that with me?'

'Probably not, but I was a lot more confident about kissing

207

strangers in my younger days, and I always drank Malibu on nights out.'

Her breathing slowed, like she was afraid of falling if she breathed too deep, as his gaze softened and he began to make his way towards her.

Wait. Should they?

Flynn stepped over to her, standing right in front of her. He put one of his hands on her shoulder, and with the other he stroked her hair off her face. 'I'm not a stranger,' he said, his lips, level with her eyes, curling into a gentle smile.

Should they, though?

August felt like time had slowed right down, all of her worries dropping over the ledge of her mind, and now it was just about Flynn's lips, inches from hers. Without turning, she placed the Malibu bottle somewhere behind her, she wasn't sure where, it could be suspended in mid-air for all she knew; she certainly was. And then she moved her hands to his forearms. 'No, you're not a stranger,' she confirmed, her voice quiet. She felt completely safe.

Chapter 36

Flynn

Holding August, touching the skin of her face, really looking at her in close-up, Flynn tried to push away thoughts of whether or not they were doing the right thing. This had the potential to change their whole relationship, and they already had a really good thing going, living together as flatmates. The more seconds that passed, the more he took her in in front of him, the deeper he thought he might fall.

The decision was taken out of his hands the moment she inhaled, looked him straight into his eyes and said, a smile playing on her lips, 'So kiss me.'

They moved closer together until they were breathing the same breath, and their lips grazed each other's, barely a kiss to begin with, more of an exploration.

They smiled into each other, Flynn's arm tightening just a touch around her waist, August's hands on his upper arms, tiptoeing upwards until her fingers touched the back of his neck and he tilted his head down further, pressing his lips a little more onto her hers.

As they discovered each other's lips, Flynn tried to keep himself in check, afraid of showing too much of what he was feeling right now, and he hadn't even had a chance to process exactly what that was himself yet. He only knew he wanted to remember everything about this moment.

This kiss was light years away from the accidental peck that time he'd first walked into their flat and he'd met Bel. That one was laced with guilt over his recently ended relationship with Yui, while this was all about August. Only about August.

Chapter 37

August

The minute their lips touched, August was swept away, all at sea in Flynn's arms. He kissed her, and she kissed him back, and it was delicious. She didn't need that liquid courage; this was so much better than a moment with a stranger in a club. She kissed Flynn with everything she had, all the happiness she'd felt since moving into Elizabeth Street with him, all the lonely moments she'd felt since James left, and she kissed him hard because she didn't want it to end but she knew this probably shouldn't happen again.

This didn't feel like a practice kiss, or a fake kiss in the name of acting, to her at least, this felt like a first kiss. Oh God.

Should they have done that?

A small bubble of nervous laughter made its way up through August's chest, and though she tried to suppress it, out it came. Flynn pulled back, the moment ending, their lips unlocking. He laughed too.

211

'I think we nailed it,' he said.

'I think you're right.' She blushed a little, and then briefly hid her face against his chest, giving herself just a few more moments in his arms.

Flynn looked down at August, and he seemed reluctant to let her go. 'We could keep rehearsing, if you want,' he suggested, his voice quiet.

August was a doer, a risk-taker, someone who grabbed onto life, or at least that's what she aspired to be. Many, many times she had just gone for what felt right rather than being someone who thought things through carefully first. And though it hadn't always worked out in her favour, she liked that about herself. Right now, a huge part of her was enjoying Flynn in this new and exciting way, and it would be so easy for her to throw her arms back around his neck and spend the rest of the day making out with him. But her conscience, that real killjoy part of her she hated to listen to, was shouting at her loud and clear today. *This is not a good idea, things could get very complicated, very fast. He's your flatmate. It will become awkward and one of you will want to move out. Don't do this.*

But –

NO. Have some damned self-control.

'I think we'd better leave it there,' she answered, eventually, and Flynn nodded, dropping his arms, breathing a little sigh of relief.

They stood beside each other for a moment, unsure what to say, until August broke the silence. 'Well, thank you.'

'Thank you,' Flynn replied.

'Fancy a cup of tea?'

'Yes, please, that would be great.'

'Great.'

'Thank you,' he said.

'Thank *you*.'

August went into the kitchen and made the tea, staring out of the window at absolutely nothing other than the memories dancing behind her eyes. She licked her bottom lip, tasting his imprint one last time.

Time to pull herself together. It was done. He'd done as she'd asked, and now the job was completed. She knew she had to go back out there with a clear mind, and not one full of his lips, his hands, his eyes. *Get a grip, Anderson*, she scolded herself, and picked up the mugs.

August entered the living room and slapped on her usual sunny smile, and Flynn stopped pacing in his tracks. He looked like he was going to say something. He was regretting it. He was going to tell her he had to move out. 'Glad we got that ticked off the list!' she said, a desperate attempt to play down what had happened. She wanted everything to go back to normal. Please, please, let everything go back to normal. They had such a good thing going.

Chapter 38

Flynn

In the living room, Flynn had also been staring out of the window, hands on hips, a million miles away. What *happened*? Something had shifted, been dislodged, that was never meant to have moved. He knew that if she came back into the room now and asked him to kiss her again, he would do it, without hesitation. He hoped she did.

Flynn, in contrast to August, had always been more of a thinker first, and only taken action when appropriate. But she was changing that about him, not through any intention on her part, but there was something about her that made him want to be spontaneous and reach for the stars, because that's where she was, with the stars as her playground. And though his head was bellowing at him to put the brakes on and think this through, his heart wanted her. He paced the room, sure that when she came back in he would sweep her into his arms and kiss her again.

When August re-entered with the teas, and declared their kiss as being 'ticked off the list', Flynn blinked, the adrenaline coursing through him screeching to a halt. She'd just been acting. Of course she had. And that's all either of them was supposed to be doing.

For a second they observed each other, both in the spotlight, until Flynn said, reaching for a tea, 'Yes. Kissing done. Well done us.'

He pushed down his bubbling feelings. He'd probably just got caught up in the moment anyway, hanging onto memories of happy relationships of the past and letting loneliness get the better of him for a moment. She would go back to being just his flatmate, August, to him, and he'd go back to being Just Flynn.

Chapter 39

August

August thought she could hear a change of tone in Flynn's voice, but figured hers was probably a bit off too; they had just made out, after all. It would be weird for them not to feel a little off-balance. She'd just have to try and restore natural order as quickly as possible.

'I think we did well there,' August proclaimed, handing Flynn his tea. 'If the situation arises that for whatever reason we need to kiss, it won't be weird anymore.'

'I'm not sure what kind of situation would come up where we'd quite need to do *that*,' he replied, taking the tea and perching on her armchair. She sat on the floor in front of the sofa, facing the window, the sunlight illuminating the pale greens in her eyes.

'No, I suppose it's unlikely, isn't it?' she mused. 'But hey, better to be overprepared for the worst, than underprepared.'

Flynn raised an eyebrow. 'The worst? I can't imagine a "worst" scenario where we'd have to kiss like that.'

But August just laughed, her big, light laughter that softened the tension in the room. 'Right? If something awful happening meant we had to snog, imagine what we'd have to do if the world was ending.' She caught herself too late. 'I mean, don't imagine that!'

Now it was Flynn's turn to snort into his mug. He wiped the splashed tea off the end of his nose and rubbed his eyes, saying, 'This has been a very strange afternoon.'

'Just another day with the Miyoshi-Andersons.' August drank her tea for a bit, and then said, 'I guess we should stick to just a quick peck from now on, when strictly necessary.'

Flynn met her eye, as if trying to read her. 'I guess so.'

'We don't want to make things ... blurry.'

'No, definitely not.'

'I'm sorry I got a little carried away,' she admitted.

'Don't be, I think we just both needed it, you know, for what it was – a one-time thing.'

'That's true,' agreed August, wondering if there was a hint of him attempting to sound more convincing than he felt, or whether she imagined it. For her, she was a helium balloon, drifting downwards from the clouds she'd touched for a while.

But while Flynn was under the impression she'd been acting when she kissed him, to August, it was only now that she was acting her heart out.

Chapter 40

August

August booked an emergency dental appointment with Bel the next day.

'You can't keep booking emergency appointments with me just to bypass the system,' Bel said, on closing her examination room door. 'There's nothing wrong with your teeth.'

'Hi, Kenny,' August said, hopping up on the reclining chair.

'Hi, sweets. How's the husband?'

'Well, I don't know about my teeth, but my mouth feels a little overworked,' she hooted to Bel, and fanned herself, her voice portraying quite the golden era starlet.

Bel gasped and Kenny sent a dental probe clattering to the ground. 'Did you kiss?' Kenny practically shouted down at her.

'Kenny, shhh,' said Bel. 'Did you kiss? Did you kiss your fake husband but very real flatmate?'

'It was all just in the name of research.'

'Researching what, exactly?'

August sat up and took a sip out of the plastic cup of mouthwash beside her, swilled it around in her mouth while she thought, and spat it into the tiny sink.

Bel put her hands on her hips. 'You know, this isn't a bar. The mouthwash is for actual patients.'

'I am a patient; I still have to pay for this appointment so I'm going to make full use of the facilities. Kenny, could you pass me some of those big sunglasses? I fancy lying back under this lovely warm lamp.'

'Fine, I might as well give you a check while you're here, then.'

'Ooh, how about a little dose of that teeth whitening instead?'

'Now you're pushing it. Lie back and tell me what the hell happened.'

August snuggled down on the seat, the huge plastic protective glasses on her face. 'We decided it would be a really good idea to try kissing each other on our own terms, in our own flat, in case the situation ever occurred that we needed to put on a kissing display. Then we'd be able to do it, no big deal, rather than it being this weird, awkward thing we'd never done before.'

'*We* decided?' said Bel, standing in front of August, holding one of those tiny mirrors on a stainless-steel rod. 'That sounds like a classic "August" decision to me.'

'What's that supposed to mean?' August challenged. 'Actually, that's probably fair. And it was me who suggested it.'

'When would you ever "have" to put on a kissing display?' Kenny piped up, coming into August's eyeline.

'Sounds like an excuse to snog your hot flatmate,' said Bel.

'And I don't blame you for a second.' Kenny agreed.

'It was not that at all, it was purely part of the act. An extra scene that needed writing, that's all.'

Bel brought her mask up to her cover her mouth and nose, and said through it, 'So what was it like?'

'It was *good*, he's a good kisser. Whoever dates him is a lucky girl.'

From over the top of her mask, August could see Bel's eyebrows raise towards Kenny.

'Hey, what's that look for?' she said, before Bel pushed open her mouth and started counting along her teeth, tapping on them with a metal thing.

'Nothing, three, two, one, one, two, three. Just happy for you that your fake husband makes you fake happy. Four, five, six, seven and eight.'

As Bel continued with the examination of her teeth and gums, August kept quiet (she had no choice), listening to Kenny humming along to the radio, which aptly was playing 'Can I Have A Kiss' by Kelly Clarkson.

Bel's face was close to August's, and their eyes met through the plastic glasses. The corners of Bel's eyes crinkled, and August knew she was smiling from behind the mask, which made her start to smile, and then laugh, and she nearly choked on the probe in her mouth.

Bel sat back and removed her gloves, throwing them in the bin, and brought down her mask. 'Everything looks great, just as it did before. No cavities, no plaque build-up, no loose dentures, all good.'

Kenny started dragging a stool over and paused to check with Bel, 'Are we done? Can we discuss the kiss more now?'

'Sure,' Bel wheeled over her own stool as well, and August removed the glasses and sat up, cross-legged, on the reclining chair, and took the cup of mouthwash in her hands like she was cradling a cup of tea. 'So how did you feel afterwards?'

'Wait,' said Kenny. 'First I want to know what the actual kiss was like.'

August laughed. 'He was a gentleman.'

'Speaking of, did you see the new receptionist when you came in? Mark?'

'I did, he seemed really nice. Did you kiss him yet?'

'Kenny,' scolded Bel, trying to keep the focus during the limited time they had. 'August, go on, tell us about the kiss.'

'It was . . . ' she lapsed into a smile before shaking herself out of it. 'It was very good and very professional. I think it would be believable.'

'Did you believe it?'

'What do you mean?' August asked her friend.

'Do you think he was just acting, or was he *kissing you* kissing you?'

That's the million-dollar question, thought August. 'I think it was ultimately just acting, but that we got quite into the scene.'

'What does that mean?' laughed Bel. 'Wait, did you go further than kissing?'

Kenny gaped.

'No, no, no, just kissing, but it was a big kiss, in a nice way, not like, tongues-and-grinding, just quite . . . smooshed?'

'I think I know what you mean,' said Bel. 'So no tongues?'

'A tiny bit of tongues,' August whispered.

'Are you going to do it again?'

'No,' said August, quickly. 'I think he was a little embarrassed, and I think he regretted it a bit, you know, crossing over that line for a minute between flatmate-slash-friends to friends-with-benefits. We've agreed to just keep things as they were.'

'Unless a public kissing display is needed,' clarified Kenny.

'Exactly.'

'Are you okay with that?' asked Bel.

'Of course. It's the right thing to do.' She was okay with it, really. Sure, she'd enjoyed the kiss – maybe a little too much – and sure, she'd have kept kissing him all day if he'd wanted to. But it was just a bit of fun, a yummy distraction, and it had to stay that way. He'd made it pretty clear he didn't want to be living with a girlfriend, and she agreed that hooking up with your flatmate was a bad idea. At least, she had felt that way. But would it really be *so* bad . . . ?

Bel looked unconvinced, but moved on. 'I do have something I wanted to talk to you about, actually, and now seems as good a time as any.' She thought about that for a moment. 'Or maybe it's the worst time.'

'Well, you have to tell me now.'

'Should I leave?' Kenny asked.

Bel shook her head. 'No, it's fine.'

'Good, because I had literally no intention of leaving. Ooh, unless you need anything from reception? August, do you need some toothpaste samples?'

'No, I'm good.'

'I'll get you some anyway.' He high-tailed out of the room.

'What do you want to talk about?' asked August.

'Now we've decided the wedding will be next summer, we'll soon start sending out save the dates. Do you want a plus one, or do you want Flynn to come with you, or should I invite Flynn separately and give him a plus one too?'

'Oh, I hadn't thought about that. Flynn won't be expecting an invite, you know, you don't need to invite him *and* a plus one to be polite, it all adds up, money-wise.'

'No, I know, but I feel like we've been getting to know him and he's a nice guy, a nice *friend*. We'd like him there.'

August mulled this for a moment. This was sweet of Bel, and she knew it would make Flynn happy. 'He could just be my plus one – or, you know, you could just invite the two of us together. Because I'll be on bridesmaid's duties for much of the day anyway.'

'All right.'

'Although, will he be lonely, then? Maybe he needs a plus one to keep him company?'

'. . . All right.'

'But I don't think he has anyone he thinks of like that at the moment. And weddings are good places to meet people, perhaps he'd make more friends if he came on his own, he might meet a nice girl.' August was putting way too much thought into this; she could feel it. And how did she know

223

Flynn didn't already have a string of women in his office queueing up to be his date? He was certainly good looking enough, and charming enough, and kind enough.

If she let herself ... yes. She could very much see what women would see in Flynn. Maybe she was beginning to see it herself.

Bel stood up. 'How about you just talk to him about it? We're happy either way you want to play it, just let us know when you know.'

'Are you sure?'

'Yes. Let's just give it a little time and see where the dust has settled after a couple of weeks. I can hold back your invites for now. You're both on the B-list anyway, so you're only in if other people decline.'

'Ha ha.'

August left Bel's dental practice with clean teeth, a spring in her step, and lips that still tingled happily from yesterday's kiss, fake or not.

Chapter 41

Flynn

While August was having her teeth checked and her soul searched by Bel, Flynn was across Bath, on the verge of getting in touch with Poppy. He was taking a short break at work, twirling his phone in his hand while her contact details lit up his display.

He'd not thought much about the redhead from the pub, and maybe shutting out all thoughts of romance, from Yui to August, would be the right thing to do. But she'd seemed nice, and fun and, like he'd thought just before he'd met Poppy, perhaps the misguided feelings he was having for August *were* just loneliness. So maybe he should give happiness a chance instead.

Convincing himself, at least partially, he sent her a text asking if she'd like to meet in the pub sometime over the next couple of weeks, if she was free.

*

During a still-warm evening in mid-October, Flynn waited for Poppy, waving to her across the pub with a little more confidence this time.

'I owe you a drink,' she declared, wandering over to him. 'Several, probably, thanks to you getting me out of that pickle with the hens!'

'You could have got away without – I didn't expect to see you again,' Flynn replied. 'I thought you must be part of a visiting hen group, to wreak havoc in this cathedral city and then head back to your homes across the country.'

Poppy tilted her head to the side, shielding her eyes from the last glare of the evening sun, her face lit up golden and her hair seeming fierier than it had before. 'Is that why you never got in touch before now?'

'Ah,' he laughed. 'Sorry about that.'

'It's fine, we shared, like, three minutes of conversation.' Poppy smiled at him.

He wasn't sure what to say to her, teetering on the edge of wanting to walk away and wanting to find out more about her, and then she spoke again.

'Let me get you that drink, Flynn, and then maybe you can tell me some of those very deep thoughts going on in there.'

Half an hour later, he and Poppy were sitting on one side of a bench in the pub garden, the furthest end from the live music, facing each other. They were onto their second drink, and Flynn was enjoying how easy it felt.

She'd asked about his situation, but not wanting to start

thinking about Yui, or what was or wasn't happening with August, he simply told her things were complicated, and that he wasn't with anyone right now, but it hadn't been long that he'd been single.

She seemed to understand – she too had recently broken up with someone and had needed to move out of where they lived. But she didn't want to talk about it. Instead they discussed simple, happy things like TV, the hen do, books, music. Talking with Poppy was like winding down after a long week, and he realised that was exactly what he was doing.

When the hour came for her to leave, this time he promised he would get in touch with her, and he meant it.

Poppy stood up, swinging her legs over the bench seat and brushed herself off. Then she fixed Flynn with a look. 'Look, I'm not looking for a boyfriend, and I think I'm right that you don't want a girlfriend, but I'm enjoying getting to know you. And I want to get to know you more, okay?'

'All right,' he replied. She had a flash of August about her in her assertiveness, Yui too for that matter, and perhaps that's what attracted him to all three women. And then, maybe in attempt to stop his mind wandering back towards his ex-girlfriend and his pretend-wife, he blurted out, 'Do you get a lunch break?'

'Sure. Do you?'

'Not really,' he laughed. 'But technically, yes. Do you want to have lunch next week, maybe Tuesday?'

Poppy nodded. 'Let me know what time and where you make a reservation. I like seafood.'

'All right,' he replied, again. 'Tuesday it is.'

'Tuesday it is,' she echoed. 'Bye, Flynn.'

'Bye, Poppy.' And just like that, Flynn Miyoshi was branching out and going on a date.

Chapter 42

August

August closed her eyes and imagined herself as a seventeen year old. 'I am Catherine Morland,' she whispered out loud. 'I'm living in *Northanger Abbey*. I *am* Catherine Morland.'

She stood in her bedroom, her wonderful bedroom in her wonderful home – seriously, it was hard to concentrate when she had to keep pinching herself that she actually *lived here* – wearing the same ensemble she'd walked the promenade in during the Jane Austen Festival. With her audition creeping very close now, August was spending every waking hour rehearsing. In the shower, she recited her lines. At work, she found herself adjusting her posture and facial expressions in accordance to the scene playing out in her head. The language she used in emails and press releases began to have a flowery, early nineteenth century ring to it.

Catherine Morland was the leading lady in Jane Austen's *Northanger Abbey*. That's right, August was going big or going home. The way she saw it was, she'd taken a chance on landing her dream home on Elizabeth Street and it had paid off. Who's to say what else she could achieve if she took the risk?

Flynn had been so busy with work that they hadn't spent much time together since the kiss, but she still found her heart jumping when their paths crossed in the mornings, or if she got out of bed for a glass of water in the night to find him hunched over his laptop on the sofa, his glasses on, his brow furrowed. She'd make him a cup of tea and leave him to it, and then dream nice dreams of him and wish he was in his own room, dreaming and peaceful. She wondered if he had been thinking about their kiss, like she had. But she didn't ask.

Instead, she worked tirelessly, fine-tuning her lines, the scene she would be reading having been sent to her by email when she registered. As the big day drew closer, until it was only a week away, tiny sparkles of hope grew inside her. She just might get this. She just might be on the verge of having her big break into theatre.

The thought was daunting, and the thought was powerfully exciting.

Chapter 43

Flynn

Flynn and Poppy met for lunch, and then met for lunch again a week later. After grabbing takeout sandwiches, Poppy insisted they use the rest of the hour for Flynn to show her where he lived. He was reluctant at first, not because it seemed like a come-on, but because of how it would look to his neighbours if he came home in the middle of the day with a pretty woman while his 'wife' was at work.

'I'm not trying to jump your bones,' Poppy said, rolling her eyes at him. 'I'm just interested. You made the view sound amazing, and we could both do with stretching our legs. When was the last time you took your full lunch hour?'

He couldn't argue with that, much as he needed to.

They approached the house and he scanned the area for neighbours, but the coast was clear. Poppy stopped outside the front door. 'Is this your humble abode?' she asked.

'This is the one,' he answered, reaching for his keys. 'How did you know?'

'You said it was at the top of the hill with a great view, and here we are.' Poppy gestured around her. 'Must be nice to live here.'

'It is,' he paused to follow her gaze, keeping his hands in his pockets to avoid any sudden and unexpected PDA from Poppy.

Poppy turned away from the outlook quicker than he would have expected, considering they'd just traipsed all the way up here. Facing the house she asked, 'Which floor is yours?'

'We're on the first floor, so the middle, if you don't count the top level – the one with the windows slightly set back. That's where the landlady lives.'

'What's she like?'

Flynn shrugged. 'Strict, but actually quite welcoming. We don't know her that well.'

'… We?'

'My flatmate and I. I told you about her – August.'

'Ah yes, your flatmate August.' Poppy walked up to the front door and then looked back at Flynn. 'You're going to show me the inside, aren't you?'

Flynn barely said a word as they ascended the stairs to the first floor, for fear of alerting the other residents. Only when he and Poppy were in the apartment and the door closed did he speak again, offering her a drink.

'Sure,' she said, and began moving through the flat, looking along the shelves.

The wedding photos. Flynn jumped into action, striding over to stand beside Poppy and turning her towards him. 'I have to show you this view,' he said, and quick as a flash while her back was turned, he managed to spin two picture frames to face the back.

'The same view I just saw from outside?' Poppy asked, her eyebrows raised.

'Yep, but it's just … wow …' Flynn gazed out of the window in wonder.

'I'll tell you what view I do like,' Poppy purred, and before he could say another word she was in front of him, pressing her lips against his for the first time.

It took Flynn a moment to appreciate what was happening. Poppy's kiss was soft yet insistent. He let himself enjoy Poppy, who was here with him now, and it was nice to get lost in the moment. Because, for now at least, he could forget about Yui. He could even forget about August, for just a few seconds.

Chapter 44

August

Inside her cupboard-slash-recording booth, August removed her headphones, rolled her neck and was about to let out a satisfied '*Mmmmm*', cooling down her voice after a job well done, when she heard from behind the door somebody else beat her to it.

'Mmmmm,' said the distinctly female voice, and August froze. The voice then spoke again, purring, 'That was nice.'

Who the HELL is in my apartment? August thought, and was about to kick open the door of her booth and wallop them one when she heard Flynn. She pressed her ear against the door.

'Can I get you that drink?' he asked.

She stopped breathing. Did Flynn have a girlfriend? How did she not know about this? Memories of their kiss came flooding back and she couldn't make sense of it all, of how while she'd been reliving the moment and thinking of him

234

as somebody who could be more than a friend, he'd been having that with someone new.

Also, Flynn was never home at this time of the day, what was going on? But then, to be fair, she would usually still be at work too, if they hadn't let her cut her day short at lunchtime to practise her lines for the audition tomorrow. August suspected it was because she kept talking to everyone like she was a Regency lady, walking about with her hands clasped in front of her, and it was getting infuriating for the rest of the team. So she had come home, and had been in the booth ever since, recording herself going through her audition piece and then listening to it back, critiquing every word.

August knew she should come out of hiding, let them know she was there. It would be so awkward because they'd assume she'd been in there listening to them kissing, but she couldn't stay in there in case they started to do more . . .

She heard the female voice closer now, like she was standing right to the side of the door, looking at the objects on their shelf, and put her hand against the door to push it open just as the voice said, 'So what's your flatmate like?'

August couldn't leave now. She tried to make out what Flynn was saying, though he was clearly over in the kitchen.

'She sounds like a good person to live with,' the woman said, sliding to her right. August felt her directly on the other side of the door now, they were face to face, and August wondered if she was scrutinising the door-shaped slits in the wall, wondering what was behind it.

'She is,' Flynn said, his voice clearer now he'd obviously moved back closer.

Wow, her recording booth really wasn't that soundproofed after all. It cut out an awful lot of background noise to the point that if nobody else was in the apartment it was completely silent, but with someone talking right outside the door, muffled though it was, you could hear exactly what they were saying. If she wanted to start working in here seriously, she'd need to fix that.

'What time will she be home?' the woman asked.

'I'm not sure,' said Flynn.

If August had to guess, she'd be willing to bet that the woman was waiting for Flynn to invite her to stay a while. But just as likely could be that they were already back to doing whatever it was they'd been doing when she first removed her headphones. Oh God, what if they were naked out there?

'Come here,' the woman said, and August was certain they were kissing up against the wall. She felt like a voyeur, and wished she'd come out of the booth immediately. She also felt a little bit lonely. She knew what that kiss felt like.

August was about to put her headphones back on when she heard the woman say, 'Thanks for showing me where you live. Maybe I could spend a little longer here with you next time.'

She held her breath as the two of them made very definite sounds of leaving the apartment. There was no goodbye, so Flynn must have left too, or at the very least be showing her out.

Quick as she could, August cracked open the door of

her booth, checked for signs of Flynn or anybody else, and army-rolled out onto the floor. She grabbed her handbag and keys, hoping to leave the apartment before Flynn came back, so she could stroll in casually a while later like she'd never been there.

August listened against her front door, and peered through the peephole, but the landing was deserted. She slid out through the door, ninja-style, letting it click softly behind her.

Racing down the stairs, she hesitated at the bottom. What if they were right outside? She opened the door a tiny slit and looked out. Nothing, the street was deserted.

Breathing a sigh of relief, August slipped out the door only to pause on the front step. The recording booth – she'd left the door open. If Flynn returned before her, he'd know she'd been in there.

Looking left and right, and left and right again, she made the decision to run back inside, taking the steps two at a time. Bursting back into her flat she hurdled the sofa, slammed the booth door closed, triple-backflipped her way back out the door (well, not quite, but it felt like that) and back down the stairs. She would exit the building, skirting down to the right and heading down the hill in the opposite direction to where Flynn was probably walking, or standing, with his mystery woman.

In her rush, August made a fatal error. She forgot to listen at the front door of the house again.

Had she listened, August would have heard Callie firing questions at Flynn. She would have heard Flynn stammering for excuses. But she heard none of this, whirling out the door and facing both of them together.

'August!' Flynn said, surprised.

'Flynn!' she replied. 'Callie!'

'August!' exclaimed Callie. 'So you *were* at home.'

'Um.'

'I thought you weren't at home and young Flynny-boy here was up to no good with that redhead,' Callie continued with a chuckle and a slightly-too-hard punch on Flynn's upper arm.

'No, no, I was here the whole time,' August smiled and caught Flynn's eye. He blushed.

'Sorry for the third degree, there, Flynn, I just saw you come out there with that girl, and she's so pretty, and I thought, oh yeah, when the cat's away, eh? I don't bloody think so, no lying to my friend August.' Callie laughed, and August's stomach twisted.

'That was just our mutual friend,' August tried to laugh it off.

'Poppy,' Flynn added. 'A lifelong friend.'

'Poppy,' confirmed August, wondering who Poppy was, and what she meant to Flynn.

Callie waved her hands. 'Problem solved, crisis averted, as you were, soldiers. I'll let you go about your day. Are you two coming in or going out?'

'I'm coming in,' answered Flynn, his eyes on August.

'I was just going to pop out for a bit,' said August, inching past them, not quite wanting to face Flynn at the moment.

'Are you sure you don't want to go out later?' asked Flynn,

full of smiles. 'I have to get back to the office but we could catch up for a few minutes now Poppy's gone?'

'Nope, I need some fresh air,' August said, and ran away down the hill.

Chapter 45

Flynn

Flynn was still stewing over the fact there was a real problem with getting any privacy, living here, when August reappeared in the flat at the end of the day, clutching a bag with doughnuts from the coffee shop. 'Peace offering?' she said, holding them out to Flynn.

He stood up from where he was sitting at the table and folded his arms. 'Nice afternoon?'

August eyed him. 'Yep. I had to get to the library, do some snogging up on – *SWOTTING up on* – Austen. So you have a . . . '

'A Poppy.'

'Right. A Poppy.'

'It's very new, that's why I hadn't . . . ' he trailed off, unsure how much explanation she wanted, or how much explaining he wanted to do. 'Where were you at lunchtime? I checked your room when Poppy and I arrived.'

August's eyes slid towards the cupboard in the wall.

'You were in there?'

'Yep. But I didn't hear anything, I promise. Well, not much, not until the . . . end. I'd been recording and I had my headphones on and my volume loud, checking all the words were clear. The first I was aware of anyone else even being in here was just after she said . . . '

Flynn asked, 'What?'

'She made a sort of yummy sound and said something was nice. And then I nearly came out, but I got worried you'd think I'd been listening to the whole thing, and that the two of you would be naked, and then—'

'Whoa,' Flynn laughed. 'She was here for literally five, maybe ten minutes. We didn't do anything. Apart from kiss.' He looked bashful at that.

'No, please, you should do whoever, I mean whatever, you want in here,' August said, flustered.

Flynn replied, just as flustered, 'No, I know, I just mean, you didn't hear anything . . . scarring.' They were both quiet for a moment until Flynn said, 'Lucky we weren't staying around for long. She just wanted to see where I lived.'

'She came all the way up that hill just to see where you lived?'

He shrugged, 'She was interested.'

'Interested in you asking her in for more than a tour, I expect,' August said, and then clamped a hand over her mouth. 'Sorry, probably overstepped enough boundaries for today by hiding in the wall and listening to you snogging, like a pervert. So how did you meet her? Is she from your work?'

'I met her a little while ago at the pub. It's . . . I don't know. I don't know what it is.'

August nodded and Flynn stared at the ground for the moment, his arms still folded, feeling guarded and a little embarrassed. He hadn't planned for this to happen today. He hadn't really planned for any of this, as far as Poppy was concerned. She was just suddenly in his life.

As was August.

He sighed. 'We need to think about how we're going to date people while we live together.'

'I really am sorry; I didn't realise you were dating.'

'No, no,' he backtracked. 'You have nothing to apologise for, and I'm not dating really, this thing with Poppy is very new and I'm not really sure what's happening with it, I just mean in general, bringing dates home, whether that's you or me, next week or next year, we just need to figure out a solution to the whole "the neighbours think we're married" thing. Another solution.'

'If it helps, I'm not seeing anyone, and don't really have any interest in seeing anyone, so you can just tell whoever that anyone you bring home is a lifelong friend.'

'That doesn't seem sustainable,' Flynn said. 'Perhaps we just tell our dates the truth?'

'How do you think Poppy would feel about it?'

He considered this. 'I don't know her very well, but I think she might run for the hills instead of get caught up in our baggage.'

August nodded. 'Pretty sure if I was dating someone who was like, *Guess what, I have a mega-hot housemate who everyone*

242

thinks I'm married to and we have to hold hands and kiss some-times, is that cool? I would probably run a mile.'

'Exactly.' Flynn met August's eyes. 'Wait, which one of us in the mega-hot housemate in your scenario?'

'I am, obviously. Flynn, did you, were you two …' August trailed off while she found her words. 'Were you two seeing each other when we, um, kissed. You know, the Malibu-fuelled-*proper*-kiss?'

Of course he knew which kiss she meant. He found himself glancing at her lips now, and then a wave of guilt rushed over him, because earlier that day he'd been kissing Poppy. He should not be thinking about August in any way other than as a flatmate. 'No,' he answered, looking her in the eye instead. 'I did meet her briefly before that, but nothing happened. We only met again, properly, after you and I, um, kissed.'

August seemed pleased about that, though did he imagine the second or so that she lingered in front of him? Did he imagine that hovering in the air between them were words left unsaid, and ghosts of kisses?

Chapter 46

August

August had the whole of the Friday off, ready for the big audition in the early afternoon. Before Flynn left for work that morning, he made her three pancakes and a thick banana smoothie, knowing she'd probably be too nervous to eat come lunchtime.

It felt weird to her that she hadn't known about Poppy, which was completely understandable and none of her business, but ... Poppy had been in her home, with her Flynn. Not that he was actually *her* Flynn, but it all just felt ... weird.

'Thank you,' she told him sincerely, trying to push these thoughts out of her mind, at least for today, as she sat at their table in front of her food, while he grabbed his coat and bag.

'Break a leg,' Flynn said, and leaned over to kiss her cheek. He hovered for a moment and she instinctively put her hand up to hold him against her. How easy it would have been for them to move their lips two inches to the side and kiss, but the moment passed and Flynn pulled away, as if he'd made a pact with himself now that he was seeing Poppy – no more flirting with August.

After he left, August watched the door through eyes with a million thoughts behind them and tucked into her breakfast, managing all but the last bit before the nervous butterflies awoke and filled the rest of her tummy. She knew they wouldn't rest until the day was over.

'Good morning,' August said. On stepping out of the house, she had been surprised to see a certain someone sitting on the wall, cup of tea in hand.

Abe jumped a little, having been lost in his thoughts when she approached, and then laughed at himself. 'Good morning,' he said, smiling the same relaxed, soft smile he'd offered just to her during the house inspection. It was so different from the straight-lipped, brow-creased one from when they'd first met at the open house. He took in her outfit. 'You look like you're heading somewhere interesting.'

'Big audition today,' she explained. 'What are you doing here? We usually only see you at weekends; don't you work in London on Fridays?'

'Yeah. Mum was feeling a bit under the weather again – I think it's the cold spell – so I came down last night on the late train.' Abe stifled a yawn. 'Sorry,' he said.

'I'm sorry to hear that, anything I can do?'

He smiled. 'No, thanks though. I just never sleep well on Mum's spare bed; it's got this huge dip in the middle. I actually – oh, it doesn't matter.'

'What?'

'Well . . .' he looked bashful for a moment. 'When Mum was having your place refurnished a little and she got that great bed for you and, um, Flynn, I tried to get her to put that in her spare room instead.'

'And give us the big dipper bed?' August chuckled. 'How kind.'

'She gave me a telling off for that,' he admitted.

August liked this easy-going Abe; he was showing more and more of his human side to her and she warmed to what she saw. It wasn't just his manner. Here in his PJ bottoms and a thick wool sweatshirt, morning stubble and scruffy hair, he actually looked quite delicious.

Abe shifted over all of a sudden. 'Do you want to join me? I don't have a spare tea out here but you can have a sip of mine if you like?'

Something made her want to sit down with him. Perhaps it was knowing that she was heading out to her audition far too early anyway. Perhaps it was because she now knew that Flynn was most definitely not thinking about their kiss in the way she had been. In fact, kissing him again was off the table. And not that kissing Abe was *on* the table, but at this point all she knew is that she wanted to sit with him.

'I will join you for a minute if that's okay; I can never say no to this view. But I won't have any tea, I just filled myself full of coffee and might wet myself.'

WHAT, why did I say that? August thought.

'Fair enough,' Abe replied, and the two of them sat side by side and looked out for a moment, while August tried to

246

recover from her mortification. She felt his presence close to her, could hear his breathing, smell his aftershave, which was different from Flynn's. He turned to look at her, and when she met his eye it was as if they were connecting, properly, for the first time.

After a moment, Abe drained the remainder of his tea and stood up, stretching his shoulders and revealing a sliver of skin above his PJ bottoms. 'I'd better get back in,' he said, ending the moment between them. 'I promised Mum I'd cook her a slap-up breakfast this morning before I head back to London.'

'You're going back today?' August asked, standing also, and admonishing herself silently for allowing the touch of sorrow to inject itself into her voice.

'Yeah, but ...' he chewed his lip for a moment, looking up at the top floor flat. He then turned his gaze onto her. 'I'll be back next weekend, I think.'

'Oh, give me a text if you want to grab a coffee or anything? Your mum has my number,' she replied before she had a chance to think about whether that was a good idea or not.

He nodded, and then reached an arm as if to touch her shoulder, but pulled it back at the last minute, placing an invisible boundary between them. 'Good luck with the audition, I look forward to hearing all about your new starring role.'

Abe turned and went inside with no more than a small wave, and August stayed rooted to the spot for a minute. There was something undeniable that moved under the surface when they talked, sunlight caught under a wave that grabbed her attention. She wanted to move on, but Abe? Her landlady's son? She realised she could hardly have picked a more complicated person to do it with.

I am Catherine Morland, I am Catherine Morland, August chanted to herself with her eyes closed. She struggled to keep her breathing centred as she sat outside the audition room within the Old Theatre Royal. She'd arrived early. Her audition slot wasn't until close to 1 p.m. but she'd arrived shortly after eleven, as soon as they opened their doors, just in case the casting team were running ahead of schedule.

A middle-aged woman had opened the door, letting in August and only two others, and she'd given August a once over, her eyebrows raised. August had taken this as a good sign – there seemed to be very little competition *and* she'd clearly made an impression. But as she heard the door opening again and saw more hopefuls walking in, the reality of the situation caused a heavy stone of worry to form inside her.

There were a lot of people here.

And August was the only one in costume.

Perhaps that was a good thing – she'd stand out, right? Show she was serious about getting the role? But all the other actresses were dressed casually, comfortably, but somehow still managing to look like delicate Georgian-era teens ready to come of age. A twist of a curl falling over a forehead here, a puff-sleeved shirt there, a floor-length skirt – but made from light cotton, not layers of stiff fabrics. It all caused August's heart to thud faster. She'd really assumed dressing the part would have been the done thing.

'August Anderson?' the woman who'd opened the doors earlier now poked her head out from the audition room.

August stood up, feeling all eyes on her as she shuffled her way towards the room, her taffeta dress making the most godawful rustling noise that cut right through the quiet murmur of people running lines under their breaths.

Come on, August, this isn't you, she scolded herself during the ten seconds it took to walk through the door and into the audition room, and in those ten seconds, she snapped herself out of her worry. August was confident, outgoing, she was great at improv and she was likeable. Sure, she felt like an egotistical twat thinking about herself like this, but nobody else in that room was going to think it if she didn't.

'Hello,' she smiled, and then, in a louder voice, boomed, 'Hi, my name is August Anderson and I'm here to read for the role of Matherine Corland!' She fixed on a pageant-worthy grin and surveyed her audience of three seated at a trestle table on one side of the room: the woman who'd let her in, the one with the raised eyebrows, another woman in glasses, and a gentleman who looked ready to fall asleep at any moment.

They blinked at her and Eyebrows raised them again.

'*Catherine Morland*,' August corrected herself with a jolt and then laughed loudly.

'Hello, August,' said Eyebrows. 'I'm Jan, the producer, this is Elaine, the director, and Bill, our prompter. He'll read with you today for your scene.'

'Fantastic, great to meet you all, I'm August Anderson, I'm here to read the role of Catherine Morland.'

Jan, Elaine and Bill all glanced at each other.

'I like your dress,' Elaine commented. 'Very ... in character.'

'Thank you, I like what you're wearing too,' August enthused, admiring Elaine's plain T-shirt and jeans.

'When you're ready, August,' Jan said, her eyebrows remaining steadfastly in the air.

August exhaled slowly. This was it; this was her moment to shine. She channelled Hilary Swank. She channelled Lea Michele in *Glee*. She swallowed, and said, in her clearest, loudest, most audience-grabbing voice, 'I have been to see your mother's room!'

August recited the lines with gusto, hoping her personality and her preparedness were shining through. This would be a bigger production than any of the amateur dramatics performances she'd done in the past, she knew she'd need a bigger voice to be heard right at the back. She'd need more stage presence than was required of her at the Roman Baths, and though she used a lot of facial expressions during her voice work, perhaps she'd better make even more use of them here, in the flesh. She only faltered when she glanced down from the imaginary upper circle she was directing her whole performance to, to see the faces of the three behind the table.

They were wincing; all of them.

August ran out of fuel. She forgot the next word, and fumbled the next line, and skipped the line after that.

'Would you like to check your script?' Jan prompted. 'It is allowed.'

'Um, no, I've memorised all of it,' August said, feeling the bile rising.

'I think we've got a good sense from there actually,' Elaine cut in.

'Really, I do know the rest.' She couldn't end on a wince, she just couldn't, she was supposed to end in applause.

'That's okay. Thank you for coming in, August.'

'Please. I can do it differently if you want.'

Elaine rested her elbows on the table, a move which caused both Jan and Bill to sit back in their chairs. A move which had to mean business. 'May I be honest, August? Because I can't always give feedback, but I can tell how much you must have wanted this.'

Must have . . . No, please no.

But out loud August said, 'Yes, please do.'

'While we appreciate the effort with the costume, and you clearly spent a lot of time learning the script, I just can't see you as our Catherine.'

'But, I am Catherine. I mean, not literally, but . . . ' August lost her words, yet again.

'What we saw today felt like watching you – August Anderson – playing Catherine Morland. What we wanted to see was simply "Catherine Morland".'

'I don't understand.'

'Although it's nice to see your personality, once you begin reading you need to know how to leave that at the door. Catherine is young and naïve and almost timid, in a way, despite her love of gothic novels. You played a totally different person to that. You practically played Isabella Thorpe.'

The penny dropped. Isabella was confident, high-spirited, flirty. August had known Catherine wasn't those things, she knew who she was, but she'd still barrelled on with a performance that was more focussed on showing off herself than showing off her acting. She felt stupid, like a rookie. Like an amateur. 'Can I try again, delivering the piece in a different way?'

She saw Jan glance at Elaine and for a second she thought she might get another shot. 'I'm sorry, we're on a tight schedule and we've already seen other actresses who got it from the off.'

'Could I audition for Isabella?' August asked, clinging onto one last hope.

'We cast her this morning,' Jan said, her eyebrows lowering, pity in her voice.

'I see.'

Elaine sat back and shuffled her papers; the universal sign for 'meeting adjourned'. 'Thank you for coming, August, pleasure to meet you.'

August managed to whisper a thank you before racing out of there, afraid that if she allowed herself to say another word she might throw up all over the floor. And the worst part was, she didn't know if things had gone badly because of nerves – because she'd put so much importance on this audition, on this play – or whether it was simply that she really was an awful actress. Oh God, it was way too big a question.

It was over. It was over before it had even started.

Chapter 47

Flynn

Flynn heard a noise in the corridor and hesitated, wondering if it was August home already. He put the bottle of Prosecco and box of Jaffa Cakes he'd bought for her as a celebration out on the side, and then changed his mind, stuffing them in a cupboard in case it was bad news. He then took them out again – if it was bad news, maybe she'd want to guzzle some fizz and eat chocolate.

He went to listen at the door, and when he realised what he could hear, he swung it open and burst out.

August was on their landing, sitting on the top stair with her face in her hands, soft sobs coming from her. Her handbag lay beside her, and appeared to have been thrown down, with items spilling out of it including the script pages, a water bottle, a lipstick and the copy of *Romeo and Juliet* they'd read from together.

'August?' he said, sitting down beside her, and she responded with an almighty sniff.

She said nothing, but turned and let him pull her into his chest, where she stayed, crying, for a while, and Flynn's heart sunk to the bottom of the ocean for her.

'I'm sorry,' she said eventually. 'I shouldn't be crying on you, that's not your job.'

'It's kind of my job as your husband,' he teased, quietly. 'Do you want to come inside?'

August shook her head.

'Do you want to tell me what happened?'

'I was . . . awful,' she choked.

While she'd mulled on this for a moment, Flynn had extracted himself and gone back into the flat to retrieve and open the bottle of Prosecco. He handed it to her now, and she took a swig from the bottle, scrunching her nose as the cold bubbles fizzed about in her mouth. 'Thank you.'

Flynn didn't push her for details. He knew August well enough now to know that if she wanted to talk she would talk for England. She'd open up about this too eventually, probably later this evening when the shock of whatever had happened had died down.

She took another swig and Flynn asked, 'How come you took *Romeo and Juliet* with you? Did you show them your Tybalt?'

'I don't know, it just made me feel brave.'

'It did?'

August nodded. 'I liked doing that scene with you, it made me overcome that weird acting cowardice I had. So it was with me for, I don't know, good luck or a motivational boost or something.'

'Did it help?'

'I don't know, kind of.' A big sigh escaped her. 'I was a bit nervous to be honest, and anxious, but I still went into it with this feeling of *I've got this*. Like I had the part already, I just had to not fuck it up for thirty minutes. But then … Oh, I don't want to talk about it. I was awful.' She sunk her head back into her hands.

'Hey, everyone has bad days but that doesn't mean you were awful. Sometimes when you're acting you just feel off. And it sucks. But it's just today.'

'I don't think you understand—' August started but Flynn stood up and held out his hand.

'Come on, I'm going to show you something.'

'What?'

'Come on. You have to come inside.'

'What is it?'

'Would you just come in?'

August lifted herself and her bottle of Prosecco off the ground while Flynn gathered up her spilled handbag, and she trailed inside after him, looking sorry for herself.

Flynn directed her to the sofa and went off to get his laptop, pausing at his door for a moment.

Do I really want to do this? Ah, what do I have to lose?

'What is this?' she asked, as he placed the laptop in front of her, and navigated to YouTube.

'This is an answer to your question. To the question you asked me weeks ago, when you asked me how I know a little about acting.'

'What?' she said. She was smiling, and his heart jumped a level just seeing that.

'Fair warning, there's no message here, no words of wisdom in what I'm about to show you. It's not meant as a success story or some kind of motivational speech. It's just, really, because I think you could use a laugh.'

He found the video he was looking for and sat back, watching her reaction more than the screen, because he knew what was about to be shown very well indeed.

As a muted-toned 4:3 video started playing, showing a montage of run-of-the-mill school kids in Britain in the late nineties, supplemented with swirling lettering, August recognised the theme music before the title even slid into fruition. '*Grange Hill*?' she said, glancing up at him, behind her. 'Why are we watching *Grange Hill*?!'

'You'll find out in about six seconds . . . ' Flynn said, and smiled as she turned back to the screen, tears dried up, leaning forward with interest.

'NO FUCKING WAY!' she screeched. There on screen, buck-toothed in an ill-fitting blazer and a dodgy-looking fringe pasted across his forehead, was Flynn. Unmistakeably, adorably dorkily, Flynn. August paused the action and leaned in, staring at his little face. 'You were in *Grange Hill*?!'

'For all of five minutes, and definitely no more than five lines,' he laughed.

August spun around to him. 'But you were actually in *Grange Hill*? This is really you?'

'It's really me.'

'You were a child star!'

'I absolutely was not. You'll see why if you keep watching.'

August was practically bouncing in her seat now, and

Flynn knew he would do anything to make her happy; a thought which surprised him, though he pushed it from his mind immediately.

She pressed play again and saw Flynn, who stood with two other boys, deliver a line about going to class, in which he stole a peep at the camera at both the beginning and the end. She laughed.

'I had a little problem with the "don't look into the lens" instruction,' Flynn explained with a chuckle. 'I was never pencilled in to be a recurring character beyond three episodes anyway, but even so, it wasn't surprising I never got called back.'

With one more *'See ya,'* from little Flynn, he was gone from the screen, and August asked, 'Do you have access to any more clips of you?'

'There is one more of my episodes on YouTube,' he reached across and typed in a new search. 'Get ready for some great egg beating in a home ec class.'

August watched, mesmerised by his younger self on screen. 'How old were you here?'

'Eleven, I think? Maybe twelve? I was playing a Year Seven, so around that age.'

'Did you do any other acting?'

'No, it was a passing phase for me. I think my next big obsession after this was playing the guitar.'

'You play the guitar?'

'Nope,' he admitted. Flynn stopped the video after his 'big scene' and said, 'See, I have no moral message to relay to you, but if it made you smile for a minute then that's the desired result.'

'It did, thank you, Flynn. Maybe I, like you, should give up on this career and turn instead to the guitar. Or law. How hard can international law be anyway, right?' she joked.

'Because of one bad audition? You're kidding, right?'

'I'm just so ... *humiliated*, Flynn. I almost wish I'd only found out about the whole audition the day before, but over these past weeks I've let the idea of getting the part rise and rise to the point I really believed it was mine. I could see myself on that stage. I'd imagined the conversation with my boss about handing in my notice. Not just taking a break, because the leading role in a professional play would have opened the door to this whole other side of my career, and it ... it would have meant I could do it. I was good enough. I'd imagined telling my mum, my friends, I'd imagined coming home today and telling you.'

'I know,' he sympathised. 'I was hoping you were going to come back with good news too. But again, it's one bad audition.'

'I am a big stupid failure and I'm chasing after the wrong career and Hilary Swank wouldn't even deem to use her Oscar to beat me out of the way.'

Flynn had no idea why poor Hilary Swank was being brought into this, but August, usually so gung-ho and confident, was steering back towards meltdown city. And he didn't have any more *Grange Hill* to show her.

'But you can act, August, you know you can, because it's what you already do – you've had loads of success in voice work and you'll be getting calls for more really soon, now your booth is set up. You *can* do this. But maybe being a stage actress takes some different skills, which you could work on.' He paused, putting a hand on her back while she gave a big sigh. 'Don't be so hard on yourself. Maybe having talent in one area doesn't automatically give you talent in the other. I know I couldn't just walk in to court as a barrister because I'm currently a solicitor, it would take time and training.'

August gasped. 'What if it's karma? What if because I short-cutted one dream, living here by lying about who I am, what if that's it for me and now—'

Flynn began to laugh at this, causing August to see the funny side too. 'You know, I'm shocked you didn't get this part because you can be dramatic as hell.'

'*You're* dramatic as hell,' she retorted. But then she turned around and wrapped her arms around Flynn, giving him a huge squeeze. He heard her whisper into his shoulder, 'You're a good guy. This new girl of yours better know how lucky she is.'

Chapter 48

August

She was in bed that night when she finally checked her phone. She looked at it with one eye, fearing the official message telling her she hadn't landed the role – although she already knew that, of course. But August's face lit up like the screen in front of her when she saw a text from Abe.

Hello, it's Abe. Just wanted to check in on how your audition went. Nice to see you this morning.

Formal, to the point, sweet. August replied, downplaying the audition – and her disappointment – but thanking him for asking.

Are you back in London now? She added.

His response came quickly, and she wondered if he too was lying in his bed, two lonely hearts across the other side of the country but under the same night sky.

Yep, back in the Big Smoke. See you, and Flynn, next weekend?

Smiling, August responded: *Sounds great. Goodnight, Abe.*

Goodnight, August.

Chapter 49

Flynn

In the house at the top of Elizabeth Street, it appeared to be a tradition to rotate get-togethers between flats monthly for awkward drinks and conversation. Flynn and August had just missed hosting one before they moved in, and tonight was their turn, so they'd been told by Callie.

Typically, the drinks were no longer than an hour, and Flynn knew that August was happy for the distraction. Even though her disastrous audition (her words) was two weeks behind her, she was still feeling at a loss with herself, wondering where her future might lie.

Flynn was pleased to host the drinks for not too dissimilar reasons. The past couple of weeks had seen his work ramp up to an almost unmanageable level. He was tired all the time and found it hard to step away. He'd barely seen Poppy, he hadn't called home to Japan to speak to his parents for what felt like an age, and he was relying way too much on August to be his sounding board at the end of every long day. She said she didn't mind, and that it stopped her having to think too much about her own issues, but even so; he knew he was snappy at times, and he could tell she was losing patience with his complaining. A forced break, a mandatory bit of social interaction, was just what he needed.

Maud and Allen from the flat below sat on the sofa. Compared to Callie – who sometimes seemed like their third flatmate, the number of times she popped over to chat to August – they didn't know Maud and Allen well. The couple kept to themselves and didn't pry. Allen in particular seemed uncomfortable around so many women, in a shy way, and mainly just chatted with Flynn about aeroplanes, keeping his head low.

August was refilling drinks when Allen grumbled softly, shifting in his seat, 'What's behind my back?' Maud pushed him forward, sticking her hand underneath the cushion.

'What's that?' August laughed, topping up Callie's Prosecco, looking at the scrunch of black material Maud had dug out of her sofa.

'It's a – *oh*!' Maud, in the manner of a magician, held the item up by one end and let it tumble down to reveal itself. And all of a sudden she held in her hand a black, very full-busted, bra. Maud, in a state of shock, shook it off her hand like it was a spider, and it landed on Allen's lap, the clasp draped in his drink.

'Oh!' he mirrored Maud, fishing it out with his breadstick and passing it towards August, his face a neon pink.

Callie burst out laughing. 'All right, Maud, it's not that kind of party! Get your undies back on!'

Maud was now also pink head to toe, as evidenced by her shaking fingers. 'It's not mine,' she exclaimed. 'It's August's brassiere.'

August accepted the bra from Allen, breadstick and all, but was lost for words for a second, because this was most certainly not hers.

At that point, Flynn pulled himself together and shouted, 'August, the drink,' and August looked down at her non-breadstick-and-bra hand, to see that she was still pouring Prosecco with the other, and bubbles were foaming out over the top like lava and pooling on the tablecloth.

Callie's mum jumped into action with the napkins, Callie grabbed the glass and placed her mouth over it, trapping the remaining bubbles, Allen began a coughing fit and Maud glared at him because she knew full well he kept glancing at the bra, which still dangled mid-air.

Flynn and August met each other's eye, and she did the only thing she could, really, given the situation.

'I am *so* sorry, everyone, hard day at work yesterday and I was having a relax on the sofa when I got home. I must have forgotten to take this back to my bedroom. *Our* bedroom.' She picked the bra off the end of the breadstick and held it in her hands like everything was perfectly normal. Like this wasn't someone else's bra.

Callie, bubbles-problem-fixed, guffawed. 'There is no way that's your bra,' she said, pointedly looking between the vixen-like cups and August's own modest chest.

'It was an audition, for an acting role,' August thought on her feet. 'I had to be a sort of Marilyn Monroe character and this helped ...' Gulp. She avoided looking at Allen. '... Create the shape.' August telepathically shot daggers at Flynn.

'Flynn, what's it like having an actress for a wife?' Callie asked, tucking into a sliver of watermelon wrapped in Parma ham.

'It's great,' Flynn replied. 'She's always doing something interesting.'

'I bet it's great,' Callie said with a crude wink, and then leaned over, holding out the appetiser plate. 'Maud, Allen, can I interest you in August's melons?'

'Just going to put this away,' August sang, and she hurried into Flynn's bedroom, with him in tow, the sound of Callie's hysterical laughter following them.

When they were out of sight, she pushed the bra against his chest. 'I think this belongs to you,' August hissed.

'That's not quite true.'

'Your girlfriend, then. When did she even – you know what?' August held up her hands. 'I don't even want to know. I don't want to know anything about it. I love that you have a girlfriend, Flynn, it makes me so happy to see you happy, but just ... well, I just ask that you stay away from my armchair if you're going to do things in the living room.'

Flynn could see she wasn't too mad, and it was kind of funny, but even as he stuffed the bra into one of his drawers and followed August back out to their guests, he wondered when Poppy would have taken that off. She'd only popped over once last week before they went out on a date, and they'd not done anything more than kiss. He had left her alone for a few minutes while he changed, though. Perhaps she removed it in anticipation? And then when things hadn't got as heated as maybe she'd expected, she'd . . . forgotten?

Back in the living room, August was back in conversational flow and Flynn looked around to see if there were any more drinks that he could top up before he sat down next to Allen again. He hadn't done a runner, though Flynn had half expected him to.

He tried to focus on Allen, but his spirits had dampened. Three days on *Grange Hill* at the age of eleven hadn't prepared him for how much work it took to be an actor. The lies, the being on edge, it sometimes felt like as much of a full-time job as his real job. He stole a look at his faux-wife as she glowed and glittered, and wondered if she ever wished to just come clean.

As his gaze swept the room, Flynn caught Callie's eye. She raised her eyebrows at him, her mouth set in a straight line, and for just a second before she readjusted her face and turned back to laugh at what August was saying, he swore she gave him the evil eye.

Chapter 50

August

August loved her days working as a costumed character at the Roman Baths. Even though she only did a couple of days a month, hopefully a few more during the peak summer season, she looked forward to them with the same fizz of excitement every time.

She often played Flavia, a Roman lady, and her role was to interact with visitors, giving them fun facts while never dropping character. It tested her improv skills and at the end of each day she had a new sense of motivation for trying to break into theatre work.

Even today, with the memory of her failed audition so fresh that she thought it would sting to be in character, it calmed her to the point that she thought maybe she could love acting still, despite her recent failure.

'That was *so cool*,' a young boy enthused to his mum as

they walked away from 'Flavia'. 'She was really from ancient Rome, wasn't she, Mum?'

August allowed a little smile to cross her face. Maybe she wasn't completely awful after all ...

With the East Baths clear of visitors for a moment, August strolled out to the Great Bath, open to the cool air, the *pièce de résistance* and the centrepiece for the whole complex. A huge pool with steps descending into the hot spa water from all sides that once upon a time Romans would have stepped down into.

Being November, the number of people milling around the venue was few, and August had a few moments uninterrupted while she sat at the side of the Bath and gazed into the warm water.

She turned her thoughts to Abe, and how they were ever-so-slowly growing closer as time went on. Far from *close*-close, but they text each other occasionally, stopped for a chat when he visited his mum, and she felt she was beginning to peek beneath what had once been such a closed-off, hard shell.

Only, thanks to this enormous lie she and Flynn were carrying around on their backs, it could never be anything more than that ... could it?

Shaking Abe from her mind, her thoughts returned to the audition again, only this time, rather than hiding from the sting of embarrassment, or the sadness of a dream down the drain, she found herself musing: *at least I'll be more prepared next time.*

Perhaps there were silver linings to be found in all of this, and perhaps she'd look for them one day soon. But not here, or now. She could hear the voices of people approaching.

August hoiked up the huge skirts of her dress and turned away from the green-tinted water of the Great Bath and into the shade, and from behind a pillar, hand in hand, out came Flynn, with a woman who she assumed was Poppy.

She gasped. 'Hello!'

Flynn took a moment to realise it was her and then laughed out loud (not cruelly) and said, 'There you are!' He reached in for a big hug, the chunky audio guide that dangled from his wrist tapping her side, and August noted Poppy watching the two of them.

'I wasn't expecting the hair, I thought we must have missed you,' he said, prodding at her towering, dark, curly wig. 'Poppy managed to drag me away from my laptop, thank God. I told her you worked here sometimes and thought we could come along and she could meet you.'

August turned to Poppy with a big smile and said, 'Greetings, the name is August,' and then whispered, 'If anyone else comes along I'll need to hop back into character, okay?'

'Hop back into character,' Poppy murmured, not taking her eyes off August. 'How many characters do you play?'

'Just one, although it's not always the same one. I'm not supposed to break character at all, that's really frowned upon, so *Shhh*,' August smiled.

Poppy looked up at Flynn, her head tilted to the side. 'Imagine having to pretend you're someone you're not at the drop of a hat.'

For a millisecond, Flynn and August met each other's eyes, before he pulled his full attention back to Poppy as if nothing had happened. 'Ha ha, imagine that,' he agreed. 'Luckily, August's a very good actress, great improvisation skills.'

'I can imagine,' Poppy said.

August brushed away the compliment, though it made her glow a little bit that he still believed in her. She then, too, focussed her attention back on Flynn's girlfriend. So this was Poppy. This was *'Mmm, that was nice'* Poppy. She *was* pretty, quite striking in a memorable way, and August wondered something. 'Are you an actress?' she asked her.

Poppy shook her head. 'Absolutely not.'

August tapped at her chin. *Where do I know you from?* 'I just feel like I've seen you before.'

Poppy said nothing, just raised her eyebrows, as if she was waiting for August to finish her speculation.

In the end, August gave up. 'Must just be one of those small-world things, we've probably stood in line together at the bus station or something.'

'That must be it.'

August shivered a little. It was frosty here, under all this shade. 'Are you two enjoying the Baths?'

'Definitely,' Flynn enthused. 'Are the Baths themselves ever open to the public to swim in?'

'No,' August replied. 'But the Thermae Bath Spa is worth a visit for its open-air rooftop pool, all warm and minerally, just like these ones.'

'Hey, that sounds nice, doesn't it?' Flynn said to Poppy.

She nodded, though if she was a local, or even a long-term resident, August suspected she'd have visited at least once. 'Anyway, we'll let you get back to work, but maybe we could all have dinner together next week or something?'

'Sure!' answered August.

'Sure,' said Poppy.

August watched as Flynn and Poppy walked away, their hands entwined, and his face turned towards her, smiling. August knew the warmth of how it felt to be on the receiving end of that smile, to be holding that hand, to kiss those lips—

August, she scolded herself.

Chapter 51

Flynn

Poppy was coming to dinner. Although Flynn would have preferred the three of them to meet out somewhere, maybe for pizza or a pub dinner, he was keen for August to get to know Poppy properly, and Poppy was quite insistent about coming to their home.

'How are you feeling about this evening?' August asked, chopping into a red bell pepper, side by side with Flynn in the kitchen, as if she were reading his mind.

'Great,' he answered.

'Liar,' August teased. 'Are you nervous?'

'A little ...' They were prepping fajitas together and Flynn had been unusually silent. A thought was niggling at him, the one he'd been getting more and more recently. When was this going to end? He could tell Poppy what was going on but he'd rather get to know her a little more first, show her she can trust him, because right now he couldn't imagine she'd be happy to know he and August role-played the happy couple on a daily basis. She definitely wouldn't like that they'd kissed – not that he'd kissed August again since dating Poppy, and he wouldn't, but that's why he needed Poppy to trust him first.

August interrupted his thoughts. 'Is it because I'm going to be here too? Are you nervous about introducing her to friends? I know we've already met, but it'll be different tonight, won't it – chatting to each other properly. I hope she likes me.'

Friends. Flynn sliced the chicken in front of him into long strips. Poppy had already met a couple of Flynn's friends from work. August was more than a friend. She was way more than his flatmate. He stole a glance at her. Like it or not, he didn't have any family left in the UK, so she was the person in the country that he felt closer to than anyone else. Perhaps that would change in time, and Poppy would become his closest confidante. But right now ...

'I hope *you* like *her*,' he answered.

'I'm sure I will,' she waved the knife hazardously in the air. 'She seemed nice enough when we met the other day. Also, you're a nice guy, so you wouldn't go out with an idiot. Do you think things are getting serious?' August gasped all of a sudden, pointing the knife towards him. 'Are you going to want to live with her?'

'*No*,' he replied. 'Like I've said before, after what happened with Yui, I'm going to take my time moving in with a girlfriend again.'

'You took your time with Yui, though; you were together

273

for a year, it's not like you rushed into it. So try not to measure everything against that, this is a completely different relationship. But also,' August added, 'take as many years as you need because I don't want you to move out.'

'I wouldn't move out anyway, you'd have to move out,' he said, with a smirk.

'Oh here we go,' she laughed. 'You'd have no sob story about living in a hotel this time, my dream home story still stands strong.' August tipped the contents of her chopping board into the wide pan and grabbed a lime to start rolling about on the counter under her hand, releasing all the juices inside. 'I still have to just stop what I'm doing sometimes and do a happy dance over living here, after all these years of wishing. I'm a lucky girl.'

'You're going to be in London so much when you get that starring role in a West End play, that you won't even need this place,' replied Flynn.

'I can't believe you'd want to piss off my dead grandmother by forcing me to move out of the home that her dying wish was for me to live in.'

'It was *not* her dying wish.'

'She will haunt you . . .'

At that moment the doorbell buzzed, signalling that Poppy had arrived. Flynn put down his own knife and gave his hands a quick wash. 'I'll go and get her up here. No talk of ghostly grandmas, okay?'

'She heard that,' August retorted. 'She says you're already on thin ice and she wouldn't want to make the dining table move across the room while Poppy is sitting at it.'

Flynn grinned and walked out of the apartment, poking his head back in quickly to add, 'Seriously though, it's *way* too early to worry about Poppy and I living together.'

Chapter 52

August

August watched Flynn go to the door and took off her apron, checking her appearance in the mirror. She was comforted by his last comment, and she had the feeling he was a bit, too.

Poppy entered the flat in front of Flynn, casting her eyes briefly around the living room before they came to settle on August.

'Hi, Poppy,' August said, greeting her warmly.

'Hello, August,' Poppy replied, a little less warmly. Was that just her way, was she shy and a little guarded? Or was she cautious about the fact that her boyfriend lived with a female flatmate? August could understand that. She'd have to put Poppy at ease. Show her there was nothing else going on.

Even if August had felt there might be, for just a moment, when she got caught up in that kiss. She realised she had to be mindful not to entangle herself in Flynn and Poppy's relationship when she was already dealing with the complexities of starting to like a man who thought she was married. She paused for a moment, thinking of Abe. How often she was flip-flopping at the moment. One minute she was telling herself she had to walk away, stop picturing herself starting up anything with him, as it was too complicated. But the next she was imagining scenarios where she told him the truth, and he was happy, and not at all mad about being lied to, and *they* were happy. Just like Flynn and Poppy.

'Can I get you a drink?' August asked, heading towards the kitchen, tipping a picture frame onto its front en route, a frame that housed one of the 'wedding day' photos of herself and Flynn embracing on the beach. She didn't think Poppy had noticed the faux pas, or the cover-up.

'Do you have wine?' Poppy asked.

'Always,' August replied. 'Red? White? I don't think we have any rosé at the moment . . . '

'Red, please.'

'Flynn? Want some wine?'

'Yep, cheers August!'

As August poured the wine, she watched Flynn and Poppy from the corner of her eye. He took her coat, smiling at her, relaxed, but not completely. She wrapped an arm around his waist. She was dressed in a stylish black jumpsuit and heels, her red hair loose and red lipstick on her mouth. She looked very cool and for a second August, in her lemon-coloured jeans and electric-blue sweatshirt, felt like a children's TV presenter compared to her. Not that it mattered what she looked like compared to Poppy.

Taking the two wines back into the other room, and fetching herself a Budweiser (she liked beer with fajitas), August joined them.

The evening went well. Well, it went *fine*. August couldn't help but feel that Poppy was being a little short with her. She was about to offer a cup of tea to the two of them, along with a comment about how they'd be doing her a favour because her eyebags would need all the cold tea bags they could get in the morning, when Flynn said, 'August, I think Poppy and I are going to pop out for a drink.'

'Great! I'm going to give my mum a call and catch up with her,' August answered. She wasn't planning to do that at all, but she didn't want them to feel they had to invite her. And actually, she wasn't sure she wanted to be invited. If August was honest – not that she'd say this to Flynn – she was getting kind of exhausted by having to work so hard with Poppy.

'Okay,' said Flynn, and he leant over and gave her a peck on the cheek, something that surprised the both of them a little, and Flynn stepped back quickly.

August saw Poppy give the tiniest shake of her head. Oh shit. She was going to be mad at Flynn now. And like the feeling you get playing Jenga, when the tower wobbles and you know it's close to crashing down, August knew the path had been laid for her to become a source of contention in Flynn's relationship. Poppy would never be happy with them being so close, with them living together so closely.

'Bye, Poppy,' August said, slapping on a smile and glossing over what had just occurred. 'Great to meet you properly.'

'And you,' Poppy replied. 'What a lovely home you both have.'

Was there a hint of something in that, something bitter or sarcastic, or did August imagine it?

August held the door open for them and Poppy exited first. As Flynn walked out, August whispered to him, oh so quietly, 'Careful when you leave the building.'

Flynn met her eye and gave a small nod. She was confident he knew what she meant: don't be romantic with Poppy until you're down the hill. On the way in, she knew he'd walked up the stairs twirling his keys. On the way out, she knew he would check on his phone for bars or pubs not too far away, walking distance-wise. It was how they'd agreed he would keep his hands occupied and avoid holding onto Poppy's.

Out on the landing, Flynn waved a goodbye to August, and Poppy too turned her head.

She caught August's eye and gave her a tight smile.

And like a flash, August remembered where she'd seen Poppy before.

Chapter 53

August

It was seeing her there, on the landing. Something about the backdrop, the flip of Poppy's red hair, the stern look in her eye. It had all come together, and August closed the door hastily, taking a moment to catch her breath.

Poppy had been here before, not when August was hiding in the wall cupboard but *before* before – she was at the open house. She was the woman who'd stormed past her and Flynn on their way in, the one who'd also known Mrs Haverley's intentions of only renting to a married couple, and she'd been pissed off.

Did Flynn know Poppy had wanted to live here before they'd moved in? Did Poppy know they'd lied to land the apartment? Would she care?

August ran to the window to watch the two of them walk down the hill. Of course she would care, *of course she would*, that's got to be why she acted so coolly around August.

Poppy looked back up at the house, right at the window August was looking out of, and like a fool August ducked. Her heart was beating fast.

Maybe Flynn had already told her, after all, and August had just misunderstood. Maybe he knew full well she'd come to view the apartment, they'd had a good laugh over the coincidence, and he'd let her in on the secret. After all, it's not like they had to pretend to everyone, only Mrs Haverley, mainly, and they'd decided to keep things clean by telling the same tale to the other residents in the property.

Ha, keep things clean. Things were beginning to prove anything but clean.

So yes, Flynn had probably told Poppy all about them and she just hadn't realised. And if he hadn't yet, she'd just nudge him to do so. It would be fine.

But there was a wringing in her stomach, a horrible feeling of worry. August stood and looked back out of the window, following the distant figures of Poppy and Flynn as they rounded the corner at the bottom of the hill, now arm-in-arm.

What if this wasn't just a coincidence? What if Poppy knew exactly who Flynn was when she'd approached him in that bar? Because that's what Flynn had said, wasn't it? That she'd hit on him?

Which led her to question ... What if the game wasn't over at all, and August and Flynn hadn't been joint-winners; what if they'd just moved to the next level, where a whole new antagonist awaited?

*

281

August spent the rest of the evening trying to distract herself while she waited for Flynn to come home. If he even came home – maybe he'd go back to Poppy's tonight. It was perfectly feasible, and she couldn't call and check up on him because it was none of her business; she *wasn't really his wife*. Nevertheless, she waited.

Sometimes she managed to convince herself that it was of course a coincidence, and also that of course Poppy had told Flynn she'd been to view the house, the first time he'd brought her here. And so Poppy hadn't landed this particular rental, she'd probably forgotten about it by the following day, and had found herself a fantastic place to live.

At other points in the evening August spiralled, weaving all sorts of imaginary hypotheses to herself about her future. Poppy had tracked Flynn down expressly to expose them. She'd go to Mrs Haverley and tell her everything. August and Flynn would need to move out but Mrs Haverley would have reported them to the police and to a renters' governing body and they'd struggle to ever find a home again and they'd have to go to court and Flynn would move back to Japan and August would have to leave Bath and then she'd be in the paper and every audition she ever attended for the rest of her life would have the casting director question, *Weren't you that girl who conned an old lady?*

Whoa.

At that point August would screech the brakes on and take some deep breaths, telling herself this was nonsense, make believe, big worries based on very little fact. And the cycle would begin again.

When she heard footsteps on the landing at close to midnight, she muted the television and stood up.

Flynn entered their flat. 'Hello, I wasn't expecting you to still be up,' he said. She could tell he'd had a couple more drinks, and he seemed cheery.

'Hi,' August answered. 'How was your evening?'

'Really nice,' Flynn answered with honesty, leaning against the back of the sofa. 'I feel ... lighter. Poppy being here, going for a drink, the fact she got on so well with you, it all felt lovely and unforced.' He yawned.

'That's good,' August said, still standing there, wringing her hands. 'Do you want a coffee or anything?'

'Better not, I'll be awake all night. Thank you, though.'

'That's okay,' August tried to move past him towards the kitchen, because she felt like she needed something to hold on to. But Flynn caught her in a hug.

'Thanks for this evening,' he said, his voice in her hair, scented with wine. And her shoulders sunk a little in his embrace, wondering if she should say anything at all. 'I know I don't need your approval, but you're my closest friend in this country.'

Friend. 'Tell me how you met Poppy, again?' she asked, as if she'd forgotten.

'In the pub,' Flynn replied, and he collapsed onto the sofa, lying down with his head on a cushion and closing his eyes.

August returned with a glass of orange juice and studied him for a moment, dark eyelashes, dark hair, lips that she knew were soft because she'd had the pleasure of kissing them, though Poppy was in charge of that now. August wondered fleetingly if she and Flynn would ever kiss again. For show, of course. But then realised it would never happen if Poppy stayed in the picture.

Flynn's eyes opened. 'What's up?' he asked her.

'I'm just thinking about Poppy,' August took a seat on the armchair, sitting forward, unable to relax.

'You like her, right? She's nice?'

'She's nice,' August agreed, trying to pick her words carefully. 'Did you know her before you met her in the pub?'

'Did I know her before I met her?' Flynn asked, but he wasn't making fun of her, it was more like his foggy brain was trying to unscramble what she was asking. 'No, I don't think so.'

'It's just that she looked familiar to me.'

'Well, you've lived in Bath for a while, maybe you'd worked together for a bit, or jived together in the discotheque.' He sniggered at his silliness.

This wasn't the right time. As much as August wanted this off her chest, it would be selfish to throw this at him now when he was tipsy and happy, just to try and make herself feel better. Instead of continuing, therefore, she said, 'Maybe that's it.'

His eyes closed again, his face content, and as she watched him for a beat his breathing slowed, the smile in the corners of his mouth relaxing, and he began to drift to sleep.

'Flynn?' she said. When he didn't rouse, she crept closer, until she knelt before him, her face near his. 'Flynn?' she whispered.

He stirred, only as much as that his hand raised and rested down upon hers, warm and heavy. 'Mmm?' he murmured.

'Do you want to go to bed?' she asked him, hoping to coax him into having a good night's rest – not on the sofa – so maybe he could be bright-eyed and bushy-tailed and she could speak to him tomorrow morning.

'With you?' he asked, confused at the question, and then fell back to sleep again.

'Never mind,' August replied, standing up and tiptoeing to her room, closing the door to the whole mess behind her.

The following morning, August was up early and in her running gear. She waited impatiently for Flynn to rise and shine, 'accidentally' being a little noisier around the flat than she would usually be.

At a few minutes to 9 a.m., Flynn opened his bedroom door and said, 'Is it Sunday?'

'It is,' she said, handing him one of his own-recipe banana smoothies. 'How did you sleep?'

'Okay once I'd peeled myself off the sofa and got into bed,' he rubbed his still-cricked neck. 'You're very awake.'

'I am. Do you want to go for a run with me?'

'Not really,' he yawned and she reached over and snatched the smoothie as he was about to take a gulp.

'This is only for runners.'

'That's harsh, who else are you going to give it to?'

'I'll drink it myself.'

'You already have one. Drink two and you'll puke

within five minutes. Last night was fun, huh? The dinner went well.'

August relented, handing him back the smoothie, but instead of answering his question just coaxed, 'Please? Come for a run?'

He yawned again, a big, long yawn, and by the time it had finished he seemed ready to take the plunge. 'Okay, but nothing massive.'

'You've clearly never run with me before,' August replied, and she drank her smoothie in small sips while he went and changed out of his pyjama bottoms.

August hadn't decided quite how to broach the subject of whether Flynn's first girlfriend after Yui might have targeted him as sabotage, but she hoped that the run, the first half at least, would pound some great ideas into her.

Chapter 54

August

Leaving the house, August was pumped, or at least, pumping herself up like she was about to start a marathon. The air was cold outside, the sky overcast. It was everything a November Sunday should be, with bare tree branches that tapped and scraped against window panes, roads dark grey thanks to a layer of overnight rain that hadn't dried fully yet, and the breeze had a definite chill, not strong enough to be considered blustery but more the kind that follows you inside, clinging to your scarf ends, causing you to exclaim about there being a 'hell of a draught out'.

Flynn had barely finished stretching before August took off down the hill. She ran a step ahead of him, dictating their path, and leading them through the length of the Royal Victoria Park, through the deserted streets in the centre of the town, and towards the River Avon behind the abbey.

August ran fast, faster than she usually did, as fast as she could manage until they reached the river. She was pink, panting, her breath rough in her upper chest. She came to a stop with a stitch in her side and sweat beads on the back of her neck, in her elbow creases and forming on her upper lip. Resting her hands on the cool stone of the wall above the river, August stretched her hips backwards, facing the ground, and wondered how she still didn't know what to say.

'Are you okay?' Flynn said, jogging to a halt beside her. 'Are you training for the Olympics or something?'

She shook her head, gulping in oxygen, and faced him.

'What is it? Do you feel ill?' he asked, seeing the worry in her eyes.

'I need to talk to you about something,' August blurted out.

'Go for it.'

She hesitated, letting the wind cool the dampness on her face, causing goose bumps to form on her arms. 'It could be nothing. It could be nothing at all, but I feel like I need to give you the information and then it's your call. Do whatever you want with it. You probably already know anyway.'

'Know what?'

'It's about . . . Poppy.'

August spotted the flicker of a smile cross his face at her name. She felt like the biggest cow for being the reason that smile would soon leave.

'What about her?' Flynn asked, concerned.

'I think . . . I *know* . . . that we've met Poppy before.'

'At the Roman Baths?'

'No, *before* before; before you started dating her.'

'Where?'

Here goes, August thought. 'Do you remember at the open house, when we first arrived and some girl came bursting out of the flat in a huff?'

Flynn crinkled his brow. 'Not really.'

'She made a comment about how *we'd* be right for the place but it had been a big waste of time for her? She was one of the people who already knew Mrs H only wanted a married couple, before we did?'

'Oh . . . ' Flynn gazed off towards the river for a moment. 'And you think that was Poppy?'

'I'm sure it was. She looked really familiar to me when you first introduced us but it wasn't until I saw her yesterday on the landing, when you two were heading out to go for your drink, that it hit me who she was.' She watched as Flynn absorbed what she was saying.

'Are you sure?' he asked.

August nodded.

'So she went to view the same house as us,' shrugged Flynn. 'She's settled somewhere now.'

'Did she mention it though, the first time you brought her over?'

'No . . . '

'Don't you think that's weird?' August said. Flynn flinched at that, like it was something he didn't want to hear, or that he didn't want August to say. She tried to smooth it over by adding, 'I just mean that I would have turned up and gone, like, *Oh, you live here? That's so funny, I came to view this flat a few months back too*, if it were me.'

289

'To be fair, August, not everybody thinks and says what you think and say.'

'I know, I just—'

'Maybe she was just a bit embarrassed because she felt like she wasn't "selected" for the flat, or whatever. Or maybe she just doesn't remember because she'd seen a hundred flats for rent that week.' He paused, regarding her, a look in his eye that she hadn't been on the end of before, like he wanted to say something but was holding back. 'Or maybe it wasn't even Poppy.'

They were all good, reasonable arguments, and August had argued with herself the same points over and over again for the past twelve hours. She didn't know what was the truth, she just knew she needed Flynn to be privy to all the same information as she was. Which is why she said, with conviction, 'It definitely was Poppy. I know it.'

Flynn ran a hand over his sweaty brow. 'It's just that I can barely remember that woman. I doubt she can remember seeing me that day.'

'Or maybe she does remember, and she recognised you in the bar, and that's why she came up to you in the first place.'

He looked down towards the river, his face hardened, his eyes searching for nothing in particular. 'I don't know what you're trying to imply.'

'Nothing,' August lied. But she hadn't been one to sugar-coat things with Flynn and wasn't about to start now; that wasn't the type of relationship they had. 'I'm just questioning her motives, I guess.'

'Her motives?' Flynn cried. 'As in, why is she with me?'

'No, not *why* is she with you – there are a hundred million reasons why she would be with you because you're *you* – I just mean, what if she's annoyed that we got the flat instead of her?'

'If she was, then she must have got over it, because she's not mentioned a thing to me.'

'She seems . . . ' August trailed off.

'She seems what?'

'Cold. Annoyed. I don't know.'

Flynn looked miserable, like this November morning. 'Perhaps she's not exactly feeling the warmth from you.'

August was afraid she was floating downriver, without Flynn, making things worse rather than being the lifeboat. 'I tried, Flynn, I'll keep trying – I promise – and I don't think I've been being weird around her, it's just that now I know who she is I can't help but worry.'

'Worry about what?' Flynn asked. He looked exhausted all of a sudden, and rubbed at his forehead like a headache was forming with a vengeance.

'I think she knows about us.'

'There is no "us",' Flynn snapped. 'You . . . never mind.'

August felt cold, the chill in the breeze enveloping her now. She knew that, of course she knew that, but it still stung her pride, and her heart. She might not be part of an 'us' with him romantically, but she meant *something* to him, didn't she? She gritted her teeth. 'I know, I'm just trying to speak to you as a friend. I think something is up.'

'Is this just jealousy? Are you worried we're not going to be able to play imaginary marriages anymore? Are you worried about your dream home? How about worrying about me and my happiness?'

'I *am* worried about you, that's the point, it's not about me,' ... Was it? No, she cared for Flynn, maybe even more than she cared about the house on Elizabeth Street, but that wasn't the question right now.

He was silent for a while, looking forward, breathing hard. Then he said, his voice low and his eyes refusing to look at her, 'I am trying my best to be happy. Trying my hardest to make a life for myself here, trying to find a reason why this wasn't all one huge mistake. I'm trying to move on from a broken relationship.' And then he added, almost inaudibly, 'I'm also trying to respect you, and move on from whatever this dysfunctional mess is that we've got ourselves into.'

August couldn't breathe for a moment. What did that mean? What was he saying? 'Flynn?'

'I need to think.' He started to back away.

She caught him by the sleeve, pushing her own confusion aside. 'I just don't trust how she came into your life all of a sudden, never mentioned that she'd been inside our flat before, and seems really suspicious of me.'

'Of course she's suspicious of you,' Flynn threw up his hands. 'Look at you; you're fun and pretty and you know me. The two of us get on in a way she and I are nowhere near to yet. Of course she'd be wary of you.'

August shook her head, getting annoyed back at him now for twisting this all around on her when she was only ever trying to be open with him. 'Don't put this down as some kind of clichéd female rivalry thing, like Poppy can't handle you having a female friend.'

'Maybe that's not the question, then. Maybe it's can you handle me having a girlfriend?'

She didn't know what he wanted her to say. She withdrew her hand from him and stepped back, ready to take herself out of the picture. This was his problem to deal with however he wanted, she'd simply been the messenger. 'Don't you *dare* try to make me look like I can't handle you having a girlfriend. I've been nothing but welcoming towards Poppy, even though she's been, frankly, an icy bitch around me. The only time I've faltered is when I realised that she might be playing you.'

'What do you think she's going to do?'

'I don't know!' August had been raising her voice but she tried to lower it back down as another couple of joggers passed them by, serving them with a look. 'I have no idea what she may or may not be cooking up, I don't have the answers, I don't even have a theory, I'm just telling you what I know.'

Flynn sighed, and not the happy, contented sigh she'd heard come out from him when he drank coffee on the wall outside in the morning sunshine, or when they'd shared a takeout pizza together, eating until their bellies were too full. He stared at her for the moment, and not with the soft, inquisitive stare that he'd treated her to before they'd kissed. This was all different, all wrong.

Eventually he spoke. 'I think the problem is, you don't really know anything.'

Flynn turned and took off in a gentle jog, as it started to drizzle. August waited until he was out of sight around the centuries-old abbey, and then set off herself, in the opposite direction.

Chapter 55

Flynn

As Flynn ran a short-cut back towards Elizabeth Street, August's words turned and churned inside his head. They mangled together, mixing with annoyance, sadness, guilt at how he'd spoken to her, and worry, in case she was actually right.

Why was August doing this? He'd so wanted her and Poppy to get on, for some reason it had seemed important to him, but now she seemed to be trying to pick fault.

Was there something about Poppy and the way they met, the keenness she'd shown in visiting his home and the interest in his relationship status. '*You're not married?*' she'd asked at the bar that first night. But that was a normal question, a good question, really, for anyone flirting to check up on. Flynn found himself trying remember if she'd asked that question with curiosity, or with surprise, and then he cursed August under his breath for making him assess Poppy's intentions, and flooding black ink into his memories of the start of their relationship.

August was his flatmate, nothing else, the rest was just make-believe. Poppy was somebody who he could maybe, one day, love in the same way he'd loved Yui, and he couldn't wait for that day to come.

But try as he might to make this all about August, ultimately, he needed to speak with Poppy. He took a brisk shower, and left the flat quickly, not ready to run into his fake wife again just yet.

Flynn saw the back of Poppy's head as he approached the park bench, her distinctive red hair immaculate with just light tendrils dancing in the cold breeze. He watched her for a short moment, trying to get a sense of exactly how he felt about her now he could see her.

On the one hand, he'd thought he was really beginning to like her. She was fun, clever, confident. She'd helped him know there was possibility to be happy again after how things had ended with Yui.

On the other hand, didn't the fact he only *thought* he was *beginning* to like her after nearly two months tell him something pretty clear? He enjoyed spending time with Poppy, and she seemed to enjoy him, but even though he'd put down the slow burn as him not wanting to rush into a new relationship, neither of them seemed to really be making much effort to stoke the fire and get it roaring. Was it possible that the 'like' was exactly where it was always going to end?

'Hi, Poppy,' Flynn said, coming around the side of the bench.

'Flynn,' Poppy said, getting up and tightening her coat around her. 'It's so frickin' cold today, why the hell did you want to meet outside?'

She went in for a kiss but he stopped her. 'Do you want to get a coffee?'

'I want you to buy me a coffee,' she grumbled, side-eyeing him, and the two of them walked to the nearest cafe, the one August was always talking about that had good breakfasts. He told Poppy this, and watched her reaction after he said August's name.

But Poppy remained stoic, not so much of a hint of a curled lip or a rolled eye. Surely that wasn't the natural reaction if you disliked someone to the extent August had made out? What was it she'd said? That Poppy had always been an icy bitch around her? But then, Poppy wasn't exactly beaming and asking after August's wellbeing today either.

Flynn pressed on. 'I went for a run with August this morning. We got into a bit of an argument.'

'I'm sorry to hear that,' Poppy said, with the warmth of a robot. 'Lovers' tiff?'

'Why would you say that?'

'Because it's a joke?' Poppy took her coffee and went to sit at one of the large wooden tables upstairs, in the corner, the furthest away from other customers. Before Flynn had even sat down, she asked, 'What do you want to talk about, Flynn?'

He raised his eyebrows. 'What do you mean?'

'I mean that last night for maybe the first time since we started this,' Poppy waved her finger between the two of them. 'Whatever *this* is, you were affectionate and touchy-feely, and I felt like you were looking at me, really looking at me, *for the first time*. Do you know what I thought?'

'What?' he asked. This wasn't how he'd been expecting this conversation to go.

'I thought, "Oh great, he's finally got the permission he's been craving from his *flatmate*, and now he's allowing himself to have a little fun."'

Flynn's blood ran a little colder at the way she used air quotes around the word 'flatmate'. Was August right? He had a feeling he was about to find out. 'She is just my flatmate, you know.'

'Maybe she was, once upon a time.' Poppy regarded him, her blue eyes hard, the curve of her mouth flattened out. She was right; last night, tipsy with a bit of liquor, happy because the evening had gone well, and, yes, because August had seemed to approve, he'd allowed himself to try and get closer to Poppy, to try and stoke that fire. That wasn't so strange, surely. At the end of the day, August was his closest friend here and he'd wanted her to like Poppy. It had made a difference to him.

Eventually, Poppy shook her head. 'And now you're all distant again, brooding even, and we're back to square one. So clearly she told you.'

He held her gaze, one hand clamped around his coffee. He was going to play dumb, ask what she meant, but they both knew and therefore it was game over.

'That's a yes, then,' Poppy sighed. 'I knew she realised who I was last night. If you want me to apologise, I'm not going to.'

'Did you know who I was when you came up to me in the pub?'

'Yes, I recognised you from the open house, of course.'

'I don't really remember you.'

'I'm not surprised, you only had eyes for the one you walked in with,' Poppy replied. 'And before you grow the biggest head, I don't remember you because you're the most attractive man in the world or anything. I remember you because the two of you looked like such a perfect couple. The dream tenants for that horrible old landlady.'

'She's okay,' Flynn said, surprised at himself for defending Mrs Haverley. A bit of deflection, perhaps. 'If you thought we were such a happy couple, what did you hope to gain by chatting me up by the bar?'

'Nothing, quite honestly. The hen party dared me to come on to you, this handsome stranger waiting at the bar, and when I looked over, I recognised you. Thinking you were a safe bet to not become creepy and clingy, because I knew you were with someone, I went along with it. And then imagine my surprise when it turns out you actually didn't have a partner.'

Flynn's mind was a muddle, he couldn't separate the reality of what happened from the events she'd manufactured yet. 'But you didn't know where I lived at that point, you didn't know I'd got the apartment.'

'No, I didn't, I just thought, Hey, this guy is actually

single, and he's pretty nice. It was the second time we met that you mentioned where you lived.' She paused to sip her coffee, her eyes never leaving him.

'Why didn't you say anything? Why didn't you just ask me how I got the apartment if that's what you were wondering. I probably would have told you.'

Poppy shrugged. 'I was curious and intrigued, and to be honest, I wanted to find out myself because I didn't know if you would have told me the truth. Besides, I was still getting to know you, and I liked you, and I wanted to see the house myself to make sure I wasn't jumping to conclusions. Because at the time it felt a little far-fetched to assume the two of you were faking being a married couple in order to beat off the competition for a rental apartment.'

'It's not as simple as that,' Flynn started. 'It wasn't just any old flat—'

'But I was right, wasn't I? That landlady only wanted to rent to a married couple. Not the likes of me, not the likes of a lot of the other hopefuls. But you two must have fit the bill when you lied your way in.'

Flynn was silent for a time, turning the facts over in his head, asking her questions that he didn't say out loud about why she hadn't confronted him, why she'd carried on the façade, but maybe it didn't matter. They'd both held things back. They'd both made this an unhealthy relationship, and him more so.

Instead, he asked – or rather stated – after a while, 'You left a bra in my apartment.'

Poppy smiled a little at that, a twinkle in her eye, just for

300

a second. 'All right, you caught me, I wanted to be a little territorial. Can you blame me? You made me feel like the other woman, like the mistress, and you didn't even have the courtesy to tell me why.'

'When did I make you feel like that?' he asked the question but he knew it was true. From his jumpiness at sneaking her in and out of the flat, to the ease and warmth he couldn't help give off towards August, even when Poppy was around.

'Well, for one thing I'd just seen the photo of you and her on the beach, looking like happy newlyweds, and I wondered what else you two got up to there alone.'

'Nothing,' Flynn said, softening, understanding her point of view.

'Nothing?' she pressed, however. 'You've never slept together, or even kissed?'

Flynn hesitated, and that was all the confirmation she needed. Poppy picked up her bag, and the remainder of her coffee.

'We have kissed, but not since you and I started seeing each other,' Flynn said, wanting to be as honest with her as he could, now. 'Are you ...' he started, and then stopped himself.

Poppy turned, her eyes narrowed. 'Am I what?'

He needed to ask, and he loathed himself for it because it was what he'd accused August of only caring about. 'Are you going to do anything with the information?'

'Am I going to do anything with the information?' Poppy repeated back at him, her voice full of scorn. 'What do you think, Inspector Morse? Do you think I'm going to tell on you to your landlady? Flynn, we've seen each other a handful of times over the space of two months, let's just leave it as something that was over before it started, okay?'

'Sure,' he answered. Flynn hung his head, ashamed under her gaze. He didn't want to ask the next question, but he knew he had to. 'When did you stop liking me? Was it after that time you came to the flat, when we first kissed?' *When August had been in her recording booth the whole time*?

'I didn't stop liking you,' Poppy explained, her eyes flicking down, refusing to let him see the hurt in them. 'I was genuinely into you; I always have been. But that doesn't mean that I'm not annoyed by this other side of you. It felt deceitful, to me, and to other people.' Poppy went to walk away and then turned, saying, 'Not everything I did was a lie, Flynn, in fact, hardly any of it was. But importantly to *us*, as much as I liked you, I could see you liked her.'

He looked up at her with surprise and was about to protest but the words caught in his throat.

She held her hands up, stopping him from trying. 'You and her, and that fake life you've created – I saw the wedding photo you'd turned to face the wall, I saw the anxious looks you'd cast up and down the street in case of any neighbours watching – that's a lie you two need to figure out what the hell you're doing with. Are you just going to pretend to be married for life, and never live your actual lives?'

Flynn left the cafe a good half an hour after Poppy had. He'd stared into his empty coffee cup, whirling her words around his head. It was over before it started, that was certainly true. Was he sad about that? Of course. Was he Yui-level sad? Of course not.

The thought of Yui, in fact, had him pining for their life together, to be back in Japan, back near his family, back where he didn't have to lie and pretend, when he wasn't completely shattered from his job all the time. Because he really was completely shattered, from everything.

He walked home, slowly, allowing the drizzle to fall on him.

Poppy's words whirled about in his mind. She wasn't wrong. He could keep trying, denying, lying, and acting. But the truth was that everything came down to August, and it was time he faced that fact with his eyes open. He'd fallen for her, and he needed to see her, because he was sinking.

Chapter 56

August

Back at their home on Elizabeth Street, August had been sitting on the wall in the rain since returning from her run. She was cold, goosebumped, and her lips had turned blue.

She hadn't wanted to hurt Flynn, of course she hadn't, but how could she have kept this to herself? Calling Poppy an icy bitch was probably a bit of an overstep, though. But August had developed a deep friendship with Flynn over the past months of living together, and if Poppy thought she could waltz in and light a stick of dynamite in their world she wasn't about to stand for it.

'What are you doing out here?' someone asked, and she turned, expecting it to be Flynn. Instead she faced Abe, who was looking at her with concern.

He was holding a shopping bag and wearing a baseball cap to shield his eyes from the rain, and he stepped over the wall to her, putting the bag in a puddle, concern causing him to remove his coat and place it around her. 'You're frozen, come inside.'

She tried to find words but instead her teeth chattered, and for a moment she lost herself in the warmth of Abe's coat, the smell of him, and the kindness of his face.

He led her inside and into her flat, and she thanked him. She headed for the shower, in the hope that the steaming water would wash her worries away. It didn't work, but it did at least warm her up. When she emerged a little later in dry clothes and with a little more colour to her lips, she was pleased to see Abe still there, sitting on her sofa, with two piping hot cups of coffee before him.

He stood up when she entered the living room. 'I hope you don't mind me staying,' he said, clearing his throat. 'But you made me a coffee when I needed it a few weeks back, so I wanted to return the favour.'

August sat down on the sofa, and he sat next to her, their proximity something neither could ignore. 'Thank you,' she said.

Abe glanced at her. 'Do you want to talk about it? About why you were sitting outside in the rain in November, looking so down?'

'Um . . .' she really did want to talk about it. August wasn't good at keeping things bottled up. But how much could she say to Abe, really? 'Flynn and I just had a bit of an argument, that's all.'

Abe shifted in his seat, and when she did the same it caused their knees to touch lightly. It was almost imperceptible, but not quite. Neither of them made any move to pull them back apart. August's breathing slowed a little.

'I'm sure everything will be okay,' said Abe, his voice quiet.

'I'm sure it will too. I just don't know if I did the right thing or not at the moment. And then I said some horrible things.'

He nodded. 'It's not fun when that happens in an argument. But I'm sure he'll know it was just in the heat of the moment.'

There was something about the way he said 'heat of the moment', how his voice cracked, how they met each other's eyes for a second. But then he angled himself away, reaching for his coffee, and the spell was broken.

August leaned forward and drank from her cup too. 'Mmm, this is perfect, thank you. And thank you for stopping me from catching pneumonia out there.'

'Of course. It's the neighbourly thing to do.'

'How's your mum?'

'She's okay. Not getting any worse, which is good, but I worry about her more over the winter months. Whether she admits it or not I think she needs me quite a bit, which is partly why I keep coming down from London at the moment.'

It hung in the air, his mention of 'partly why'. It hung suspended within this heavy tension that surrounded them, with him thinking she was a married woman, and her caught in her own lie. August couldn't bring herself to ask what his other reason might be, as she was afraid in case it was her. She was also afraid to ask in case it wasn't. Instead she said, 'If I can help, in any way, you can always call me and I'll go and check on her?'

'Thank you,' he said, with a smile. She felt a compulsion to lean her head on his shoulder, and she decided to go with that feeling. August felt Abe flinch under her touch, but he didn't move away. It felt good to be close to him.

'It's the neighbourly thing to do,' she murmured.

With the coffee warming her from the inside, Abe from the outside, and the rain falling gently beyond the window, August was lulled into a sense of calm. So much so that she jumped when the door to the flat opened.

Flynn walked in, his shoulders hunched and his hair wet. She shifted away from Abe a moment too late. Flynn's eyes swept across the two of them, and it stopped him in his tracks.

Chapter 57

Flynn

Abe stood up, fast, and nodded at both August and Flynn, looking flustered, before making his way out of the apartment. But Flynn had seen them snuggled together. He'd seen how August was taking comfort from their argument in his arms. And he knew it could have all been different if he'd just admitted what was going around his mind earlier. That's not to assume she would have 'picked him', of course, but perhaps he would have been able to live his life with a bit more clarity. As it was now, he felt so far below the murky surface he could think of only one way out.

'Are you two . . . ?' Flynn asked August.

'Me and Abe? We're just friends.'

'Does he know about us?'

'No.'

There is no us, Flynn's own words echoed back at him, and

he could tell by the tiny frown that crossed her face that she was remembering them too.

'Have you seen Poppy?' August asked, walking around the sofa to face him.

'Yes.'

'And?' August held her breath.

Flynn moved away from her and towards the sofa, where Abe had been, his mind full of the image of the two of them together. Once again, he felt the weight of his exhaustion. He was just *exhausted*. He put his face in his hands, sighing. 'You were right, it's over between me and Poppy.'

'Oh, Flynn.'

'It doesn't matter,' he said, though it actually did. 'She's not going to tell Mrs Haverley. But perhaps you need to decide what you want to tell her son, if you're thinking of getting involved with him.'

She bristled. 'I told you, we're just friends, and I don't need your advice on what I should think about.'

'You're right,' he said, the clouds fogging up his mind again in a way he hadn't meant them to. 'You don't need my advice, and I don't need this right now. I'm so tired, of work, of lying, of failed relationships, of having to look both ways every time I leave the house in case I need to concoct some new fabrication about us.'

'I'm tired too,' said August, raising her voice a touch. 'You don't think I want us to just live like normal flatmates? You don't think I hate seeing you overworked and used? You don't think I hate lying to everyone? I thought living here was the answer to all my problems, like it would be the start of something amazing, and I'm so gut-wrenchingly disappointed it's not working, Flynn.'

It wasn't working anymore. That was the truth of the matter, the only truth in all of this.

'I'm sorry things didn't work out with Poppy,' August added.

'It's not just about Poppy. Or Abe.' Flynn rubbed his face. 'It's everything.' He took a moment. When had it got so bad? And how could he get out of this? His head was full of confusion over his feelings for August, annoyance about Poppy and that whole deceitful relationship, stress from work, and this marriage lie was just too much on top of everything else.

Sighing, August said, 'I never forced you into this.'

'I never said you did – you're the only one who's ever been fixated on that. But . . . ' pausing, Flynn stood, and he looked hard at August. He took in her face, her everything, committed her to memory, along with all the thoughts of what might have been. Then he said, 'I think we need some time apart.'

A tear fell onto August's cheek. She swept it away quickly, her mouth set in a stiff line. She sighed, clearly frustrated with herself. 'I never thought I'd cry in this house, and now I am. Because of you.'

'Good,' he said.

'Good?'

'Yes, good. Because if you're crying, you're living, you're feeling something and it's real. Ever since we moved in here it's been such an endless masquerade ball that I often don't even know when you're being the real you.'

'I've always been me around you,' August stated.

'Have you?'

She took a deep breath, and then crossed the room to him, slowly, with her eyes locked on his. When she reached him she took a moment as if she, too, were capturing his image. Then she nodded, just once, and put her arms around him, though he was damp from the rain. They held onto each other for a moment, the rope holding them together on its last threads.

Chapter 58

August

As August had always done, when she had big life decisions to make, she sat on the wall in front of what was now her home. Wrapped in warm clothing to shield her from the late November frost, she tried to use the breathing exercises from her yoga class to focus on what she needed to think about, one thing at a time: how to fix her friendship with Flynn, her tangled feelings for Abe, her need to come clean, especially to Callie, dear Callie, oh and the small matter of her career, which she kept pushing aside.

She and Flynn had barely spoken since their showdown, so she didn't know quite what he was thinking in relation to them having time apart. He seemed so busy with work that to be honest, she barely saw him anyway.

'Hello, August,' came a female voice. Welcoming the interruption, August opened her eyes to see Mrs Haverley.

'Hello,' she replied. 'It's a bit cold out here, isn't it, Mrs Haverley. Is everything okay?'

'I'm perfectly fine,' Mrs Haverley insisted. 'Are you well? You look burdened, if you don't mind me saying.'

'Oh, it's just ... I've been trying to muster up some motivation for the next steps in ... my career, nothing interesting.'

'Would you like to come up and talk it through?' Mrs Haverley offered, and August almost fell off the wall. She'd never been invited up to Mrs H's before. Let alone been invited for chit-chat. But ...

'Okay ...'

At the top of the stairs, after a slow ascent, Mrs Haverley opened her door. 'Come on in, I was experimenting earlier and trying to make eggnog but I made an awful mess and gave up.'

August had assumed Mrs Haverley's flat would be pristine but formal, like a room in a manor house inside a Jane Austen novel. What she actually found was a layout similar to her own apartment, but with smaller windows ever so slightly tilting towards the sky. White walls and pale grey furnishings, vases with fresh lilies, well-thought-out accent pieces like a small sculpture here and an appliance there, a huge TV and a wall full of Andy Warhol art prints.

It seemed that Mrs Haverley's old-fashioned ways didn't extend to her living quarters, where she was, apparently, a thoroughly modern Millie!

'Can I give you a hand with the eggnog?' August asked, knowing nothing about the drink.

'No,' said Mrs Haverley. 'Let's just have a glass of Advocaat instead.'

August took a sip of the custard-like alcoholic drink while Mrs Haverley directed her to a round table under one of the windows, where they could see for miles. Mmm, Advocaat was tasty.

'How's the world of theatre, these days?' Mrs Haverley asked. 'Did anything become of that audition you were preparing for when I performed the inspection on your apartment?'

August shook her head. 'No, I messed it up. Better luck next time, I guess.'

'What is next for you?'

'I don't know, really. Ultimately, I still want to do acting, and there are a lot of things I could do to help me get there, but my ego took a bit of a bruising. So to be honest I've been stalling.'

'So you aren't pursuing your career at all at the moment?'

'I wouldn't say *at all*, I just also wouldn't say ... much.' Rather like when she lived in London, really. And rather like when she'd first lived in Bath. Dear God, she hadn't come up here for a scolding.

But it was as if Mrs Haverley observed the barriers and backed off, ending that topic of conversation with, 'When I'm faced with a lot of things I could do, I find it sometimes easier to focus on one small change at a time.'

That was true. August's mind drifted while her gaze lolled through Mrs Haverley's room, pausing on cute photos of Abe throughout the years. She thought about what would be the easiest, most immediate step she could take, and it was obvious really. She could certainly put herself out there more than she had been, and follow up with contacts she'd made over the years. She could start to reach out and make links with like-minded people, put herself out there rather than hiding away.

Perhaps when she got back to her flat she'd do something she'd been meaning to do since arriving in Bath, really. She'd update her social profiles, make her Instagram public, find some fresh new people to follow and connect with, maybe even update her headshots with the help of Bel's photography skills (and she'd pay her, nothing like investing money to force August's hand into taking action).

She would install those proper soundproofing tiles she'd bought off Amazon after the whole listening-to-Poppy-snog debacle.

She'd build a repertoire of characters and make a demo reel.

Easy steps. But at least they were *steps*, and they made something sparkle inside her.

'Did you mention once that your grandmother lived in Bath?' Mrs Haverley asked. She closed her eyes for a moment to enjoy the drink while August was thinking.

'I did,' said August. 'She lived not far from here, actually. At the bottom of the hill and round a bit, there's a cottage, painted yellow, loads of trees around it.'

'I know the one.'

'She lived there for years – certainly my whole life and for a long time before that I think.'

August observed Mrs Haverley staring at her, her eyes sharp and curious. It was a similar look to the one she'd given to August all those months ago at the open day, like she'd started to take notice. 'Your grandmother lived in that cottage?'

'Yes,' replied August. 'She used to bring me up this hill so many times. I even came in this house once, when I was really small, because she wanted to drop something in to a friend of hers. It must have been before you moved in.'

'What was her friend like?' Mrs Haverley asked with a smile.

'To be completely honest, Mrs H, I don't remember anything about her. I was too spellbound by the house itself. That I remember every detail about.'

'What was your grandmother's name?'

'Pearl. Well, no it wasn't, it was Penelope but for some reason we all called her Pearl,' August laughed then, thinking about names. 'And for some reason I want to say her friend who lived here was called Windy Day, but that can't be right.'

'That sounds exactly right, actually,' Mrs Haverley answered, getting up and pulling a large photo album off her shelf, before bringing it, and the Advocaat bottle, back to the table with her.

'Did you know her?'

'Your grandmother or "Windy Day"?'

'Either.'

'How about both?' Mrs Haverley started flicking pages in the photo album, thick, stiff pages with photographs glued directly onto the card. 'It turns out you and I have been friends far longer than I realised, August Anderson.'

She slid the open photo album towards August. August felt her face light up into a beam on seeing her grandmother's face looking out at her. Pearl's hair was darker in the photo than August remembered it being, curled around her face. She was laughing, standing in a river, the water up to her ankles. Her tea dress was hoiked up around her knees and she held both it and a cigarette in one hand. The other arm was linked with another girl's, someone younger, who was doubled over with laughter, her eyes scrunched shut and the sun illuminating her skin. But even in the split-second capture of what looked like a wonderful summer's day, August knew exactly who it was.

'This is you! And my grandma!' she said, delighted. 'You and my grandma were friends?'

'I've lived in this house a long, long time, August. Before it was separated into apartments, before your grandmother moved to Bath.'

'So you're, um, Windy Day?'

'I'm actually *Wendy* Day – or at least I was before I married – but your grandmother delighted in calling me Windy Day.'

August sat back in her chair and stared at Mrs Haverley. 'But . . . you're a lot younger than my grandmother.'

'I was back then, too,' Mrs Haverley joked. 'But when we met we were both single and had enough friends in common that the fact I was barely twenty and she was, I think, early thirties didn't matter. We had a lot of fun and laughs.'

'Did the two of you fall out?'

'Oh no,' Mrs Haverley said with a firm shake of her head.

'Over the years we lost the closeness to the point of being no more than acquaintances I'm afraid. But that's just how life works. Pearl was older, she married and started a family before I did, long before I did, as it happens. Though I remember she thought I was the one who was the 'old soul' and stuck in my ways. We just drifted apart. I do remember her bringing you here that day though.'

August watched Mrs Haverley talk. She'd known her grandmother. She'd been *friends* with her grandmother, to the point that she also called her Pearl. A tear spilled onto a cheek which August tried to wipe away so Mrs Haverley wouldn't see it, because though it warmed her heart to have this connection to her past, a guilty cannonball sank inside her. Mrs Haverley – old-fashioned, austere Mrs Haverley – had been her beloved grandmother's *friend*. And August had lied to her.

In an attempt to shake away the feeling of shame, August turned back to the photo album and silently pledged to no longer view Mrs Haverley as just an old-fashioned landlady, but to see her and hear her as a person. Starting with today.

'Mrs H, I'm going to make that eggnog for us, and then will you tell me the story behind these photos?'

Mrs Haverley smiled at August, colour in her cheeks, and said, 'I would love that, August.'

November's long and drizzly stretch eventually turned into December. August watched as Flynn's work didn't let up, and occasionally she wondered when he'd last seen daylight. He left home in the dark, he came home in the dark. She guessed his lunch breaks were non-existent, as was his social life.

He and August didn't talk about Poppy, or their argument, and sometimes a sadness appeared to envelop Flynn that he couldn't seem to shake. He barely noticed things like the Christmas lights being switched on in the city centre or the market that had popped up, or the festive music that had begun to be the background soundtrack to everything outside his office walls. He seemed lonely, longing to come up for air.

August watched Flynn from the sidelines, wondering how to help, wishing she could take some of his burden off his hands. The more he worked, the less she saw of him, but what she did see seemed sad and withdrawn.

One evening, mid-December, when she was nearly ready to hit the sack but poor Flynn hadn't even made it home yet, an idea struck her. If she could get him home at a normal time, just for one evening, she was sure she could inject some much-needed Christmas spirit into him.

'A Christmas party?' Bel asked down the end of the phone. 'Of course I'm in – where?'

'My house,' August explained. 'Just a small party – my friends, his friends from the office, just something to help Flynn forget work for the night and let the festive spirit in.'

'Would your landlady allow a party in your flat?'

'We'd keep it low-key, and it's not like I can see any of us doing keg-stands on the landing or anything.' The more August thought about the idea, the better it felt. Flynn needed some fun, some friendly faces, and yes, a couple of them would be from his work but she knew he hadn't spent any chilled evenings with them in the pub for a long time. 'I think he needs this, Bel.'

'Do you think he's blue about not going home to Japan for the holidays?'

August had wondered about that, but hadn't had a chance to speak to him about it. 'Maybe. I was wondering whether to ask him if he wanted to spend Christmas together.'

August's mum had decided to go away for Christmas this year, on a Baltic cruise with her sister, August's aunt. They'd asked August if she wanted to join them, but she couldn't really afford to get her own room, and wasn't sure three of them in one cabin for nine days would be anyone's idea of a Merry Christmas.

'That would be nice, he'd probably appreciate it,' Bel answered.

'So would you come to the party? With Steve of course, and Kenny if you like?'

'Of course, count us in.'

When August hung up the phone, it was as if the Christmas lights had been switched on inside *her*. Finally, she had a reason to feel festive, and a Christmas present for Flynn she thought he would really like, and maybe even need: a chance for a little bit of festive fun.

Chapter 59

Flynn

'What are you doing next Thursday evening?' August asked Flynn as soon as he returned from his morning run. His eyes immediately flicked towards his work laptop, worried about what emails he might have missed from just being gone an hour.

August tapped his arm. 'Don't say you'll be stuck at work. What if I told you you *had* to give yourself the evening off?'

'If my hand were being forced, I can't say I'd complain,' he said, without commitment. He watched as she went about the motions of making him one of his banana smoothies, Ariana Grande singing Christmas music from the radio in the background. It was sweet – he hadn't asked her to, and she wasn't making a big deal out of it trying to earn brownie points or anything, it was just . . . kind. But it didn't change anything. He still had to go, he just didn't know when.

'Good.' She whirred the blender and continued bopping

along to the track. She knew the melody so well that she could keep dancing, even though she couldn't hear it over the noise. 'Because we're throwing a Christmas Party. No – *I'm* throwing a Christmas Party. For you.' She handed him his smoothie.

'You are?'

'I am. It's all arranged, your friends from work are coming, plus my friends who are now basically your friends too. It's not going to be a rager, just maybe fifteen people, a few drinks and nibbles.'

'You've already arranged all this?' Flynn couldn't believe it. 'For me?'

'For you,' she said, nodding. 'And because I think you need a little Christmas spirit, otherwise I'm basically living with the Grinch.' She winked to show she was teasing.

Nobody had ever thrown Flynn a party before. And of course, this wasn't purely a 'Happy Christmas to Flynn and only to Flynn' event, but it meant a lot that she'd go to the lengths of planning it, picking the date, contacting the guests, all because she thought he needed some cheering up.

In that moment, for just a second, he forgot the pained thoughts that had been growing in him. He forgot how he kind of hated his job, how he missed Japan, how he missed Yui and felt like a fool for jumping into the thing with Poppy too quickly.

'So are you in?'

'Sure, I'm in,' he answered. 'Do you think we should forewarn the neighbours?'

'On it!' she sang. 'Just before you got home I delivered a

322

box of Christmas cookies to each of them, along with a card to say we were having a gathering and would keep the noise down, and that it would all be over by eleven.'

Flynn nodded his head approvingly.

'So all you need to do is show up, okay? This is my Christmas present to you, and you taking a night off from the grind can be your Christmas present to me.'

True to his word, Flynn showed up. In fact, just knowing there was a string of Christmas lights at the end of the tunnel kept him going through the long days and nights of working. Just knowing he would have an evening off – a proper evening where there would be no temptation to look at his work emails – made him excited. And despite everything that was brewing under the surface, he found in himself a whisper of longing to spend some proper time with August. He couldn't deny it.

'Your friends from work don't think we're married or anything, do they?' August said, hobbling out of her room shortly before seven on the evening of the party. She was wearing a bright red dress with a flared hem, silver glittering eyeshadow, and, at that moment, a single white stiletto. She was jamming some big white orb earrings that looked like snowballs through the holes in her ears.

Despite the distance that had grown between them since Flynn told her he needed space, she still managed to take his breath away for a moment. He pulled himself together and answered with a, 'No, so no pretending needed tonight.'

'No pretending,' August smiled, catching his eye. 'So how do I look?'

'Great, except I think you're missing a shoe? Unless this is a new trend I'm not aware of?'

'I'm getting to that one,' August breezed, and flicked on the Christmas playlist she'd created on her phone, her speakers filling the apartment with Wham!

Flynn made them both a snowball cocktail while she sang along unselfconsciously to 'Last Christmas'.

The thing about Christmas parties, as evidenced throughout history and documented in many movies and novels, is that the rules are different, there's magic in the air; anything can happen, and usually, it does.

Chapter 60

August

Their guests arrived in quick succession, appearing
generally in threes and fours, sharing taxis to the top of
Elizabeth Street to avoid walking too far in their smart –
and most likely uncomfortable – shoes, and in the frosty
December air.

August surveyed the scene with warmth in her soul. Sia's
'Santa's Coming for Us' was playing in the background, the
snowball cocktails were a hit, Flynn's work friends were
mingling seamlessly with hers, and, most importantly, Flynn
looked relaxed. His face glowed in the soft glimmer from the
fairy lights, and his eyes had more sparkle than the drapes of
tinsel August had strung around the window panes.

There was a knock on the door, interrupting her thoughts,
and she bopped over to open it, finding Callie and her mum,
bedecked in sequins and reindeer antlers, waving her card.

'A *Christmas Party*!' Callie exclaimed. 'Hell, yes. This

was such a great idea, thanks August! Ooh, are these your friends? *Hell-o*.'

Uh-oh.

Callie was inside her flat, making a beeline for one of Flynn's workmates, a man named Joe. Callie's mum handed August a bottle of red and danced her way inside as well, and August darted a glance to Flynn. Their eyes met in joint panic mode, and without further ado, Flynn rolled off the back of the sofa and twirled in front of both Callie and her mum, taking one hand from each of them and spinning them both to face away from the bedrooms. August reached the rooms in three strides and whipped both doors closed, containing their separate sleeping quarters behind them.

Flynn caught up with August by the kitchen. 'Erm,' he started.

'I swear, I didn't invite them,' August hissed. 'I clearly said on the card *we* were having a small party and that we wouldn't disturb *them*.'

'We can't ask them to leave,' Flynn said. '... *Can* we? You do it!'

'No, we can't ask them to leave, we just have to stop them talking to anyone.' Even to August that was easier said than done, knowing Callie. 'It'll be fine, it'll be fine! Most of my friends know we're having to live this lie anyway,' It was becoming harder to admit that was what they were doing these days. 'I'll go round and let them know to play along if needed. Do you want to warn any of your work friends?'

'Not really, not here, but I will if it becomes necessary.'

August forced a smile back on her face. 'It's no big deal

though, right? We'll just make sure Callie and her mum are always talking to you, me or Bel. Let's get back to enjoying the party.'

'You're right,' Flynn nodded. 'It'll be f—'

'Gotta go,' August interrupted him and flew across the room to grab Callie who was circling Joe like a predator and her prey. August grabbed Callie's hands and led her in a mid-living room jive to 'All I Want For Christmas Is You'.

Callie looked so happy to be dancing and August felt a rush of warmth towards her, which may have been fuelled by the cocktails. Callie really was a great friend to her.

Bugger it. August opened her mouth because she couldn't hold the secret any longer. And Callie was fun, she'd understand, maybe she'd even find it hilarious. Over the music she called, 'Callie, I've got something really funny to tell you.'

Chapter 61

Flynn

Flynn was just about to get back into the swing of the evening when there was another knock on the door.

'Allen, Maud,' he greeted them, because of course they were here too. 'Merry Christmas.'

'Merry Christmas, lad,' Allen said. 'I feel like I've barely seen you around the place lately, so we couldn't miss the opportunity for the party.'

'Oh, there's a lot of young people here,' said Maud, taking a cautious step into the flat.

Flynn nodded, trying to look disappointed. 'I know; we'll completely understand if it's not your scene.'

'Nonsense!' Maud said, and started shuffling in.

Allen surveyed the scene with a beam on his face. 'We haven't been to a Christmas party like this since we lived in Stratford in our younger years.'

'Ah, you're an East Ender, Allen, like I was for a while.'

He nodded. 'Maybe I'll try and make some acquaintances this evening.'

Flynn's eyes widened and he called out loudly, 'Great! *August, look who's arrived*!'

August looked like she was about to say something to Callie, but stopped dancing while her gaze fell on her down-stairs neighbours. Her grin didn't falter for a minute, but Flynn knew her well enough now to know that behind the fake smile was a very real *Oh, shit*.

'Callie, look,' she said, 'Here's our other lovely neighbours. Why don't the three of you have a catch up while I get you all some drinks. Where's your mum gone?'

'We see each other all the time,' Callie waved her away and zeroed her focus in on Joe again.

Flynn caught her this time, taking her into his arms and dancing her in the general direction of the kitchen, i.e. the opposite end of the room to Joe. This was also where Callie's mum was. She in deep conversation with Kenny, who was delivering a monologue about how beautiful Flynn and August's wedding had been.

Kenny winked at Flynn in camaraderie, and continued saying, 'I was Flynn's best man and I managed to convince the whole wedding party to go swimming in the sea right before the ceremony.'

Flynn managed to unhook Callie's hand from his shoulder, placing it onto Kenny's instead and swung back around to help August with Allen and Maud. En route, he whispered in Joe's ear, 'If anybody says anything to you this evening about August and I being married, please just go with it.'

Joe's eyes crinkled at the edges and he started to laugh, his loud, booming laugh that made his whole beard shimmy. 'What—'

'No time to explain. I'll owe you one.' With that, Flynn returned to Allen just as he was about to open the door to August's room. 'You all right there, Allen?'

'Just looking for your bathroom, if you don't mind?'

'That door there,' Flynn pointed and off Allen shuffled.

Flynn caught August's eye across the room, where Maud was showing her photos on her phone of her grandkids, and August mouthed to him, 'I'm sorry.'

He shook his head at her and smiled. It wasn't her fault. Spotting Callie's discarded card on the side, he picked it up to read the wording.

We're having a Christmas Party! We hope you like parties, but just in case you don't we'll keep the noise down. From 7 to 11 in our flat (the middle), ready for you to have a 'silent night' afterwards. Merry Christmas! Love, August and Flynn x

Well, it was certainly enigmatic. He wasn't surprised the neighbours thought they were invited. This was going to be an interesting evening.

Chapter 62

August

August needed some air, just for a minute. She'd just got away from Maud, who was lovely, but was in full flow about her grandkids and where they lived, and when August happened to mention that she too used to live in West London it started a whole fresh batch of pictures to be brought out. Not to be unkind, but it was kind of killing her party buzz.

She stepped from the apartment, closing the door behind her and nearly colliding with Abe as he descended the stairs from the top floor.

'Abe!'

'Hello, August.'

'M-merry Christmas,' she stammered. It had been a while since she'd seen him, the last time being when he was in her apartment, and she'd rested her head on his shoulder. Since then, she'd felt his distance, noticed he hadn't been around as much, missed him finding reasons to text her, and vice versa. He was such an unexpected sight on the corridor; one, because she hadn't been expecting to see anyone out here, as most the residents were safely (or not safely) in her flat, and two, because she'd come out here for a breather, and not to have her breath taken away.

He looked relaxed in dark jeans, Nike trainers and a grey hoodie. His sandy hair seemed a little longer now, and he was a little stubblier, but not in a too-busy-to-shave way, more in a, I'm-just-taking-a-few-days-to-chill way. He stopped, right in front of her, his hand on the bannister, his body close.

'Merry Christmas to you,' he replied. And then, quietly, 'How are you doing?'

'I'm good,' she smiled, her gaze falling on his lips. She saw Abe glance at her door, where the sound of Jackson 5's 'Santa Claus Is Comin' to Town' could be heard within.

'We're having a little Christmas party, mainly for friends ... but um, some neighbours have shown up too. Would you like to come in?'

He hesitated. 'Well, I'm just on way down to the coffee shop at the end of the street to get Mum some pastries. Do you want anything?'

'They're open now?'

'It's Thursday, late night shopping. If I'm remembering correctly from last year, they stay open late too. Come with me if you like.'

'That's nice,' she paused. How she'd love a walk down the hill right now, a bit of cold air and space to think, but she couldn't leave Flynn dealing with the guests on his own.

'I'd better stay. But drop in on your way back past, it's good to see you.'

'Maybe,' he said.

'I hope we aren't being too noisy for your mum?'

'Not at all. It's funny, she was quite a social butterfly once but prefers quiet now; that's why she won't have come down. She'll have liked that you were all getting together though.'

'I can believe that, actually.'

Abe smiled. 'She's not the battleaxe she appears to be. At least not all the time.'

He waved goodbye and went off down the stairs, and August found herself watching him as he went. And hoping he came back.

'Wahey, look what I've got!' Callie shrieked. She'd legged it from the flat about five minutes ago and August pulled Flynn aside to seriously suggest locking the door behind her. She felt awful; this was supposed to be a stress-free, fun night for him and it had turned into a game of cat-and-mouse with the neighbours.

It simply shouldn't be this hard. Living a normal life in your own home *shouldn't be this hard*.

Then Callie had reappeared, throwing open August and Flynn's front door again, and swinging a massive bunch of mistletoe over her head.

'Yes,' cried Kenny, and August caught him shooting a thrilled look between her and Flynn.

Callie kicked off her heels and stood up on the sofa, attaching it to the light fixture hanging from their ceiling.

As soon as it was secure, she pointed across the room at Joe and said, 'You. Me. Under the mistletoe.'

Expecting Joe to run a mile, August saw Flynn's eyes widen when instead Joe strode over and said, 'Why not, eh? It's Christmas!' and planted a wet one right on Callie's mouth.

'Callie ...' Callie's mum shook her head and drank Prosecco straight from the bottle.

Bel and Steve hopped up and had a sweet smooch, where Steve dipped her like a *Strictly Come Dancing* finalist. This then prompted Allen to go one better with Maud, and lead her across the room in a tango before their own kiss.

There was so much cheering, August was almost able to pretend she didn't hear Callie's shout of, 'Now for the local newlyweds, come on Aug and Flynn!'

August laughed, acting like she was oblivious and racing towards the kitchen where she collided with Abe, and—

'Mrs Haverley!' She looked from her landlady back to Abe, untangling herself from his arms, their hands lingering together a moment longer than necessary. 'Abe! You both came! How *lovely*.'

'It's a very nice party,' Mrs Haverley said, holding onto her son's arm. 'I should have warned you about Callie's mistletoe obsession though. It was hung all over the building last year.'

The landlady looked tired, paler and more fragile than she had when August had been up in her apartment, though she'd made an effort in a long, beaded skirt and pearl-scattered blouse. Her hair contained a jewelled candy cane slide and there was red lipstick on her mouth. Her hips swayed to the music.

Abe looked into August's eyes for a moment and August could have sworn something passed between them.

But perhaps ... perhaps it was just those snowball cocktails.

All of a sudden Callie was beside her, dragging her away with a quick, 'Merry Chrimbo!' to Abe and Mrs Haverley. On Callie's other hand was Flynn, and she dragged the two of them into the centre of the room.

'Come on,' Callie slurred. 'Prove to me that love still exists; that you're still happily married.'

August jolted, meeting Callie's eye, and wondering if she imagined the millisecond of determination in her friend's face. She shook it off. Callie was tipsy, and already she was hungrily looking back over at Joe.

August tried to hide her sigh and tilted her cheek to Flynn for him to peck, and the crowd went wild ... with frustration.

'Oh, give her a real kiss,' shouted Callie. 'She's not your mum!' Then she turned to her own mum and said, 'Sorry, Mum.'

Flynn murmured to her, 'Well, who knew? There really is such a thing as an emergency kissing display.'

But this wasn't right. None of this felt right. The room seemed to spin with the lies and the pretence and there was Flynn in front of her – her Flynn, no attachments, waiting to kiss her. And across the room was Abe, who she barely knew but somehow felt she wanted to know more, and she couldn't stop herself thinking of him watching her. Like he would be able to tell somehow. Like she didn't want to kiss Flynn in front of him.

August felt dizzy and exposed under the mistletoe.

Chapter 63

Flynn

Flynn had been wanting to kiss her again for months, even if he'd only admitted it to himself recently. All his frustrations, all those other dates he'd gone on, all his pent-up feelings were a kiss away from drifting away, and he wanted to kiss her, not for show for others, but because he wanted to show *her* how he felt.

But she stopped him with a hand on her chest, a 'no' in her eyes, and within seconds she'd stepped away from him and become the laughing, gracious party host yet again, batting away protestations at the lack of a kiss with topped up drinks and compliments on the guests' dancing.

Flynn tried to compose himself, pretending to laugh along at Callie and her mum try a lindy hop to 'Rockin' Around The Christmas Tree', but he was crushed. She was definitely pulling away.

It seemed that was exactly what he had to do too,

enough was enough. He had no right to ruin her night or make demands.

She was perfectly okay without him.

When the Christmas party ended, and for the next week, both August and Flynn were subdued. What was meant to be a carefree night had felt jarring and difficult. Warm Christmas wishes had felt wrapped up in ribbons of deceit.

Flynn wasn't angry at August, of course he wasn't – far from it – but his feelings for her seemed impossible to live with.

He needed to talk with her, tell her about what he planned to do, but there never seemed to be a good time. And when he finally did have space with just her, it was Christmas Day.

They spent Christmas together, neither mentioning much about their absent parents, or about the strange void that had opened up between them. August and Flynn simply whiled away the day with quiet companionship, watching Christmas movies and going to their rooms for phone calls with loved ones. At the end of the day, they took glasses of mulled wine together onto the wall outside the house, and when they draped a blanket over the two of them to keep out Jack Frost, it felt like the first time they'd been in close proximity since their near-kiss.

'Merry Christmas,' Flynn had smiled, holding August's gaze.

'Merry Christmas, Flynn,' she replied. And as her head came to rest on his shoulder, he wasn't sure if everything was going to be all right, or whether his heart was going to slip and break at any moment.

Chapter 64

August

New Year's Eve had arrived, the 31st of December daylight hours whizzing by as if the calendar was excited to jump into January.

While Flynn had to work, of course, August had spent a quiet day in the flat, trying to tell herself that these strange feelings of discontent would be gone soon, a new year always makes things feel fresh again.

That evening, August was heading to a pub in town with Bel, Steve, Kenny, a few other familiar faces and friends, and hopefully Flynn, though at seven-thirty he text her to say he was a long way off finishing for the day.

August called him in return. 'That sucks,' she said, upon him answering.

Flynn sighed down the line. 'Tell me about it; sometimes I wonder if they sacked ten people before they hired just me to cover the work.'

'How long do you think you'll need to stay for?'

'I'm sure I'll be done by ten . . . '

'*Ten*?' she screeched. 'But it's New Year's Eve! Can't you just quit instead?' She was only half joking, because how much happier would Flynn be if he just packed it all in?

He laughed at that. 'Unfortunately, I ended up living in a flatshare with a steep rent, so I'd better not.'

'All right. Well, I'm heading out to meet the others soon, but come to the pub as soon as you can. I'll text you if we move on anywhere else.'

'Will do.'

'Enjoy lawyer-ing.'

'Enjoy partying like it's 1999.'

'Hey,' she said. 'It's not a party until you get there, okay?'

On the other end of the phone she heard Flynn stifle a yawn before saying, 'That's definitely accurate.'

'Are you and Flynn going to kiss again at midnight?' Kenny asked later that night, a wicked glint in his eye, shouting to be heard over the crowd of New Year's revellers inside the pub.

'Not if he never makes it out of work,' August shouted back, and then added quickly, 'But still no, I don't think that would be a good idea.'

'Why?' Kenny demanded.

'We're not in front of our landlady right now, or our neighbours, so why would we?'

Kenny roared with laughter at this, causing Bel to turn around and ask, 'What's going on?'

'She asked why on earth she would kiss Flynn at midnight!'

Bel thumped Kenny on the leg. 'Shut up, Kenny, or I'll fire you.' This just made him laugh more. 'Any news on that flatmate of yours?' she asked August.

August checked her phone – 10.45 p.m. Poor Flynn, that boy was not getting even a drop of work-life balance at the moment.

She went to the bar to get another drink for herself and Bel, and found herself wondering what Abe would be up to this evening over in London. Probably at the top of a skyscraper in the City at an eye-wateringly expensive bar, drinking champagne and surrounded by models.

August shook her head, now she'd tried to picture it that seemed a highly unlikely thing for Abe to be doing.

Perhaps he'd be reclining in a leather armchair with a cigar within the mahogany-panelled walls of an exclusive gentlemen's club. No, that didn't seem Abe's scene either. In fact, did gentlemen's clubs still exist? Were strip clubs now referred to as gentlemen's clubs?

'Two gin and tonics, please, and a couple of Budweisers,' she said to the barman, removing thoughts of Abe, and how he might or might not be spending New Year's Eve, from her head. She turned her attention back to her phone and sent Flynn a quick text: *Still no sign of coming up for air? I've got a beer here waiting for you, but should I get it Deliveroo-d to your office so you can catch up?*

A message came back shortly after: *Can you add a massive pizza to that order? I'm starving!*

Poor guy. *Are you serious?* she asked. *I can send some food and drink your way for real if you like?*

No, don't worry, I'll hopefully leave soon.

At eleven-fifteen, August made a decision. She picked up her coat and leaned over to Bel. 'I'm going to go and drag him out of that office,' she said, speaking loudly into her ear.

'You're leaving?' Bel cried. 'But it's nearly midnight.'

'I'll try and be back before then, but if I'm not, you guys have a great time.'

'Did you say you're going to try and get Flynn?'

'I'm going to try – even if I have to drag him from his work by the tie.'

Bel raised her eyebrows at that image.

August explained, 'He's had a tough year – a big break up six months ago, moving to the UK and not knowing anyone, his insane job, the whole Poppy debacle.'

'I know, I know, it's okay, go and meet him,' Bel laughed.

'I don't feel responsible for him or anything, he's a grown man,' August clarified.

'And he's your friend. I'm not judging you; stop judging yourself.'

'You're sure you don't mind?'

'No, I don't mind, go and drag him into the new year. If anyone can get him there, you can.'

August left the pub, skittering past a group of women about to raise a toast of towering champagne flutes and into late night Bath. The ground was wet but the winter drizzle had paused and now the sky was clear and starry, suggesting it wouldn't be coming back.

Walking past pubs and restaurants with their doors open and revellers spilling onto pavements, August strode through the city she knew so well, weaving through short-cuts and via alleyways until she reached Flynn's building. It was now twenty-five minutes to midnight, and she needed to get him out of there. It didn't matter if the ground was shaky beneath them right now, he was still Flynn, and he'd held her up enough times since they'd moved in together, she wanted to support him now.

August phoned him.

'Hey, I'm so sorry—' he started, but she cut him off.

'Are you still at work?'

'Yes, I really thought 10 p.m. seemed a long way off when we spoke earlier, but I've been lumped with a huge stack of case files for something high-profile going to court next week. Because of the skeleton staff covering the office between Christmas and New Year, there's nobody else here. Then I realised there was something I hadn't thought to check for and have had to go back over everything I've been doing today.'

'That's enough,' she interrupted him.

'I have to do it, August.'

Gentler this time, she pressed, 'Flynn, that's enough. I'm outside.'

Chapter 65

Flynn

Flynn, two floors up, looked through the window to see August standing on the street outside his office. Into the phone he said, 'What are you doing here? You should be in the pub with your friends.'

'You're my friend too, and if you can't make it to the pub, I've brought the pub to you.' She held up two bottles of Budweiser she'd carried with her. 'It's New Year's Eve, are you going to let me in?' He saw her surveying the front of the office, with its shutter down. 'Because if you're not ... I do know how to pick locks and I think I can get in here.'

He laughed. 'Of course you do. I'd better let you up, hadn't I?'

'Yep.'

A moment later, Flynn reached the side door, meeting her eye through the glass, unlocking the various bolts and keys. He opened the door and there she was, in pink sequins and

344

a gold headband emblazoned with the words *Happy New Year!!!!* Her eyes were pink and blue glitter, her shoes turquoise ankle boots. Against the backdrop of the dark night and damp street, she was like a bunch of flowers.

'Happy New Year!' she cried, handing a bottle to Flynn and shoving past him through the door. She stopped mid-stride, freezing on the spot and asking, 'I'm not going to set off a security alarm or anything, am I?'

'No,' he laughed. 'Want to see my desk?'

'I want to see all of it,' August answered, wandering on ahead of him, her eyes adjusting to the darkness of the rest of the open plan office. That is, until she banged against a table and nearly bent double, narrowly avoiding smacking her nose.

Flynn reached for her hand, which was both so familiar to him now but also felt unnatural in his, thanks to their shift at the Christmas party. He led her through the building towards his desk, where his lamp illuminated a great pile of papers and notes, Post-its scattered and highlighter pens with missing lids. 'Happy New Year,' he finally replied. 'Are you sure you want to be here?'

August handed him a beer. 'Of course I don't, but I also don't want you to be here. Can't you forget about it tonight and put in a couple of hours tomorrow?'

'I don't know, the thought of having to come back to it again tomorrow . . .' he sunk his chin onto his hand and tipped the beer into his mouth. He knew he looked as glum as Eeyore. Flynn then turned his eyes towards August, cracking a smile, and said, 'Jesus, I bet you're glad you left the party to come here!'

'I am!' August declared. 'Where else would I rather be, bedazzled up to the eyeballs in the pinkest, most sequinned dress Bath has ever seen?'

'You're right,' Flynn stood up. 'It's New Year's Eve ... It's New Year's Eve, for another—' he checked his watch. '—Fifteen minutes! Can you give me five minutes to pack my stuff and lock up?'

'To go where?'

'Back to the pub?'

'We'd be pushing it,' August admitted. 'And it's so crowded in there that come midnight we'd be fighting our way to try and make it back to Bel and the crowd.'

'Ah, August, I'm sorry. Is there somewhere nearer we could go?'

August fiddled with her phone for a moment, and all of a sudden Prince's '1999' burst into their atmosphere. She put the volume on full and used the last of her raspy voice to call loudly to Flynn, 'We can go right here.'

Grabbing her beer with one hand, and Flynn's shirt sleeve with the other, she pulled him up out of his chair and danced with him through his deserted office, her dress twinkling in the near dark as it reflected the bulb from his lamp.

Flynn was an awkward dancer next to August, his inhibitions a stark contrast against her abandon. And although he presumed she'd had a few drinks, and good for her if she had, it wasn't like that was her catalyst. This – this dancing, sparkling, colourful, laughing, zany woman who could act off the cuff or think things through long and hard – this was August. And he liked her, oh, a lot more than he should.

'Come on, we don't have time for self-consciousness, we have ten minutes to fit a whole night out into, and I didn't bring any extra beer, so you're just going to have to get into it.' August reached up and put her headband onto his head, smiling up at the result.

'It's okay for you, you're an actress, you're a lot more able to get into character than I am. My brain is still on data and evidence.'

She put a finger up to his lips and untucked his shirt from his trousers, her fingers grazing his stomach for a millisecond causing him to suck in his breath. 'Excuse me,' she purred over the music. 'I know your secret now.'

'You do?' he stopped dancing, his eyes fixing into hers for a moment.

'Yes,' she grinned. 'I know you're an actor too. Channel that *Grange Hill* spirit I saw on screen.'

'I don't think I danced a lot on *Grange Hill*,' he laughed, but he got what she was saying. 'I think I've done way more acting and dancing around topics in the last six months, actually.'

'You're a pro, then,' August clanked her beer bottle against his, and the music changed to Flo Rida's 'Club Can't Handle Me' from a few years back. August cheered. 'What a perfect song for us right now! Hey, do you have any secret stashes of whisky in your desk drawer?'

'No, this isn't *Suits*. Oh, but do you know who might?' Flynn took off across the floor, opening the door to his manager's office. Sure enough, on a side cabinet was a bottle of port, a Secret Santa gift from someone, which Flynn knew he'd seen in Sainsbury's so could replace it easily.

It was just like how it was when they first moved in together: easy, fun, seemingly uncomplicated. But back then it was their secret to keep from the world, and now he felt like it was him keeping something secret from her.

'I've got 'Auld Lang Syne' all cued up ready to play when we hit the countdown,' she told him, as he reappeared and poured big slugs of port into faded corporate retreat mugs from the staff kitchen.

He watched for a second as August danced about on her own, oblivious almost to the fact they weren't in a crowded bar or a club or even a party. It didn't seem to matter at all to her that she was spending New Year's Eve in an empty office, with just him.

Chapter 66

Flynn

A little before one in the morning on what was now New Year's Day, Flynn and August lay on their backs on a large table in one of the boardrooms, talking. He'd angled a projector away from the blank white wall and onto the ceiling, hooking his work laptop up to it and playing an ongoing YouTube video of fireworks. They burst into sparkling colours above the two of their heads, and they watched and admired with as much gusto as if they were on the riverbanks of London.

New Year's Day. That meant Flynn had been in the UK for six months now. Six months away from Japan, from his family, and from Yui, who was on his mind tonight more than usual these days.

'You work too hard,' August said.

'I know.'

'And you don't enjoy it.'

'I know ...'

'Was it ever like this at your job back in Japan?'

He thought about it for a moment. 'My immediate thought is no; it definitely wasn't this bad. But Yui may disagree with me about that. She always thought I worked too much.'

'Did it bother you?'

'No, she wasn't being a nag, she was right. It's just that now I look back and it feels like I had it easy,' Flynn gave a small smile, and August glanced over in time to see his face illuminated by a bright blue firework reflecting off the ceiling. 'It's ...' Flynn started a sentence he didn't know whether to finish, but after a while, unprobed by August (who knew he would finish it at some point), he continued.

'It's possible I ruined tonight without meaning to.'

'What do you mean?'

'I mean ... I hadn't really been looking forward to New Year's Eve, so maybe I buggered it up on purpose, but I didn't mean to drag you into it.'

August rolled her head to the side to really look at him now. 'What's wrong with New Year's Eve?'

'Last New Year's Eve I proposed to Yui.'

August gasped and sat up. 'You two were engaged?'

'No. She turned me down.'

'What?'

'Yep. She said we'd not been together long enough, and also, I think she thought the celebratory atmosphere had taken over my soul or something because it wasn't prepared, I didn't have a ring or anything, but I had meant it. So it still stung.'

'Was it downhill from there?'

'No, I don't think the proposal really changed the course of anything, it just certainly didn't push us on an upwards trajectory, that's for sure. New Year's Eve just brings back memories that I didn't want to think about, that's all.'

August lay back down and found his hand in the dark, slipping her palm against his, and remaining quiet while he let his thoughts position themselves.

Flynn spoke again. 'It's been six months; I just wish I could move past things.'

'Are you still in love with Yui?' August asked, her voice delicate.

'No,' Flynn said, knowing he sounded both honest and defeated. 'But I don't seem to have been able to move on, for some reason. I keep comparing everything to *her*. Comparing my life now to how it was then.'

'I'm no expert,' August started, 'But doesn't the act of getting over someone have to relate back to that person?'

'What do you mean?'

'Well, I don't see how you could have spent the last six months blocking out all thoughts and feelings about Yui, refusing to think of her at all. That's just not how the mind works, is it? And your feelings would probably have come back with a vengeance. So you take steps forward, and you meet new people, and you try new things, and you do it all with the thoughts of that person still with you. But those thoughts eventually begin to dilute, until one day they're just part of you, and your history, but no longer the biggest part of you.'

Flynn put a hand on his forehead, squeezing August's with his other. 'You're probably right. But right now I just can't help but wonder if all of this was a mistake.'

'A mistake?'

It pained him deeply to admit such a thing, especially to her while she, and happiness, felt within reach. But he couldn't put all of his happiness on her shoulders. How would that be fair? He sighed, and took his time saying the next part. 'Coming back to England.'

Chapter 67

August

August's heart broke a little in that moment, for him but also for her. Was she part of his mistake?

'All my family are in Japan now, I enjoyed my job *a lot* more, I had Yui and maybe it wouldn't have worked out anyway but at least I'd know. And you and I, well ...'

August held her breath, waiting to hear his thoughts.

Flynn continued. 'Sometimes I just wonder why I left.'

'Because you wanted a change, and a new adventure. There's nothing wrong with following that,' August said, trying to smother the desperation in her voice, because this wasn't about her.

'But where's it got me? A job that takes up so much time I hardly see anything outside the office walls. A new girlfriend who ran a mile.'

August gulped. 'Can't you think of one good thing about being here?'

He looked towards her, meeting her eyes in the darkness. 'You, of course. Of course meeting you and living with you has been incredible, and crazy, and hard work, and hilarious. Don't doubt that. But we can't deny that it's caused a few problems.'

'Do you feel bad about ... you know ... lying?'

'About us, to everyone in the building?'

'Yes.'

'Yep,' Flynn answered. 'Do you feel like it's been a lot harder than we thought it would be?'

'Yes,' August replied with a chuckle. 'You?'

'So much harder. And so much more fun as well, at times.'

'We have had some good times,' she smiled at him.

They lay in the dark, hands held, looking into each other's eyes with faux-fireworks overhead – which felt pretty consistent with a lot of their relationship – and neither realised they were both thinking how easy it would be to kiss the other right now. Or maybe they did suspect it, but taking that action, when it wasn't for an 'audience' or for 'practice' would change everything.

'Why do we keep doing these romantic things?' Flynn asked, holding his breath as soon as the words were out of his mouth.

'I don't know,' August let out a tinkle of a laugh, though inside she had a million thoughts, she just didn't know how to express them. Besides, it seemed clear to her that he had some real figuring out to do about a few things before she muddied his thoughts with her own confusion also. 'Do you really feel like you made a mistake coming here?' she asked him.

'Honestly? Probably not. But I feel homesick, Aug, which kinda tells me England isn't really my home anymore.'

August was losing him, this guy she'd become so fond of, had relied on so much, and had fallen in love with, in a way, even if the love she felt *was* just . . . friendship.

'August?' he said, interrupting her thoughts.

'Mmm-hmm?'

'I need to tell you something.'

August was silent, staring at the ceiling and the fireworks, waiting for him to tell her what she'd already been suspecting.

'I'm going to go back to Japan—'

'What?' she gasped. 'I thought you were going to say you'd move out, not go home!'

'Do you want me to move out?' he asked.

'No! Do you?'

'I don't know.' He squeezed her hand tightly. 'But I meant what I said after we had our argument: we need some time apart, out of our bubble. I have to do some thinking about what I want and I need it to be away from our flat, and work, and everything. And I think you should do the same.'

'But would you be moving back to Japan?'

'No, not initially, but I can't promise you I won't. I'm going to start with going back for a couple of weeks, to visit my family, maybe talk to Yui. I need a break from all of this.'

'Find yourself,' August said, quietly. This felt like it could be the end, but she could see he needed this.

After a while, Flynn voiced a concern. 'What if I decide I want to stay out there?'

'I think you're already trying to decide that, aren't you?'

Flynn agreed. 'I guess I am.'

'Just go for it, let yourself really think about it without any pressure.'

'Will you be okay if I go?'

She smiled, as genuinely as she could muster. 'I survived a long time without you, Flynn Miyoshi, I can survive again with you gone.'

He sat up and moved over to her, pulling her up to seating too, the fireworks still popping overhead, and wrapped his arms around her. 'You're a good friend, August Anderson.'

'I know,' she said into his chest, breathing him in. 'Just bring me back some of those matcha KitKats, okay?'

'Deal.'

They embraced and it was for more than friendship, it was for reassurance, for a goodbye. It was to share the curiosity about what could have been. It was for a fresh start and for happiness.

When Flynn broke free and helped her off the table, he asked, 'What will we tell the neighbours, if they ask?'

August hopped onto the floor and gathered up the mugs and bottles, and followed Flynn back through the office, where he packed away his things, yawning, both of them ready to call it a night. 'I'll just say you've gone for business – and that's why I haven't gone with you – but you thought you'd stay on a bit to visit family while you were there.'

He looked at her face as they stepped into the cold night air, she watched as his eyes trailed over the shape of her eyelashes, her nose, her lips and she wondered if he'd ever tell her truly what he was thinking. The street was now quieter than when August had run up it an hour and a half ago, though some people were still partying strong. 'And what if I go for good?'

'Then I guess we get a divorce,' August replied, and it took everything she had but she kept that smile in place.

'I don't want to divorce you,' Flynn said.

'You don't know what you want,' she teased in return, and extracted herself from the moment before either of them allowed whatever always drew them together to become a cloud across his thoughts right when he needed a clear head. 'Now let's go home, get some sleep, and tomorrow you need to book that much-needed time off work.'

'Yes, boss,' he said.

When they arrived home, they crept through the building quietly, and it wasn't until they were inside their flat and were about to leave each other at their respective bedroom doors that they spoke again.

'Happy New Year,' August whispered.

'Happy New Year,' Flynn replied. He paused at the door, as if this were the beginning of the end. 'Am I doing the right thing?' he asked August, though he was also, really, asking himself.

August nodded with confidence. 'Yes, one hundred per cent. I think you owe it to yourself to do this. It's your life.'

After he'd disappeared into his room, August moved not in towards her own bed, but to the living room window, looking out at the nightscape of Bath that she'd grown so in love with. It wouldn't change, even if he went, even if she couldn't live here anymore. But knowing that her time to share this with him was trickling away caused her to turn away from the view.

Chapter 68

August

Over the first two weeks of January, while Flynn prepared for his trip to Japan, August threw herself into her work. It was one thing for her to tell Flynn he needed to take back control of his life and decide what he wanted, but she knew she needed to face that in herself too.

She said yes to opportunities for voice work that she'd previously shied away from, following her failed audition; things that were challenging or out of her comfort zone. She found a local amateur dramatics group and called them to see if they could meet at some point. She updated her online profiles and started chatting to other actors and agents on social media. The Tony felt a long way off, a *very* long way, but it felt good to work for something.

The more time she spent in her booth, now fully sound-proofed, the more she remembered how much she loved voice acting, but it also allowed her to block out what was happening in her apartment. And she wondered … if things hadn't gone so terribly during her audition, would she have found this sparkle for her work again?

Flynn seemed lighter, happier – he said knowing he would soon be having a break from work to go home and see his family was the tonic he needed. But although August was sure that was all true, she also wondered whether potentially rekindling things with Yui – and moving back to Japan to be with her – was also playing a part in his change of mood.

One thing was clear: the romantic thoughts about Flynn that had bobbed to the surface time and again since they'd moved in together had to be pushed down. This was not about her or her journey or her feelings, there were things Flynn needed to figure out by himself. She needed to step away.

When the time came for Flynn to leave for the airport, early in the morning on a cold Saturday in January, August held back her sorrow.

'I'll see you in about three weeks,' Flynn said, hugging her goodbye.

'Have a good time, you deserve it.'

'Thanks.'

August punched him lightly on the arm, which felt awkward and unnatural, but hey, it was done now. 'Go and sort your head out,' she instructed.

Flynn gave her a smile and she took in his face one last time.

Once he'd gone, closing the door softly behind him, his suitcase disappearing from view, the apartment was quiet.

Quieter than when Flynn was just out for the day, it was almost like the walls held their breath, afraid to move in case they came crumbling down. August climbed into her grandma's armchair and allowed herself a cry.

She cried because she didn't know if Flynn would be coming home.

The following day, August rose early and treated herself to a Sunday morning bath, and then she made a coffee in her travel mug and left the house on Elizabeth Street early to take a walk as the sun came up. Slowly, the frost on the ground melted and the crisp sky became an ice blue, and August walked and walked, tiring out her legs long after the coffee was drained.

Flynn would be in Japan now, at his parents' house, which he'd mentioned was somewhere not that far from Tokyo. She wondered what he was doing, but tried not to dwell. Instead she focussed on the here and now – *her* here and now – and savoured the cold, minty air, the sounds of the birds waking up, the yawning of the Bath buildings as they woke up and stretched under the winter sunshine.

And when finally she returned to Elizabeth Street, rounding the brow of the hill, she saw something unexpected; something that made her smile.

Chapter 69

Flynn

Though it was morning in England, it was early evening in Japan, and Flynn was struggling to stay awake at his parents' house, desperate to not let jet lag get the better of him this time. His journey back had been a wonderful contrast from his journey to the UK – smooth, on time, no delays, no turbulence, and by the time he'd touched down he already felt like his work stresses were a million miles away.

And so was August, but he needed to at least try not to think about her too much while he was here.

He took a can of iced coffee from his parents' fridge and padded outside on to their decking to take in the countryside, with Mount Fuji rising in the distance. It was very different from Bath, but every bit as beautiful.

He felt like he was home.

Chapter 70

August

'Morning, Abe,' August said, approaching the wall in front of the house.

He looked up and beamed. 'Good morning. I'm back!'

'I can see that. I haven't seen you since the Christmas party. How have you been?'

'Good. And you? Happy New Year.'

'Happy New Year to you.' August sat next to him on the wall, keeping a little gap between them this time, unsure what Abe thought of her even though she had her suspicions. 'How's Mrs H?'

'Eh ...' he trailed off, lost in thought for a moment. 'She's okay. She was telling me about your visit to her a few weeks ago?'

'It was nice,' August replied. 'She had Advocaat, which I hadn't had since my gran was alive.'

'She loves Advocaat; her mum – my gran – always had it

around too. She mentioned your gran actually, weren't the two of them friends?'

'Yes,' August cried. 'I can't believe I didn't realise the whole time I lived here that actually Mrs Haverley, your mum, was the "Windy Day" my grandma brought me in here to visit when I was little. I don't think they were super close – your mum was a bit younger than my gran, but they were definitely friends.'

'That's funny. Did my mum remember you coming over when you were little?'

'She says she did, but I'm not so sure, and I wouldn't blame her, it was a long time ago.'

'It's nice that you had that connection,' Abe commented, and drifted into his thoughts for a second before saying, 'Mum's got more closed off over the years and sometimes it's good to remember who you were in the past—' He stopped, and cleared his throat, as if he was getting a bit deep. 'So anyway, thank you. Where's Flynn?'

He caught her eye again at the mention of Flynn, and August had to look away. 'He's away at the moment, in Japan.'

'Japan! Business or pleasure?'

'A bit of both,' she said, fixing her gaze forward, not comfortable lying to Abe after the truthful moment he'd just shared with her.

The two of them made their way back inside, and on the stairs Abe said, 'I'll be back next weekend. If you need anything while your, um, Flynn's away just let me know.'

'See you next weekend,' she whispered after him, looking forward to it already.

Chapter 71

Flynn

Flynn had spent the best part of a week in Japan, relaxing with his family, catching up on sleep, visiting with old friends, before he took the trip into the centre of Tokyo to see one of the main people he needed to reconnect with.

A Sunday morning in Tokyo can feel as busy as a Saturday morning in other parts of the world, and Flynn loved it. He stood on the pavement facing the tower block where he lived for a year, the bright white January sky glinting off the panes of glass. As he stood still, around him, people went about their days, enjoying their leisure time, wrapped in layers to protect them from the bitter weather.

It was nice to be home.

But this particular building wasn't his home anymore, and with a glance at his watch, he moved on, saying a final, silent goodbye to the window that once had been his, all those storeys up.

He wondered if Yui still lived there. He'd soon find out.

Flynn had thought about visiting Yui at home, assuming that was still her home, but had changed his mind shortly before getting in touch with her. It wasn't about the flat they'd lived in, it was about them, it had always been about them, and he didn't want to muddy his thoughts by feeling nostalgia for a home that was no longer his.

Instead he'd kept it simple, and told her he was in Tokyo to visit his family, that he'd really like to talk to her, and could they meet up for a walk in Koishikawa Korakuen gardens, one of their favourite places to take an al fresco coffee. He'd waited a full day and night for her to respond, and when she did, it was in agreement.

Entering the park, Flynn felt like he had the koi from the pond leaping about in his stomach. For most of their relationship he'd seen Yui every single day, and that had been stripped away to him not seeing her now for over six months. Not speaking with her. Not looking at pictures of her. Would it be like reuniting with an old friend, or a stranger?

He sat on a bench and pulled out his phone while he waited for Yui to arrive, scrolling back through his photos, letting his eyes fill with images of Bath, and he settled on one of August sitting on the wall outside their house, drinking her morning cup of tea, that he'd taken from their living room window. He wondered what she was doing at that moment.

Chapter 72

August

At that moment, actually, August was sleeping. It was one in the morning in the UK, and August had spent her Saturday doing two things she couldn't have even imagined doing a few months ago.

One was that during the week she had landed her first audiobook to record in her new booth – an eerie thriller – and today was the day she'd been planning to get started. Or, get started again, because she only realised after five chapters in the day before that her jewellery was making a load of background tinkles in an otherwise tense scene and she had to remove it all and start over.

And two was that she spent the day hanging out with the landlady and her son.

Moments before shutting the door of her booth on Saturday morning and closing out the sounds of the world, August had heard Abe on the stairs with his mum, a full week after she'd last seen him. August dived from the booth, leaving behind the audiobook and oh-so-subtly zoomed from her flat to run into them as they descended.

Mrs Haverley was slow, gripping the railing with the determination of someone who might bite your head clean off and spit it down the hill if you so much as muttered the suggestion of a chair lift being installed. Abe walked beside her, carrying her bag, holding an arm aloft in case she needed it. Mrs Haverley looked up at the sound of August tumbling out of her door below them. 'Is that August or Callie?' she barked, keeping her eyes on the stairs.

Abe glanced down and met August's eye, a smile spreading across his face that she echoed. 'Hello,' he said, greeting her with a warm tone, like hot chocolate.

'Hey, welcome back,' she replied.

'Oi,' Mrs Haverley hissed at her son, not very quietly. 'She's married, you know. Now give me that arm.'

'Mum, I know,' Abe cried, and August held back a chuckle. 'We're heading down into town, to the Fashion Museum. Mum wants me to pick her out a funeral gown.'

'I do not, stupid boy.' She thwacked him one, but August could hear the gentle teasing in both of their voices. Mrs Haverley rounded the staircase onto her landing at that moment and looked her up and down, taking in her lime green leggings, baggy grey sweatshirt with huge Disney castle motif, and neon yellow hoop earrings. 'You look like a girl who appreciates ... fashion ... would you care to come with?'

'Oh,' August tugged on her sweater. 'I think I'm actually very unfashionable, but what I do appreciate is colour.'

368

'Then you'll enjoy the frocks, let me tell you,' Mrs Haverley said, and without a pause, she continued her descent and barked, 'Come along.'

August glanced at Abe who shrugged and continued after his mother down the stairs, but when she didn't move he turned back and whispered with a smirk, 'Come along!'

She didn't feel at all dressed for a fashion museum, and she really had some work to do, but after only a moment's dilly-dallying August grabbed her coat and her ankle boots, and hopped down the stairs after them.

'Were you going somewhere?' Abe asked as the three of them took a slow walk down Elizabeth Street towards the town.

'When? Now? Am I not coming with you?' August asked.

'No, before. You looked like you were just leaving your flat before we accosted you.'

'Oh right. Erm. No, I was just going to run outside and see what the temperature was like.' What a lame excuse – Abe knew full well she had windows in her flat.

'Right,' he answered. 'How's Flynn getting on in Japan?'

'Flynn is in Japan?' Mrs Haverley shrieked as if she'd never heard such madness. 'That's the other side of the world! Has he left you?'

'No, no,' August replied, keeping her eyes forward. 'His family lives out there and he was taking a business trip, so ...'

'When will he be home?'

'Another couple of weeks, actually.'

Mrs Haverley tutted, but didn't follow it up with any more

comments, so perhaps she hadn't quite known why she'd done so any more than the rest of them.

'Have you been all right?' Abe asked, seeming to choose his words carefully.

August waved him away. 'Yeah, fine. How are you? How was your week in London?'

'All right, same old. I went on a Jack the Ripper walking tour on Wednesday evening.'

'You did?' asked August. 'I played one of his victims once, in an am-dram play on the street in Whitechapel. It was quite gory, really, now I think about it.'

'I told you she was an actress,' Mrs Haverley said sharply to her son.

'I already know, Mum,' he said.

'Was the walk good?' August asked. She couldn't quite imagine Abe, sweet but serious as he seemed, taking himself off for a guided two-hour history jaunt.

'It was great,' he enthused. 'Really informative, and so strange to stand on the cobbles where those poor women were murdered.'

'Why were you doing such a thing?' Mrs Haverley asked, pausing to take a break at the bottom of the hill.

Abe looked a little abashed. 'I just felt like it, I was bored.'

He was lonely, August thought. She knew, because she used to do the same kind of thing. 'When I lived in London I often had times when I felt a bit . . . bored, or at a loose end, or whatever. I used to do those walking tours sometimes. They're so affordable and *so* good. Another thing I used to do was visit the museums in Kensington. If I wanted to kill an hour or two I'd go with the sole purpose of hitting just one gallery on that visit and doing it really properly. I never got around to doing all the galleries in all the museums though, by the time I left.'

'I like that idea,' Mrs Haverley gave a nod of approval, and August noticed she raised her eyebrows at Abe much to say, *you like it too, don't you, boy-o.*

'Have you been to the Fashion Museum before, Mrs H?' August asked and then cringed; she must stop calling her Mrs H in public, she didn't want to sound rude.

'Oh yes,' Mrs Haverley smiled, the same smile she'd shown when August had chatted with her about her grandma, the one that shined across her whole face. 'I worked there for many years. I started back in the seventies; it was called The Museum of Costume back then.'

'Did you enjoy it?' August asked.

'Very much. The fabrics, the detail, the colours,' she winked at August.

'Did you work there until you retired?'

'Not quite,' Mrs Haverley answered. 'I left for a while after this one was born,' she motioned to Abe.

The three of them made small talk as they wove their way down towards the Fashion Museum, housed within the beautiful coffee-coloured Assembly Rooms on Bennett Street, which always tickled August's Austen-loving heart. As they walked around the museum, admiring the collections and after August had insisted that even if nobody else was, she was going to try on the Georgian gown on the dress-up display, Abe held back, putting his hand on August's arm. Mrs Haverley walked on ahead, lost in thought and memory.

'Thanks for coming to this,' he said to her, his hand still on her arm, which she was more aware of than all of the swathes of gold and silver threads around them.

'My pleasure,' she replied. 'I'm having a nice time.'

'Are you?' Abe asked, and his eyes fixed hers for a moment, before he slowly removed his hand and lowered his gaze to the floor also.

'Yes, I am,' said August. And she really was, though six months ago she couldn't have in a million years imagined being close enough with the battleaxe landlady to be taking a trip out with her and getting along like old chums. Callie had been telling the truth: Mrs H really was kind of fun.

But also . . . with Flynn on the other side of the world, possibly reuniting with his ex-girlfriend, being with Abe really felt like it might be a chance for her heart to stop fannying about, fluttering around Flynn like a confused butterfly. She hadn't been looking for a man to replace Flynn, she hadn't been looking for a man at all, but it just seemed to be working out that way.

Except for that one little, tiny detail, that caused her to sigh out loud and Abe to look through his lashes at her again. He thought she was a married woman. And if she told him the truth, that they'd been lying to him and to his mother this whole time, would he still want to touch her arm like that?

The rest of the afternoon was pleasant. More than pleasant: it was fun. August enjoyed Abe's company, and, much to her surprise, Mrs Haverley's as well.

By the time she climbed into bed that night, and drifted off to sleep, and it reached one in the morning, she was enjoying a dream about playing Harry Potter himself in the stage show of *The Cursed Child*. And she was nearly, almost, successfully managing to not think about Flynn too much at all.

Chapter 73

Flynn

'*Ohayo*, Fujio,' a familiar voice said, sounding out his real first name and interrupting his thoughts.

There she was. Yui stood in front of him as familiar as the day he'd said goodbye, in everything except the expression on her face. She didn't look pained or angry, she didn't even look distant, which had been his biggest worry, he now realised. She looked content.

He stood up, and after a moment's hesitation on how to greet each other, she made the first move to hold out her arms and they embraced, softly, quickly, and accompanied by a small laugh.

'I bought you a coffee – a matcha latte – is that okay?' Flynn asked, handing her one of the cups on the bench.

'Of course, that's perfect, thank you,' Yui replied, warmly.

They of course spoke in easy Japanese, something Flynn was enjoying flexing his vocal muscles around again. He was enjoying a lot about being back here, and stealing a glance at Yui, he knew he was enjoying her company again as well.

'How are you?' Flynn asked.

'I'm good, very well. How are you? How is England?'

'It's . . . different.'

'Different? Do you mean different from when you lived there before?'

'Different from here,' he clarified. 'Everything feels very, very, different.'

'Are you not happy?' Yui asked.

'Not really,' he admitted. He felt foolish doing so, partly wishing he was back here telling Yui that everything was great, that it was the right decision. But he was tired; he'd done a lot of pretending, one way or another, over the past few months. And so he confessed, 'Sometimes I wonder if this was just one huge mis-step.'

'Why?' Yui asked, seeming genuinely puzzled. 'It's never a mistake if there's an adventure beside it. Aren't you having an adventure?'

'There never seems to be time for adventuring because my job is so busy. I had this image of learning all about the history of the city of Bath, taking trips around the UK, visiting old haunts and new roads. Then having weekends away across Europe, seeing all the countries I'd never made it to before in big, bright detail. But I've barely done any of it. All I see in detail are legal documents, spreadsheets, the walls around my desk.'

Yui was silent for a while, sipping her drink, digesting

what he'd said, until she said, 'You were the same here too, you know.'

This surprised him. 'What do you mean?'

'When we first got together, you talked about the excitement of moving to Japan a couple of years previously, how there was so much you wanted to see here. You were going to snowboard in the north and visit your grandmother down in the south. You were going to jump on planes and visit China and Taiwan. You were going to eat at every restaurant in Tokyo.'

Flynn felt a sadness at all the missed opportunities, all the things he'd never done when he lived in Japan. This was all the more reason to come back, permanently, right?

'Don't look so glum, that isn't why we broke up,' Yui continued, giving him a nudge. 'You never promised me we'd do all those things, and they weren't the reason I was with you. I'm just ... pointing out that this situation isn't new for you. It's not a bad situation *because you moved to England*.'

They walked in silence for a few minutes, with Flynn wondering what to say. He had a million questions he wanted to ask her, about her family, their friends, her life, but they all felt like the kind of questions you ask when you haven't seen someone in a few weeks, not half a year.

'How's your work?' he settled on eventually. It was an extremely dull question, and he had the flash image of August swatting him with a magazine for being so beige among all of this colour and beauty in the gardens, and next to Yui.

'It's fine, same as usual,' Yui said.

'And your family?'

'Everyone's doing well.'

'Do you still live in our apartment?' he asked, needing to know.

'No,' she shook her head. 'I moved out a month or so after you'd gone. It wasn't right for me anymore. I'm now in a place by myself, it's really nice. Small and cosy and has a view over the Sumida River.'

'That sounds perfect for you,' he answered. She'd always loved the water. In their worst days, when they seemed to argue whenever they had a rare moment together, Yui would take herself off for long jogs from their apartment block and alongside the river.

'It is, it suits me.' The way she said it felt dipped in sentiment, like she was trying to tell Flynn in the kindest possible way that *he* hadn't suited her, that *he* hadn't been right for her anymore. 'What is your home like in England? Do you live on your own?'

'No . . .' he paused. 'I share the flat with a woman, actually, but she's just a flatmate.' *Just a flatmate.*

'Does she find your early-morning banana milkshake habit as annoying as I did?' Yui asked, and chuckled.

Flynn thought of August, and how at the sound of the blender she'd always appear, no matter how early, in the kitchen, sniffing at the air. He knew now to always make enough for her to have one too. Bananas had been added to the 'shared' shopping list long ago. 'Luckily for her, the blender we have is much quieter than the one you and I owned.' Flynn remembered that blender well, a gift from

Yui's parents which she'd never quite forgiven them for, that churned and ground away like a pneumatic drill was being used inside the apartment.

'What's her name?'

'August,' Flynn handled her name with care, unsure how Yui would respond to it.

'August . . . ' Yui turned the name over in her mouth. 'Like the month?'

Flynn only nodded.

'Do you and August live in a tall building, like you and I used to?'

'No, it's a house converted into flats, just a few neighbours sharing the same roof.'

'And does it have a view?'

'It does, you can see the whole city stretched out before you. I can see why some people would climb all the way to the top of the hill again and again, year after year, just to look at the view.'

'So the city is beautiful, you have a nice place to live, good company, good health, the only real problem is the job?'

'And I don't have you,' he confessed.

'Fujio . . . ' Yui put her hand on his arm, signalling him to come to a stop. They paused on a low wooden bridge, a stream running underneath it, babbling softly. She took a deep breath, and Flynn already knew what she was going to say, he could see it in her face, kind though her expression was.

Yui took a beat before speaking. 'You wouldn't have me, even if you came home. You know that, right? Even if you'd stayed in Japan and never left, you still wouldn't have me, not anymore.'

His shoulders sank, not with the weight of his sadness, as he'd thought they might if Yui said this, but with relief. Relief to finally *know* the answer to the question that had troubled him for months. It was still sad, of course, and would take some adjusting to, but if anything it was now like a weight had finally been lifted..

'It wasn't working, was it?' he asked, leaning down on the railing of the bridge, but turning his face to look at her. 'We weren't working.'

Yui simply shook her head.

'You don't think it would have made any difference if I'd stayed?'

'Do you?' she asked, a half-smile on her lips.

'I honestly didn't think I knew the answer to that this whole time.'

'I think deep down you knew it before you accepted that job. I don't believe you would have taken it – you probably wouldn't have even applied for it – if you hadn't already known we were lowering the curtain on us.' Yui said this without judgement, without bitterness. Flynn could see she'd moved on, and now he just needed to catch up with her.

'You seem happy,' Flynn stated. 'Are you?'

'I am. Is that the answer you came all the way across the world to hear?' she joked.

Was he happier knowing she was happy? It didn't make sense to him, because if she was happier now than she'd been when they'd been a couple, shouldn't that make him sad? Shouldn't he feel resentful and even more lonely? Maybe he should; who's to say how a person 'should' feel? But he didn't. If anything, Yui's happiness gave him permission from himself to let go. And so in reply to her, before they went away from the Japanese gardens in two different directions, he told her, 'Yes.'

Chapter 74

August

August poured Abe a glass of wine. Another week had passed, or close enough, and he was back in Bath again, this time coming down early for the Thursday evening. He'd knocked on her door on his way up the stairs, carrying a duffel bag and wearing his work suit, and had asked how she was.

'I'm good,' she said, cursing her straggly hair and the yellow monster feet slippers she'd bought on impulse during the week and had barely taken off since. 'How are you? Is your mum okay?'

'She's fine, well, not fine, but no different. So, still seems a bit unwell, really, I suppose.' He lingered in her doorway.

'Do you want to come in or do you need to go straight up?'

'I could come in,' he answered immediately.

'Wine?' she asked, picking a bottle out of the rack. She wouldn't usually drink on a work night but ... who was she kidding, yes she would.

'Yes, please,' he answered, and took a seat on the arm-chair. He then moved to the sofa, and then back to the armchair. He stood up when she brought the wine over. 'Where should I sit?'

'Anywhere you like,' she answered. She glanced at the bedroom doors; both were closed. It had become a habit that she and Flynn kept their doors shut now, in case anyone popped by, but it still didn't hurt to check. She also mentally clocked the rest of her surroundings. Wedding photos upright: check.

Abe took a seat on the sofa in the end, so August squashed down on the armchair, feeling like the two of them together on the sofa might send him running.

He seemed distracted though this evening, focussed on something else, more like he was the first time they met than the last few times, especially last weekend. 'Are you okay?' she asked him.

'Hmm? Oh yes, I'm fine,' he said, and took a gulp of his wine. 'How are you? How was work today?'

'Good, actually, I finished a bit early and came home to do a bit of recording and found out I'd been booked for another job, voicing a cartoon character for an episode of a new Netflix series!'

'That's amazing!'

'It's just on one episode, not like, a recurring character, but still.' August couldn't help but beam. She'd never voiced a cartoon character before, and she nearly hadn't gone for the role. But she'd had a photo text from Flynn during his first few days in Japan, showing a pile of interestingly flavoured

KitKats he'd bought for her, and she'd taken the colourful animal characters on the front of some of them as a sign.

'I think that's very cool,' Abe nodded, and then drifted back into silence again.

'Are you sure everything is all right with your mum? You seem ... distracted,' asked August.

'Yes, well. Is Flynn still in Japan?'

'Yep, for another week-ish,' she answered, her answer feeling loaded.

'Great. I mean, not great, for him. But.' Abe stopped talking and stood up in front of her as if he was about to declare something, before backing off and leaning against the back of the sofa, maintaining a distance between the two of them.

Eventually he spoke, his voice soft, his eyes downcast. 'I feel stupid. Because I came home early this weekend, not for Mum, she's probably sick of the sight of me by now, but ... to see you.'

August held her breath. *What did this mean?* 'To see me?'

He nodded and rubbed a palm across his forehead, before gulping at his wine again. 'I'm so, so stupid, and I'm sorry, I didn't mean anything by it, I'm not trying to muscle in on anything just because Flynn's away. I'm just lonely and we get on, that's all.' He stood up, flustered.

August stood too. Abe liked her. She was sure this is what he was saying. Wasn't it? Or was it just like he said, that he was lonely and he saw her as a friend, but felt like that was encroaching on a boundary?

She should tell him the truth. Right now. She could just let the words spill out that she was single and then whatever he was thinking would be okay. She and Flynn had spoken about how this couldn't go on for ever, after all ... sort of. She opened her mouth but the words caught in her throat.

Abe went to the door. 'I should go up to Mum. Let me know if you want to hang out at all this weekend. Or not. As friends, of course.'

'Abe—' she stuttered and he turned, looking at her with a sadness that made her want to wrap her arms around him. Those words were right there: *I'm single. I'm not really married to Flynn. Do you like me?* But instead she said, 'Shall we get dinner or something tomorrow, and just chat?'

Abe nodded at that, his lips parted like he wanted to say – or do – something else, but he then clamped them shut and turned to walk out the door.

'Tomorrow, then?' August clarified.

He looked back at her. 'Tomorrow.'

August wasn't sure what they'd both agreed to, exactly, but she had until tomorrow to decide what she wanted.

Chapter 75

Flynn

The third time Flynn nearly sliced into his finger instead of a mushroom, his mother took the knife out of his hand and replaced it with a beer. 'You're no use to me in this state, Flynn,' she scolded, softly. 'Just leave it to me.'

Flynn sat on a bar stool in his parents' kitchen, their window facing out onto a lake, Mount Fuji's peak visible in the background on a clear day, like today. His father was in the garden, finding extra fresh vegetables to add to their lunch, and Flynn had spent the morning, well, actually the whole time since he'd boarded the train and returned from Tokyo last weekend, thinking about his future. And his past.

'Can we talk about Yui yet?' Mrs Miyoshi asked. She spoke to him in her native English, just as happy to utilise that language as Flynn had been to use his Japanese when he arrived back in the country.

Flynn laughed at that. 'Of course, what do you want to know?'

'Oh, I don't know,' his mum said. 'How is she? How did it go? Are you still in love with her?'

'She's fine, good even. Happy, actually. It was nice to see her – and no, I'm not still in love with her.'

'Oh.'

'Oh?' he questioned.

'I just . . . ' she trailed off for a moment. 'I presumed she was the reason you came back.'

'She was, in a way, in the same way you and dad are, and Japan in general is. I just missed my life.'

'Your life now isn't so bad, you know,' she replied, raising an eyebrow at him as if to say, *Millennials*.

'Agreed, agreed, I'm just doing some thinking about what I really want.'

'But you weren't thinking about Yui, just now?'

'No,' he replied with honesty. He'd been thinking about August.

'What's the smile for?' Mrs Miyoshi probed. 'Do you have a girlfriend in England?'

He shook his head. He hadn't told his parents about Poppy, and now it was over before it had ever really begun, there seemed little point. Instead he tried to change the subject, seek some advice. 'Do you think I should quit my job?' he asked, just as his dad walked in the room.

'Quit your job?' Mr Miyoshi parroted. 'In England?'

'Yes,' Flynn replied, switching back to Japanese.

'For another job?'

'Or to come back here.'

'Why would you come back here?' his father asked, bluntly, as his wife took the handful of vegetables from his hands. 'Fujio, are you happy?'

He thought about it, but he didn't have to think for long. 'No. But I worry it's just because of all the changes.'

'Change is fine, it's part of life,' his mum said, echoing words to him that she and his father had always lived by. 'We can still appreciate the past and enjoy its memories. But you need to be happy, that's what is important.'

'Why can't you be happy at the moment?' Flynn's dad asked. 'Why do you think you need to quit your job?'

'Because I'm tired and overworked.' *And because I've fallen for my flatmate, who isn't interested in me like that.*

His mum, who had always been a big believer in following the heart instead of the head, which was how she'd spent her life between two different continents, said, 'There is happiness in time-affluence, Flynn. If you don't have the time to do the things that make you happy, then working all the extra hours and earning all the extra money isn't going to make you wealthy.'

'You're very wise, Mother,' Flynn said, thinking about what she'd said.

And so Flynn got in the car. He drove towards Mount Fuji and parked where he could see her shoot straight up into the air, white tipped and full-skirted. He had so much of Japan he still wanted to explore that he'd never given himself the freedom to do so. He wanted to climb in the Japanese Alps,

387

travel far to the snowy north, take a plane to the tropical islands in the south, visit the temples and shrines and cities and villages. He wanted to do it all.

And one day he would.

Because he also wanted to visit the remote lochs of Scotland, just like he'd described to August for their imaginary honeymoon. He wanted to visit Rome in the summer when it was so hot your gelato melted down your hands. He wanted to drive through Germany and campervan around Cornwall. If he left England now, he'd be making exactly the same mistake he'd already made here in Japan – making plans and goals and wish lists and not fulfilling them. And what then? Wouldn't it just be an endless cycle?

Coming to Japan had been just what he needed. He'd seen his family, he'd had closure with Yui, he'd cleared his mind, and now he could go home. His new home. And one day he'd come back here and call Japan home again.

But not now.

Suddenly he knew what he wanted: to spend his last few days of leave with August, really figuring out what they meant to each other, and deciding what else he could do when he quit his job.

He checked his phone. He wasn't due to leave Tokyo until early next week, but perhaps he could change his flight. To tomorrow.

Chapter 76

August

August took a half day on Friday and went shopping. She couldn't concentrate at the press office because she still didn't quite know how to handle things with Abe tonight.

What if she told him the truth and it ruined everything? Her brain was so muddled. If only Flynn were here to talk this through with, then they could both make the decision.

Sometimes, when the brain is trying to work through a difficult problem, it can become fixated on a solution to something else entirely, just to feel productive. This was certainly the case with August, at least. And that's why she found herself standing by the sale rack of a fancy clothing store in Bath's city centre, holding up a slinky slip of a dress. If she dressed like an elegant grown-up for her dinner with Abe tonight, she reasoned, then perhaps she'd be able to remain level-headed and grown-up about the whole situation.

Touching the fabric of the dress, in this store she didn't quite belong in, she felt a wash of loneliness, just as she was predicting about Abe, and she wanted to be close to him, she liked the way he looked at her. It hurt to think of Flynn wrapped up with Yui right now.

August wanted to be close to someone.

When August got home, she tried on her new dress again. It was beautiful, and it looked beautiful on. The satin fabric, a deep teal shade with matching teal lace detailing, wrapped her body like a Christmas present. It accented her curves, and didn't squish or hide her imperfections – it made her feel sexy and celebrated. The back of the dress had been fiddly, with ribbons and lace trailing down her spine, but it was worth persevering with in the end, and thanks to the fanciest underwear she owned, a teddy she'd purchased on a whim a few years ago that was now layered underneath, she stood proud in front of the mirror.

August gave herself a satisfied nod, struck a quick pose, and then reached behind her to start undoing it all, ready for it to be fresh on tonight.

Although … it might be overkill, mightn't it, showing up for a 'friends' dinner dressed to the nines? Abe would probably run a mile.

As the doubts crept in, August's fingers fiddled with the looping ribbons down her back, her mind elsewhere. *Hmm.* Something was wrong, and the dress wasn't slipping off as easily as it had in the shop changing room.

August twisted in front of the mirror to try to get a better look, but she couldn't really see. Something was wrong, right where the ribbon looped into the lace and kissed the ticklish centre of her back. She just … couldn't … quite … get it undone.

As she tugged, her limbs contorted, she heard the sound of threads tearing. '*Shit*,' she muttered, and carefully pulled the delicate straps over her shoulders so the dress dangled from her ribcage, tangled hopelessly in the equally intricate underwear. What was she going to do? Sure, she could keep it on for the rest of the day and then wear the damned thing straight out to dinner, but there were only two possible endings for this garment as things stood. Either she'd need to politely ask Abe to help her remove it after dinner, which would be a big expectation to place on a man who thought she was married, or she'd be in this exact position late this evening and need to rip it off herself anyway. And she really didn't want to rip it. August's budget didn't allow for drawerfuls of luxury garments, or lingerie for that matter, so this little number was intended to be pulled out again and again.

August needed help getting out of it *now*, by someone who would untangle the snarled fabric and wouldn't judge her. And Bel would likely have her hand in somebody's gob at the moment, so she probably wouldn't appreciate dress-gate for the emergency it was.

Wrapping her dressing gown around herself, August stepped onto the little balcony off her bedroom, checking there was nobody staring up at her from the park and hissed upwards, 'Callie?'

She could see Callie's window was open, so she tried again, calling up a little louder. 'Callie?'

August was about to give in and go up to Callie's flat in person – though she really didn't want to have to explain all this to both Callie and her mum, that would be too mortifying – when Callie stuck her head out the window.

'Who's that?' she called out towards the park.

'Callie, down here, it's me.'

'Hello, August, what's up?'

'I need your help with something.'

Callie's mum stuck her head out of the window, next to her daughter. 'Hello, love.'

'Hiya,' August answered, pulling her dressing gown around her.

'Everything okay?'

'She says she needs my help with something, Mum.'

'Oh. Do you want to come up, love? We've got cake up here.'

August smiled. 'Thank you, but it would be really helpful if Callie could come down here, actually.'

'All right,' said Callie. 'Just me, or me and Mum?'

'I think just you, just on this occasion.'

'On my way.'

Moments later, Callie knocked on the door, holding two plates with big slices of cake on them. 'From Mum,' she explained. 'Oh, one was for me and one for you, but I can get more if Flynn wants some?'

'No, he's still travelling,' said August, ushering her in. 'Callie, I've got a bit of an embarrassing problem.'

'Brilliant,' she replied, settling down with the cake. 'The best kind of problem. What can I do you for? Plucking an unwanted hair? Ointment application? Lost tampon?'

The way she reeled them off had August wondering if she was the go-to fixer in Elizabeth Street. 'No, nothing like any of those, this is more of a wardrobe malfunction.'

Callie's eyes travelled down to August's dressing gown. 'What have you got on under there?'

'Not much, to be honest.'

'And what's the problem?'

'The problem is that what little I have got on I can't get off.'

'Why didn't you wait for Flynn to come home? Surely the point is for him to take it off you anyway?'

August felt herself pink, both at the shame of still lying to Callie, and moreover at the thought of Flynn taking it off her, which flashed into her mind as rather a pleasant fleeting image.

She regained her composure and said, 'Well, this is supposed to be a surprise, for another time, I was just testing it out. And now something's gone wrong with the ribbons on the dress and, I think, the hook and eyes at the back of the underwear because I can't get it off and I can't really reach it and something's beginning to tear.'

'All right, love, well, let's have a look, then.' Callie sat back like a punter at a striptease.

'Don't laugh, okay?' August cautioned.

'Bloody hell, what is it under there, a mankini?'

'No ...' August stood up and shyly removed her robe, revealing what was underneath.

Callie didn't laugh, she didn't even make some sordid comment, which August half expected, and wouldn't have blamed her for. Instead she said, 'Hon, you look beautiful. Absolutely beautiful. That's a lovely dress, I'm guessing, when it's on properly, and that's some pair of undercrackers. Flynn's a lucky guy.'

'It's at the back, around the middle. I can't really see . . .' August changed the subject but then added, 'Thank you, though.' Callie was a good friend, way more than August felt she deserved. In the spirit of this new and improved August, she was going to tell Callie the truth. Soon. Just as soon as she'd spoken to Flynn and given him the heads up.

Callie got up and had a look, then bent down to scrutinise further. 'I see what the problem is, the hook on your undies has gone through the fabric of the dress right where one of the ribbons crosses in the centre of your back here. It's completely mangled.'

August's heart dropped. 'Do we need to cut me out?'

'No,' Callie said. 'I can get you out of this, I'm sure. And I reckon I can save it so you'll be able to put it back on again afterwards, but I might need to make a couple of little adjustments.'

'You can?'

'I can. Have you got some little scissors, maybe nail scissors, and a needle and thread and maybe . . . a spare button?'

'Yes, probably, one moment.' August threw her robe back on to run into her bedroom, where she kept a medical kit with some sewing supplies and small scissors. She also made Callie a quick cup of tea to go with their cake.

And while this was going on, she didn't even notice how

Callie's eyebrows raised and her gaze lingered on the open door of her bedroom.

Back in the living room again, robe on the floor, August stood with Callie kneeling behind her, the dress pulled up with the skirt hooked under August's arm. August was rather aware of how close her neighbour was having to position herself beside her bottom.

'Thanks so much for this Callie, I owe you one.'

'It's no problem, hon,' Callie replied, holding a needle out of the side of her mouth. 'I had a look on your Instagram the other day, by the way. I was showing Mrs H your new headshots.'

August froze, feeling a chill cross her skin that was nothing to do with being half naked.

'They're lovely,' Callie commented from behind her. 'You don't show Flynn much on there, do you?'

'No ... no, he's not a big social media person,' August replied. How could she have been so stupid? She knew Callie had sent a follow request back when her Instagram account was private, she just forgot when she made it public. And no, Flynn was not on there much, in fact, he wasn't on there at all before six months ago. Before that, James certainly was featured though.

August tried to take a calming breath and change the subject, relieved when Callie seemed to move on too. 'How's your mum doing?'

'She's good, thanks. She's so into yoga now, I'm telling you, she's been talking about doing this Bikram course where you do it every day for, like, a month and go off on a retreat with the whole class. She wanted me to do it but I was like, Mum, I don't even like staying in the bath too long if it's too warm, I would not cope well with steaming-hot exercise.'

August was so focussed on listening to Callie talk, and the feel of being lightly jostled from the back, that she didn't hear anybody coming up the stairs or nearing the door until it opened.

And as the fabric freed itself and the dress pooled to the ground, there he was: Flynn. Not in Japan, but right there in front of her.

Chapter 77

Flynn

Flynn dropped his keys, his head turning quickly to the side so he wasn't looking at August. He'd already seen it though, just for a second, the vision of her standing in the middle of the living room wearing some kind of sexy, slinky swimming costume. He was pretty sure, actually, that it *wasn't* a swimming costume. For a millisecond he wondered if she'd been wearing it for him, but then he heard her gasp in surprise and then Callie's voice called out, 'Oh, hello, neighbour!'

'I'm so sorry,' Flynn fumbled, his eyes closed, using his hands to search for the door and close it.

August started to drop to grab her gown but Callie shrieked. 'Don't move now or the whole thing will spring open. Not that you'd mind that, would you Flynny-boy?' She cackled.

'Oh my God,' whispered August.

'Don't worry about it, so it isn't a surprise any more, that doesn't matter. Come on, Flynn. You might as well appreciate your wife while she's all gussied up. I'm nearly done here; we're just doing a little maintenance. How was your trip?'

'That's okay, I'll just go, um, back out again,' Flynn then started navigating his way back towards the door, banging his suitcase against the wall. But his eyes were clamped closed, so he ricocheted towards his bedroom instead.

'What's the problem?' asked Callie, as he flung open his door, about to jump in after his case. 'Look how lovely she looks.'

'I-it's okay,' August stammered, probably feeling very, very naked. 'He'll look later, he's probably just jet-lagged, or embarrassed that you're here.'

'Don't be ridiculous, Flynn. Tell her she's a stunner.' Callie nudged August and hissed, 'Let him check up on it, as they say.' Callie then looked around August towards Flynn, and said, confused, 'What's going on? Why won't you look at her?'

During all of this, thanks to his tightly shut eyes, Flynn didn't even notice that Callie's scrutiny had moved off him and was now resting at the view just past his right shoulder. His bedroom.

Without warning, Callie turned away from Flynn and stared at August, as if trying to read her face. 'Is it the redhead? That girl he kept bringing over here?'

'What?' both August and Flynn said in unison, Flynn still with his eyes closed.

'Has he been cheating on you?' Callie said, looking at August with deep concern before snarling at Flynn. 'Are you having problems? Is that what's happening here? I've been there, if that's what this is, if you're trying everything, gussying yourself up, trying to get his attention and he won't even look at you.'

'No, no, that's not what's going on at all,' August insisted. 'Flynn, look at me. What do you think, honey? Welcome home!'

Flynn cracked open one eye and looked at August's face, only her face, to see if she was being coerced. But she smiled at him, gave a minute nod of her head, and rolled her eyes. She then struck a playful pose like a pin-up girl, giving him permission to lower his eyes.

'Wow,' he murmured. 'You look beautiful.' She really did, though he didn't look down. His eyes stayed on her laughing lips, her hands reaching into her caramel curls, the brightness of her eyes. He couldn't look away from that happy face, even though it pained him to know that all this must not be meant for him.

He wondered if August and Abe had become closer since he went away. Did Abe now know their secret? It didn't matter, the fact was, she wasn't doing this for him. If he'd ever had one, he'd missed his chance. Now he had to step aside so she could be happy.

Chapter 78

August

He came back. He came home. Standing there, dishevelled from his flight, shirt loose, a day of stubble, hair messy, Flynn looked perfect, and August had to remember to breathe.

Just before she told Flynn to look at her in her lingerie, she'd thought, *Oh, bugger it*. He'd seen it all when he came in anyway, let the boy out of his misery. So she stood tall, lifted her chin and spoke through only slightly gritted teeth.

August was shy under his gaze, even though he pulled it away after only a brief admiration and instead met her eyes again. Something passed between them and she wished in that moment she could be standing there for him, after all.

Behind her, Callie sighed, and it brought August back out of her own mind. Callie. Wonderful, kind, helpful Callie who'd been through so much and who trusted her. August turned her head to meet Callie's eye, to say ... well, she wasn't sure what, but in that moment she felt like she just wanted to be honest and tell her the truth, more than anything.

And then Callie beat her to it. 'Something isn't right,' she declared in a quiet voice.

'With the dress?' August asked, though something had shifted, Callie wouldn't meet her eye, and there was a sadness to her voice.

'Not with the dress, that's fine, I've got you untangled and I'm going to head back upstairs now. Feel free to drop it up and I'll do the alterations, like I promised.' She stood up and gathered her things, heading for the door.

'Callie, can we talk for a bit?' August held her breath.

'Not right now. Maybe some other time. Let's talk after the neighbour drinks tomorrow night, okay?'

'Callie—' August stopped. Neighbour drinks? Oh FFS, she'd forgotten all about them. It was their turn to host again.

Callie held her hands up, but still refused to look August or Flynn in the face, and August would have given anything in that moment to go back to the first day they moved in, to when she met Callie, who was immediately kind to her, outside the building, bringing her tea, smiling and open and honest. She wished she'd told the truth right there and then, rather than watch Callie leave, and for August to become the villain in her own story.

Chapter 79

August

August was left staring at the closed front door. Callie knew something was up.

No, no, Callie couldn't have put two and two together based *only* on that debacle. That would be impossible. At the most, Callie must think they have marriage troubles. Flynn dived into the shower, and so she went to her room to get dressed, and it was then she noticed both of their bedrooms on full show. Was it that that had given them away to Callie?

August changed, slowly, listening for sounds of Flynn, taking comfort in knowing he was back home again.

He was back, he came back. Of course he had, all of his things were here, but the real question was would he stay?

Her stomach fluttered, thoughts of Flynn tumbling and jostling for space, pushing those of Callie aside, because having him back on the other side of the wall made her happy. It was really, *really* nice to see him.

She pulled on some pink leggings and a snuggly ice-blue sweatshirt, and placed her hand on the wall, straining to hear his voice as he sang softly to himself inside the bathroom.

Her phone began to ring.

Abe. Abe, of course, she was supposed to be seeing him tonight, he was the whole reason for the fancy outfit, not Flynn. 'Hey, Abe,' she sang down the line, stealing a glance towards the bathroom where the shower was still running.

Why did she feel like she was cheating on her husband, when he wasn't even her real husband? He'd probably just spent the last two weeks getting it on with his ex-girlfriend.

'Hello, August?' Abe said, as formal as ever, and she rolled her eyes. The reason it felt like cheating is because if she was right about the spark she and Abe shared, and if she did something about it, in his eyes she *would* appear to be a cheater. An adulteress even.

'Hey, what's up? Still on for dinner?'

He cleared his throat. 'I'm ever so sorry, my mum's not feeling good at all this evening, and I think I'd better keep an eye on her. Would it be all right with you if we rescheduled, perhaps I could come back to Bath again next weekend?'

'That's fine,' she said, hoping he didn't hear the disappointment in her voice. 'Of course. Is Mrs H okay?'

'Yes, I'm sure she'll be absolutely fine, but you know how it is . . .'

'Of course. Is there anything I can do? I could bring dinner up for both of you?' She still wanted to see him, she realised, she still wanted to be near him. God, she was a mess at the moment.

Abe hesitated, and she listened to his soft breath down the phone line for a second. 'No, that's all right, August. I think it will be better to wait to see each other until next week, and then maybe Flynn could come along as well . . .'

'Flynn's back, actually, Abe. He came home early.'

'I see,' he replied.

She understood what he was telling her, though it took her by surprise. He was breaking up with her, in a way, or at least breaking the threads they were beginning to form. He didn't want to be the other man. He was stepping away from her, and what might have been.

August moved out towards the living room window, the sound of the shower still running, wondering if it was even true about Mrs H feeling unwell, and that if not, he'd felt he'd had to lie to her to let her down gently. She needed to figure her shit out, and pick a lane: did she want Abe to think she'd cheat on someone for him, or did she want to tell him the truth?

Did she want to finally tell all of them the truth?

Was she ready?

If anybody passing the house on Elizabeth Street at that moment had looked up they would have seen a woman gazing out of her window on the first floor, lost in thought, or just lost. And if they'd turned their eyes upwards, not one, but two, floors higher, they would have seen a man looking much the same.

Chapter 80

Flynn

'I'm sorry about that,' Flynn said, re-entering the living room after his shower and seeing August curled up on her big green armchair. His flight home had been smooth sailing, way nicer than the trip over last summer. Perhaps it was because, back then, he had been leaving the familiar and entering the unknown. This time he was returning to August.

'About the underwear thing? Don't worry about it.' August stood up and faced him, and it was as if neither quite knew how to behave, like there was an invisible layer of ice to crack through before they could get back to normal. 'How was Japan?'

'It was . . . ' Flynn couldn't find the words, not because he didn't know them but because he lost himself in her face. So instead he smiled, and pulled her into a hug. 'Hi.'

'Hi,' she laughed against him, the tension breaking. 'Welcome home.'

They broke apart and Flynn sat on the sofa while she returned to her chair. 'Japan was good, great even, you were right, it was exactly what I needed.'

'I'm so glad,' she replied, and he searched her face to try and guess what she was thinking. 'You look happier.'

'I think I am.'

'Did you manage to see Yui?'

'Yes, it was really nice.' He paused, wanting to tell her all about it, to open his heart to her about how he felt, but she seemed a little distracted. Was it because of what just happened with Callie? August was close with her, so if Callie felt betrayed it was bound to be playing on her mind. 'How are you? How have your last couple of weeks been?'

'Good,' she smiled. 'Actually, I got to know Abe a little more, he's been visiting his mum a lot while you've been gone.'

Did he imagine it or was she holding her breath, waiting for his reaction?

'You did?' Flynn swallowed.

'Yeah, he's a good guy, actually. We get along well.'

His indecision, his lack of spontaneity, all these things about himself he so desperately wanted to change, but was it all too late? Had he lost her?

Not knowing how to respond, he changed the subject. 'That thing with Callie just then . . . that didn't sound good.'

August grew sad and serious all at once; it was a face he rarely saw.

'I feel bad, Flynn,' August admitted, knotting her hands together. 'Callie definitely knows something's off. I feel really bad for lying to her, and Mrs Haverley, and our other neighbours. Do you?'

'I do, I have for a while,' he answered.

'How would you feel . . .' August paused, unable to form the words. She gulped, and let the words blurt out; as was always her way. 'How would you feel about us coming clean? Telling everyone the truth? Stopping this façade?'

'Is it because of him?' Flynn asked, quietly.

August took a beat. 'Abe?'

Flynn and August locked their gaze, and he knew the answer without her having to say it. He wasn't angry – what right would he have had to be angry? – but he missed her without her even taking a step away from him. He missed the way she'd kissed him, he missed her climbing into his bed, he missed the way she was unafraid around him and how she brought his life colour.

Everything would need to change if she and Abe became a couple. Even if they kept living under the same roof, for a while, that wouldn't last for ever.

August spoke, breaking him from his thoughts. 'It's a little bit about Abe, but it's mainly just about us. I don't want to pretend and lie and live my life this way anymore. Do you?'

Chapter 81

August

August let Flynn sleep off his jet lag the next day, and took charge buying some supplies for the neighbour drinks that evening. She didn't buy much – to be honest she was hoping to have everyone in and out in under an hour, so she could have a good talk with Flynn.

He'd come back, and she didn't know what that meant, but she knew she was more pleased to see him than anything else she felt right now.

In the afternoon she crept into his room, where he was snoring softly, and climbed onto his bed.

'Flynn?' she whispered. She watched him, not in a creepy way, but just for a minute so she could remember him like this if it turned out they needed to go their separate ways.

Here he was, this man who had barrelled into her life over a spilt cup of coffee, and become her friend, her confidant, her flatmate and her fake husband. He was warm, from his kisses to his soul, and more than anything she wanted him to be happy.

The room was dark, but not pitch black, the daylight straining to find its way through the closed curtains. 'Flynn?' she whispered again, lying down next to him. 'You need to wake up or you'll never sleep tonight.'

He murmured, a smile flittering across his mouth, and without opening his eyes he draped an arm over her. 'Jet lag is winning,' he said, his voice sleepy.

'It sure is. Do you want to wake up?'

In the gloom, his eyelashes fluttered, and then he was looking at her, next to him, their breathing synced. Flynn's hand moved to her arm and he rested it there. She should move. If she didn't want anything to happen between them, she should move right now, because all signs pointed to him thinking about kissing her. August didn't move.

But after an eternity of holding in the moment, Flynn exhaled, and dropped his hand. 'Okay, I'm awake,' he whispered, and he smiled, rubbing his eyes.

'Good,' August rolled onto her back and watched the ceiling for a second, composing herself. 'The neighbours will be over in a couple of hours, I've got everything we need – wine, cake, crisps.'

'Thanks, Aug.'

'No problem. Consider it a really lame welcome home party.'

Up until their guests arrived, bang on 5 p.m., August and Flynn shuffled around each other, polite, a little confused, very much in need of a good heart-to-heart once this was out the way.

Allen and Maud arrived first, full of chit-chat and wanting to know all about Flynn's trip to Japan. Callie and her mum came shortly afterwards, and though Callie gave August a slightly guarded look, she whispered, 'Sorry for storming out yesterday, hon, we'll have a catch up when we can and you can tell me anything that's been bothering you. Maybe over a yoga mat, okay?'

August nodded, pleased that Callie wasn't furious, but more determined than ever to admit the truth to her.

Flynn was about to serve up the rest of the cake – he too was clearly hoping for a short and sweet neighbour get together this evening – when someone mentioned Mrs Haverley.

'Mrs H, of course!' August stood up. 'I was going to take her up a piece of cake because she's not been well. Shall I pop up now?'

'That's a nice idea,' Maud said. 'Flynn, you go with her and say hello and we'll pour another round of wines.'

August and Flynn nipped up the stairs armed with a glass of red and a slab of cake. They delivered it to Mrs H, who was in a chair in the living room, trying to figure out how to turn off *Love Island*, which she claimed not to actually be watching, on her newly installed Netflix. She was on her own, as Abe was out picking her up some medical supplies from the Boots in town. August and Flynn stayed a few minutes, helping her switch off Netflix, and showing her how to switch it back on again, should she change her mind, before leaving to return downstairs to their guests.

From the staircase, August could see their door was open, though she was sure Flynn had closed it on his way out.

She heard voices as they descended, so the neighbours hadn't left ...

Then August heard one voice she hadn't expected, and it turned her to stone, icy air washing over her like the February frost had been let right into the building and found its way to her feet, legs, arms and heart.

August gripped Flynn's arm and he came to a stop beside her, and they met each other's eyes.

'What is it?' he asked.

This couldn't be happening, August thought, frozen on the staircase. *She never just* popped over.

The voice rang out louder, a dominating annoyance the vocal equivalent of stamping one's foot:

'I think I would know and I can assure you, my daughter is *not married*.'

August took off, jumping the rest of the stairs two at a time, and skidded into her flat with Flynn right behind her. Standing there in a huddle in front of one of their framed, fake wedding photos was Mrs Anderson, August's mum, her smart coat still buttoned up, her gloves in her hand, and her lips pursed together.

'August Anderson, what is going on?' her mum demanded, facing her daughter. 'It can't be true. Can it? I've told them you're not married. That you would have told me, but ...'

All of them faced her: Allen, Maud, Callie's mum, Callie.

'What are you doing here, Mum?' August asked, her heart thudding in her chest.

'You're always telling me to pop over, I had an appointment in Bath, and since I knew your flatmate was away, I thought we could have dinner together. Or should I say your *husband*, according to the photo I saw as soon as your friends let me in?'

'It's, um—' Flynn started, but he was as lost for words as August, and they both stood there with mouths opening and closing like a couple of fish out of water. August moved her eyes to Callie, who shook her head and turned her gaze away.

'Callie …' August pleaded, her voice quiet, but Callie refused to look up.

'What is this?' Mrs Anderson continued, holding the photo in the air. 'I thought it was just you two having a bit of fun until this one—' she jabbed the picture towards Allen '—told me it was a picture from your wedding day. Imagine my surprise! I certainly don't remember an invite to your wedding!'

'Perhaps they eloped?' Maud suggested and then backed away from August's mother's death stare.

'Yes, maybe it was a long time ago and they forgot to tell you,' Allen added. Maud swatted him for his ridiculous suggestion.

Mrs Anderson tutted. 'They did not elope, they are just flatmates, they didn't even know each other before they moved in here.'

'They didn't,' Callie said, but it sounded less like a question and more a quiet confirmation, like she'd suspected as much, somehow.

'Look, August, I know you like playing the actress, but this has clearly gone far enough. Either you're pretending to be married to him for some reason, or you've completely left

412

me in the dark about the relationship you two really have. So come on, who are you lying to. Them? Or me?'

Them. Or her.

There were really only two choices here. Either August and Flynn confessed to the lie, or they dove even deeper into it by starting a whole new lie to her mum. It was a no brainer, of course, and with all the exhaustion August had felt from carrying around this secret for the past six months, she slid her eyes back towards the neighbours and whispered, 'I'm sorry.'

Flynn found her hand, hanging limply at her side. 'I'm sorry, too. It was all my fault.'

Maud and Allen left first, heads down, mutterings of 'let's leave them to it, dear, we can find out the truth tomorrow.'

Callie's mum collected up her and her daughter's belongings, without looking at Flynn or August, and made for the door.

Callie was silent for a moment, hurt in her expression, the weight of the deceit rooting her to the spot. And then she walked past August without another word.

'Callie? Let me explain.'

'Not now,' she said, and closed the door behind her.

August faced her mum, who put the picture down on the shelf again. 'I don't know what that was all about,' she said, eventually. 'But perhaps one of you can make me a cup of tea and I can lend you an ear. Honestly, August, it's tall tales like this that make me feel your grandmother is back with us, sometimes.'

Chapter 82

August

The following morning, on Sunday, August lay in bed after a restless night wondering how she'd let the web she'd woven get destroyed, instead of untangling it herself when she had the chance. Because let's be honest, she'd had a lot of chances. They both had.

Now they all knew, and they all probably hated her and Flynn. But even if they did, even if there was no way she could make up for the lies and deceit, the least she could do was make sure there weren't any more.

She and Flynn had agreed, yesterday evening, that they would tell Mrs Haverley together, after she confessed to Abe first. She wanted to be the one to do that, alone.

But first she wanted to talk to Callie.

August crept out of her room and listened at Flynn's door to see if he was awake, but the apartment was silent. So she

414

left him a note. A note, rather than a text, felt like it had just the right blend of personal touch and dramatic flair.

Morning, Flynn,
    I've decided to go up and talk to Callie about us. I hope you don't mind that we haven't done this together but I want to clear the air with her, if I can, as soon as possible. I hope you understand.
    So this is it … the truth comes out today.

She hesitated, not sure whether or not to write the next bit. But it felt right, and it felt like the truth, so she went for it.

    Whatever happens, Flynn, you've been the most amazing first husband a girl could ask for. Thank you. For everything.
    Aug xx

August picked up her yoga mat, and left the apartment.

August knocked on Callie's door, lightly, in case she or her mum were still sleeping. But Callie opened it a moment later, her hair in an eighties-style side-pony, a mug of tea in hand.

'Hi, Callie.'

'Hi, August.'

August took a deep breath. 'I have some explaining to do. Will you come out into the back gardens and do some morning yoga with me?'

Callie regarded August for a moment, before turning to look out the window behind her. 'It's freezing out there.'

'Good point . . . ' she hadn't quite factored in that yoga in five-degree weather might not be the most relaxing.

But then Callie held the door open for her. 'Bugger it, let me whack on a few jumpers and we'll go.'

Down in the gardens, the two of them found a sheltered spot in the morning sunshine, where it wasn't too chilly. They sat opposite each other with their legs crossed in front of them, and Callie watched August, expectantly.

Callie stuck a leg out to the side to stretch it, and August mirrored her, and said, 'Callie, you were right.'

Over the next ten minutes, August explained everything, while Callie stayed silent beside her. As August talked, Callie dictated the yoga moves, which got more challenging the more August spoke, so by the time she'd covered everything she was teetering on one leg in a shaky tree pose that she was pretty sure the rock-solid Callie was forcing her to hold on purpose.

'What I don't understand, Aug,' said Callie, moving into warrior two, 'is how you could lie to me so easily, after I'd been nothing but honest with you.'

August nearly toppled over with the weight of her shame. 'I was so wrong. I was lost in a complete fog thinking about how nobody wanted to live here more than me, and that my only chance to fulfil my dreams was to start them from inside this house. To begin with it felt like an acting job, like it wouldn't hurt anyone, but I know now that it was selfish.'

'Yes, it was.'

'I know this is no excuse, but I *did* want to tell you so many times.'

'To be honest, love, that doesn't help much. That's a little bit like what my ex-husband said to me when I caught him in *his* lies.'

August nodded and sat down, giving up on the yoga, and instead burying her face in her hands. 'You're right. I'm awful. I'm so sorry, Callie. I'm going to talk to Abe today, and we're going to tell Mrs Haverley as soon as he says she's well enough. Whatever happens after that, I hope you can forgive me one day, because you're an amazing friend and I'm lucky to have you in my life. And that's the *truth*.'

Callie took a few moments, sitting down herself and slowing her breath, and rolling her neck, before saying with softness. 'We'll get there. You're still *you*, right.'

'I am, I've always been me, authentically me, aside from the whopping great secret life. I really need to leave the acting to the day job; I know that now.'

Finally, Callie smiled at August, and August thought that maybe, give it a little time, things might be okay between them.

'Your mum's a force to be reckoned with, isn't she?' Callie commented, her eyebrows raised.

'Isn't she just? Want to trade?'

'No, thanks.'

'I think you would have liked my gran, though,' said August.

Callie nodded and then said, 'Abe might be quite happy about all this.'

'What do you mean?'

'You two have a spark, you know it.'

'Maybe,' August shrugged, blushing a little.

'But then, that's what I always thought about you and Flynn.' Callie stood and picked up her mat. 'I'm going to head in now, my fanny's getting frostbite. Are you coming?'

'I'll be in in a moment,' August replied.

'All right, see you soon, love,' and with that, Callie left the garden, but August thought, hoped, she wouldn't be leaving her life for ever.

Chapter 83

Flynn

Flynn was stepping out of the building when Callie came around the front with her yoga mat.

'Oh hi, Callie,' he said with caution. 'I was just nipping down to the coffee shop, do you want anything?' He'd been heading to get August one of those hazelnut coffees she liked, and an almond croissant, in case she needed cheering up after her confrontation. No matter what, he still found himself wanting to do anything he could, big or small, to make her happy.

'I'm fine, thanks,' Callie replied. 'Listen, August told me everything.'

Flynn dropped his voice. 'Callie, I'm sorry, I hope you know our lies were never meant to hurt anyone. We just got . . . '

'Caught up, I know, she told me.' She smiled at him, not her usual easy smile, but one that maybe told him she'd be okay after she had some time.

'I'm sorry,' he repeated. 'We're going to tell everyone the truth now. I know Aug's really anxious to tell Mrs H, and ... Abe.'

'Do you have feelings for her?' Callie asked Flynn, looking at him with a directness he wasn't used to.

Flynn hesitated, because he'd never said aloud what he now knew. 'It's complicated.'

'Complicated isn't bad,' Callie replied, and moved to go past him before stopping and taking a deep breath, seeming to draw something from deep inside her. 'Maybe take the complicated option instead of the easy one. Believe me, nobody wants to feel like they're the easy option.'

Chapter 84

August

It was like a plaster now; August had started ripping and she just wanted the whole thing off. She needed to know where she stood, with the house, with Abe, with Flynn.

She called Abe later that morning and asked if he wanted to take a walk, somewhere a little away from the house. It was still cold, but maybe if she bundled up warm, and then she'd tell him everything and he'd just laugh and forgive her and kiss her and wrap his arms around her so they were both warm and it would start to snow.

Is that what she wanted though? Because a part of her kept thinking about Flynn. Did she want Abe? Or did she just want company and comfort at a time when she was afraid Flynn had found that with Poppy, or Yui?

Before she left she shared almond croissants with Flynn and asked, 'Can you believe it's all about to come out? Life as we know it might be about to change.'

'I'm ready,' he gave her a half smile. 'I really am ready.'

'You are?' that was a relief, to hear him so certain.

Flynn continued. 'We spent so much time prepping for how to explain our past that we didn't even think about our future. How was it ever going to work to *actually* live our lives when we can't date without complications, we can't holiday without syncing our calendars, we can't bring around friends and family without asking them to lie for us as well.'

'I know. Turns out having an imaginary marriage takes a lot of work.'

'They say a real marriage does too.'

'Can I just say one thing?' she said, brushing crumbs from her fingers and placing one hand on the door handle, ready to leave.

'Of course,' Flynn replied.

'About all of this, the last six months, everything we've been through . . . ' she trailed off and Flynn tried to jump in.

'I told you, it's not your—'

August stopped him. 'This isn't an apology to you. I've been a shitty person to a lot of people, but I didn't force you into this. So it's not an apology, it's a thank you. Thank you for agreeing to this hare-brained scheme. Thank you for helping me fulfil a dream. Thank you for becoming one of my closest friends, my confidant, my one-time kissing partner.' She laughed then, avoiding his eye, because she hadn't exactly meant to bring that up. 'Just, thank you.' Before he could say it back, she opened the door and stepped onto the landing, looking back long enough to add, 'So I'll go, then? I'll tell Abe the truth? Because once he knows that's practically Mrs H knowing, and our house of cards could topple.'

Flynn nodded, and she left him in their home.

'Abe, I need to tell you something,' August said, as soon as she met him at the wall outside Number Eighteen. He stood tall in a smart overcoat, a maroon scarf and neat jeans. He looked like the polished version of himself today, but he was just as handsome in his PJs. She quite wanted to climb into that coat with him actually, the wool looked jolly warm.

Focus, August.

'How's your mum been over the weekend?' she interrupted herself, remembering he'd said she wasn't feeling great on Friday evening, and that he'd been out getting her some medication when they'd gone up the evening before.

'She's okay, better than Friday, sorry for cancelling.' Abe smiled down at her and they began a descent of the hill. She felt his presence close to her, so magnetised that she had to stop herself from leaning her arm against him. She felt it from him too, like he wanted to touch her, like he was clasping his hands together in front of him to stop himself reaching out. 'How's Flynn? Did he have a good flight?'

'Yep,' she replied, noticing the strain in his voice.

She took a breath, wondering what this would mean for the two of them. What did she want it to mean? He was kind, they had a spark, but once the lie was set free and they could be together, would they actually want to?

Or were they just two lonely people looking for reassurance after all?

There was only one way to find out.

'Listen. About Flynn.'

'I don't want to—' he started.

'Abe, wait. Do you remember that day of the open house, when you let Flynn and I in together?'

'Of course.'

'Well . . . We were never there *together* . . .' August opened up and told Abe the truth about the months she'd been living in Elizabeth Street, and about her relationship with Flynn, or, moreover, the lack of one. As she spoke, she watched his face for a sign that he was somehow happy because it meant she was single. They were free to date. But no such look came.

'So what I'm saying is,' she finished. 'We both wanted to live here so much that we made a stupid mistake that we thought would land us the apartment. I made the mistake, mainly, it was my idea. I'm sorry for lying.'

Abe walked silently beside her, his eyes on the ground.

'We're going to tell your mum, and whatever she decides she wants us to do we'll do, but I wanted to tell you first, because . . .'

He stopped and faced her. They were on a quiet, deserted street, not far from her grandmother's home, and shaded by trees. August's instinct was to try and fill the silence with more babble, or apologies, but she kept her mouth shut. She let Abe, thoughtful, considered Abe, work through his thoughts.

He took a step closer to her.

'So are you and Flynn . . .'

'There is no me and Flynn,' August answered, although the admission caused an ache deep within her, and she wondered whether it was even true.

'I don't think I can do this,' Abe said, his voice quiet, and he broke her gaze by looking down at the ground.

August touched Abe's arm and like a spark igniting he looked up at her. And she thought about what it would be like to kiss him.

She imagined how it would feel if he grazed his fingers against her skin, if he pulled her into him. She remembered the longing they'd both felt over the past month. Part of her wanted, needed, the barrier to smash and for them to kiss, sweet and new and the most wonderful closure for the both of them.

But two lonely hearts don't make a right. Instead of kissing, after a moment, they both stepped down and he said, 'I'm glad I know the truth. But you know I need to back away.'

'I know,' August whispered back, trying to stop staring at his lips, because he was right, this was the right thing to do. But that didn't stop him being quite yummy.

'You've been lying to my mum, to everyone, for over half a year. Messing with their feelings. Callie adores you and calls you the 'dream couple'. My mum trusted you with her house. I . . . I liked you and I felt awful for that, and for Flynn. And I do understand why you did it, but she's still my mum. I know she can be stuck in her ways and old-fashioned, but she's *still* my mum.'

August let his words sink in, agreeing with everything

he said. She *was* his mum, of course he would be angry at anyone who wronged her.

'Do you think if this had never happened you and I might have . . . ?' They were still close, her hand on his arm, cherishing these soon-to-be-over moments.

He shook his head, and then swept his gaze over her lips, a parting ghost of a kiss in place of the real thing, before saying, 'If that had never happened, then I wouldn't have even known you, and I'm glad I do.'

August breathed him in, and finally let him go.

Stepping back, he transformed back into Abe Haverley, landlady's son, though they let their fingertips linger against each other until the end.

Abe turned to walk the other way, and August began to make her way back to her home.

Tomorrow. It was time to tell Mrs Haverley, so she'd let the dust settle and tomorrow she'd ask Abe if Mrs H was well enough to hear the news, and then she and Flynn would go together.

She accepted it now: she was the villain here. Because of her own blinkered goals. Not Mrs Haverley for only wanting to rent to a married couple, not the other neighbours for nearly unearthing her secret, not Poppy for seeming to threaten to blow their cover, but her. August. She'd concocted a life of lies to people she truly liked and respected all to fulfil her own needs. She was the villain in her own story. Whatever happened now, there would be no more lies.

426

Chapter 85

Flynn

August and Flynn awoke at the same time in the middle of the night, sometime during the dark hours between Sunday and Monday, August upon hearing voices in the corridor outside the apartment, Flynn from the blue lights that flashed repetitively on the street outside, illuminating his walls through the curtains.

They both came to their bedroom doors, their eyes meeting.

'What's happening out there?' August asked Flynn, her voice scratchy from interrupted snores, one bed sock lost somewhere during a dream. She looked perfect.

Flynn moved to the living room and looked down, where the unmistakeable luminous yellow form of an ambulance was parked outside their home, its lights silently rotating. 'There's an ambulance here,' he explained, though it didn't offer much of an explanation.

August unlocked and opened their front door and stepped out, reaching the bannister and craning her neck up, following the sound of the voices.

Callie's face appeared from the floor above, also looking upwards, and August called, 'Callie? What's going on? Is it Mrs Haverley?'

Callie looked down, revealing two large, charcoal, mask strips pasted to her under-eyes. 'It must be,' she replied, and looked back up.

Flynn appeared next to her, having covered up his bare torso with a sweatshirt. 'I'll go up and see if I can do anything. Maybe she'll need a bag packed or something if they're taking her to hospital.'

'No, I should go,' August began to protest, putting her hand on his chest, when she spotted Abe on the top landing. 'Abe!' she called.

He looked down, nodding at Callie, his worry lines softening just a touch at seeing August's face. 'Hi, August. Hello, Flynn.'

'What's going on? Is your mum okay?'

'Um,' he looked back towards his flat and there was the sound of footsteps and shuffling. 'Not really. She's got to go to hospital.' With that, a stretcher emerged and two paramedics began descending the stairs with ever such a lot of care.

August gasped; though she and Flynn only caught a glance of Mrs Haverley's face, it was long enough to notice that her eyes were closed, her mouth covered with an oxygen mask, the skin on her forehead smooth and unwrinkled.

Abe followed the stretcher down the staircase, distracted with worry, and didn't look back at August or any of the other residents.

When the door closed behind them all, Flynn gently led August back into the flat, where she stood in the darkened living room, her hands to her mouth.

'August?' he pressed. 'She's going to be all right, she's with the best people now.'

'She just looked so small,' August choked, and tears over-spilled. 'I didn't realise she'd got so much worse. She looked just like my grandma.'

Flynn held her, not being able to give answers, but just to be there for her.

Flynn slept crumpled on their small sofa with August in his arms, not closing his eyes until she'd finally dropped off. She'd twitched and murmured in her sleep (more than usual), and when she woke up she looked at him through tired, worried eyes.

'I was dreaming of my gran,' she explained, not bothering to untangle herself from Flynn. 'She was laughing with Mrs H, with their feet in a stream, like in a picture she showed me. And I was floating away from them, like a leaf, and no matter how much I opened my mouth and tried to call, my grandma wouldn't come and rescue me.' She rubbed her eyes and looked up at Flynn, her face close, propped up on his chest. 'Did you stay with me all night?'

'Of course,' he replied.

'Did you sleep?'

'Enough.' He lingered for a moment, part of him not wanting to break this moment where she was so close to him that he could have counted her eyelashes. She breathed into him, and he into her, and for a moment he could almost feel their hearts searching for each other in the darkness. Eventually though, Flynn admitted to himself this wasn't the right time and so he carefully moved her and asked, 'Can I get you a tea?'

August nodded and reached for her phone. 'I'll text Abe to see if he's okay, and if there's any news.'

Chapter 86

August

August spent the next few days, and some of the nights, running her hands over the walls of the apartment, pacing the floors, and gazing from the windows at the frosty landscape beyond them. She was savouring the house and its memories in case it all came crashing down, but there was also another reason for these rituals. Showing Mrs Haverley's home some love made her feel a little closer to her landlady.

Flynn, who still had a few days booked off work since he was meant to be in Japan until the middle of the week, stayed by her side, sensing the deep worry inside her, and sharing in her shame.

August kept in touch with Abe, just a few simple texts over the week, and eventually he contacted her one evening to say his mum was on the mend, suspected angina. She was remaining in hospital for now, but according to Abe, sparklier and more of 'her usual, fierce self'.

Can I visit her? August replied.

She'd like that.

The following morning, August knocked on Flynn's door.

'Come in,' he said, sounding sleepy, but he sat up in bed as soon as she came in. She climbed on his bed beside him now, without thinking, and only paused when she accidentally moved his duvet a little, revealing his bare chest.

'Sorry, I'm sorry, I'll speak to you when you're up.'

Flynn reached out and touched her arm. 'It's fine, Aug, what's up?'

'I'm going to go and see Mrs Haverley today in the hospital.'

'All right, do I have time to jump in the shower?'

'No it's okay, I'm going to go alone.' August wished he wouldn't mention him having a shower now, since she was trying to keep her mind on track. 'If you don't mind. It's just that after everything, and her being in there, I don't want to overwhelm her.'

'But you've dealt with everything so far, let me take some of the weight.'

'Do you fancy dinner tonight? Here I mean?' she asked by way of reply. She realised she was longing to see him, be with him, talk with him properly like she'd barely done since he came home. She missed him. 'It might be our last supper,' she semi-joked.

'Yes, leave it to me,' he said, and smiled that smile.

There was a moment where they were silent, together, like a pendulum that could start swinging either way. Maybe it was the threat of their closeness ending, maybe it was the realisation they were about to be free to live again, but it made August's skin tingle at his closeness.

She broke away. She had to stay focussed on the job at hand. After that ... who knew what would happen.

August took the bus to the hospital and was in the ward soon after visiting hours began, directed by a nurse to the bed which Mrs Haverley occupied.

'August!' Mrs Haverley croaked, her eyes open but glassy, her upper body propped upright in the bed but a look of fatigue enveloping everything about her.

'Hi, Mrs H,' August said, sitting down beside her. She resisted the urge to pat her hand. Until she came clean, every movement felt like part of her lie.

'Is Abe with you?'

'No, I wanted to have a quick word with you on my own if that's okay ... '

'August, please tell me you're here to take me home,' Mrs Haverley grumped, but seeing as she was still hooked up to various machines, it was clear to August she was at least half-joking. That was a good thing, because that sparkle was back, her cheeks had some pink in them again.

'You look well, Mrs H, how do you feel?' August commented.

'What's wrong with you?' asked Mrs Haverley in reply.

August blinked. 'What do you mean?'

'I mean, why do you have the expression and complexion of someone who is about to regurgitate their breakfast upon the floor?'

This was quite accurate, because August felt like she might, in fact, do just that any second. It wasn't so much a fear of being kicked out of the apartment on legal grounds, it was the shame of the lie, the backlash it might cause, the guilt. It was all of what was stewing inside and making her want to squeeze her eyes closed.

And so she did. She took a deep breath, and did what she did best. Blurted it out before she could think about it any longer. 'Mrs Haverley, I know this is awful timing, but if I may I'd like to tell you something about Flynn and me. We've not been entirely honest with you. We ...'

August steadied her breath, opening her eyes and gazing at the ceiling, at the one, two, three, four ceiling tiles overhead. And then at the five, six, seven, eight tiles over there to the right. And then at the nine—

'Spit it out, girl, I don't want to die here of boredom.'

Looking directly at Mrs Haverley, August said it. 'I'm not married to Flynn. We aren't married. To each other.'

'Have you separated, darling?'

'No, it's not a divorce, because it was never a marriage.' August paused and added, just to make it absolutely clear, 'We lied to you, Mrs Haverley, and I'm sorry.'

Mrs Haverley took that in for a second. 'You aren't married, but you are a couple.'

'No, we lied about all of it. I heard you, at the open house, telling Abe you only wanted to rent to a solid, dependable, married couple, and I wanted to live in that house so much, and Flynn needed somewhere to live because he'd just moved here from Japan, and we were selfish and entitled and

434

instead of respecting your wishes we barrelled on ahead.' Wow, it was flowing out of her now. And Mrs Haverley, whose gaze was unwavering, her mouth unsmiling, just lay there listening to it all.

So August continued rattling on. 'We feel awful, Mrs H, and rightly so, because we lied to you and everyone in that building, just so we could get what we wanted. We see it now, both of us, and I'm sorry it took months for us to come clean – I think we actually both knew we should come clean some time ago, but we were scared you might kick us out – but when I really started to get to know you, and found out that you knew my grandma, that's when . . .'

Mrs Haverley sighed in thought as August trailed off. 'All the hand holding . . .'

'Fake,' August explained. 'I mean, you know, we were holding each other's hands, not like, mannequin hands, but it was fake in terms of the feeling behind it – you get it.'

Mrs Haverley's eyebrows were furrowed. 'You share a bedroom.'

'Not really, we don't.'

'You kissed at the Christmas party.'

August blushed at that. 'Actually we only *nearly* kissed in the end, all of them have been near-kisses, apart from, um, well we did rehearse one once.'

'I'm sure you did,' Mrs Haverley muttered. 'But the wedding photos?'

'Fake.'

'I knew that was Weston.' With that, Mrs Haverley lapsed into silence for a while, her gaze towards the window. 'Tell me, August,' she said eventually, pulling herself to sit more upright and shooing away August's attempt to help. 'What do you think your grandmother would have thought of all of this?'

August felt chastised, and rightly so, and the mention of her grandmother stabbed at her soul. 'To begin with, I thought she would have found it comical. But when I realised you meant something to her, well, I now think she would have been pretty disappointed in me for lying to her friend and treating you like this.'

Mrs Haverley was quiet for a long time, to the point August was about to take her leave. Maybe she could come back tomorrow and see what – if any – amends she could make.

And then Mrs Haverley spoke, her voice quiet, but clear. 'I don't think that's true.'

August looked up from her hands, to find Mrs Haverley fixing her with a soft stare. 'What do you mean?' she asked.

'I remember Pearl quite well and to be quite honest, August, I think I agree with your initial feeling – I think she would have found the whole thing a hoot. In fact, I think she would have done the exact same thing herself in your position.'

'You do?'

'Don't you?'

She thought about it, hard, and actually . . . she did believe her grandma would have seen the funny side. She would have demanded August confess to everything, and insisted she give a proper apology, which would have included anything that could make amends, but she probably would have been just a little amused by August and Flynn's scheme.

'Did Pearl ever tell you about Dear Richard?' Mrs Haverley asked.

'No, who was that?'

'Dear Richard was her sweetheart before she got married. A brute who was in the Navy and away a lot. He was all muscles and military training and had the ability to ravish her like nobody else could whenever he came to town.'

'What the hell?' She'd never heard of 'Dear Richard' in her life. 'Was this before she and my grandad got together?'

'Your grandad stole her from him.'

Wow. August's grandad must have been quite the Lothario to steal another man's girl like that. Especially from someone who was ravishing her like never before. Vom.

Mrs Haverley continued. 'Pearl fell in love with your grandad and told him that she would end things with Dear Richard as soon as he next got off the boat. What boat she never said, Pearl didn't know a thing about the Navy.'

'Was Dear Richard mad?'

'Hardly,' Mrs Haverley let out a small tinkle of a laugh. 'He was completely made up.'

'He was *what*? Why?'

'Pearl created this whole character, even cut a photograph out of a magazine of a strapping young naval officer and put it in a locket around her neck. Dear Richard's sole purpose was as a deterrent for the unwanted advances of men. Until your grandfather came along, and Pearl decided she'd quite appreciate his advances. So Dear Richard had to be retired, as it were. Well, not quite.'

August soaked in this information about her grandmother, happy tears springing to her eyes. What a funny, creative woman she was; she'd always been.

Mrs Haverley continued. 'I used to say to her, "Pearl, why don't you just tell these other boys 'no'?" but she, rightly, argued that sometimes a no doesn't get them off your back. It should be enough, but it isn't always. It was a different time.'

'Hmm, not that different, unfortunately,' August said.

'That's probably true. Callie is often showing me something she calls "DMs" filled with men getting quite cruel if she says she's not interested. All sorts of name calling. Stupid behaviour.'

It made August smile to think of Callie up in Mrs Haverley's apartment, having a chin-wag and discussing the pitfalls of online dating. 'What did you mean by Dear Richard not quite being retired?'

That laugh came again, and Mrs Haverley said, 'I remember your grandmother telling me that when she and your grandfather first got engaged to be married, she told him, 'Dear Richard will always love me, and if you treat me badly I shall write to him and he'll come and show you what's for and then whisk me away!' She kept Dear Richard in her back pocket, just to keep your grandfather on his toes.'

August shook her head. Grandma and her stories, honestly. She felt quite proud of old Pearl though. To think, she'd had an entire imaginary relationship also.

But August's smile faded. 'Nevertheless, what my grandma did, with the whole Dear Richard thing, wasn't doing anyone else any harm, it was just something she did for herself, that only really affected herself. What I did was selfish, and I was a complete cow for acting like your wishes didn't matter.'

'We all have our reasons we do the things we do, and when you're within a breath of reaching your dreams it's easy to get caught up in doing whatever you can to grasp them.' Mrs Haverley stopped talking for a moment, her thoughts swimming back to her younger days. She then carried on, saying, 'I'm not saying I'm not angry at what you did, and what Flynn did, and I feel used and embarrassed. But I think I'll get over it. I was also at fault for trying to discriminate, as Abe has told me numerous times in the past couple of days – now I understand why – and for that I'm sorry.'

Abe had stood up for them? He was a nice guy, he deserved to find someone really special. August sent him a little piece of her heart as thanks, in that moment. 'But you should get a say in who lives in your house,' August said.

'Well, only up to a point.' Mrs Haverley adjusted herself on the bed, and her eyelids appeared to grow heavy. 'Darling, I am pleased you told me and I'm not banishing you in any form, but this has been a lot of information, and I need to get some rest. Once Abe gets here in the afternoon he does go on; he's insisting on reading me the complete works of Austen at the moment, even though he knows I prefer a good Jackie Collins bonkbuster.'

August nodded and stood, picking up her bag. 'Thanks

for listening, Mrs H. And I'm – we're – truly sorry. We'll understand, whatever you decide to do.'

'Hold on, you said Flynn had just moved here from Japan. You and Flynn have started seeing each other now though, haven't you?' Mrs Haverley asked, all of a sudden.

'No,' August said. 'We literally met on the day of the open house and nothing's happened, we're just friends.'

'You wouldn't give two hoots if he met someone new?'

'No . . .' August replied, though her heart thudded in her chest. Because she would. She would. The thought of him reuniting with Yui was one thing, because she wanted him to be happy, but he'd chosen to come back the UK and now the thought of him choosing to move on from what they had was making her wobble.

'Do you think it hurt him to see you with Abe?'

'No,' August said, quieter than before. *Did it?*

Mrs Haverley's eyes began to close again. 'This is very gallant of you both to start screaming your truths from the rooftops, but maybe you need to start being truthful with each other.'

'We're just friends,' August said.

A smile played on Mrs Haverley's lips. 'You could have fooled me.'

With her defences crumbling, August felt her resolve rebuilding, and with every moment that passed she became stronger, more sure than ever of what she wanted.

It was time to be brave. Because August was fooling nobody anymore, least of all herself.

Chapter 87

August

Leaving the hospital and exiting into the brightness of this winter Saturday, August stretched. It was cold out, but she decided to take a long walk home, and have some time to listen to her thoughts.

She weaved her way back through the tree-lined streets on the outskirts of Bath and then alongside the river, where sunlight glinted off the water as if inspecting it before the temperature dropped to add a smooth layer of ice on top overnight. She walked with no rush, just her thoughts for company.

There was a very real chance she would be moving away from Elizabeth Street soon. What a shame that would be. But what a ride it had been.

While she'd lived there, she'd rebuilt her voice acting career.

While she'd lived there, she'd pushed herself to go on her first big theatre audition.

While she'd lived there, she'd found the part of her that wanted to reach for her goals again.

While she'd lived there, she'd reconnected with a part of her grandmother's past.

While she'd lived there, she'd made friends that she hoped would give her another chance.

While she'd lived there she'd fallen for a guy she was playing house with, a guy who was kind, who challenged her, who was more adventurous than he gave himself credit for, who wore glasses when he read (*ohmygod yum*), and who made her heart race every time she came home to him. When he looked at her, she forgot all pretences. When he kissed her she forgot everything.

With every step that took her closer back to Flynn, August pictured the memories and life they'd built together since last summer.

All of this had happened while she lived on Elizabeth Street, but now it could all be taken away, she wasn't worried. The drive to be the person she wanted to become had always been in her; if she lost the apartment, that wouldn't change.

When she reached Elizabeth Street and started ascending the hill, her pace quickened. She needed to tell Flynn how she felt, it was time for her truth to him to be set free. What it would mean for the two of them, she didn't know. Much like a lot of these truth-bombs, she couldn't predict, or control, or influence, or fake her way through the consequences.

On the way up the hill she savoured every tree, every house, every memory she'd made on this street in her lifetime and the lifetime of memories she'd made living within her home since last summer. She breathed in the cold winter air, smelled the smoke circling overhead from wood burners up and down the road, touched her hand along the railings, imagining, as she always did, all those Austen-like people who had done this two hundred years ago.

August had wanted to live in the house on Elizabeth Street for so long, and even if it all ended tomorrow, it had been a dream come true.

Chapter 88

Flynn

Flynn paced the apartment, waiting for August to arrive home, waiting to tell her what he should have told her months ago.

When she'd sat on his bed that morning, he knew he couldn't keep doing this dance with her. If he'd learned one thing from going back to Japan it was that now was the time to be brave, to take the adventures.

Who had inspired him to take this whole crazy adventure of a marriage pact in the first place? August.

She was the one who brought the person he wanted to be out of him. And he wanted to be with her.

The door opened and there she was, his flatmate, his faux-wife, his friend. August had flushed cheeks like she'd been walking fast in the cold air, her hair misted into tangles in the breeze. Her bright clothing was like a summer's day no matter what the weather.

'I need to tell you something,' he blurted to her.

'OK,' she replied, her soft smile lighting up the apartment as she closed the door.

A thickness settled in the air between them, a thousand unspoken words, a future in other people's hands, and more than anything in that moment he wanted to stride over to her and kiss her.

But he couldn't, he didn't know how she felt, only how he felt, so it was time for him to brave telling her.

'I'm going to tell you something,' he started. 'I want to hear how it went at the hospital, I want to hear everything, but first you need to be the one to listen because no matter what's about to happen, you need to know something.'

August raised her eyebrows and removed her coat, hanging it without taking her eyes off him.

His fear melted away as he looked at her, because this was August. If it all came crashing down at least she would know somebody loved her.

Flynn took a breath. 'Because of you I feel alive and ready to see all the things I want to see. I want to take control of my life, and have adventures, and laugh, and love, and bring the woman I love on a sleeper train to Scotland with me.' He paused, searching her expression. 'Because of you, I'm happy. And not because you've changed me, because you've inspired me. And you need to know that you should never change. You're impulsive and daring and you're sunshine. I'll always think that about you, no matter what you say next.'

'Flynn—' she started to interrupt, taking a step forwards.

He held up his hands. 'I know you and Abe have got close,

and I respect that and I'll back off and move out or whatever needs to be done, but I can't keep being your flatmate.' Flynn started to move towards her, he couldn't help himself. 'Even if the neighbours hadn't caught us out, I don't think I could have kept pretending to be married to you anymore.'

He stood in front of August and reached out a hand to graze against hers. 'I can't keep holding your hand. I can't keep putting my arms around you. I can't keep kissing you.' His eyes moved to her lips and her breathing slowed. She tilted her chin towards him, her eyes on his mouth also. He swallowed, and said quietly. 'I can't keep having you climb in my bed.'

August nodded, a tiny movement of her head, her gaze moving from his lips up to his eyes.

Flynn moved a fraction closer to her and said, 'I'm in love with you, August. So I can't do those things anymore if you don't feel the same.'

She smiled at him, and moments before their lips touched after what felt like too long but also just the right amount of time, she whispered, 'You took the words right out of my mouth.'

This kiss felt right. It felt like everything it had been back when they were practising, and more. The room seemed to be spinning, they touched each other's faces, backs of necks, they breathed against the lips before them, and they gave their hearts to one another, fully.

'Are you ready for this?' August whispered, when they pulled apart. 'Because this is real life now, no more curtains dropping or scenes ending, this is us.'

'I'm so ready,' Flynn replied. 'I'm ready for us to take the next step in our relationship, and move from husband-and-wife, to boyfriend-and-girlfriend. Are you?'

She pretended to think for a moment. 'I don't know, sounds a bit risky . . .'

Flynn laughed, and before he swept her into another kiss that would take them a long time to come out of, he let his eyes take her in, wanting to remember this moment for all of his life.

Chapter 89

August

Later that evening, while Flynn fixed them dinner, August's phone rang. Seeing Abe's name, she went to her room to take his call.

August took a deep breath; this was it. But you know what … it was okay. She and Flynn had found each other, they were each other's home, they'd picked each other. They'd picked *themselves* and their happiness and their futures, no matter where they ended up living.

'Hi, Abe,' she answered. 'How's your mum been this afternoon?'

'She's doing fine,' he said. He sounded more like himself again – the more relaxed version of himself that she'd got to know over the recent months. She liked that voice, and she hoped he could forgive her one day so they could be friends. 'I just came from the hospital, actually, and listen … She's handing the management of the building over to me, so she wanted it to be my call whether we ask you to move out or not.'

'Oh.'

'I told her we didn't really have any legal grounds to ask you to move out, and of course we got into the same discussion we always do.'

'It doesn't matter about legalities, Abe, if you and your mum want us out, we'll understand and we'll go.' Saying it out loud stabbed August in the heart, but she would stick by her word.

'Well, Mum did give me her recommendation. But she also said that because of us – me – my complicated feelings and "sad, lonely, womanless life in London" as she so aptly put it – I had to make the final call.'

August looked around her room, at her little balcony and her pile of scripts and then at herself in the mirror. 'And?'

'And . . . you and Flynn can stay.'

Her heart did a somersault before her ears asked her to check in case they were malfunctioning. 'Did you say we could stay, as in, keep living here?'

'I did. You're good tenants. Neither of us particularly wants to start the search again, and Mum said something about a pearl being angry at her from up there if she kicked you out, whatever that meant. So if you two want to stay, I'm happy for you to stay.'

'Are you sure?' asked August, keeping her voice quiet. 'Abe, I don't want you to feel weird.'

'Really, August, I will be fine.' He paused, before saying quietly, kindly, 'Go and be happy.'

'You too, Abe.'

When August hung up the phone she held it to her for a second, holding Abe for just a moment like she'd barely had a chance to in real life.

She then let him go.

August sat for a few minutes in her surroundings, in her bedroom, with her Flynn on the other side of the door. She wouldn't take any of this for granted again. From now on, August Anderson would use the drive she knew was in her to work for her dreams.

That said ... she'd never give up her adventurous streak.

Thanks to that, a whole new adventure was about to begin.

She flung open the door and Flynn looked up from where he was carrying a bottle of wine to their small table in the living room.

He had his glasses on, he must have been reading a cook book, and it made her melt a little. 'Everything all right?' he asked.

'Abe – and Mrs Haverley – are happy for us to stay living here.'

Flynn put down the wine and reached August in two strides, kissing her so she was lifted off her feet, or at least it felt that way, she wasn't sure.

'Dinner will be two minutes,' he said, breaking away, and then, with an adventurous glint in his eye told her, 'Wait in your room, I'll come and get you.'

She did as she was asked, leaning her back against her closed door and thanking her lucky stars, her fate, her kind and forgiving neighbours and friends, her grandmother and her own self for giving her another shot.

There was a knock on her door and August turned, opening it, and there was Flynn, dressed in his suit, his loose-collared pale blue shirt that he'd been wearing that first day she met him that still had the coffee stain on the front, despite being washed. He'd kept it.

He smiled down at her, leaning against her doorframe and motioning to the laid table behind him. 'August Anderson? I'm Flynn Miyoshi. I'm here to pick you up for our first date.'

Epilogue

Dreams have a starting point, but they don't ever have to end if you can keep nurturing them, helping them to grow, adding to them and enjoying them.

Flynn quit his job, but not law altogether. He found a new firm with a strict work-life balance policy, and began to love the wide world that his field opened up, once again. He made sure to video call with his relatives in Japan weekly, and that included his grandmother, all the way down in the south on her tropical island.

Callie's mum, Allen and Maud all met the news about Flynn and August not being married with surprise, but all would admit it didn't really make any difference to them either way. As far as they were concerned, the love birds in the middle apartment were exactly who they had always thought they were. Callie, in time, forgave August for her deception, and their warm friendship resumed.

Mrs Haverley returned to her top floor flat from hospital,

feeling better than she had in years. She was now a keen walker – so keen, in fact, that she joined August and Bel on the Regency Costumed Promenade at the next Jane Austen Festival, parasol and all.

Bel and Steve finally married after a long engagement, and Kenny finally got to be the best man that Bel always knew he was. His plus one, and *his* best man, was Mark the receptionist, and neither of them could stop beaming their pearly whites at each other all day.

Abe returned to London, where his life quickly became less sad and lonely than before. Feeling motivated by the emotions that August had awoken in him, and wanting to feel them again, he started dating a woman called Maya, who loved to join him on trips to Bath to visit his mum.

August gave up the notion that the house was a portal to her dreams, and that by living there and having her ultimate dream come true, all the others would just fall into place. Instead she stoked the fire within her, and focussed on furthering her career, allowing fear to fall away as she found success with her expanding demo reel, and enrolling in a weekend drama school to learn how to become a better, classically trained, stage actress on the side. She still had every one of her dreams; and this time, she was willing to work for them.

As for August and Flynn's relationship ... Well, no fake divorces were needed. They remain in their home in Elizabeth Street, now sharing just the one bedroom. They still like to practise kissing, often. And though neither of them knows it yet, in the not-too-distant future they'll be replacing those make-believe wedding photos with the real deal.

Acknowledgements

Thank you, wonderful readers, for moving in with August and Flynn and keeping their secret with them through the pages of this book. I hope you enjoyed living in the house on Elizabeth Street – I certainly liked hunkering down under the imaginary chandeliers to write it for you. Although the house and the road are made up, Bath itself is one of my favourite cities in the UK, and it's been great to visit again, at least in my mind (thanks Covid-19 for putting a stop to research trips ... sigh).

Special thanks to my lovely editor Bec Farrell at Sphere for helping mould this novel and for all your sparkling enthusiasm. And to the rest of the team at Little, Brown and beyond, in particular Frankie, Thalia, Vanessa and Bekki, Robyn Neild for the beautiful cover illustration, and Anna Acton for beautifully narrating another Isla tale – big big thank you, I couldn't do this without you.

Thank you to my literary agent Hannah Ferguson and the

team at Hardman & Swainson. Hannah, you're a star, can't wait until we can meet up again!

Thank you to the magical Louise Andrée Douglas for her help visualising the wonderful world of auditions, and to voice artist Penny Scott-Andrews for helping break down the beats on how to work in this industry. Thank you Rob for the marvellous research help and thank you Emma for always reading through my rough drafts, even when they're sometimes verrrry rough!

Thank you, family and friends – Phil & The Bear for being my real husband and dog and for being the best parts of 2020 (and every year). Mum & Dad who I've missed during all the lockdowns but who've always been on the end of FaceTime. Paul, Laura, Beth, Rosie, Indy, Mary, David, Jude, Robin, Eleanor, Peter – miss you and hope we can all get together again soon.

And a big thank you to Holly & Belinda. We might be in a global version of an escape room this year, but you two never fail to encourage me towards unlocking my dreams.

ISLA GORDON

A Season in the Snow

'Heart-warming and full of hope. I loved it'
HEIDI SWAIN

Escape to the mountains and fall in love this Christmas ...

Alice Bright has a great life. She has a job she adores, a devoted family and friends she'd lay down her life for. But when tragedy strikes, she finds her whole world turned upside down.

Enter, Bear, a fluffy, lovable – and rapidly growing! – puppy searching for a home. Bear may be exactly what Alice needs to rekindle her spark, but a London flat is no place for a mountain dog, and soon Alice and Bear find themselves on a journey to the snow-topped mountains of Switzerland in search of a new beginning.

Amidst the warming log fires, cosy cafes and stunning views, Alice finds her heart slowly beginning to heal. But will new friends and a charming next door neighbour be enough to help Alice fall in love with life once more?

**'The most beautiful, heart-warming story.
Gorgeously cosy, uplifting ... utterly lovely book'
Holly Martin**

'But, apart from that,' he said, 'I think she did me a favour. I got out of it, and it was nobody's fault.'

'Well, except for the fact that it was *your* fault.'

'Yes, God, you're right, aren't you? It was completely my fault. I suppose what I mean is, I'm glad I'm not the one who came across as a heartless bastard. Because I'm not one, really. Well, I don't think I am.'

'I don't think you are either.'

His hand still rested on my forehead.

'Why did you come round here?' I asked.

'To see you,' he said simply.

'Oh.'

He looked down and took his hand away.

'You and Angus . . . I'm sorry, I know it's completely none of my business, but is – was – well, anyway, there's not anything going on, is there? He said there wasn't, but I thought he might be trying to spare my feelings. He's like that.'

'I know,' I said. 'And no. There never was, really. I was . . . well, I hope I didn't hurt him. I think one of the reasons I liked him – not the only reason, because then I really, really liked him, you know, I think he's brilliant . . . But, well, I think, well, he kind of reminded me of you.'

His mild eyes blinked twice in surprise.

'Is that true?'

'Yes,' I said, swallowing the lump in my throat.

'You . . . well, me, well, you know . . . ?'

'Ehm, yes,' I said, trusting that that was the right answer.

His grip on my hand tightened and he brought his other hand down to cup my cheek. Outside the window, the snow was falling again.

'Eventually I realized . . .' he began. 'I realized that I was terrified you'd be with him, and make him happy and not me. I was so jealous.'

I gazed up at him.

'You were jealous? You were getting married!'

'I know. It just didn't seem fair to me that he got you because his timing was on and mine was as off as it could possibly be. As if I didn't have enough to worry about.'

I couldn't believe I was hearing this. I put my hand over his hand.

'I met a psychic on the train,' I said, smiling. 'I didn't believe it. Total nutcase. Do you know, she told me to go back to Alex.'

'You did,' said Fraser.

I looked at him enquiringly.

'Alasdair. It's my middle name. It's Gaelic for Alexander.'

I pulled out the handkerchief. D'oh! F.A.M. That mad woman had probably seen the 'A' when I was clutching it like a maniac, and gone for the educated guess. Unless, of course . . . I looked up at him, shiny-eyed.

Almost in slow motion, we began to touch each other on the arm and the face, discovering each other for the first time. I felt his strong shoulders through his white shirt. All the hairs on his forearm had raised themselves up from the cold air, and the closeness of

370

us. I tentatively touched one of his buttons.

'If I cry any more, I think I'll go blind,' I muttered, trying to hold back.

'That would explain what you see in me then.'

'Ho ho ho.'

Suddenly I felt his strong arms clasp my waist, his grip tighten. The expression on his face was tentative, excited, nervous, unsure – well, actually, fairly sure.

I looked straight at this man.

'You know, if this was a book,' I said, 'it really should have ended with a wedding.'

'Not necessarily,' he said. 'It could just have ended with a kiss.'

And it did.

Epilogue

We wanted to sneak away immediately. We had a lot to discuss and a lot to do. Somewhere in the country, we thought, where we could walk, and talk and, well, the other thing. I was lit up like the Christmas lights outside. I grabbed together some warm things in a bag and we made our way to the door. On our way out, I heard the phone ring. Linda picked it up.

'Oh,' I heard her say. 'Mel!'

'I don't think I want to get that, do I?' I said to Fraser.

'Don't tell them I'm here either,' he said.

'Oh my God. I haven't even thought about trying to explain it to people.'

'Shh . . .' From behind, he put both arms around me

and leaned on my shoulder. 'There's plenty of time to worry about all that.'

'Mel!' Linda yelled. Linda yelling! What a day this was turning out to be. 'It's somebody called Nicholas! He wants to know if you're free this . . . hang on . . . tonight or the rest of the weekend?'

I raised my eyebrows at Fraser. He shook his head vehemently.

'I think that's going to be a "no", Linda,' I said.

There was a pause. Then she popped her head round the door.

'He's asked me out instead!' she said breathlessly.

'Oh . . .'

Well, how bad could it be? He was well off, he had a nice car, he was tall, he wasn't . . . well, he wasn't the heart of pure evil, and Linda needed to get out of the house.

'Why don't you go?' I said kindly. 'He's all right. It could be fun.'

Linda looked at me quizzically.

'That eight foot, wanky, dog-breath accountant? What the FUCK do you take me for?'

Do You Remember the First Time?

Life doesn't have a rewind button.
Ever wished it did?

As her best friend Tashy cuts into her wedding cake, 32-year-old Flora realises she is disillusioned with life. Suddenly, her well-paid job, cosy flat and stable relationship with sensible Olly don't amount to a whole lot. Flora wants to be 16 again. She closes her eyes and wishes. Her wish has come true.

Waking up the next morning is a shock. But now Flora has the chance to right some wrongs. Trading crows feet for pimples and dull dinner parties for house parties where White Lightning and snogging are the order of the day, Flora revels in a life where things are far less complicated and just much more… FUN.

It's not all laughs though. Will what she does change the future? How can she get back to the present and her ordinary life? And does she even want to?

Turn the page to read an extract!

Chapter One

The rain was beating down on the windscreen, as we tried to navigate (rather damply) along the winding country road.

'I hate the country,' I said gloomily.

'Yes, well, you hate everything that isn't fifteen seconds from an overpriced cappuccino,' said Oliver crossly, although in his defence he had been driving from London for six hours.

'I don't hate everything,' I said. 'Only . . . those things over there.'

'What things?'

'Those . . . oh, you know.'

'Cows?'

'Yes, that's it.'

'You can't recognise a cow?'

'Remind me.' He used to think this was really cute.

'It's where your latte comes from,' he said, sighing.

Oliver does like the country. He was born, bred and boarding-schooled here. He couldn't understand why someone who'd lived their whole life in London wouldn't want to get out of it once in a while. I had patiently explained to him several times the necessity of all-night Harts the Grocers, proper bagels, and the choice, if one so wished, to pay six pounds for a bottle of mineral water in a nightclub, but he would bang on about fields and animals as if they were a good thing.

I examined his profile in the dimming light. He looked tired. God, he *was* tired, very tired. So was I. Olly worked for a law firm that did a lot of boring corporate stuff that dragged on for months and was fundamentally big rich bastards (Ol excepted, of course) working out ways to screw other big rich bastards for reasons that remained mysterious, with companies called things that sounded like covers for James Bond. I worked as an accountant for a mega firm – there were thousands of us. I tried to tell people it was more fun than it sounded, but I think after eleven years they could tell by my tone of voice that it wasn't. It had seemed like a nice safe option at the time. It was even fun at first, dressing up and wearing a suit, but recently the sixty-hour weeks, the hideous internal politics, the climate of economic fear, and the Sundays Ol and I spent with our work spread out over the kitchen table were, you know, starting to get to me. I spent a lot of time – *so* much time – in the arid, thrice-breathed air. When we were getting to the end of a deal I'd spend twelve hours a day in there. That was about seventy-five per cent of my waking seconds. Every time I thought about that, I started to panic.

It wasn't that we didn't have a good lifestyle, I reflected, peering out through the rain, and thinking how strangely black it was out here: I hadn't had much total darkness in my life. I mean, we both made plenty of money – Olly would probably even make partner eventually, as he worked really hard. But the shit we went through to get it . . . Jeez.

We took nice holidays, and Olly had a lovely flat in Battersea that I practically lived in. It was a good area, with lots of bars and restaurants and things to do, and if we got round to having kids, it would be a good place to bring them up too. Parks nearby and all that. Good schools, blah blah blah.

Good friends too. The best, really. In fact, that was why we were here, splashing through the mud in the godforsaken middle of nowhere. My oldest friend from school, Tashy, was getting married. Even though we'd both grown up in Highgate, she'd come over all *Four Weddings* when she and Max got engaged, and insisted on hiring some country house hotel out in the middle of nowhere with no connection to either of them.

I was glad she was getting married, give or take the bridegroom. We'd planned this a lot at school. Of course, not until we were at least twenty-two (we were both now thirty-two). In the manner of Princess Diana, if you please (although I'd been to the dress fitting and it was a very sharp and attractive column-style Vera Wang, thank you very much), and we'd probably be marrying Prince Edward (if we'd only known . .) or John Taylor.

Olly caught me looking at him.

'Don't tell me – you want to drive.'

'Do I fuck.'

He grimaced. 'Look, I know you're tired, but do you really have to swear so much?'

'What? We're not driving the Popemobile. We're all grown-ups.' I wrinkled my nose. 'How would you start to corrupt a lawyer anyway?'

'It's just not nice to hear it.'

'From a lady?'

He sniffed and stared through the windscreen.

I hate it when we get snippy like this, but really, I was exhausted. And now we'd have to go in and be super jolly! And Fun! All Evening! So I could keep Tashy's spirits up. I wondered who else was going to be there. Tashy was a lot better at keeping in touch with people than I was. When really, all I wanted to do on a Friday evening was pour an enormous glass of wine, curl up in front of the TV and drift off before the best of Graham Norton, which might, just might, mean I woke up rested enough either to go to the gym or have sex with Ol (not both).

Oliver stayed quiet, staring out into the darkness. I turned up the radio, which was playing 'Colourblind' by Darius. Eventually he couldn't stand it any longer.

'I can't believe you still listen to music like that.'

'I'm breaking – what – the after-thirty pop music bill of rights?'

'It's just so childish.'

'It's not childish! Darius wrote this all by himself!'

Ol gave me a look. 'That's not what I mean.'

'I'm not listening to Dido, OK? It's not going to happen. I'd rather die.'

'At least she's your age.'

'And what's that supposed to mean?'

Ol shrugged it off, and I let him. I knew why we were squabbling anyway, and it was very little to do with the respective ages of pop musicians.

It put a lot of pressure on a couple, especially our age, when one's friends baled out and got married, I reckoned. I mean, who was next? I was worried it was going to be like musical chairs, and we'd all sit down at once, wherever we happened to be.

'Turn here?'

I looked at Ol, who knew already I wouldn't know. He turned anyway, and a hedge brushed the window. It was very dark.

I mean, everyone was rambling along, having fun, working their guts out all week to get ahead, and pissing away the weekends for fun . . . then suddenly, ding dong, the first thirtieth birthday party and engagement bash invites had fallen on the doormat all at the same time, and we kept finding ourselves trailing round Habitat, buying the same vase over and over again.

I knew Tashy would try to do things slightly differently – everyone does, even if it's just a new place to stencil their initials ('Aren't the salt and pepper cellars in the shapes of our names adorable? And so reasonable!'), but it was still a wedding, wasn't it? There'd be a traditional Church of England service, the one everyone likes with the 'have and holds, for richer for poorer' stuff in it, even though our Sunday religion is strictly the *Observer* and the *People*; there'd be champagne on a lawn somewhere, there'd almost certainly be cold wild salmon at some point, and twelve-to-fourteen hours of pointless drinking before we had to stumble back to some horrid b. & b. somewhere for three hours before pulling ourselves out of bed to stuff full English breakfasts down our necks before piling back on to the motorway, leaving the bride and groom somewhere in a plane en route to the next forty-five years of togetherness, early nights, screaming babies and moving to Wandsworth because the council tax is cheaper and the schools aren't too bad.

Which was fine, of course. Lots of people did it. In fact, at the moment, it seemed a hundred per cent of everyone was doing it. I glanced at Olly. I had a funny feeling in the pit of my stomach that he might be thinking it was about time that he, too, did it. Just little things. Like he took over my bill paying because it would make it more convenient. (It did too; for an accountant I'm shocking with my money, like all those dipso doctors telling you to cut down on the booze. I always leave it till somebody's threatening to come round and total my kneecaps.) Or, maybe we should get a kitten? (If I wanted a small malevolent creature crawling round my kitchen demanding food I'd have a baby, thank you.)

Of course, my mum loved him. He was nothing at all like Dad; he was smartly spoken, and well off – oh – and hadn't left her.

'Not long now,' Olly said then, rubbing my knee in a making-up gesture. And I believed him. It wouldn't be long. Until Olly and I did what Tashy and Max were doing, and all our other friends were doing. Which should make me a lot more excited than I felt.

I shivered involuntarily.

'Are you cold?'

'Do you ever feel old, Ol?'

'Erm, cold or old?'

'Old.'

'Oh,' he said. 'Yes, of course. Well, I suppose, not really. I mean, I thought it might be a bit strange when I turned thirty, but it was all right really. I'm pretty much where I expected to be, don't you think?'

I was surprised at this. 'What do you mean, where you expected to be?'

'You know – by this stage in my life.'

'You mean, when you were younger, you thought about how close to a corporate law partnership you'd be in your thirties?'

He shrugged. 'Well, I took the A levels to get on to a law degree course, so I suppose I must have done.'

'You didn't just take your A levels because your parents wanted you to, but secretly you were going to be a rockstar or a footballer?'

'No! I think I knew by the time I was sixteen I wasn't going to make it as a footballer.'

'Really? I didn't give up on being a gymnast until last year.'

'The only gymnastics I've ever seen you do is accidentally falling out of bed.'

'That's not the point, is it? Don't you ever wonder about how we ended up just here?'

Olly was slowing to a junction, and as he stopped he turned to me and took my face in his hands.

'And what's so wrong with right here?'

The lights of the country hotel were twinkling ahead. Inside were old friends and good company. Here at my side was a decent man. Nothing was wrong at all.

* * *

'Flo! Ol!'

Tash had that massive, slightly manic grin people get when they've been welcoming people for hours. She looked splendid, as well she should, given the draconian diet she'd been on for the past six months 'so my bingo wings don't flap all through the service'.

I gave her a huge hug.

'Elle Macpherson or Martine McCutcheon?' she asked, turning round 360 degrees.

'What, are you kidding? Kate Moss,' I declared.

She beamed even wider. 'Excellent.'

We'd been spending quite a lot of time, in the last few months, going through celebrity magazines and slagging off people getting married. We particularly liked those who go rather – ahem – over the top, like Posh Spice and Catherine Zeta-Jones. Max thought we were being incredibly childish. Oliver didn't know about it, in case he thought I was trying to give him hints, which I wasn't, in a way, although I was also getting to the point where I thought it might be a bit embarrassing if he didn't ask, which I know isn't very romantic.

Tashy is small, occasionally a bit chunky, but thanks to the no-fat, no-bread, no-booze, crying-oneself-to-sleep-with-hunger-pains regime she's been on lately, there was not a pick on her. Her hair was currently extremely glossy and straight, though was, once upon a time, very wild and curly, and her sparkly green eyes betray her past when she went through a career a week and was constantly getting into scrapes. Now she'd settled into being a software designer, which sounded more glamorous than it was (and doesn't sound *very* glamorous at all, really), and was marrying Max, who also worked in computers and who was tall, bald, and very, very dull, but a much better bet, on the whole, I suppose, than the good-looking unruly-haired rogues Tashy had spent most of her twenties waiting to call her, then get off with somebody else. And her boho look had gone too. Feather earrings and deep plum clothes had given way to a slightly more appropriate look for a nice middle-class North London girl. In fact, Good God, was she wearing Boden?

She grabbed me by the arm. 'Come on! Come on! They can't mix a Martini, but I'm getting married so we're starting on the champagne we towed back from France.'

'Yes, but you're getting married tomorrow. Isn't not having a full-on death hangover meant to be part of the whole big idea?'

'Oh, sod that. One, I'm not going to get any sleep anyway, and two, someone's coming in with that full body foundation spray thing Sarah Jessica Parker uses. Believe me, you won't be able to tell if I'm alive or dead underneath it. You won't believe the work that goes into making all us haggard over-thirties brides look like freshly awakened virginal teenagers.'

'You want me to take the bags up then?' said Olly, standing grumpy in the chintzy hall, which was filled with copper kettles and random suits of armour.

'Well, do you mind?' I said guiltily.

'Then what am I supposed to do whilst you two go off and cackle like witches for three hours?'

I stared at him. I looked into his big likeable face. Why was everything he said tonight really irritating me?

'Can't you go and talk to Max?'

Olly dislikes Max in the way that you're always a little chippy about people in whom you recognise a bit of yourself. Plus, he loves Tash to bits and has always been overprotective, vetting anyone she goes out with.

'Is that Ol?' came Max's loud voice from the bar. 'Thought I recognised that clapped-out XR5.'

'I've got some work to catch up on,' said Ol. He yawned ostentatiously, winked and headed upstairs.

'Don't work too . . .' my voice petered out.

* * *

I heard the general sound of merriment through the big oak doors that led to the original ye olde trusty inne section, and sighed.

'Can we not go to the bar?'

'I think if there was ever a good minibar-emptying excuse it's tonight,' said Tash.

I rolled my eyes. 'Yes, because we usually require a parental consent form.'

'How's the lovely Ol then?' she asked as we quietly crept upstairs to avoid the revellers. 'Getting in a romantic mood?'

I think it's a bit insensitive to ask after someone else's love life when you have a big white dress hanging on the back of your door.

'It's fine,' I said. 'I think we must have one of those relationships where you bicker a lot to show you care.'

'Is that true?'

'Yes. People who are too affectionate are overcompensating,' I said blithely. 'Apparently.'

'OK,' said Tash.

'I took a test in a magazine.'

'OK!'

I bounced on the bed in her honeymoon suite. 'Well? Are you excited then?'

'Do I look excited?'

'Not as much as I'd expected, actually.'

She threw herself dramatically on the bedspread to join me, widening her eyes. 'Oh, Flo, I just can't believe it . . . you know. It's the dreamiest thing that's ever happened! I'm the luckiest girl in the whole wide world.'

'Oh, shut up. You know what I mean, though. You must be a bit nervous, or something.'

'I am. I really am. It's just, what's as exciting as it's cracked up to be? Nothing.'

'Getting into our first nightclub?'

'Yeah, we were twelve.'

'It was very exciting.'

She grinned. 'Still. It is quite cool.'

'You're actually doing it!'

'I know!'

'That's better.'

I rolled over onto my stomach. 'So is it not going to be what we always thought it was going to be?'

Tashy stuck her lip out a little as we remembered the many hours we'd spent sprawled over her bed (I always liked going to hers; her slightly sluttish mother let us eat in front of the TV) in pretty much the same positions, discussing how it would be.

'Well, I suppose I've had sex already . . .'

'You haven't! You filthy bitch!'

'So that's out of the way. And, also, he's not royal and there aren't six million people lining The Mall with flags to cheer us on our way.'

We were quiet for a moment, and I jumped off the bed and ceremoniously declared the minibar open. It even had Baileys in it. Ooh, we used to love that. Sugary milk!

'Hey – remember these?'

Tashy eyed one up balefully. 'A feature of my first night of unmarried intercourse . . . and, possibly, my last.'

I tore them open and we toasted each other.

'To true love,' I said.

'Aha-ha-ha.'

Actually, I'd meant it. I took a swig.

'Just think – you'll never have to make love to a man who slaps you on the rump and calls you a filly ever again!'

'Neiighhhh!!!!'

'Or date ANYBODY SHORT.'

Olly and Max were both very tall. These were our minimum requirements. We'd always reckoned that short men for girls were the equivalent of that horrible joke blokes tell – 'What have fat girls and scooters got in common? They're both fun to ride, but you wouldn't want your mates seeing you with one.'

'Or snog anyone for a dare.'

'Or sympathy.'

'Christ, yeah. Remember Norm?'

'It was charity work,' I replied indignantly. 'Helping the less blessed in the world.'

Norm had been something of a mistake, something of a long time ago.

Norm had been a snuffling pig, outright winner in an ugly pig competition.

'Anyway, why are you starting, Bridezilla? What about Pinocchio?'

Pinocchio told a lot of lies and had a very long narrow woody.

'Pour me some more Baileys immediately,' demanded Tashy.

'I don't want to give you a headache.'

'Are you joking? We've booked singers from the local choral society to sing the hymns. No one's getting out alive without a headache.' She rolled over.

'It's turning out all right, though, isn't it?'

'We thought that at sixteen.'

'Oh yeah, when we hadn't gotten pregnant. God, we knew nothing.'

'I think we thought that was it, didn't we? That we'd cracked it.'

'And at any moment, the knight in shining armour was just outside putting money in the meter . . .'

'Can you believe both of our Prince Charmings are going bald?' said Tash meditatively.

'Yours fastest,' I said defensively.

'It's all the testosterone building up from me being too tired to shag him after planning this damn wedding.'

'Does not shagging them make them bald? We could have saved Prince Edward after all.'

'No we couldn't.'

The thing is, when your friends fall in love – seriously – it gets very difficult to discuss the boys with them any more. It's fine to completely and totally dissect someone you've seen twice because they look a bit like Pierce Brosnan and can get gig tickets, but once it creeps into the full time – watch telly with, wash socks of, etc. – it becomes impossible. It's like discussing somebody's naked dad.

Max was just so sensible, so safe. He just . . . he just didn't get it. And he didn't seem to know the lovely Tashy I remembered, haring down the seafront at Brighton with her heels in her hands at four a.m., or marching us off through

Barcelona because she thought she knew the way and was buying the sangria, or dancing all night on top of a bar, or taking her stuffed rabbit on holiday until she was twenty-six . . . I know people think this about all their friends, but Max . . . he was all right, but I didn't really think he was good enough for my her. I wanted someone who could match her, dirty giggle for dirty giggle, not someone who could help her work out her SERPS contributions and had strong views on the education of children.

Of course I knew this was how it was going to work. We'd even devised the Buffy scale of life relationships: you start off wanting Xander, spend your twenties going out with Spike and settle down with Giles. Which seemed to mean Tashy had never had a chance at an Angel. And, I suppose, neither had I. I didn't believe in angels, anyway. I didn't believe in much.

* * *